T0195998

HER VERY OWN SCOTTISH RAKE

"I don't know Lord Vale well, of course, but Lady Felicia was speaking of him, and I couldn't help but think he sounds like just the sort of gentleman I need," Lucy said.

Need? She *needed* Vale? Something dark and tangled rose in Ciaran's chest and crowded into his throat until he was struggling to breathe past it.

"I know he's a bit of a rake, but he's warm-hearted, I think, and Lady Felicia says he loves mischief. He might think a pretend courtship was good fun."

Ciaran's hands clenched into fists. Oh, he'd find it good fun, all right. A pretend courtship with a beautiful lady was just the sort of fun Vale would appreciate.

"You are *not*," he said, biting off each word through clenched teeth. "Asking Sebastian Wroth to pretend to court you."

Her eyes went wide. "I'm not?"

"*No.*" He took a step closer, raising her chin higher so she had no choice but to meet his gaze. "Let me make myself perfectly clear, Lucy. Vale isn't going to be your pretend suitor. Not Vale, and not any other man."

"Well, why not?"

Lucy jerked her chin out of his grasp, and planted her hands on her hips. "Well, Ciaran? Why shouldn't Lord Vale be my pretend suitor?"

"Because *I'm* going to do it."

Books by Anna Bradley

LADY ELEANOR'S SEVENTH SUITOR

LADY CHARLOTTE'S FIRST LOVE

TWELFTH NIGHT WITH THE EARL

MORE OR LESS A MARCHIONESS

MORE OR LESS A COUNTESS

MORE OR LESS A TEMPTRESS

THE WAYWARD BRIDE

TO WED A WILD SCOT

FOR THE SAKE OF A SCOTTISH RAKE

Published by Kensington Publishing Corporation

For the Sake of a Scottish Rake

Anna Bradley

LYRICAL PRESS
Kensington Publishing Corp.
www.kensingtonbooks.com

LYRICAL PRESS BOOKS are published by

Kensington Publishing Corp.
119 West 40th Street
New York, NY 10018

All Kensington titles, imprints, and distributed lines are available at special quantity discounts for bulk purchases for sales promotion, premiums, fund-raising, educational, or institutional use.

Special book excerpts or customized printings can also be created to fit specific needs. For details, write or phone the office of the Kensington Sales Manager: Kensington Publishing Corp., 119 West 40th Street, New York, NY 10018. Attn. Sales Department. Phone: 1-800-221-2647.

Lyrical Press and Lyrical Press logo Reg. U.S. Pat. & TM Off.

First Electronic Edition: February 2020
ISBN-13: 978-1-5161-0970-8 (ebook)
ISBN-10: 1-5161-0970-8 (ebook)

First Print Edition: February 2020
ISBN-13: 978-1-5161-0971-5
ISBN-10: 1-5161-0971-6

Printed in the United States of America

Chapter One

Brighton, England
May 1818

If a proper lady intended to engage in a shocking impropriety, a fashionable seaside resort wasn't the place to do it. Lady Lucinda Sutcliffe had only arrived a few days ago, but she'd already discovered there were more gouty old men and phlegmatic old ladies in Brighton than there were grains of sand on the beach.

Dozens of aged invalids meant dozens of pairs of rheumy eyes, all in search of scandal.

Not in this part of town, though, and not at this time of day. It would be an hour or two before fashionable Brighton roused themselves from their beds, and when they did venture out, they wouldn't come here. Lucy had been watching the tidy patch of sand behind their rented villa for days now. It was as close to a deserted beach as one could find in Brighton.

Location, timing, and privacy—these were the first three of the four necessary elements of any successful impropriety.

The final element? Don't hesitate.

A lady had to seize her opportunities when she could. This might be Lucy's first opportunity, her first adventure, and the first time she'd seized anything more exciting than an extra lump of sugar for her tea, but that didn't make the rule any less sound.

She peered down the long stretch of beach to her right, then her left. She scanned the low outcropping of rocks to her east, but there wasn't a soul to be seen. Ah, splendid! A smile spread across her face, and she rubbed her hands together in anticipation. This was the most brilliant idea she'd ever had—

"This is the most ridiculous idea I've ever heard of, Lucy."

Lucy raised her gaze to the sky and prayed for patience before turning to face her accuser. She recognized the look on Eloisa's face. It was a special look her cousin seemed to reserve for Lucy alone.

Two parts fascination, three parts horror. Even Eloisa's eyebrows looked scandalized.

"You'll get caught," Eloisa fretted. "Then what do you suppose will happen? My father will keep us locked in our rooms for the rest of the month, and all our pleasure will be spoilt."

Lucy didn't bother to argue that point. Pleasure did seem to shrivel and die in her Uncle Jarvis's presence. But surely that was reason enough to pursue it with single-minded determination behind his back?

Anyway, she wouldn't get caught. "Who's going to see?" Lucy waved a hand at the empty beach. "No one ever comes to this side of town." If her uncle had understood just how unfashionable a neighborhood this was, he never would have taken the villa, but it was too late to change now.

Eloisa dropped the towels she'd been carrying onto a rock. "What if Father saw us leave the villa?"

"He didn't. You said yourself he never rises before noon. You don't suppose your mother saw us, do you?" Lucy's aunt suffered from sleeplessness and was often awake at odd hours, but she usually kept to her room.

"No. She dosed herself with laudanum last night. She'll sleep for hours yet." Eloisa sighed. "Her nerves are overset."

Yes, well, they would be, wouldn't they? Lucy's own nerves had been forged in fire, but after days of being trapped in a coach with her Uncle Jarvis, she felt as brittle as glass and as liable to shatter. Traveling with her uncle felt very like how Lucy imagined being buried in her grave would feel—that is, cramped and airless, with mounds of damp earth pressing in on every side.

Except instead of earth, Lucy was pressed on every side by mounds of damp flesh.

She'd spent the past five days flattened against the carriage door, but as much as she squeezed, she couldn't escape Uncle Jarvis's creeping girth. No sooner did she inch away from him than a pudgy knee or fleshy arm would fling itself into the sliver of open space. He'd been chasing her across the seat since they'd left Devon. By the time they'd reached Brighton, Lucy was ready to hang by her fingernails from the window to escape him.

But she didn't want to think of her uncle right now. The beach stretched before them, the waves flirting with the sand at the water's edge. "Come, Eloisa. We're here now." She gave her cousin a hopeful smile. "The water looks lovely. Don't say you're not tempted."

Eloisa gazed at the water for a moment, her mouth turned down in a frown. "I don't see why we can't simply go out this afternoon in a bathing machine. That's how it's done, Lucy. Ladies don't simply hurl themselves into the ocean."

Well, for pity's sake, why not? Growing up in Devon, Lucy had spent many happy hours of her childhood splashing about in the waves. Oh, it had been years since she'd been swimming, but she had vague memories of how glorious it felt to float along, her body cradled by the cool water around her.

She couldn't experience that joyous freedom if she was tethered to a bathing machine. "There's no pleasure in being dragged from a bathing machine by a large woman who plunges you into the water and knocks you about like a pile of soiled linens while your skirts billow like hot air balloons."

Eloisa folded her arms over her chest. "Well, I don't know how to swim, so I'd just as soon have a dipper, thank you."

"We'll go in the bathing machines later, with your mother." For her aunt's sake, Lucy had dutifully submitted to an hour's tedious dipping every afternoon since they'd arrived. "But floating about like an overdressed corpse isn't swimming, Eloisa."

"Lucy! What a ghastly thing to say!"

"For now, I'll be your dipper." Lucy ignored Eloisa's outrage, and gave her cousin a wheedling smile. Poor Eloisa. A lifetime spent pinned under her father's thumb had bled her of every last drop of spirit. It wouldn't do. One way or another, something would have to be done about Eloisa's listlessness.

"Come, Eloisa. You don't have to swim. You can paddle about in the shallow part. I won't let you drift out to sea. I promise. Not that there's much chance of that in this secluded little cove."

The look that flashed across Eloisa's face this time was three parts affection, and two parts exasperation. "You're a regular hoyden, Lucy."

Lucy shrugged. If a chance to swim unencumbered made her a hoyden, then so be it. "Please come in, Eloisa. It won't be any fun without you."

Eloisa's face softened. "Your father did you a grave disservice, Lucy, letting you run wild as he did, but you've a good heart, for all that."

Lucy choked back a laugh. Run wild? She couldn't remember the last time her father had permitted her to run at all, wild or otherwise. By the end he'd hardly suffered her to stir out of doors at all, even for a stroll in the gardens.

"I'm not one to speak ill of the dead, and perhaps the less said about your father the better," Eloisa went on, "But he wasn't well."

The laugh died in Lucy's throat. No, he hadn't been well, but he'd been a loving father for all his flaws and freakish whims, and that was how she chose to remember him. There didn't seem to be much sense in arguing about it now, however. Eloisa had made her mind up about Lucy's father years ago, along with the rest of England.

"If we continue to stand about like this, we'll lose our chance." Lucy loosened the tie at the neck of her cloak, tugged it off, and tossed it down on the rock next to the towels.

When Eloisa caught sight of the dark blue linen bathing costume Lucy wore under her cloak, her face paled. "Oh, Lucy! You can't really mean to do this? Someone will see you, and it will cause a scandal!"

Lucy sighed. Everything caused a scandal, it seemed. "Why should it? I'm wearing a bathing costume, for heaven's sake." It was prickly as a hedgehog, too. "Though I don't see why the ladies must be bundled up in scratchy linen when the gentlemen are permitted to swim about nak—"

"Lucy! I will not stand here and listen to you talk about gentlemen who are…gentlemen without their…unclothed gentlemen. It's not proper."

Lucy was tempted to laugh at Eloisa's prudery, but then Eloisa would get into a snit, and Lucy would never be able to coax her into the water. "Then let's not stand here at all. Are you coming in?"

Eloisa glanced at the water again, hesitating. Lucy waited, hope surging at her cousin's longing look, but then Eloisa's teeth sank into her lower lip and she shook her head. "No. I'll go in later this afternoon, the proper way. I should never have let you lure me into this mad scheme in the first place."

Lucy's heart sank. Her childhood had been a lonely one, and she'd always longed for a sibling. When she found she had a cousin only a few years younger than she was, she'd dreamed they'd grow to love each other like sisters. But at eighteen years of age, Eloisa behaved as if she were already an old maid. She was prim and cautious, whereas Lucy was…

A hoyden? Perhaps, but there were worse things one could be.

A recluse, for instance.

She was twenty years old. Twenty years, and she'd hardly set foot beyond her father's estate for the last four of them. So far, she'd seen little else since they left Devon aside from the inside of a cramped coach, and the row of graying teeth at the back of Uncle Jarvis's gaping mouth each time he released a deafening snore.

Now, by some miracle she was here, mere steps away from the ocean.

After years spent wandering the halls of a dusty house with no one but her father and the servants to talk to, new adventures had at last presented themselves. Lucy intended to seize them with both hands.

But perhaps it was for the best if Eloisa didn't join her. Despite all her planning, Lucy couldn't be certain no one would see them. Risk couldn't be entirely eliminated—that was what made this an adventure. If they did get caught, Eloisa would suffer for it far more than Lucy would.

After all, Uncle Jarvis wasn't *her* father.

Lucy seated herself on the rock and kicked off her shoes. "Very well. You may as well go back then, before someone sees you. I'll follow soon."

Eloisa looked ready to scurry away that instant, but she hesitated. "Are you sure? If the water should become rough—"

Lucy waved a hand toward their villa. It was close enough to the slice of secluded beach Eloisa might be able to see her from their bedchamber window. "Watch me then, if you like, but it's all right, Eloisa. I'll be careful, and I won't go far."

"If anyone should ask for you, I'll tell them you haven't risen yet," Eloisa said, anxious now to be helpful.

"Fine. I'll return within the hour." Lucy didn't wait for Eloisa's response, but picked her way over the sand in her bare feet, her bathing costume flapping around her shins. She closed her eyes and sucked in a quick breath when her toes touched the cold water. When she opened them again and turned around, Eloisa was gone.

Lucy moved forward until the gentle waves rose to her knees, then her waist, and then in one dive she went head first into the water. She kicked her legs until she was close enough to the bottom to grab a handful of sand in her fist. The water wasn't deep, but deep enough when she was upright her feet dangled into a void. Water surrounded her on all sides, a flowing, surging cocoon. The cold waves caressed her skin, leaving a spray of sparkling wet goose bumps in their wake.

When she broke the surface the second time, a shout of sheer joy burst from her lips.

She'd been quiet all her life, it seemed, but now her cry echoed in the clear silence of the morning. Exhilaration shot down her spine and stole her breath for a moment, but in the next instant she filled her lungs and dove under again. She pushed against the gentle current, each strong stroke taking her farther away from the beach. Her limbs burned with restless energy, and she went under again and again, surfacing only to grab a few breaths before she plunged again, making a game out of diving deep enough to touch the sandy bottom with her fingertips.

When she surfaced at last, she swept the wet hair from her eyes and tipped over onto her back for a long, lazy float, her gaze fixed on the rosy sky above her. The sun had just crested the horizon. She'd have to go soon, but goodness, how delicious it felt to be in the outdoors, to spread her arms wide and feel the silky glide of the water against her back.

She'd come back tomorrow, and every day afterward for the month they were to remain in Brighton. How silly Eloisa was! Despite her cousin's dire warnings, no harm had been done this morning. Now Lucy had had her swim without all of Brighton erupting in a scandal, perhaps she could coax Eloisa to—

"Oh!" A shocked cry tore from Lucy's lips. God in heaven, what was that? Something had brushed against her leg. Seaweed? No, it felt like... it felt like...

A creature of some sort had taken hold of her foot! For one terrified moment visions of enormous octopi swam through Lucy's head, but no, it wasn't an octopus. That was impossible, because this creature had wrapped its fingers around her ankle. Octopi didn't have fingers, only tentacles.

It wasn't *something* that had grabbed her foot.

It was *someone*.

A man, judging by the size of the hand. A man, and perhaps a murderer, because whoever he was...

He was trying to pull her under.

"Let go!" Lucy kicked out and her foot connected with something hard and spongy at the same time.

"Oof!" There was a pained grunt. He dropped her ankle and Lucy tried to kick away from him, but the next thing she knew he'd grabbed a handful of the wet linen at the neck of her bathing costume and flipped her over onto her back. He wrapped an arm under her neck, dragged her body on top of his, and...

Dear God, he was enormous! His arm, corded with muscle, was like a vice against her windpipe, and his hard chest was at least the twice the width of her back. She kicked out wildly, but just when she'd managed to squirm free he hauled her back against him and wrapped one long leg around her thighs. "Stop squirming!"

Lucy's mouth fell open in shock. An enormous man had just appeared from the depths of the ocean and wrapped his arm around her neck. This was *not* the time to stop squirming. "Let go! You're choking me!"

The arm around her neck loosened at once, but instead of letting her go he anchored his palm under her chin and tilted it up, so her face was away from the water and her head tipped back against his shoulder. "You're all right, lass."

Lass? Was her murderer Scottish?

"Keep still, and we'll be on the beach in no time."

There was no mistaking that lilt—not when his deep, soothing voice was right next to her ear. That and the calm authority in his tone made Lucy pause just long enough for the worst of her panic to recede. She let her limbs go loose, and her body relax against his.

She felt more than heard an approving rumble come from his chest. "Aye, that's better." He unwrapped himself from her lower body and began to kick toward the shore, his long legs slicing through the water with ease. "You'll drown us both if you thrash about."

Drown? *Oh, no.* Surely, he didn't think—

"There's a good lass. I've got you."

But of course, he *did* think it.

Dash it, why should he jump to such a conclusion? Just because a lady chose to have a swim…alone, that is, in the dark, before the sun had risen…

Very well, it *was* a trifle unusual, perhaps. There was *some* chance, just a tiny one, he'd mistaken her shout of joy as a cry for help. He must have seen her from the beach, or perhaps from the low rock wall. From there it might have looked as though the waves were dragging her down each time she dove under.

This poor gentleman had thought—not without reason, she had to admit—she was drowning, and he'd dived in to rescue her.

Lucy let out a low, despairing moan. Goodness, what a tangle.

"There, it's all right now," he murmured, clearly mistaking her moan of embarrassment for a terrified whimper. "We've made it to the beach."

"Yes, yes, so we have. Oh, no! There's no need to—"

He brushed her feeble protests aside and rose from the water with her in his arms. "Yes, there is. You've had a shock."

She had, indeed, though not how he supposed. Still, there didn't seem much point in objecting *now*. He'd already executed a daring ocean rescue. Was she really going to begrudge him another few moments of heroism?

Lucy surrendered, and he carried her onto the beach. He lay her down in the sand and knelt down next to her to catch his breath. "Are you all right?"

She lay on her back with her arm over her eyes for a moment, then turned to him with a sigh. "You're very good, sir. I assure you, I'm—oh, my goodness! You're bleeding!"

Watery red streaks stained the front of his white shirt, and a fresh stream of blood poured from his nose. He pressed a hand to his face, and his palm came away covered with it. "Aye, so I am." He tried to staunch it with his sleeve, but it was positively spouting, and the wet linen was no match for it.

Lucy jumped to her feet to fetch one of the towels Eloisa had left on the rocks, then hurried back to him. "Here, take this. How did you…"

Oh, no. Lucy wished she could sink into the sand beneath her feet. In the water, when she'd been struggling to get away, her foot had connected with something hard.

She'd kicked him in the face. Hard. If the blood seeping through the towel was any indication…

"I've broken your nose, haven't I?"

He shrugged. "It's not broken. Just bent."

She bit her lip. "But there's so much blood."

"Noses bleed."

Lucy couldn't see his face because it was hidden by the towel, but his big shoulders moved in another shrug. He didn't sound angry. Despite her mortification, a grin tugged at the corner of Lucy's mouth. "A dousing, a kick to the face and a broken nose? My, you're taking all this quite well."

A muffled laugh came from behind the towel. "Better a broken nose than a drowning."

Lucy winced. "Um, yes. Well, about that. You see—"

"In any case, my nose isn't broken." He lowered the towel from his face, then rose to his feet until he was towering over her, his hands braced on his hips. "It's hardly bleeding at all anymore."

Lucy stared at him, eyes wide.

Goodness. He was quite…that is, he was rather…well, it wasn't as if she could ignore it, since he was soaked to the skin, but even if he'd been dry, there could be no denying he was unusually…

Robust.

She was no expert on a gentleman's anatomy, having scarcely set eyes on any gentleman but her father, but she doubted many of them could wear a wet shirt quite as well as this one did. His torso was…well, she'd never seen so many lovely angles and grooves in her life. The thin, transparent fabric of his shirt clung to his hard chest and taut belly as if it were proud to be there, and his dark blue breeches were plastered like a second skin to a pair of long, muscular thighs.

Thank goodness *they* weren't transparent, or she might have fallen into a swoon.

Lucy's face flamed with sudden heat as it dawned on her she was standing in front of him in nothing but her bathing costume. He seemed to notice it at the same time. His eyebrows rose as his gaze swept over her body. He had straight, dark eyebrows, and lovely eyes—a bright, ocean blue—but they narrowed as he stared at her, realization flickering in their depths.

"Tell me, lass. How did you end up in the ocean? Did you fall in?"

Lucy chewed on her lip as ten different responses flew through her head, each a more elaborate falsehood than the last. Really, what use was the truth in this instance? She couldn't tell this poor gentleman he'd taken a blow to the nose and nearly drowned them both to save a lady who didn't need saving.

It would be dreadfully rude.

Very well, then. A lie it was. "Yes, I'm afraid I'm quite clumsy. I fell in, and the next thing I knew I was fighting for my life in the pounding surf."

A bit dramatic, but it would do.

"Were you, now? How terrifying. Did you fall from the wall?" He pointed to the ring of rocks lining the tiny cove.

The wall? Yes, that seemed plausible. "I did, indeed. Tumbled right over the edge of it."

The blue eyes twinkled down at her. "Ah, I see. How did you happen to land in the water instead of in the sand?"

Blast it. "Well, you see, I didn't so much fall as I…what I meant to say was I was walking on the wall, but then I came down to the beach and—it was foolish of me, I know—I thought I'd put just a toe into the water, but the current overcame me, and the next thing I knew, I was fighting for my life in the pounding surf."

His lips twitched. "The pounding surf again? It must be powerful this morning to drag you out by a single toe. But there's one thing I can't quite make out about your story."

"Is there, indeed?" Lucy widened her eyes and tried to look innocent, but she was as guilty as a thief with a pocketful of guineas, and she had the racing heart to prove it. "What's that?"

"I just wonder how, between dipping your toe into the water and being swept out to sea by the pounding surf, you had time to change into a bathing costume?"

Lucy opened her mouth, then snapped it closed again without a word. Try as she might, there was simply no reasonable explanation for the bathing costume.

"That's your cloak and your shoes on that rock over there, isn't it?" He pointed over her shoulder, then held up the towel she'd handed him. "And another towel?"

Really, what could she say? That he'd been determined to save her, and since he was as big as a horse and twice as strong, there'd been little she could do to stop him? That his perfectly executed, daring rescue was entirely unnecessary? "Well yes, but—"

"Ah." The blue eyes glinted with humor. "You came out for a swim, didn't you?"

Lucy fidgeted with the skirt of her bathing costume. "Perhaps I did, but—"

"Tell me, lass. Are you a strong swimmer?"

She loosened her grip on her skirt and met his knowing blue eyes. "Yes, but even a strong swimmer—"

"Even a strong swimmer can drown in the pounding surf? Is that what you were going to say?"

"Well, yes."

"Aye, that's one explanation. The other is you weren't drowning at all." He toyed with the towel, running it through his fist. "So, which is it, lass? Were you one gasp away from sinking to a watery grave, or is there some other explanation for my broken nose?"

Chapter Two

"You just told me it isn't broken." Wide, dark brown eyes narrowed suspiciously on his face, drops of water still clinging to her eyelashes. "Is it, or isn't it?"

Ciaran choked back a laugh. "Forgive me, ma'am. I should have asked if there's some other explanation for my unbroken but severely injured nose."

He crossed his arms over his chest and waited while she decided whether or not to continue with her lie. They both knew he'd caught her out, but he could see she was considering carrying on with it, just the same.

Dogged, daft little lass, wasn't she?

He couldn't decide if he was impressed by her persistence, or offended she thought his male ego was too fragile to bear the truth. He knew one thing, though. After that tale she'd just told about the pounding surf dragging her out to sea by a single toe, he was eager to hear what she'd say next.

The slight quiver of anticipation in his stomach felt odd. Damned if he could remember when he'd last looked forward to anything with even a flicker of interest. If he'd resisted this trip to Brighton with half as much enthusiasm, he wouldn't be here now. "Well, lass? Which is it? A morning swim, or a near drowning?"

She bit her lip and cast him a measuring look from under her damp lashes. "It depends."

Ciaran didn't know whether it was the lady, the blood loss, or the shock of cold water so early in the morning, but a rusty laugh knocked loose from his chest. "On what?"

"On whether your nose is actually broken or not."

Ciaran wriggled his nose a bit. It bloody well felt like it, but he hadn't heard the telltale crack. No crack meant no break, but he wasn't going to admit that to *her*. Not yet, anyway. "It's difficult to say. Now I think on it, I may have heard a bone snap when you kicked me. It *has* taken a beating. It's bruised, and likely to swell."

"Swell?" Her brows drew together in a guilty frown. "Do you think so?"

Ciaran hastily stuffed the towel back into his face, and made a great show of holding it there and looking as pitiful as possible. "Yes. No doubt it will swell to three times its size and turn black and blue."

"Oh, dear." She winced. "Is it terribly painful?"

"Aye. The nose is a sensitive organ, lass, and that was a vicious blow you dealt me." Ciaran hid his grin behind the towel. "The worst of it is I'll certainly have to wear a plaster on it. The gentlemen will laugh at me, and the ladies will refuse to dance with me at the assemblies."

"Surely people won't be as cruel as that?" She wrung her hands. "Why, you saved a lady in distress. Your actions were heroic—"

"Were they?" He lowered the towel and took a step toward her. "Because I've an idea I saved you from nothing worse than your morning swim. Come now, lass. Tell the truth."

She raised her chin. "You believed I was in distress and you risked your own safety to rescue me. The truth is, it doesn't matter one whit whether or not I was frolicking in the waves or drowning. Either way, you behaved like a noble gentleman."

Ciaran raised an eyebrow at this passionate speech. "I'll have the truth between us just the same, if you don't mind."

She threw her hands into the air. "Oh, very well, if you must. I wasn't one gasp away from succumbing to a watery grave, as you put it. But if anyone has the nerve to laugh at your plaster, I'll tell them I was."

This time Ciaran gave in to his amusement, throwing his head back with a hearty laugh. "That's generous, but if I were you, I wouldn't tell a soul about this."

If anyone in Brighton found out she'd been out swimming alone in the early morning hours, she might as well pack her things and go home now. He didn't used to give much of a damn about propriety, but that was before he'd come to England and seen with his own eyes how much damage even the smallest slip could make to a lady's reputation.

And this wasn't a small slip. It was a reckless dive straight into scandal.

She tapped a finger against her lips. "Yes, perhaps we'd better keep this morning's adventure to ourselves."

Ciaran might have let it go at that, but he felt obligated to give her a stern warning first. He wasn't much of one for stern warnings—either delivering them, or heeding them—but it wasn't just her reputation at risk.

It was her safety. It was dangerous for even a strong swimmer to go out alone. If she'd been overcome by the current she might really have been swept out to sea by the pounding surf, and no one would ever have known what had happened to her.

His amusement faded at the thought. What was the chit doing out here alone? Who were her people, and why didn't they keep a better eye on her? What the devil was she about, scampering about Brighton like a wild thing, risking everything for a bit of fun?

He eyed her, then asked in as firm a tone as he could manage, "If I happen to wander this same stretch of beach tomorrow morning, you won't be here again, will you, lass?"

She didn't reply, but Ciaran noticed the sudden, stubborn thrust of her chin, the telltale flush on her cheeks. His eyes narrowed. "I asked you a question. This morning's swim is your last, isn't it?"

She tossed her damp hair over her shoulder and gave him a bright smile. "Well, as to that, who can tell?"

It wasn't the answer Ciaran wanted to hear. "*You* can, lass. You can tell me you won't come out here again, or you can keep this up until someone catches you at it, and they tell all of Brighton."

"Yes, I suppose they might do that." She cocked her head to the side, as if considering it. "*If* they catch me."

"They will." They always did. It was a bloody miracle she'd made it through the morning unscathed. She wouldn't be so lucky a second time. "Why would you take the chance?"

She'd turned away from him to gaze out at the water. Goose bumps rose on her skin, but she didn't seem to notice. "Because I've waited a lifetime for a chance like this," she murmured, more to herself than to him.

What the devil did that mean? "A chance to go swimming?"

She waved a hand toward the ocean. "A chance to see things. Why should it be shocking to want to see things?"

It shouldn't be, but Ciaran didn't say so. It would only encourage her. He dragged a hand through his wet hair, a defeated groan escaping his lips. If she didn't reassure him this was her last swim, he'd be out here every bloody morning before dawn looking for her.

Damnation.

Sleeping until sunset was the only thing that made Brighton bearable. "If you insist on swimming, can't you bring someone with you? A brother, or a friend? It won't do a damn thing to protect your reputation, but at least you won't drown."

"I'd like to have a friend to swim with. It would be a great deal pleasanter that way, wouldn't it?" Her plump lips turned down for a moment, but when she faced him again, her smile was back. "But you needn't worry about my drowning. I was very young when I learned to swim, and I've never forgot. I'm quite a capable swimmer."

Ciaran huffed out a breath, nettled to the last degree. It was another nonanswer. She was good at those. He'd been good at them at one time, too. His older brother Lachlan had usually been on the receiving end of those half-answers. Whoever would have guessed how annoying they were?

"You know what will happen if someone sees you out on the beach alone in the dark in your bathing costume, don't you?" *Jesus.* He sounded like a prig, but damn it, he'd never get another wink of sleep until she reassured him. "It'll be a—"

"Don't say scandal!" Her face darkened with a scowl.

Ciaran blinked at her, surprised. "All right. I won't say it, but that won't make it any less of one if you get caught."

She sighed. "It's just...well, everything seems to cause a scandal, doesn't it? Everything worth doing, anyway."

Ciaran opened his mouth to argue, realized he agreed with her, and closed it again.

"It's utter nonsense. Why should I have to apologize for wanting to do things?" She turned her wide dark eyes on him. "I'd far rather risk the scandal than just meander along, peeking into the edges of my life as if it doesn't belong to me at all."

Her words sliced through Ciaran, unexpected and unwelcome, and something painful and bitter swelled inside him in response.

Meander along the edges of my life...

Wasn't that what he'd been doing in the months since he'd left Scotland? Meandering along the edges of his life? Wasn't that how his brothers had wheedled him into this Brighton nightmare in the first place? Because Ciaran hadn't had the energy to protest?

Or was it just that it didn't matter to him where he was anymore? Wherever he happened to be, he never felt as if he belonged there.

"I make no promises not to swim tomorrow," she said, startling him from his thoughts. "Despite what you may think, however, I don't court scandal, sir. I'm fully aware of the precariousness of my position, but as I said, some things are worth the risk—worth the scandal. Don't you agree?"

Did he agree? He would have once, when he'd still believed risk led to reward. Now, he wasn't so certain. So, he said nothing and stared at her instead, trying to make her out.

She was an odd lass, to be sure.

She was younger than he'd first thought, with a dainty jaw, creamy skin, and coppery red hair drifting around her temples. He might have called her delicate, but that kick she'd dealt him earlier said otherwise. She couldn't be any older than nineteen or so, yet here she was, this tiny little lass, seizing her chances as they came, despite what anyone might think of it.

She made him ashamed of himself.

He should be grateful to her for it—for forcing him to see himself so clearly, but he wasn't. Instead he felt exposed, and all at once he wanted to escape her. How had he come to be standing about on the beach in wet breeches, arguing with some troublesome chit who was chasing scandal, anyway? His nose ached like the devil, and icy water was dripping down the back of his neck.

He wanted a bath, and his bed. "Come, I'll escort you home."

She didn't move, but gazed up at him, her expression thoughtful. "Do you come to the beach every morning?"

"Why do you ask?" She wasn't the only one who knew how to dodge a question.

"Well, since we're friends now—"

"Friends! Beg your pardon, lass, but I hardly know you."

She gave him an impatient look. "Not *yet*, no, but that's easily remedied. You could come down here to the beach in the mornings, if you liked. It's one way to reassure yourself I won't drown."

Ciaran gazed down into her dark, hopeful eyes, and some long-forgotten part of him struggled to the surface. What was the harm in accepting her invitation? It would give him something to do, anyway. But he smothered the impulse before he did something foolish, like agree to meet her here tomorrow. It wasn't a good idea. It would be bad enough if she were caught out here alone, but far worse if she had a gentleman with her.

Especially one of his reputation.

He shook his head. "There's only one way to make your morning swim even more scandalous, lass, and that's by inviting me to join you."

She shrugged, not in the least perturbed. "I already told you. Some things are worth the risk."

Ciaran laughed, but there was a hard edge to it. "Maybe, but I'm not one of them."

She stared at him for a long, quiet moment, but then she turned away to pluck up the cloak spread neatly across the rock. She laid it across her knees as she perched on the edge and took up the pair of shoes beside it.

"I suppose we won't be friends after all, then. It's a pity. You would have been my only friend in Brighton."

She didn't speak again, but finished with her shoes and rose from the rock. Without asking, he took the cloak from her and brushed the sand off it. When she held out her arms, he helped her into it. It was a fine gray wool one, with a bright green satin lining.

"Thank you." Her hair had dried a bit in the breeze, and she pulled the bright mass of curls into a haphazard knot at the back of her head. He'd never seen hair that color before, so bright even the weak morning sunlight was drawn to it, toying with the loose strands around her face and turning them one by one toward the light to study each color.

She drew up her hood to hide its dampness, and tugged the neck of the cloak tighter about her chin. Ciaran caught himself admiring the way it framed her features. She was a pretty thing, with those deep, velvety brown eyes.

He cupped her elbow and began to guide her across the sand. "Where are your lodgings?"

She pulled her arm gently from his grasp. "I don't need an escort, sir. You're very kind, and I'm, ah…grateful for your heroic efforts on my behalf, but I'd just as soon make my own way home."

Ciaran drew back, strangely stung by this rejection, though he hadn't any right to be. If he had any sense at all he'd be relieved to be rid of her, but instead uneasiness rolled over him, as if he'd never see her again if he let her walk away now.

"Wait!" He took a few halting steps after her. "You didn't tell me your name."

"No, I didn't." She didn't offer it now, but only lifted her hand in a wave. "I'm sorry I nearly broke your nose. Goodbye."

She turned without another word and began to pick her way daintily across the beach, leaving Ciaran standing there alone. The cool breeze blowing off the water sliced through his damp shirt, chilling his skin. His nose was still burning, and he could taste blood on the back of his tongue.

None of these things were at all pleasant, but as he turned to walk back to his lodgings, he wondered—for the first time in a long time—if it wasn't better than feeling nothing at all.

Chapter Three

Brighton Racetrack
Two days later

It was amazing what a lady could get away with if she only dared to seize her opportunities when they presented themselves.

Lucy had spent the morning at the Pump Room with Eloisa, and her Aunt Jarvis. She suspected her uncle had been in a temper the night before, because her poor aunt was having one of her bad days. When they'd returned to the villa, Aunt Jarvis had heaved herself out of the carriage, a muttered prayer for the recovery of her nerves on her lips, and disappeared up the stairs. Eloisa had flown after her, her brow furrowed with concern.

As for Lucy's uncle, well…he took little notice of his wife, even less notice of his daughter, and none whatsoever of Lucy. Especially when he was in his cups, which was often. By the time Lucy came back downstairs after seeing her aunt comfortably settled, Uncle Jarvis was sitting alone in a dim corner of the tiny parlor, his bleary gaze fixed on the glass grasped in his meaty paw.

And beyond him an open door, light spilling through it like a beckoning hand.

It was an opportunity, and Lucy couldn't resist seizing it any more than Uncle Jarvis could resist a bottle of port. A dozen steps saw her through the courtyard. She paused when she reached the road, but a quick glance over her shoulder told her no one had taken any notice of her departure. She'd just have a quick stroll down the road, and then return before she was missed.

She hurried along the road, her heart fluttering with anticipation. The shouts grew louder as she drew closer to the tangle of wagons and horses she'd noticed earlier. She'd been on the far side of the carriage when they passed, and the windows had been shut tight against the dust of the roads, so she hadn't been able to see what all the fuss was about, but she'd seen enough to know there were a great number of people wandering about. She'd heard the muted sounds of shouting and laughter, and sensed the air vibrating with suppressed excitement.

Was it a village fair, perhaps, or some local holiday celebration? Whatever it was, Lucy knew with utter certainty she'd never been to one before.

As she drew closer, she noticed that despite their haphazard appearance, the carriages and wagons were arranged into a rough, oblong sort of ring around a large, open space. The bulk of the crowd was huddled tightly together inside the ring, their gazes riveted on something happening in the center. Something wildly entertaining, if she could judge by the delighted roars of the surrounding spectators.

It wasn't just gentlemen, but men of every class and description, all of them shrieking and howling like a pack of wild beasts. Lucy saw a few women here and there, also shouting and shaking their fists, but no ladies. It looked to be a crowd of several hundred, and not a lady among them.

Not a fair, then, or a local celebration. A race of some sort? A cockfight? That would explain the shrieks and howls rising from the crowd. Men were always at their most savage when blood and wagering were involved.

Lucy passed through the clustered wagons, but paused at the edges of the crowd. This was the moment when a proper young lady would deduce this was not an event meant for proper young ladies. Lucy was much more concerned with adventure than propriety, but she'd told herself she'd only take a quick peek, and then she'd be back on her way to her villa before any harm was done.

Instead of retreating, she drew closer, and closer still...

She was within two dozen paces of the center ring when she encountered her first obstacle. Dash it, she couldn't see a thing except a row of broad backs. Many of them were draped in billowing cloaks, the skirts of which further obscured the view.

No, no. This wouldn't do at all. She didn't fancy the idea of watching a cockfight, but she'd come this far, and she wasn't leaving until she'd had a peek at whatever was unfolding.

She scanned the row of conveyances at her back. If she stood in a wagon bed she'd be able see over the rows of shoulders, but that much height would make her rather more conspicuous than it was wise to be, under the circumstances.

A carriage wheel, then—ah, yes! Just there, a smart black carriage with gold fittings and a green and gold crest, and the coachman nowhere in sight. Surely Lord whoever-he-might-be wouldn't begrudge her a perch.

Lucy braced her foot on the hub of the back wheel, grasped the edge to haul herself up, then managed to turn herself around and balance her backside against the side of the carriage. Ah, there! Comfortable as could be. Now she could see what was so fascinating, and—

Lucy's eyes went wide, and a choked gasp lodged in her throat.

God in heaven.

Blood pounded through her body and rushed into her head with such force she nearly toppled off the wheel. She grasped at the spokes with one hand and covered her open mouth with the other.

Two men, both stripped to the waist, were in the center of a roped-off section of ground, and they were—

Lucy pressed her hand harder against her mouth as one man slammed his fist into the other's face. His hand came away dripping with blood, but the man he'd hit—who should, by every law of anatomy have been rendered unconscious by the blow—only turned aside, spat out one of his teeth, then gave the thunderous crowd a ghastly grin as a red stream of blood spurted from his nose and mouth.

They were pounding the life out of each other.

She'd stumbled across a bare-knuckle boxing match. A pair of half-naked men, their fists flying, faces contorted with pain, blood gushing from places Lucy had never seen blood gush from before.

Knuckles, fingernails, ears, and was that…dear God, it *was*.

An eye, gone all wobbly in its socket.

A proper young lady would have fallen into a faint. Or, if she did manage to stay conscious in the face of such brutality, she would scramble down from her perch at once, gather her skirts in her fists, and run back to her lodgings without a backward glance. She'd retire to her bedchamber, lock her door behind her, dose herself with laudanum, and vow never to tempt fate again.

Alas, Lucy didn't aspire to propriety, and she wasn't a *young* lady at all. She was nearly twenty-one years old, and until she'd come to Brighton, she'd been nowhere, and seen nothing. She wouldn't be stopped now by a pack of shrieking villains and a dangling eyeball or two.

Still, there was no reason to be pea-brained about it, either.

Lucy craned her neck around and peered over the roof of the carriage she'd climbed. A wagon stood a few paces behind, and beyond that was a sleek new phaeton. Neither was near enough to block the way into the open field beyond. If someone did happen to notice her, or the crowd grew too boisterous, she'd simply climb inside the carriage and exit from the door on the other side. A quick dart across the field, and she'd be back on the road in a trice.

It would be the easiest thing in the world.

So, she stayed where she was, one hand clutching the carriage wheel, her eyes wide as she took in a scene that would have made her Aunt Jarvis's blood run cold.

* * * *

"It's astounding, isn't it, how much the human nose can bleed?"

Before his opponent could recover, Tom Belcher, hero of the Fancy, landed another blow to the man's face with a second quick jab of his fist. *Crack!*

Ciaran winced. Ah, there was the distinctive snap. No mistaking it. His own nose had been abused enough times he knew it when he heard it. "Broken nose."

"What, is that all?" Sebastian Wroth, Lord Vale, pulled his hat from his head and drew his coat sleeve across his glistening brow. "With that much blood, you'd think the man's head had been ripped from his neck."

"I hope you don't have a weak stomach, Vale. It's about to get bloodier." Ciaran jerked his chin toward the ring, where Belcher had just landed a third punishing blow to his challenger's face—a big, strapping Scot named McEwan. "Belcher's got him, but I'll say this much for the Scot. The man knows how to take a blow."

Vale nodded approvingly. "Seventeen rounds, and he's still standing. Not every man who gets into the ring with Belcher can say the same. Shame we didn't wager, Ramsey."

Ciaran glanced around them. The bout would be over in another round or two, but the crowd at the Brighton Racetrack continued to swell. "Good Lord. Would you look at this pack of scoundrels, Vale? Every villain and blackguard within thirty miles of Brighton is here."

"Here, foxed, and spoiling for a brawl." Vale nodded at a group of seedy-looking fellows cursing and shoving at each other. "It'll get ugly before it ends. The smell of blood always sets them off, and the Scot is oozing from every orifice."

Ciaran didn't have a chance to reply before the big, bloody Scot in the ring managed at last to land a fierce blow. Tom Belcher's head snapped sideways. He swayed, then dropped to his knees in the dirt. The crowd howled with rage to see their favorite brought so low by a damned Scot, and it might have gotten ugly right then, but Belcher was able to rise for the next round, and the dark rumbling of the crowd turned again to enthusiastic cheers.

"Ah. That's lucky. Brawl averted, at least for now." Vale shoved his hat back onto his head, then dug into his coat and retrieved his pocket watch.

"It's nearly three. Isn't Lady Felicia expecting you back at the Abbey this evening?" Ciaran asked, referring to Vale's country seat in Lewes. Vale lived there with his three younger sisters when he wasn't running amok in London.

"She is, and I will be. Why don't you come to London for the season, Ramsey? It could be good fun, and God knows you've nothing better to do. It might get you back in Felicia's good graces."

Ciaran snorted. "Nice of you to invite me to share your misery, Vale, but I'll have to decline. I'm not in the market for a wife."

Ciaran had coaxed Vale to join him in Brighton with promises of shameless dissipation and wicked debauchery. Lady Felicia, the eldest of Vale's sisters, hadn't been pleased to see her brother go. She'd extracted a promise from him to return within a week to begin preparations for her second London season. Vale had promised, and for all his frivolousness, no one could accuse him of being an undutiful brother.

No one could accuse Ciaran of it, either. Lachlan had used phrases like "refreshing change of scenery," and "invigorating sea air" when he'd wheedled Ciaran into taking this trip, but Ciaran hadn't been fooled.

There was nothing invigorating about spending a month in Brighton with Lady Chase, Lachlan's sharp-tongued grandmother-in-law, and Lady Chase's bosom friend, Lady Atherton. Even so, Ciaran hadn't put up much of a fight. Not because he relished the idea of a month in Brighton with two cantankerous old ladies, but because Vale was right.

He didn't have anything better to do.

"Belcher has him." Vale nodded at the ring just as Belcher forced his fist into the Scot's ribs. The crowd shouted with glee as the giant staggered backward and lost his footing. "It won't last more than another round or two."

"Just as well. Damn shame to ruin such a lovely afternoon with a riot." Ciaran crossed his arms over his chest and ran a practiced eye over the crowd. Vale had the right of it. They were a rough lot. They surged closer to the ring with every blow, shoving and pummeling at each other to get a closer look. Nothing but a bloodthirsty mass of writhing rogues as far as the eye could see, except for—

Ciaran snapped to attention, his spine going rigid as he rose to his full height. A flash of something bright had caught his eye, and for a moment he'd thought it was…

Another flash of color, a familiar bright green satin, lining the hood of a lady's dark gray cloak.

Ciaran blinked, stunned. Good Lord, it *was.*

She'd pulled her hood low over her face. He couldn't see much of her aside from a heart-shaped chin and a few stray tendrils of hair, but there was no mistaking it.

No mistaking *her.*

That stubborn mouth, and those coppery red curls…he'd only ever seen one lady with hair that color. It was the troublesome chit from the beach. The lass with a kick so vicious it could put a mule to shame.

Of course, it was her. Who else could it possibly be?

First a near-drowning, and now a violent brawl. He shuddered to think what she had planned for next week. Highway robbery?

"What the *devil* is she doing here?"

"Who?" Vale turned to follow Ciaran's gaze. "I don't see…" His voice trailed off, and he lapsed into a stunned silence. Ciaran glanced at Vale to find his friend shaking his head as if to clear it. "Well, I'll be damned," he muttered, staring at the redhead.

"But…" Try as he might, Ciaran couldn't force his brain to supply a reasonable explanation as to why she should be at Brighton Racetrack, alone, once again risking her reputation and her safety. This was a bloody prizefight, for God's sake, not a tea party.

"I don't—what the *devil* is she doing here?" He sounded like a fool, repeating himself like this, but damn it, *what the devil was she doing here?* No other question made sense.

"She's, ah…it looks as if she's…well, confound it, Ramsey, that's a foolish question. The answer is as plain as day. She's watching the bout."

An incredulous laugh escaped Ciaran's lips. "Damned if she isn't."

This ladylike little chit, with her delicate face and cloud of red curls, was as riveted by the grisly spectacle unfolding in the center ring as any one of the dirty, screeching villains in their midst.

The crowd let out a roar just then, and Ciaran turned back to the ring in time to see the Scot slam a fist into Belcher's face. There was another crack of breaking bone. Blood burst in a fountain from Belcher's broken nose and splattered onto his bare chest.

Ciaran swung his gaze back toward the redhead, his muscles tensed to run for her in case she swooned. She pressed a hand to her mouth, but otherwise she didn't flinch. Not a wrinkle marred that smooth brow, not even when the Scot seized his advantage with a half-dozen lightning-quick blows to Belcher's torso, which landed with the sickening thud of fists against flesh.

"She's steady, that one," Vale said, impressed. "Strong stomach."

The crowd wasn't as steady as she was, however. They let out an infuriated roar as Belcher crumpled like a rag doll tossed aside by a careless child.

"Here comes your brawl." Vale pointed at a throng of angry men rushing toward the ring, fists flying.

Ciaran's gaze snapped back to the redheaded lady, who was still clinging to her perch, her two dainty feet balanced on the hub of the carriage wheel. "Damn it. Devil of a time to play hero, but we can't just leave her there."

The thickest part of the crowd was a good distance from her. She still had time to get away, but this sort of violence would spread from one man to the next like a contagion. "What's wrong with the chit? Why doesn't she *go*?"

"She doesn't see it, Ramsey. It's doubtful she's ever been in a crowd like this before."

"She shouldn't bloody be here *now*—"

"Thief! Thief!" Ciaran jerked his head away from her just in time to see one man grab another by the throat and throw him to the ground. "Bloody thief! Check yer pockets, lads!"

The man's outraged howl split the air, and a small knot of men broke free from the squirming mass of bodies near the ring and leapt on top of the two men grappling on the ground. Within seconds they were engaged in a vicious exchange of blows, shoving and pushing each other closer to the lady's carriage.

Ciaran's breath froze in his lungs as the horses lurched in their traces to escape the mob, and the carriage pitched beneath her. She made a quick grab for the edge of the wheel and managed to steady herself, but she might not be so lucky next time. The frenzied brawlers continued to push toward her, their shouts and curses growing louder with every second. It was only a matter of time before the horses took fright and bolted again.

"Jesus, Ramsey." Vale's face had gone white. "She'll be dragged down into the swarm and trampled under their boot heels before she even has a chance to scream."

"Go. Hurry, Vale. Fetch my carriage. I'll get her, then I'll find you."

Ciaran didn't wait for an answer. Vale's shout faded behind him as he plunged into the brawl. A man smashed his fist into Ciaran's mouth, then seized his coat and tried to throw him to the ground. No doubt he was intent on snatching Ciaran's blunt, but Ciaran slammed an elbow hard into the scoundrel's stomach, and the man dropped to the ground with a grunt.

Ciaran didn't pause, but shoved his way through the pack of villains. His mouth was rusty with the taste of blood, his gaze fixed on the place where he'd last seen a headful of red curls, and a dark gray cloak lined with green satin.

Chapter Four

A startled cry left Lucy's lips as the carriage jolted beneath her.

She gasped as one of her feet slipped and she tottered on her perch, but she managed to grab the wheel in time to keep herself from tumbling to the ground.

Oh, dear. It looked as if her adventure was coming to an abrupt end.

The crowd had gotten closer and become more frenzied. The noise had startled Lord-whoever-he-might-be's horses, and the shouts and curses were growing more deafening by the moment.

If the horses should take fright again, and she should fall…

Dash it. She'd have to go at once. It was her first prizefight, likely her last, and she'd be obliged to abandon it before it concluded. It was vexing, but there was no help for it. If she were to be injured in a fall from Lord something-or-other's carriage at a bare-knuckle prizefight, all the laudanum in England wouldn't be enough to sooth her Aunt Jarvis's frazzled nerves.

She reached behind her, bracing her palms against the top of the carriage wheel. She twisted her body around toward the door and stuck her head through the open window. Ah, good. Just as she'd thought. There wasn't a scoundrel in sight on the far side of the line of carriages. All she had to do was squirm close enough to reach the door handle, open the door and scramble out the other side of the carriage. Just a bit closer, and she'd have it—

"What the devil do you think you're doing? Can't you see you aren't safe here? Come down from there at once!"

Lucy whirled around with a gasp as two enormous hands closed around her waist. Dear God, a villain with blood dripping from his mouth was trying to tear her down from the carriage! "Unhand me at once, sir!" Lucy kicked out at him, and her foot connected with his chest.

He grunted and staggered back a little from the blow. "Another kick, lass? That's twice in one week. I'm beginning to think you don't like me."

Another kick? What did he mean, another—

Oh, no. Lucy's eyes went wide. He wasn't just *any* bleeding villain. He was *her* bleeding villain. That is, not hers exactly, but he was the same very large, very Scottish, excessively heroic gentleman from the beach!

"Can't say I enjoy being kicked in the chest, but I'd rather that than my nose again. It still hasn't recovered from the last time you kicked me."

Lucy cringed as she recalled the heel of her boot slamming into his chest. Whatever else might happen, she had to make a vow to stop assaulting the gentlemen of Brighton.

Not that the kick had done the least bit of good. The blasted man was still holding onto her. "Sir! If you'd be so kind as to let me go, I could—"

"Don't be a fool, lass." He glanced over his shoulder at the frenzied crowd, then turned back to her. "Come down now, and I'll get you safely away before it's too late."

"I'm perfectly able to get myself safely away!" Lucy stuck her head through the carriage window again. The opposite side of the carriage was still clear. There wasn't a thing to be seen but wide, open fields, and just beyond it, the empty road leading back toward the villa. It was by far the safest escape route for them both—far safer than him having to drag her through that crowd of wailing villains.If her misguided hero would only release her she could scramble through the near door and out the other side. She'd disappear down the road, and it would be as if she'd never been here at all.

She turned to her captor and spoke in the most reasonable voice she could muster. "I assure you, sir, you needn't worry about me. I don't need rescuing. If you'd be so good as to release me, you can be on your way."

He didn't reply, but looked up at her without speaking, his dark eyebrows arched over those blue, blue eyes. A long moment of silence passed as they stared at each other, neither of them moving. Then, without warning, his brows lowered, and his lips turned down in a stubborn frown.

The hair on Lucy's neck rose in alarm. "Don't!"

She thrust out a foot to stop him, though to stop him from what, she wasn't quite sure. Something in the shifting expression on his face told her he'd made up his mind to rescue her. Not just from the crowd of shrieking miscreants, but also from herself.

"Enough." He wrapped his arms around her waist and tugged.

Her foot slipped off the wheel, but before he could drag her away like some wounded animal, Lucy instinctively snatched hold of the wheel in both her hands. She wrapped her fingers around the spokes and held on like a barnacle attached to a wet rock. "For pity's sake! If you'd only listen for a moment, I'd be happy to explain myself."

My goodness, how calm she sounded! Perhaps she was growing accustomed to being dragged about by giant Scottish gentlemen. A handy skill, really. Even so, it was humiliating to be clinging to a carriage wheel with a large man attached to her waist. It occurred to her perhaps Eloisa and her aunt were right about her hoydenish ways. She didn't like them to be right, but wrestling with a bleeding man at a prizefight wasn't precisely ladylike—

"Keep arguing, lass, and you'll get us both killed." He leaned over her, pressed his chest against her back and hissed in her ear. "Look behind us." He kept an arm around her waist and jerked them both around. Her feet met the ground, and he gripped her chin in hard fingers and turned her head toward the crowd. "See that? That brawl is about to become a riot, and in another moment you're going to be trapped in the middle of it."

Lucy's mouth fell open. Dear God, what a swarm of scoundrels! While she'd been arguing with the Scot, the crowd had gotten closer. Fists flew as they rained blows down upon each other. Not four paces away from her a man was hunched over, his hands on his knees, spitting blood onto the ground.

Lucy shuddered, but before she could look away another man caught her eye and gave her a grisly leer. Then he slammed his fist into the side of the hunched man's head and sent him sprawling face-first into the dirt.

"Now then, lass. I'll ask you again." The Scot tightened his grip on her chin and turned her face back to his. "Do you want to get yourself killed?"

Lucy swallowed. "No, I'd, ah…I'd just as soon not." At least half a dozen savages now stood between her and her escape route. She could either succumb to another round of excessive heroics, or die a violent death.

"There's a clever lass." Without another word he jerked her roughly into his arms and began to shove his way through the crowd. Lucy sputtered in protest at this high-handed treatment, and he glared down at her in warning. "If you squirm, I'll have to toss you over my shoulder."

Lucy stilled, considering this. She'd come out this afternoon in search of adventures, and dangling head over heels across a gentleman's broad shoulder certainly qualified as one. Still, as thrilling as it might be to be thrown over his shoulder, this situation hardly called for more excitement. "Very well. Where are you taking me?"

His long-legged strides ate up the ground. "To my carriage."

His carriage? That didn't sound quite proper either, but she supposed she'd lost the right to quibble over propriety when she'd come to a bout and gotten caught in the midst of a brawl. "What then?"

"Once we're free of the crowd I'll take you back to your lodgings, and hope to God you're canny enough to keep away from deserted beaches and bare-knuckle bouts in the future."

My, he was determined to save her, wasn't he? For a brief second Lucy wondered whether she *needed* saving, but then dismissed the idea. She wasn't some hazy-eyed debutante, but a grown woman. She was a trifle naïve, yes, but that was what had led her out this afternoon in the first place.

She had a great deal of lost time to make up for.

"Over here!"

The Scot swung around with her still clutched in his arms. Lucy caught sight of another gentleman—this one also tall, with fair hair—standing next to a carriage that had been freed from the tangle of conveyances and stood waiting, horses at the ready. The man waved his hat in the air with one hand and beckoned to them with the other.

"Just in time."Her captor, or rescuer—Lucy hadn't yet decided which—hitched her higher in his arms and strode toward the carriage. "Be still, and we'll be out of here soon enough."

Before they could take more than two steps toward the carriage, however, a man in a mud-stained shirt came out of nowhere and grabbed Lucy's ankle. "That's a pretty little bit ye got there." He leered down at her, then smirked at her Scot. "Care to share 'er? Plenty to go around, ain't there?"

The broad shoulder under Lucy's palm went rigid. "Take your hand off the lady. *Now.*"

Lucy's eyes widened and a shiver darted up her spine at the icy warning in that voice. She wasn't easily cowed, but she wouldn't think to defy a command spoken with such menace.

But the scoundrel, who was more than a little befuddled with drink, chose to ignore the warning. He gave her foot a sharp tug and nearly sent her toppling. "Don't s'pose she's a lady." He spat on the ground. "Not a proper one, leastways. Not 'ere."

Lucy felt a low, furious growl vibrate in the Scot's broad chest, and knew at once he wouldn't issue a second warning. Oh, dear. Now they'd get into a brawl, and the Scot would have to put her down to trade blows, and if he should be beaten to a pulp she'd be left alone with a villain who was intent on grabbing far more than her ankle.

It would have to be another assault, then. "Proper enough, I promise you." Lucy jerked at her ankle with such sudden and unexpected force the scoundrel was caught off guard. He lost his grip, and once she was free of him, she didn't hesitate.

She kicked him as hard as she could in the chin with her heel.

Hoyden, indeed. She'd been in Brighton less than four days, and she'd already kicked two gentlemen in the face.

The man staggered backward, but he managed to keep his feet under him. He ran a hand over his bruised chin, his furious gaze on Lucy. "Bloody wench."

He moved forward to grab her again, but the Scot—who was much more agile than one might assume, given his size—lunged for the man with Lucy still in his arms. He caught him just behind the knees with a vicious kick, sending him flat to his back on the ground. Then he delivered a second kick to the man's ribs to ensure he'd stay there.

Lucy peered down at the man writhing on the ground, then turned to the Scot with wide eyes. "Well done."

He only grunted in reply, but his gaze met hers for a brief instant before he looked away. He really did have the loveliest pair of blue eyes she'd ever seen. Why, what a waste it was for a mere man to have such luxurious eyelashes! She was burning to find out whether they were really as dark and lush as she thought, but he didn't spare her another glance.

By the time they reached the carriage, the fair-haired gentleman was red-faced and muttering curses. "Christ, you've cut it a bit close, haven't you?" He nodded toward the tangled, heaving mass of men surging closer every minute. "I beg your pardon, miss," he added, with a polite bow for Lucy that looked rather ludicrous, given the circumstances. "I'm Lord Vale, and your disheveled champion here is—"

"Never mind, Vale." The Scot dropped Lucy unceremoniously to her feet in front of the carriage door. "This isn't a ballroom. There's no need for introductions."

"It's a pleasure to make your acquaintance, Lord Vale." Lucy felt a bit foolish curtsying while a riot raged next to her, but gentlemen such as these—fashionable, handsome, and titled gentlemen—were used to impeccable manners, bloodied mouth and brawls notwithstanding. Besides, if Aunt Jarvis ever discovered she'd met a pair of lords and hadn't curtsied, a riot would pale in comparison to her wrath.

Lord Vale slid a solicitous hand under her elbow. "Are you quite all right, miss? No danger of a swoon?"

"Certainly not."

Her dark-haired rescuer snorted. "She nearly laid a man flat with a kick to the chin, Vale. I don't think she's the sort who swoons."

"Did she indeed?" Lord Vale's gaze roamed over her with new appreciation, then he turned back to his friend with a smothered laugh. "Then *she* rescued *you*, didn't she?"

"Oh, no, my lord," Lucy hastened to clarify. "Not at all. You see, I did kick that man, but it was this gentleman who—"

"Beg pardon, lass, but can we chat another time? We're steps away from being dragged into a riot." Her dark-haired rescuer yanked the carriage door open, wrapped his hand around Lucy's arm, and urged her inside. "Any way you choose, Harrison," he called to the coachman, "Just get us out of here. Come on, Vale."

"No. I rode Horatio from the Abbey, remember? He's tethered just there, at the crest of the hill. I'll fetch him and ride directly home. Might even make it back home by three if I hurry, and escape a scold from my sister Felicia."

The Scot nodded. "Right. Good man, Vale."

Lord Vale slapped him on the back with a grin. "Deuced awkward time to decide to be a hero." He leaned through the window and smiled at Lucy. "It's been a singular pleasure, Miss. Good day."

Lucy waved as the blue-eyed Scot leapt into the carriage and slammed the door behind him. They watched until Lord Vale reached his horse and swung safely up into the saddle, then the Scot pounded a fist against the roof. The carriage jerked into motion and began to pick through the tangle of frenzied men and frightened horses.

Lucy turned to her new friend and tried a cautious smile. "Only think of the odds against us meeting twice, and under such unusual circumstances. It's remarkable, isn't it?"

"That's not how I'd describe it." He raised one dark eyebrow at her, sat back against the squabs, and crossed his arms over his chest. He didn't say another word, but fixed Lucy with a stare that had her squirming against her seat.

She frowned. He wasn't much like the dashing Scottish heroes she'd read about in Sir Walter Scott's novels. That is, she didn't deny he'd acted bravely, but he wasn't a bit gallant or charming. It was a pity, because he had the look of a hero. Tall, broad shoulders, dark hair, strong jaw and chin, and, of course, those blue eyes.

Surely, no man with such pretty eyes could be so utterly unappealing. She gave him a hopeful smile and tried again. "Fate has made herself clear on this matter, sir. She demands we become friends."

For a moment she would have sworn a corner of his lip twitched, but the flash of humor was there and then gone. He didn't respond, but continued to stare at her. The dim light in the carriage chased the blue from his eyes, leaving them a deep, shadowy gray.

As lovely as his eyes were, Lucy didn't care to have them fixed on her with such damning intensity. "We may not like it much, but I don't see we have any choice in the matter."

Not a word fell from those stubborn lips. The silence in the carriage dragged on until Lucy couldn't bear it any longer. "You look rather like a rakish sort, but that doesn't concern me. I'm certain rakes make the most amusing friends."

He let out an irritable sigh, jerked his hat from his head and tossed it onto the seat beside him. "Is that why you came here today, lass? For amusement? You nearly got a good deal more than you bargained for. Whoever is responsible for you should never have let you out of their sight."

Lucy lifted her chin and met his stony gaze with a defiant look. "I'm responsible for myself."

Legally speaking, that wasn't *quite* true. She wouldn't reach her majority for several weeks yet. Until then her Uncle Jarvis was responsible for her. Her, and her fortune. He was her guardian, he administered her trust, and he'd continue with both until she turned twenty-one.

Bitterness coated her throat, just as it always did when she thought of the terms of her father's will. His affection for her was equal parts fear and love—too much of both, perhaps. It smothered her even now, nearly a year after his death.

The Scot ran a hand through dark hair matted with sweat. "If you're so responsible, how did you end up in the midst of a brawl?"

Lucy bit back her retort and settled for an angry twitch of her skirts instead. It was provoking indeed to be accused of carelessness when she'd be safely tucked away in her villa even now if it weren't for his tedious heroics. "I had a perfectly good plan in place to protect myself from harm, but you were so determined to rescue me you dragged me right into the middle of the chaos before I had a chance to execute it."

His dark eyebrows shot up, and he let out an incredulous laugh. Now he'd found his tongue, he had plenty to say. "Ah, so it's my fault you were nearly trampled to death, is it? Plan or no, I can't think of a single good reason why you'd be—" He broke off as his gaze fell on the sketchbook and pencil still clutched in her hand. "Were you *drawing?*"

Lucy looked down. She was so used to carrying her notebook about she'd forgotten she was still holding it.

She'd only had time to make a series of quick, bold strokes on a blank page of the small sketch book, but a few more rough lines—a gaping mouth here and a clenched fist there—and it was done.

She was no artist, but long ago she'd gotten into the habit of scratching out rough sketches on little bits of paper. It amused her father, who'd been a great admirer of James Gillray's satirical prints. Her sketches were unremarkable. She lacked skill, and she'd never had much in the way of inspiring subject matter.

But this sketch was different.

Two sweating, bloody combatants at the center of the ring and the jeering crowd surrounding them…yes, she could already see how it would take shape on the page.

"You were drawing a sketch of the bout," he repeated, his voice flat.

She turned the page toward him with a tentative smile. "Well, yes. You see, I've never been to a bout before, or to a brawl, or anywhere, really, and there's no telling if I ever will be again, so I thought I'd better seize my chance while I had it."

It seemed like a perfectly reasonable explanation to her, but he didn't seem to agree. His mouth opened, then closed. Finally, he shook his head. "You must be mad."

Lucy stiffened, and resentment rose like a dark cloud in her breast.

Mad. Dear God, how she detested that word.

She turned her head away as her face heated with a painful mix of shame and embarrassment. Half of England likely did think her mad, or they would soon enough.

As soon as they knew her name.

Her father's name.

No one ever said the word "mad" in her presence. Not her father, not the servants, and not the few friends they'd had left at the end. Indeed, they'd all done their utmost *never* to say it.

Mad. Daft. Insane. Dicked in the nob. Bedlamite. Lunatic.

To hear this handsome, blue-eyed Scot say that word so boldly, right to her face…

Lucy knew he didn't mean anything by it. He couldn't know that of all the things he might have said, it was exactly the wrong one. She didn't blame him, really, but at the same time any urge she'd had to befriend him faded into nothingness.

She drew in a deep breath and turned from the window to face him. "I'm quite sane, I assure you. Stop here, please. I'd rather walk."

The villa was still a little way down the road, and her companion hesitated. He looked as if he was about to refuse her, but her expression must have made him change his mind. He reached up and pounded his fist on the roof of the carriage.

It jerked to a halt. Lucy opened the door, prepared to scramble out, but she hesitated, then turned reluctantly back to him. She wanted nothing more than to escape this carriage, but once she did, she'd rather not have a reason to reproach herself for her behavior. "Thank you for your assistance, sir. Once again, I'm grateful to you. Good day."

She pasted a sweet smile on her lips, then leapt out onto the road before he had a chance to say anything at all. She closed the carriage door in his startled face, and set off down the rutted pathway in the direction of the villa.

Mad.

Well, let him think it, if he chose. He wouldn't be the only one, or even the only one to say it aloud. Anyway, what did it matter what he believed?

There were hundreds of people in Brighton. He'd soon be on his way back to London—or wherever it was handsome, blue-eyed Scots spent their time. With any luck, she'd never lay eyes on the man again.

It wasn't until much later, when she was tucked safely into her bedchamber at the villa, that she examined the pocket of her cloak and found it empty. Her notebook, with its dozens of sketches, was gone.

Chapter Five

Three days later

"Well, well, Ciaran Ramsey. Here you are, out of your bed before dusk at last, and you look to be in as black a humor as I've ever seen you. What ails you, boy?"

Ciaran turned from the glass to face Lady Chase. A sarcastic retort rose to his lips, but he choked it back with one final, vicious tug on his cravat. She wasn't one to indulge his darker moods, and in any case, it wasn't her fault he was such a wretched devil. "Musical evenings put me in a temper."

That much was true, but it wasn't the reason he was in a black mood.

No, it was that damned redheaded chit.

He patted at his chest, where he'd tucked her notebook into the inside pocket of his coat. He'd flipped through every page of it. Not very gentlemanly of him, but after the beach and the bout he was too curious about her to resist. Her sketches were rough, but she treated her subjects with a sly humor that brought a grin to his face.

His favorite was the one she'd taken of the bout that day. Aside from a hideously detached eyeball, she'd drawn the two boxers in the ring realistically enough. But she'd exaggerated the bloodthirsty appearance of the crowd surrounding them, so it looked as if the real battle was taking place outside the ring. She'd scrawled a line at the bottom of the page. "The Famous Battle between Dozens of Unknown Scoundrels, Fought at Brighton in Sussex, May 1818." The title was a take on Gillray's celebrated print of the "famous battle" between Humphreys and Mendoza in Hampshire. Ciaran couldn't deny the clever reference amused him.

He'd been carrying the blasted notebook around for three days, hoping to return it to her. He'd searched for her in all the obvious places—the

Pump Room, the Assembly Rooms, the promenade—but he hadn't laid eyes on her since the bout.

It wasn't surprising, really. What would such an unruly chit want with the Pump Room or the promenade? Damn shame there wasn't a duel or a public hanging to hand. No doubt he'd find her *there*.

Once or twice he'd been tempted to return to the beach, but he'd resisted. It wouldn't do her any good to be seen in his company. She was doing an efficient job of ruining her reputation on her own, without any help from him.

Not that he imagined she wanted his help, or anything else from him. He'd been a horse's arse to her at the bout. Now, three days later, he was more miserable about it than he would have thought possible. He didn't give much of a damn about anything these days. He couldn't think of any reason why *she* should be the one to pierce the haze of listlessness that surrounded him, but whatever it was, he couldn't shake her loose. It was bloody frustrating. He didn't want her there, but she was like a flea burrowing into his skin. No matter how much he clawed, he couldn't get her out.

Maybe it was only that she'd surprised him. God knew a bare-knuckle bout was the last place in the world she should have been. Or maybe it was that kick she'd dealt the scoundrel who'd grabbed her. One didn't often come across a young lady with such impressive reflexes. Then there'd been the precision of the thing. She'd left a heel print on the villain's chin. Ciaran couldn't help but admire such a well-executed blow.

Maybe it was her red hair. He'd had a weakness for red hair ever since he was a lad. He'd never seen her shade of red before, and he'd grown up in Scotland, where gingers were as common as sheep. Or maybe it was because ladies with such fiery red hair generally had blue eyes, or green.

She had neither. Hers were a deep, velvety brown. Wide, long-lashed, and glinting with mischief.

"If you please, Mr. Ramsey!" Lady Chase rapped her cane on the floor to get his attention. "Lady Atherton and I intend to leave Brighton at the end of this week. You could return to Buckinghamshire with us, but you're sure to be as bored there as you are here. Why not go to London? A change of scenery would do you good."

Ciaran frowned. First Vale, and now Lady Chase. Why did everyone keep trying to send him to London? "Why would I want to go there?"

Lady Chase gave him a shrewd look. "The season's begun. I daresay some of your acquaintances are already in town. That awful Lord Vale is going, isn't he? I don't approve of Lord Vale, as you know—he's a perfect scoundrel—but between the two of you, you should be able to stir up enough trouble in London to keep yourselves amused."

Good Lord. Was Lady Chase sending him off on a debauch? "I must be dismal company indeed, ma'am, if you're fobbing me off on Vale."

"Hush, you wicked child. I'm doing no such thing. Still, London is bound to be more entertaining for a young, foolish rake like yourself than either Brighton or Buckinghamshire."

Ciaran shook his head. London, Brighton, Buckinghamshire—it was all the same to him. What his family didn't seem to understand was his lethargy hadn't a damn thing to do with his location.

It had to do with *him.*

"You'd stay at Huntington House, of course," Lady Chase added, when Ciaran remained silent. "You'd be doing your brother a favor if you went. The house is undergoing some repairs. He wants someone there to keep an eye on things, but he and Iris don't intend to go this season."

Ciaran's sister-in-law Iris, wife to his eldest brother Finn, the Marquess of Huntington had recently given birth to a baby girl. Georgiana Elizabeth Knight, otherwise known as Georgie. She was a plump, pink and white little lass, with a gummy smile destined to render every man she encountered her willing slave, starting with her Uncle Ciaran. The happy little family planned to stay tucked snugly up at the country estate for the time being.

Ciaran scraped together a half-hearted smile. "I'll think about it."

But he knew damn well going to London wouldn't solve anything. Short of a return to Scotland nothing would, yet there was no point in going *there*, either.

That was the trouble. There was no point in being anywhere.

Lady Chase frowned. She was an astute old thing, and she knew an empty promise when she heard one. Ciaran braced himself for an argument, but before Lady Chase could get a word out, she was interrupted by a murmur of feminine voices coming down the stairs.

Lady Atherton and her lady's maid stepped onto the first-floor landing. "Here we are, my lady." The maid led Lady Atherton down the final flight of stairs and turned her over to Ciaran with a bright smile. "Why, you'll be the envy of Brighton with such a handsome escort."

Lady Chase peered up at Ciaran and let out a dry huff. "Handsome, is he? With that sour face? Humph. He looks like he just swallowed a bug."

Ciaran grinned in spite of himself. He was a jaded, selfish rake and Lady Chase was a bad-tempered harridan, but they kept each other amused. He doted on her, and though she would have died before admitting it, he knew he was secretly her favorite.

He offered her an exaggerated bow. "Not a bug, my lady, only a nip or two of port. You don't object to an escort who's in his cups, do you?"

"Eh, whatever keeps the smile on your face, my boy." Lady Chase wrapped her skeletal fingers around his arm and turned to Lady Atherton. "Shall we go? Come along, Albina."

Ciaran ushered his two elderly companions out the door and into the carriage. He didn't expect to get much pleasure out of the evening, but thanks to Lady Chase at least the start of it had proved more amusing than he'd expected.

As it happened, the rest of it turned out to be…if not pleasurable, certainly more interesting than most musical evenings. It started when they reached the New Assembly Rooms. Since the day of the bout, Ciaran had gotten into the habit of searching for a headful of shining red hair wherever he went, and tonight was no different. As soon as they entered, he glanced from one corner of the room to the other, looking for a glint of copper.

He hadn't expected to actually *find* her. He'd half-reconciled himself to the possibility she'd left Brighton altogether.

She hadn't.

He came to a complete stop, gawking at her like an utter fool. It was certainly *her*—there was no mistaking that hair—but what with being kicked in the face and bleeding all over himself, he hadn't really gotten a proper look at her before.

Now, he went still and just stared at her.

She was wearing a pale-yellow gown that brought out her vivid hair, and Ciaran realized with a start her delicate face was the most perfect example of refined, ladylike English beauty he'd ever seen.

Except for her mouth. That stubborn tilt, the full lower lip—it was too sensual to be considered respectable. A trickle of sweat inched down Ciaran's neck. Jesus, that mouth was almost indecent. How the devil had *that* escaped his attention before?

He had an absurd urge to rush over to her before she could vanish again, but they hadn't been introduced, and then there was that tiny problem of his unforgiveable behavior at the bout the other day.

No, he'd have to bide his time for now, and hope for a chance later in the evening. "This way, ma'am." He led Lady Chase and Lady Atherton to chairs just to the right and a few rows back, where he could keep an eye on his redhead.

Then he simply sat back and watched her. She held her bright head high, her face directed toward the front of the room where an ensemble of glee singers gathered around a lady seated at a pianoforte. When he'd first come upon her on the beach, there'd been a spark in her dark brown eyes, and he imagined it there now as she absorbed everything around her, alive to every note, every vibration of the music.

Just...alive.

Maybe that was why he'd resisted the idea of a friendship between them. Half-dead things tended to resent live ones. Live things were, after all, a great deal of work. She'd already irritated him into giving a damn again. What was next? Laughter, hopefulness, a returning interest in life? Because it sounded exhausting—

"Pretty thing, isn't she?" Lady Chase nudged him in the ribs.

"Who?" Ciaran asked, dragging his gaze to her.

"Who?" Lady Chase snorted. "Do you suppose I'm blind? The young lady you can't take your eyes off, of course."

Ciaran swallowed. No use denying it. "Do you know who she is?"

Lady Chase raised her quizzing glass to her eyes. "Hmmm. That red hair...unusual, isn't it? She looks vaguely familiar, but I can't quite place her face. I'm certain I've never laid eyes on her companions before."

Ciaran had been so preoccupied with his redheaded lady he hadn't noticed her companions, but now Lady Chase mentioned it he saw she was sitting next to a pretty, dark-haired girl about her own age. He'd never seen the girl before, and he also didn't recognize the pinch-faced matron on her other side.

"Albina, what do you think?" Lady Chase leaned over Ciaran and tapped Lady Atherton's arm with her fan. She nodded toward the redhead. "I vow I've seen her face, but I can't quite recall where. It's excessively provoking!"

"My dear Anne, don't you know? Why, Lady Essex was talking about her just this morning in the Pump Room." Lady Atherton leaned across Ciaran, lowering her voice. "That's the Earl of Bellamy's daughter."

Ciaran straightened in his seat. An earl's daughter? It was the very last thing he'd expected to hear. He'd met scores of earl's daughters last season in London, and this lady wasn't like any of them. Not many earl's daughters hung about at bare-knuckle prizefights.

"Bellamy! My goodness. She doesn't look much like old Bellamy, does she? At least, not what I remember of him. She must resemble her mother." Lady Chase lowered her quizzing glass with a sigh. "Poor thing."

Ciaran's brows drew together. "Poor thing? Why?"

Lady Atherton echoed Lady Chase's sigh. "I suppose she's off to London for the season once she leaves Brighton. She hasn't even arrived yet, and already the *ton* is gossiping about her. I'm afraid they won't be kind to her, given the rumors about her father."

Ciaran jerked his gaze toward Lady Atherton. "What rumors?"

Lady Atherton didn't answer him. She was deep in consultations with Lady Chase, and both of them appeared to have forgotten he was there. "Does she have any money?"

"Old Bellamy had plenty of it. Never had occasion to spend it, did he? Well, it will be a great deal easier for her if she's possessed of a grand fortune. The *ton* will overlook a good deal if she's a wealthy heiress, even madness."

"Madness! For God's sake, she isn't mad!" She was unconventional, yes, but there was no crime in that. Ciaran's own sister Isla was unconventional, and she was the sanest person he knew.

His voice must have been sharper than he realized, because Lady Chase raised an eyebrow at him. "Oh? And how would you know that, sir? Have you met her?"

"No, I...no." It wasn't *quite* a lie. They'd never been introduced. He didn't even know her name. "That is, I spoke to her once, by accident, and I tell you she's perfectly sane."

Lady Chase noticed his distress, and reached over to pat his hand. "Of course, she is, but people will call her mad, just the same. Her father wasn't quite right in the head, and they'll imagine the same of her, even if she's as sane and sober as a judge."

People will call her mad...

Ciaran closed his eyes, pinching the bridge of his nose.

Bloody, bloody, bloody hell.

He'd called her mad—the day of the bout, after Vale left and he'd been alone with her in his carriage. He'd noticed the notebook and pencil clutched in her fist, and he'd said something about how she must be mad to be drawing in the middle of a brawl.

And she...

Ciaran's jaw went tight as he recalled the way her dark eyes had dimmed, and the smile had fallen from her lips. She'd gone very quiet, and a few moments later she'd asked to be let down from the carriage.

He smothered a groan. Had she thought he was mocking her, or her father? She'd never told him her name, but if the old ladies in Brighton were already gossiping about her, she might have believed he recognized her.

"What's her name?" Ciaran asked, his voice hoarse.

"Lady...lady, er..." Lady Chase turned to Lady Atherton. "Albina?"

Lady Atherton looked as puzzled as Lady Chase. "I couldn't say. I've only ever heard her referred to as Bellamy's daughter. One doesn't hear much about her, does one, aside from in relation to her father. The girl's always been rather a mystery. I don't think she'd ever been out in company before she came to Brighton."

Damn it. If she'd appeared that suddenly, she could disappear just as quickly. This was the first time he'd seen her since the bout, and there was no telling when she might turn up again. If he didn't speak to her now, he might not get another chance. He just needed a quick word, a chance to offer an apology, or at least an explanation.

Lady Chase tapped his arm. "If you wish to speak to her, you'd best do it at once. It looks as if they're leaving."

The concert wasn't over, but her party had risen from their seats and were making their way toward the exit. Without thinking, Ciaran shot to his feet. His sudden movement caught her attention, and her head snapped toward him.

Their gazes locked, and the room seemed to blur around him as they stared at each other.

Such dark eyes...

Dazed, Ciaran took a step toward her, but a single step was as far as he got.

She blinked, her face expressionless, and then...then she deliberately dropped her eyes, and turned away.

* * * *

"Lucy, who is that man staring at you?"

"Nobody." Lucy took her aunt's arm, but as she hurried her toward the door Eloisa paused and turned to glance over her shoulder. It caught Aunt Jarvis's attention, and she stopped as well.

She let out a little gasp as her gaze fell on Lucy's dark-haired tormentor. "My goodness, he's a handsome, gentlemanly looking sort, isn't he? Have you an admirer already, dear?"

Lucy smothered a snort. Her reluctant hero was still staring at her. He had a decidedly odd look on his face, but she doubted it was admiration. Disdain, perhaps, or some sort of gastric ailment. This was Brighton, after all. Didn't everyone here have gastric ailments?

"No, Aunt. I've, ah, never laid eyes on that gentleman before. He must have mistaken me for another lady." Lucy flinched at the lie, but she could hardly tell the truth, could she?

He saved me from being trampled to death in a brawl at a bare-knuckle boxing match.

No, a lie would have to do.

"It's very rude of him to stare like that." Lucy sniffed, trying once again to herd her aunt and cousin out the door.

But Eloisa refused to be herded. "Are you certain, Lucy? Because he's still watching you, and he looks a bit, oh, I don't know...dejected?"

Dejected? Lucy was tempted to look back at him to see for herself, but she resisted the urge. What was the point? It wasn't as if the two of them were going to become friends. She'd already tried to befriend him, and he'd rejected her both times. She had too much pride to offer a third time, and anyway, she'd changed her mind about him.

She didn't care for rude gentlemen who so carelessly tossed about words like *mad*, no matter how pretty their eyes might be. "Yes, yes, I'm quite certain. Come along, Eloisa, before your mother becomes fatigued."

Aunt Jarvis had had a good day today, and Lucy wanted to keep it that way. Uncle Jarvis had taken himself off somewhere, and her aunt's spirits had risen with every hour of his continued absence.

Lucy didn't suppose it was a coincidence.

It was true her Aunt Jarvis could be tedious, with her dozens of bottled cures and hosts of imaginary ailments, but underneath her fits and palpitations she had a good, kind heart. On her best days, Lucy could see glimmers of the mother she'd lost in her aunt, and she was growing quite fond of her.

Aunt Jarvis sighed. "I am indeed fatigued, but my nerves are a bit agitated. I'm afraid I won't sleep tonight."

Lucy had taken Eloisa's arm to hurry her out the door, and she felt it stiffen under her fingers. Whenever her aunt complained her nerves were agitated and she wouldn't sleep, it meant she intended to dose herself with laudanum. Aunt Jarvis's appetite for the stuff alarmed Eloisa. So much so her cousin would now insist on staying at her mother's bedside all night to watch over her.

No, no. This wouldn't do. Aunt Jarvis was becoming dozy and dull-witted, and Eloisa was worrying herself to a frazzle. "Never mind, Aunt. I have just the thing to soothe your nerves." Lucy patted her aunt's hand.

"Have you, dear? What is it?"

"It's ah...it's called Dr. Digby's Healing Tonic." The lie rolled so easily off her tongue Lucy wondered if she shouldn't be ashamed of herself. "You've heard of Dr. Digby, of course."

Aunt Jarvis gave her a blank look. "No, I can't say I have."

"Indeed? How curious. Everyone in Devon knows of him. He's dead now, but in his day, he was one of England's most famous apothecaries. His tonic was said to cure every ill."

"Every ill? Even the headache? You know how badly I suffer from the headache, Lucinda."

Lucy did know. A headache that could be traced directly back to Uncle Jarvis. "I know, Aunt, but I'm certain Dr. Digby's tonic will set you to rights. Shall I make up a batch for you tonight, to help calm your nerves?"

"Can't we simply go to the apothecary and fetch a bottle tomorrow?" Aunt Jarvis asked.

"Oh, well, as to that…er, you can't buy it anymore. Dr. Digby has been dead for some years now. My father was friends with him, though, and the doctor was good enough to share the recipe with him. I made it for my father countless times, and I know it by heart."

Eloisa made a small, choking sound. Lucy glanced at her cousin out of the corner of her eye and saw the tiniest smile on Eloisa's lips.

"Indeed, Mama, it sounds like just the thing." Eloisa cleared her throat. "I think you should try it."

"I daresay I will, if Lucinda doesn't mind taking the trouble to make up a batch for me."

Lucy hid a grin. "Not at all, Aunt."

"Well, well. You're a good girl, Lucinda." Aunt Jarvis settled her arm more comfortably against Lucy's. "Shall we go, then?"

Lucy could feel a pair of blue eyes boring into her back as they made their way out the door of the New Assembly Rooms and toward the line of waiting coaches. She shivered as the hair on her neck rose, but she didn't turn around.

With any luck, she'd never lay eyes on the man again.

Chapter Six

The following day
Five o'clock in the morning

"For God's sakes, Ramsey, be still, will you? You're as jumpy as a scalded cat tonight. You're distracting me from my cards." Lord Godfrey slammed his fist down and the mess of discarded cards, coins, and slips of paper scattered across the table jumped from the force of the blow.

Ciaran's head jerked up. He'd been restless all evening, fidgeting and cursing over his cards, and if the scowls on the faces of the other six gentlemen at the table were any indication, Godfrey wasn't the only one who was distracted.

Something hot and angry flickered in his chest, and his jaw went tight. He glanced from one face to the next, his eyes narrowed.

I don't want to be here.

Just like that the truth burst upon him, as sudden as it was undeniable.

He hadn't wanted to be here for days now. He was sick of this cramped room in the back of the Castle Inn. Sick of the smoking fire, and sick of the haze of snuff dusting the air. Sick of the company. Especially Lord Godfrey, who was slipperier than a muddy London street and about as honest as a pickpocket.

Sick of himself.

He tossed his cards face down on the table, snatched his coat from the back of his chair, and slammed out the door without a word of explanation to anyone. He turned left on Castle Square and kept walking until he disappeared into the small, winding streets off Lewes Road.

He wasn't going anywhere in particular. Just a random stroll, to clear his head. He didn't have a destination in mind, or someplace special he needed to be.

Or so he told himself, as he wandered the darkened streets.

If he gave any conscious thought to his direction, he wouldn't go. He'd been fighting the urge to return to the lonely little stretch of beach since the morning he'd dragged her out of the water. He didn't want to go there now, but he knew he'd never have another moment's peace until he did.

He couldn't say whether he hoped she'd be there, or if he hoped the opposite. He wasn't sure it mattered. Either way his footsteps led him there, to the rock wall circling the beach where he'd last seen the troublesome redheaded chit who, despite his every attempt to banish her, still haunted his thoughts.

He didn't *want* to be her friend. Between the prizefight brawl and her ill-advised swimming adventures, he couldn't imagine a more troublesome young lady. But he found he no longer had a choice.

He couldn't stay away.

He scanned the surf, straining for a glimpse of a dark, wet head bobbing among the rolling waves. It was some time before he caught a quick movement out of the corner of his eye, and turned just in time to see her toss her head to clear the mass of wet hair from her face.

As soon as he saw her, the tight thing he'd been carrying inside for days unfurled and loosened. He filled his lungs with the crisp sea air and tried to remember the last time he'd taken such a deep, cleansing breath.

He watched her for a while as she kicked and frolicked in the water, then he leapt from the rock wall to the beach. He waited until she rose dripping from the waves, looking like some sort of mythical ocean creature with her bright hair lying in tangled curls down her back. A harmless mermaid, or a dangerous siren. Ciaran wasn't sure which, but after days of struggling to stay away from her, he no longer cared.

She emerged from the sea, water streaming from her hair, and began to make her way up the beach. Ciaran saw the moment when she noticed him, but she didn't stumble or stop, nor did her expression change. She wandered toward the rock where the gray cloak and length of toweling were folded neatly, just as they'd been that first day. She didn't speak to him, or even spare him a glance until she'd run the towel over her hair, tugged her cloak on, and laced her boots. Only then did she turn to him. She fixed him with a look that was both bland and penetrating at once, and asked, "What are you doing here?"

Ciaran's cravat suddenly felt as if it were choking him. He had to resist the urge to slide a finger underneath to loosen it. "I, ah…I have something of yours. I wanted to return it."

It wasn't the real reason he'd come, but she looked so forbidding he couldn't bring himself to tell her he'd changed his mind and wanted to be her friend, after all.

Wanted it with the sort of desperation he hadn't felt in months.

"My notebook." She held out her hand.

Ciaran swung the coat off his shoulder, dug around in the inside pocket, and placed the small book in her palm.

Her fingers closed around it. "Did you look through it?"

He briefly considered lying to her, but that was no way to start a friendship. "I did. They're very good."

She frowned. "No, they aren't. You needn't flatter me. I don't pretend to be an artist."

"But they are good, though not in the usual way." Why should they be? Nothing else about her was in the usual way. "Shall I tell you which are my favorites?"

She hadn't expected that. Her brows rose in surprise. "If you like."

"The older gentleman, with the thick, white hair and the flushed cheeks. He looks both disapproving and delighted at once. Is he your father?"

"No. Our butler, Popple. He was trying to teach me the quadrille, but I'm afraid I'm an indifferent pupil."

"An excellent swimmer, though." Ciaran offered her a hesitant grin.

She tried to resist a return smile, but her lips gave an unwilling twitch. "An excellent swimmer, yes. Do you have any other favorites?"

"The Famous Battle between Dozens of Unknown Scoundrels Fought at Brighton in Sussex, May 1818," Ciaran answered at once. "Clever reference to Gillray's print."

Another reluctant twitch of the lips. "My father was fond of Gillray."

They stood there staring at each other. Her expression was faintly puzzled, as if she didn't know what to make of this encounter, but after a moment she drew up her hood. "Thank you for returning the notebook to me. You're very kind," she said, before turning away.

Ciaran watched her stroll down the sandy beach, a slender, hooded figure, a few strands of her red hair blowing in the breeze. She'd made it halfway—just far enough for an odd sinking sensation to squeeze his chest—when he gave in to the sharp urge lodged somewhere under his breastbone.

Before he could talk himself out of it, a shout burned its way up his throat and flew out of his mouth. "Tell me your name, lass!"

She turned back to him, hesitating, but just when he'd given up any hope of an answer, she cupped her hands around her mouth and shouted something to him.

"What?" He couldn't make it out. He started toward her, but she waved him back.

"My name is Lucy!" she called again.

When she lowered her hands from her mouth, Ciaran saw she was smiling, and his lips curved in response.

"Just Lucy?" he called back.

He was certain she'd heard him, but she didn't reply—only resumed her trek across the sand. Once she reached the road she paused, then turned and gave him a small wave before disappearing around a corner.

Lucy. The Earl of Bellamy's daughter. It wasn't much to go on. It would be difficult to find out much about her until he discovered her full name.

Ciaran was halfway to his lodgings before it occurred to him she didn't want it to be easy. This was just the way she'd intended it.

* * * *

The following day

Five forty in the morning.

Lucy rested her arms on her bent knees and squinted at the bluff, her bare toes curling into the sand. She'd been coming out to the beach for her sunrise swim every morning since her arrival in Brighton, but this morning she didn't venture into the water.

She was waiting.

She'd have to return to her lodgings soon. Her Uncle Jarvis didn't generally wake before noon, but she wouldn't tempt fate, just the same. The servants didn't pry into her comings and goings, but if her uncle found out about her solitary jaunts to the beach he'd fall into a dreadful temper, and her cousin and aunt would feel his wrath just as surely as Lucy would.

Ten more minutes, and not a second longer—

"Haven't drowned yet, lass?"

The deep, lilting voice came from behind her. A delighted smile rose to Lucy's lips, but she tamped it down before she turned to glance at him over her shoulder. It wouldn't do to look too eager. "No. I haven't gone in this morning. I was just sitting here watching the sky, and..."

Waiting for you.

It was the most natural thing in the world, the way those words rose to her lips, but Lucy didn't speak them. It wouldn't do for him to think she'd been breathlessly awaiting him, her heart thudding with anticipation in her chest.

"And?" He ambled over and plopped down beside her in the sand.

Lucy eyed him. He looked like a dissipated wreck, and she wasn't much better, clad only in her bathing costume with her cloak draped loosely over her shoulders. It was a bit late for maidenly shyness *now*. So, she took a breath and told him the truth. "I was waiting for you. I was afraid I'd miss you entirely if I went in, and you see, I was right."

Lucy peeked at him from the corner of her eye. He looked like the very picture of a wicked rake, with his hair standing on end and a shadow of dark stubble across his jaw. Between that and his rumpled clothes and heavy-lidded, bloodshot eyes, he looked as if he'd been on an infamous debauch the night before, and hadn't yet been to his bed.

No doubt that was precisely the case, but Lucy kept the thought to herself. This friendship—or whatever one chose to call it—was a strange and fragile thing, and she didn't want to test it just yet. If she scolded him, she might frighten him away.

He'd been staring out at the water, but now his blue gaze met hers. "Would you have been disappointed if you'd missed me?"

Lucy hesitated. She'd offered him her friendship before only to be rebuffed, but he was *here*, wasn't he? She took a deep breath and plunged ahead. "Of course, I would be. You're the only friend I have in Brighton."

Not *just* Brighton, but all of England.

He raised one dark eyebrow. "If we're truly friends, then why won't you tell me your name?"

"I *did* tell you my name. It's Lucy, remember?"

A brief smile drifted across his lips. "Your *last* name, lass. You have one of those, don't you?"

She had one, but she'd hardly made it out of Devon before she realized revealing it would do her more harm than good. Lucy bit her lip and jerked her gaze away from him before he could coax the truth out of her with that playful smile and those teasing blue eyes. He might look harmless, but she suspected he was dangerously charming under that mussed hair and careless attitude. Rakes generally were, weren't they?

Lucy grabbed a handful of cool sand and sifted it through her fingers. "Why are you so determined to know?"

He stretched his legs out in front of him and leaned back on his hands with a shrug. "Why are you so determined to hide it, unless you're some sort of criminal who's escaped from your gaolers?"

She *had* escaped from her gaolers, though not in the way he meant. "Nonsense. Do I look like a criminal to you?"

"Well, you've assaulted me twice, so there's that."

Lucy choked on a laugh. "It's not a proper assault unless there's a broken bone."

"It's not a proper friendship if we don't know each other's names," he countered, blinking innocently at her.

"Proper? You've seen me in my bathing costume. I nearly broke your nose with a kick to the face, and now we're here alone on a deserted beach. We're long past any concerns about propriety, sir."

"Ciaran."

"I beg your pardon?"

He glanced at her, his dark hair fluttering around his face in the morning breeze. "My name. It's Ciaran."

"Ciaran." Lucy rolled the name over her tongue, testing it. It was shorter in her mouth than in his, blunted. She preferred the way he said it, with his lilt exaggerating the vowels.

Still, she nodded in approval. "It suits you. Yes, I suppose it'll do."

* * * *

The following day
Four fifty-five in the morning.

"I suppose it doesn't matter that you won't tell me your full name, Lucy. It's not as if we can truly be friends, in any case. Gentlemen and ladies never can be."

They'd been lying quietly on the sand, but Ciaran's sudden announcement startled Lucy out of her thoughts. She squirmed into a sitting position and pulled her cloak more securely around her shoulders. "What do you mean, they can't be friends? Of course, they can."

Ciaran rolled over onto his side and propped his head in his hand. "No, they can't. Etiquette, manners, a lady's modesty—even a gentleman's honor all forbid it."

It was on the tip of Lucy's tongue to point out their odd friendship wasn't based on either etiquette or manners, and least of all her modesty, but instead she merely shot him a disdainful look. "That's the most absurd thing I ever heard in my life."

Ciaran shrugged. "True, nonetheless. A gentleman and a lady might be courting, or in love, or betrothed, or lovers, but not friends."

The trace of bitterness in his voice made Lucy pause, but she balked at letting such a statement go unchallenged. "Have you ever had…"

A lover who wasn't a friend?

No, no, she couldn't ask him that. Despite the sheltered life she'd led—or maybe because of it—she wasn't prudish about such things, but even she knew better than to quiz a man about his past lovers. "What sort of man becomes betrothed to a lady, much less marries her or takes her as his, er…lover, if she isn't also his friend?"

His lover. Dear God, Eloisa would fall into a swoon if she could hear this conversation.

Ciaran gave her a look that was both amused and pitying at once. "Every sort of man there is, I promise you. Don't be so naïve, lass."

Lucy was quiet for a moment, considering this. She'd never had a friend at all, never mind a betrothed or a lover, so she was hardly qualified to hold an opinion on the subject, but even so, she wouldn't allow him to be right about this. It was simply too disheartening for her to acknowledge it as the truth. "That's utter nonsense."

"Is it? Tell me then, Lucy. How many gentleman friends do you have?"

You're the only one.

Not just her only gentleman friend. Her only *friend.* And not just for now, but for as long as she could remember. Lucy looked away from him, out toward the ocean, and lifted her face to the breeze. Before she'd come here, how long had it been since she'd felt the wind on her cheeks, or listened to the gentle swell of the waves as they rolled up to the beach?

So long, she couldn't remember the last time.

As far as friends went, well…a lady who wasn't allowed to leave her father's house didn't have friends, did she? What would Ciaran think if he knew before she'd come to Brighton, she hadn't spoken to a single soul in two years aside from her father and their servants?

She didn't want him to know. Not him, or anyone else. So, she kept silent.

Ciaran took this as agreement and flopped back down on his back in the sand. "It's no wonder, is it? As soon as a gentleman even glances at a lady, some fool or other is shrieking at him to marry her. It's not worth the risk."

This causal pronouncement made a prickle of irritation dart down Lucy's spine. Ciaran must have a great many friends to be able to dismiss friendship so carelessly. "A true friendship is worth any risk." She held up her hand when he tried to interrupt. "Never mind. If that's your only objection, then there's no reason in the world *we* can't be friends. I'd never agree to marry you, no matter who might shriek about it. I don't intend to ever marry."

Ciaran sat up again and cast her a quizzical look. "What, never?"

"That's right. Never."

He studied her, his brows lowered suspiciously, then his face cleared and he shrugged. "You say so now, but you'll change your mind. In the end, every lady chooses to marry, whether or not she has any real affection for her victim…er, her betrothed, I mean."

Lucy frowned, studying him. The way he'd said that—about a lady having no real affection for her betrothed—it sounded as if he was speaking from experience. "Have *you* ever been betrothed?"

He was quiet for so long she thought he wouldn't answer her, but eventually he did. "I've been in love."

Lucy couldn't help but notice he hadn't really answered the question. "Were you her friend?"

His laugh was bitter. "Yes, but she wasn't mine."

The hurt in his voice made Lucy pause. Whoever this mysterious lady was, she must have broken his heart. She let the silence stretch between them for long moments, the only sound the soft splash of the waves breaking on the beach. "Well, I'm nothing at all like most ladies. I won't ever marry, despite what you may think. There are a great many things more important to me than marriage."

Ciaran raised an eyebrow. "Like what?"

"Like freedom." Lucy bit out the word between gritted teeth. Her father had kept her locked in a gilded prison, and he'd called it love. Maybe it was a sort of love, too—the only sort he could offer her—but even as she'd adored him, she'd never willingly return to that half-life she'd lived. And what was a husband, if not another master? "I'm not the sort of lady who's likely to fall in love, in any case."

Ciaran studied her without speaking. Finally, a faint smile drifted across his lips. "I don't believe you are like every other lady, Lucy. Not like any other lady I've ever known."

He rose to his feet and brushed off his breeches, then held a hand out to her. Lucy took it, and he helped her up. When she gained her feet, they were standing far closer than she'd anticipated they would be. So close she could breathe in the faint scent of the ocean breeze clinging to his skin, and see the black starburst at the center of his eyes.

That's why they're so blue.

She stared up at him, a peculiar breathlessness in her chest she'd never felt before. That shade of blue made her think of the ocean stretched out behind them, the waves curling endlessly onto the beach.

Lucy cleared her throat. "Friends, then?"

Ciaran grinned down at her, a smile warming his eyes. "Friends."

* * * *

The following day

Five twenty in the morning

Despite his promise of friendship, every morning after he parted from Lucy, Ciaran never consciously planned to return to the beach again the following day.

It just happened.

He and Lucy never discussed it, but somehow an understanding had sprung up between them. He would come to the beach every morning, and every morning she would be there, waiting for him.

This morning, he'd kept her waiting longer than usual.

When he approached, he found her sitting on the beach, her legs curled underneath her, her face and hair hidden by the deep hood of her cloak. "Don't say I've missed this morning's grand bathing excursion?"

Ciaran gave the back of her hood a playful tug, drawing it down so he could see her face. The soft breeze brushed damp tendrils of hair around her rosy cheeks, and he was aware of a low hum of pleasure in his belly. Lucy was his friend, and he didn't aspire to make her his lover, but he couldn't deny she made his skin prickle with awareness.

Even when she looked cross, like she did right now, with one eyebrow arched, and her mouth tight.

"What?" Ciaran held his hands up innocently. "What have I done?"

"You *did* miss the bathing excursion." Her voice was tart, and her dark gaze narrowed as she took in his wrinkled coat and the soiled cravat hanging limply around his neck. "Your debauchery has kept you later than usual this morning. Are you onto something new?"

Ciaran made a half-hearted effort to smooth his clothing and tame his mussed hair, but gave it up as a lost cause. He tried a wheedling grin instead. "No, just the usual, dull debauchery. Wagering, drinking, ladies of questionable virtue. That sort of thing."

He kept his tone light, but aside from the questionable ladies, this account of his evening wasn't far from the truth. Lucy seemed to recognize it as a confession, because the disapproving pinch of her lips deepened.

"Don't be angry, Lucy. I beg your pardon for being late," he offered meekly.

"I'm not angry because you're late. I'm angry because you behave like a wastrel. It's just as well I don't know your last name. I'm certain you're the worst sort of rake, and I don't want my conscience pricking at me to give you up."

He lowered himself onto the sand beside her with a sigh. "That's what rakes *do*, Lucy—they waste their time. I recall you saying once you hoped I was a rakish sort, because they're the most amusing friends."

"I don't mind a rake, but I can't abide a gentleman who squanders his time in such pointless pursuits. Surely there's something more useful you could be doing?"

Ciaran opened his mouth to defend himself, then closed it again. He'd spent every night since he arrived in Brighton wagering and getting foxed. Before that, he'd spent months in Buckinghamshire doing the same thing. He *was* a wastrel, and he'd yet to find any point in it. "Like what? What would you have me do?"

"You could attend your poor, sickly grandmother. Isn't that why you came to Brighton in the first place? You use her very ill, Ciaran. Indeed, I feel quite sorry for her."

Ciaran snorted. Lady Chase, poor and sickly? The only debilitating condition she suffered from was chronic bad temper. "Don't waste your pity on Lady Chase, Lucy. She's as strong as a horse, and bound to outlive us all. In any case, she's not my grandmother. My two eldest brothers' wives are her granddaughters. Such a convoluted relationship doesn't demand constant attendance."

Lucy made a disgusted noise. "Is that so? Well, I daresay your brothers imagined you would attend her, or they wouldn't have asked you to accompany her to Brighton at all."

Ciaran let out a short laugh. "That's not why they sent me to Brighton."

Talking of his brothers depressed him. It wasn't that he didn't love his family. He did, more than he could say. But his siblings were married, with lives of their own. Somehow, Lachlan and Isla had managed to move on from the wreckage they'd left behind them in Scotland.

Only Ciaran hadn't. Somehow, he'd fallen behind.

"Why, then?" Lucy asked.

"To get rid of me." Ciaran winced, aware of how sulky he sounded. Lachlan and Finn hadn't truly sent him to Brighton to get rid of him, but if they had, could he really blame them? No doubt they were as sick of him as he was of himself.

Lucy frowned. "Why should they wish to get rid of you?"

Ciaran tossed a pebble toward the water with a sigh. "Because they're tired of watching me laze about in Buckinghamshire, drinking up all their port and being useless."

"Well, that's easily remedied." Lucy sat up and dusted the sand briskly from her hands. "Don't be useless."

* * * *

The following day

Five forty in the morning

"Are you going to scold me again this morning, Lucy?" Ciaran asked, easing himself flat onto his back beside her in the sand.

Lucy studied him for a moment, then lowered herself onto her own back, imitating his posture, even as she knew she'd spend the rest of the day trying to shake the grains of sand from her hair. "Do you deserve to be scolded?"

He stared up at the sky for a while without answering, his arms folded behind his head, then muttered, "Aye."

Lucy shifted her gaze from his profile to the water. They were both quiet as they watched the first rays of sun peek over the horizon. Lucy closed her eyes against the light, but it continued to press insistently against her eyelids. She didn't have much time left this morning. "I won't scold, but I do have a question for you."

He rolled his head toward her. "What?"

"You told me you'd been in love before. What did it feel like?" Lucy drew in a breath. "That is, how did you know you were in love?"

He lifted one shoulder in a shrug, but his tone was wistful. "I just knew. She was the first lass I ever kissed. I was only nine years old at the time, but I remember thinking I'd marry her someday."

"Why didn't you?" Lucy asked softly.

His mood shifted, went darker.

"It was more that *she* didn't marry *me*." He let out a weary sigh. "It's a long story, lass. There were some difficulties with my family, and we were forced to leave Scotland in a hurry. I haven't been back since."

Difficulties...

He didn't say what sort of difficulties, but he'd stiffened beside her.

A lady he'd known since he was a child, a lady he'd grown up with, fallen in love with—a lady who'd perhaps broken a promise to love him in return. Was she the reason Ciaran's smiles never lingered for long and rarely reached his eyes? If he was cynical about friendship and love, perhaps it was because he had reason to be.

Lucy hesitated. It didn't sound as if he wanted to talk about this, but there was one more thing she wanted to know. "Do you ever think about going back to Scotland?"

He didn't look at her. Instead he grabbed a fistful of sand and watched as it drifted through his open fingers. "Aye."

Lucy wanted to ask why he didn't, but she held her tongue. Something in his voice when he uttered that one word warned her not to prod any further.

Chapter Seven

One week later

Four twenty-five in the morning

The next week flew by in a blur of sand, ocean breezes, and plump, stubborn lips quirked in a smile. Ciaran spent every morning on the beach with Lucy, his back flat against the sand, spouting whatever nonsense came into his head.

It was as if he'd known her forever. As if they'd been friends all his life.

She never indulged or coddled him. Instead she scolded and challenged him, needled and poked and prodded until he couldn't decide whether to tease her, shout at her, or dissolve into laughter. It felt good, all those impulses and emotions fluttering to the surface again, like blood surging under his skin.

The only time in his day he didn't feel either deadened or restless—the only time he felt he was exactly where he was supposed to be—were the moments when he was with her. During those dark, quiet mornings on the beach with Lucy, he found himself again. Not the man he'd become since he'd arrived in England, but the man he'd been before. The Scotsman who'd spent his childhood running free on the moors. The man who'd fallen in love with a dark-haired Scottish lass, and dreamed he'd marry her one day.

He'd thought that man was gone forever, a ghost wandering the Great North Road, lost somewhere between Scotland and England. He'd grieved for that man—thought him long since dead and buried, along with all those childhood dreams he'd once cherished. But they weren't dead. The spark had been there the whole time, just buried under layers of scar tissue.

Lucy had brought that guttering spark to life again. He didn't know why it had been her, or even how she'd done it. His own family had been trying to drag him back to life for months now, without any success. But then that was the way of things sometimes, wasn't it? Sometimes a stranger could offer you something more than the family you loved ever could.

Or maybe that wasn't it at all. Maybe it was just *her*. Maybe it was just that it was impossible for a man to stay numb and frozen when he stood so close to a burning flame. She'd jarred him from his stupor, dragged him kicking and screaming back into the world of the living.

She was the best friend he'd ever had.

He couldn't explain how Lucy had come to mean so much to him in so short a time. He didn't even try to. It didn't matter why. What mattered was he'd been letting the tide toss him from one wave to the next for months now, as if he were helpless to choose his own direction.

He wasn't helpless. That was a lie. A lie he might still believe, if it weren't for Lucy.

And so, this morning when she laid a hand gently on his arm and asked, "What is it you want most, Ciaran?" he wanted to tell her. He just had to find the words.

When he didn't answer right away, Lucy's fingers tightened on his sleeve. "Whatever it is, all the drinking and wagering and debauchery in the world won't take its place. If you don't want to be in Brighton, or in Buckinghamshire, or in London, then where do you want to be?"

Ciaran swallowed. It had taken him so long to admit the truth to himself the words felt awkward leaving his lips. "Scotland. I want to go back to northern Scotland, to the village where I was raised, and see if there's anything left for me there."

As soon as he said it aloud, something gave way inside him. The tightness under his breastbone loosened with the words, and God, it felt good, that hesitant swell of hope that took its place.

His brothers wouldn't like it. Lachlan in particular had insisted they leave Scotland behind after their mother died, part of a past that was better forgotten. That they leave behind all the ugliness and betrayal of their final few months there.

But when Lachlan left their home—the only home they'd ever known— he hadn't left the woman he loved behind.

Ciaran had.

Dark-haired, blue-eyed Isobel, the lady he'd loved for as long as he'd been old enough to understand what love was. The lady he'd always thought he'd make his wife someday.

The lady who'd betrayed him.

Even now, so many months later, he still couldn't believe she'd turned her back on him. Isobel had been his friend as well as his love. He'd trusted her. She'd been the first person he'd gone to after James Baird's untimely death. When all their friends had been cursing Lachlan as a murderer and Isla as a whore, Ciaran had turned to Isobel for solace.

He'd never dreamed she'd abandon him.

But that was what had happened. He'd been stunned, heartbroken, and at an utter loss to understand *why*. Had she truly believed Lachlan was a murderer? Or had it simply been easier for her to condemn his family, just as all their other friends were? Had it been a moment of fear and weakness, or had she always been weak, and he'd been too blinded by love to see her for who she truly was?

He had to return to Scotland. Nothing would ever be right for him until he did. He needed to see Isobel again, and find out why she'd left him when he needed her most. To hear, from her lips, whether there was any hope left for them. Otherwise he'd keep thrashing helplessly in the water, drowning in a sea of bitterness, confusion, and regret.

How could he ever trust again while memories of the promises Isobel had made to him still haunted him? Promises she'd broken...

Lachlan had a wife now, one he loved with all his heart. He had a life here with Hyacinth. He'd come to England, and all his dreams had come true. The same was true of their sister Isla, who'd found her own love in the Marquess of Pierce, who doted on her and made her blissfully happy.

Only Ciaran had been left adrift. He'd never been able to turn his back on Scotland as his siblings had. He hadn't been able to forget the past. Until he did—until he either forgot it or embraced it—he didn't have any chance at a future.

Lucy was right. He was wasting his time here.

Her cold hand slid into his palm. "Then you should go. If that's what will make you happy, Ciaran, you should do it."

Her voice was so quiet the wind tried to snatch it up and drown it in the waves, but Ciaran heard her. Without thinking, he laced their fingers together, squeezing gently to warm her. Her slim, elegant bones shifted slightly under his grip, and all at once a rush of gratitude rolled over him, so powerful it robbed him of his breath.

He wanted to thank her. To tell her he'd leave Brighton a different man than he'd been when he arrived, and she was the reason why. Impulsively, he lifted her hand to his lips and brushed a soft kiss across her knuckles.

Lucy sucked in a shaky breath, and gently drew her hand away. She was quiet for some time. When she did speak again, her voice was unnaturally bright. "Well, then. You're for Scotland, and I'm for London for the rest of the season. I expect to be half-smothered with rules and restrictions once I'm there."

"You will be. I spent last season in London, for my sister's debut. Thankfully she's married now and I'm not obliged to go back." Though it hadn't been so awful, really, his one London season. He'd kept himself entertained well enough. But young, eligible gentlemen were in great demand, particularly those who were brother to the Marquess of Huntington. It was far more difficult for young ladies to navigate the season.

Ciaran frowned. He couldn't picture Lucy in London.

She didn't seem to be able to, either, because she let out a forlorn little sigh. "No prize-fights or brawls. No swimming. I confess I don't fancy it, but I would like to see my cousin safely married. I suppose I'll have to go everywhere with her, won't I? It's bound to be a trial. I don't even know how to dance properly."

"Come to the ball at the New Assembly Rooms tonight, and I'll teach you." Ciaran brightened at the thought. It wasn't much, but it was something he could do for her.

Lucy's dark eyes lit up, and her lips curved in a dazzling smile. "Will you? Oh, I'd love that above anything! I warn you though, Ciaran. It won't be easy. I'm truly dreadful."

Ciaran chuckled. He'd spent every evening of last season dancing with London's wallflowers. He'd escorted so many neglected ladies to the floor the *ton* had dubbed him the Wallflower's Gallant. Between one young lady and another, he'd quite literally seen all there was to see. "I'm not worried."

Then again, if there was one young lady in England who could surprise him, it was Lucy.

* * * *

He never got the chance to be surprised.

Lucy didn't come to the New Assembly Rooms that evening. Ciaran waited for her for hours, his eyes moving over the room again and again, straining for a glimpse of red hair.

It was all in vain.

She didn't come, and neither did he see her pretty, dark-haired cousin or her aunt, the lady who'd accompanied them to the musical evening. Ciaran was disappointed not to have the chance to dance with Lucy, but he told himself any number of things could have happened to prevent her attendance.

He told himself there was no reason to be concerned.

It worked, at first.

But any calm he'd felt the night of the ball deserted him the following morning, when he arrived at the beach for their usual rendezvous and found it empty. She wasn't there the next day, either, or the one after that. He escorted Lady Chase and Lady Atherton to the Pump Room and to the assemblies each night, hoping he'd find Lucy, but she was never there.

She didn't seem to be anywhere.

He didn't admit to himself she'd left Brighton until he went to her lodgings, desperate to find her, and discovered the villa silent and empty. There was a notice on the door informing passersby that the rooms were to let.

Lucy had disappeared.

Ciaran spent the rest of that day on the beach, watching the waves rolling against the shore, thinking about Lucy. Now he'd made up his mind to return to Scotland he wanted to leave right away, yet...

He thought about the first time he'd seen her, alone on a dark beach, risking her safety for a sunrise swim. Then the second time, the day of the prizefight at Brighton Racetrack, perched on a carriage wheel as a brawl raged around her. Even now, he wasn't sure she understood how much danger she'd been in that day. How close she'd come to being pulled down into the crowd and trampled.

Lucy might insist she could take care of herself, argue there was nothing scandalous in wanting to experience things, but Ciaran knew the *ton* wouldn't see it that way. Lucy had no idea what she'd face in London, no real concept of how cruel people could be. Brighton was its own sort of jungle, but if she dared to set even a toe outside the line in London, the *ton* would pounce on her like wild animals. They'd tear her to pieces.

And she *would* dare. He knew that without question, as surely as he knew the *ton* wouldn't overlook the fact she was the Earl of Bellamy's daughter.

Barmy Bellamy. That was what the gossips in Brighton called Lucy's father. Ciaran had heard it himself, whispered with malicious glee. He prayed Lucy didn't know of it, but even if she'd escaped it here, she was sure to find more of the same in London.

The same, or worse.

He'd jumped into freezing sea water when he'd thought she was drowning. He'd risked a beating to snatch her free of a brawl. He'd taken blows to the face and chest, and gagged on the gushing river of blood she'd kicked from his nose.

If Lucy were here, she'd tell him to go off to Scotland at once. She'd get angry with him, and insist she didn't need saving. Maybe she didn't, but Ciaran had already made up his mind. There was no way he could jaunt merrily off to Scotland until he was sure she was safe.

By the time he rose from the sand, the sky above his head had gone dark and moonlight glittered on the crest of the waves. The long case clock on the second-floor landing was just announcing the ninth hour of the evening when Ciaran strolled through the entryway of their lodgings.

"Home already, are you? I didn't expect to see you until tomorrow afternoon." Lady Chase stood at the bottom of the staircase, one hand on her cane and the other on her ample hip, glaring at him.

"I can't think why." Ciaran closed the door behind him. "Brighton's entertainments are dull enough."

Lady Chase gave him a sour look. "Well, you didn't seem to find them so before tonight. Goodness knows you've spent enough of your time prowling about the darkened streets of Brighton, looking for whatever wicked entertainment is on offer."

A grin tugged at Ciaran's lips. "Whatever is on offer here isn't wicked enough, I'm afraid. I'm bored to death. No, if I want satisfying debauchery, I'll have to go to London to find it."

"Now you listen to me, young scoundrel." Lady Chase pointed her cane at him, ready to dress him down, but then she stopped short, eyeing him suspiciously. "Wait. Did you say London? You mean, you intend to go to London?"

She looked tremendously pleased at this idea—so pleased Ciaran had to struggle not to roll his eyes. No doubt Lady Chase had developed this sudden, intense desire to see him in London because she hoped one of the young ladies out this season would catch his eye, he'd fall madly in love with her, and put his family out of their misery.

He might have saved them the trouble. He'd only ever loved one woman. Whatever might happen in Scotland, that would never change. He might discover there was nothing left for him and Isobel, but he'd never love another.

Ciaran gave Lady Chase a bland smile. "I'll escort you and Lady Atherton to Buckinghamshire, then I'm off to London for the rest of the season. You did say my brother needed me at Huntington House."

"Yes, yes, so I did. Well, well, I always said you were a good boy, despite your lurid debaucheries."

"Is that why you waited up for me to come home this evening, my lady? To quiz me on my lurid debaucheries? Because I'd be happy to go into detail if you—"

"Hush, you dreadful boy. I don't care a whit for your debaucheries, as you put it, and I most certainly wasn't waiting up for you. I just, er...came downstairs to fetch a book from the library."

Ciaran gave her a pointed look. "I don't see any book."

Lady Chase huffed out a breath. "I couldn't find what I wanted, if you insist on knowing every detail of my evening. I was on my way back to my bedchamber when you came in."

"May I take you up?"

He offered her his arm, but she waved him off. "No, no. I'll go myself."

He watched as Lady Chase shuffled up the stairs. Once she was gone, he let his head fall against the door at his back. He'd go to London, just as he'd told her he would. He'd stay long enough to make certain Lucy was safe. Before he left, he'd speak to Vale about keeping an eye on her once Ciaran was gone.

What he didn't tell Lady Chase—what he wouldn't tell anyone in his family—was he didn't intend to stay in London for the season. As soon as he reassured himself Lucy would be taken care of, he was bound for Scotland, to see if he could find anything to salvage in the wreckage of his past life.

At best, he'd find love. If not, at least he'd find peace.

Chapter Eight

London, England
Eight days later

    Le Pantalon, L'été, La Poule...

Lucy studied the dancers as they moved through the figures of the quadrille, her heart sinking. She did her best to follow the steps, but all those prancing feet seemed to tangle together until all she could hear was her dancing master's despairing voice echoing in her head.

    No, no, no, Lady Lucinda! Your entire set is falling into disarray!

She glanced down in despair at the fan clasped between her gloved fingers. After her disappointing performances at Thomas Wilson's Dancing Academy this past week, she and Eloisa had decided to write a few discreet dance instructions on the back of Lucy's fan, in case she forgot the steps again.

Well, she'd forgotten them, and the fan wasn't any help at all.

She darted a forlorn look at the blur of black-clad legs and pale skirts whirling across the ballroom, then back down at the tiny, cramped letters written on the bottom of her fan. Her brows drew together in bewilderment. She didn't know how it was possible, but the steps made even less sense to her now than they had before yesterday's ill-fated lesson with Monsieur Guilland. She'd made an utter fool of herself, stumbling about and tripping over her own feet as if she were a drunken lord.

Now she was about to do it again, except this time it would happen in front of all of London. It was the very first ball of her very first London season, and it was already a farce in the making.

Not for the first time since they'd arrived and taken up their lodgings in Portman Square, Lucy's heart pinched with longing for Brighton. Everything had been so much simpler there—every day alive with the promise of something new. It had felt...miraculous, as if she were a bird, soaring through a wide-open blue sky for the first time.

Now, here in London, her wings had been well and truly clipped.

She missed the beach, the gentle splash of the waves kissing the shore, the smooth, cool glide of the ocean against her skin.

She missed *him*.

She'd known she would—that she'd miss him terribly—but as with so many things, the reality was far worse than anything she could have imagined. It was a sharp, painful ache deep inside her chest, the fissure there wide and empty even now. He should have become nothing more than a pleasant memory, but she still carried him with her everywhere.

Lucy's heart had never been broken before, but this felt just how she'd always imagined a broken heart would feel. Could it break your heart, to lose a friend? Or was it true, what her heart told her when she lay in her lonely bed at night, the house silent around her?

It was a whisper still, but growing louder with every day that passed.

Ciaran was more to her than a friend, so much more—

"Smile, Lucy," Eloisa hissed from between gritted teeth. "If you keep scowling like that, no one will ever ask you to dance."

Lucy forced her attention back to her cousin. "*Dance*? You must be jesting, Eloisa." She glanced again at the dancers moving gracefully across the floor and shook her head. It was a crush. If she made a mistake—and she *would*—she'd send them all toppling like a row of dominoes. "I can't risk it. No, I'm afraid I'm destined to be a wallflower."

Aunt Jarvis had been settling her ruffles, but at the word "wallflower" she turned an anxious gaze toward the card room. Uncle Jarvis had disappeared into it the moment they'd entered the ballroom this evening, leaving Lucy and Eloisa to the tender chaperonage of Aunt Jarvis. "Wallflower? Oh no, my dear. Your uncle won't like that. You must dance, or else you'll put him into a temper."

Lucy didn't much care whether her uncle liked it or not, but she held her tongue. Aunt Jarvis was as much a victim of Uncle Jarvis's fits and pets as Lucy and Eloisa were. There was no point in taking her poor aunt to task for Uncle Jarvis's tyranny. Lucy reached out to give the bony hand a reassuring squeeze. "It's just the quadrille, Aunt. I daresay I can manage the country dances well enough."

Not *well*, but well enough.

Aunt Jarvis patted her hand. "You're a good girl, Lucinda. I realize your uncle can be, ah…a bit trying at times, but you mustn't think too badly of him. For good or ill, it has fallen to him to make you fit to take your place in London society."

Lucy held back a snort. For a man devoted to his niece's social triumph, Uncle Jarvis spent a good deal of his time in the card room.

Not that it made much difference. Unfortunately for all of them, she was as ill-suited to London society as she'd dreaded she would be, and Uncle and Aunt Jarvis were equally as ill-suited to guide her through the many pitfalls of a season. Of the four of them, Eloisa was the only one who showed any promise of flourishing. She'd taken to London with the grace and aplomb of a natural belle.

"The heat, girls!" Aunt Jarvis flapped her fan in front of her face. "Thank goodness for Dr. Digby's Calming Tonic! It's done wonders for my nerves. Even so, I'll be astonished if one of us doesn't succumb to a swoon."

Lucy hid a smile. Dear Dr. Digby. His tonic was proving to be quite a magical cure. "You look very well tonight, Aunt."

"You do, mama. The very picture of good health," Eloisa chimed in. Lucy occasionally lost patience with her aunt's megrims, but Eloisa was unfailingly loyal to her mother, in the way of two prisoners who'd been years under the command of the same particularly brutal gaoler.

Aunt Jarvis flushed with pleasure. "Indeed, Lucinda, the tonic is every bit the miracle you promised. I can't recall the last time I felt so well."

Lucy thought it likely it had been before her aunt married Uncle Jarvis, but once again, she held her tongue.

Eloisa leaned close to whisper in Lucy's ear. "What's in the tonic, really?"

"It's saffron tea with crushed hyssop, a bit of orange flower water, and a drop of honey. If my aunt should find herself failing again, Dr. Digby also has a warm bath oil to sooth inflammations and nervous disorders. It smells lovely. Like lavender."

"You're very good to her." Eloisa slid her hand into Lucy's. "I'm truly grateful."

Lucy squeezed her cousin's fingers. The blossoming friendship between them was another of Dr. Digby's miracles, and the one for which Lucy was the most grateful.

After circling Lucy warily for the first few weeks of their acquaintance, Eloisa had eased into a cautious affection for her new cousin. She still thought Lucy very odd, and was often scandalized with her unconventional behavior, but at some point, she'd cast aside her doubts. Since then, their relationship had thrived.

Eloisa turned to speak to her mother while Lucy's gaze roved over the assembled crowd. She'd had high hopes for a pleasant evening, especially when Uncle Jarvis disappeared into the card room, but they'd been sitting here for an hour now without a single person venturing near them. Their hostess, Lady Ivey, who'd been a dear old friend of Lucy's mother had kindly introduced them to one or two of her other guests, but since then, no one had offered them as much as a nod of welcome.

Lucy sighed. Well, at least one good thing would come of being ignored. She'd be spared the humiliation of dancing, since it wasn't likely anyone would ask her.

"Perhaps it would be wise if we left early, Aunt," Lucy suggested, after another twenty minutes passed without anyone glancing in their direction. "We don't want to overtax your nerves. It's our first ball of the season. There's no sense in wearying you on the first night—"

"Look, Lucy. It's Lady Felicia Wroth!" Eloisa clutched at Lucy's arm. "We met Lady Felicia at Thomas Wright's Dancing Academy yesterday, Mama."

Aunt Jarvis peered over Lucy's head toward the other side of the ballroom. "My goodness. Her party looks very grand. Who are those two gentlemen with her?"

"The taller, fair-haired gentleman is her brother, the Earl of Vale," Lucy said. "We met him yesterday, as well."

He'd arrived at Thomas Wilson's to collect Lady Felicia in a smart black phaeton with gold-spoked wheels and extravagant royal blue upholstery, his hands steady on the reins of a matched pair of spirited grays. He'd leapt down from the carriage with a flourish and tossed the reins to a boy loitering in the street.

As soon as Lucy laid eyes on him, she'd fallen into a panic. She'd recognized him as Ciaran's friend—the gentleman she'd met briefly at Brighton Racetrack. Indeed, one couldn't help but remember Lord Vale. He was the epitome of the fashionable London gentleman.

He hadn't forgotten her, either. One glance, and he knew her at once as the scandalous lady who'd attended the bare-knuckle bout. Much to Lucy's relief, he hadn't betrayed her secret. Aside from a rather wicked glint in his blue eyes, he'd behaved as if they'd never met.

Aunt Jarvis was watching him now with wide eyes. "Oh, my. He *is* very… well, my goodness. He rather catches one's eye, doesn't he? I suppose he's quite the gentleman about town?"

"Yes, very fashionable, indeed." Eloisa's gaze lingered on Lord Vale. "Lady Felicia is fond of him. She speaks of him with great affection. I don't know who the other gentleman with them is, but he looks a bit stern, doesn't he?"

Lady Felicia was holding her brother's arm, but on her other side was another gentleman, nearly as tall as Lord Vale, with chestnut hair and a firm, unsmiling mouth.

Eloisa fingers tightened around Lucy's arm. "Lady Felicia just nodded and smiled at me, and—look, they're coming this way!"

Lucy turned a curious eye on her cousin. Eloisa sounded positively breathless, and her gaze was still riveted on Lady Felicia's tall, broad-shouldered brother. Lucy could hardly blame her. Lord Vale was a handsome, dashing creature, the sort of gentleman who'd turn any lady's head.

"Lady Lucinda, and Miss Jarvis." Lady Felicia and her two gallants stopped in front of them. "How do you do? I'm ever so pleased to see you both again." Lady Felicia offered them each a shy smile, then waved a dainty hand toward her companions. "You know my brother, Lord Vale. This gentleman is our friend, Lord Markham."

"How do you do?" Lord Markham's stern face softened, and he bowed politely.

"Lady Lucinda, and Miss Jarvis." Lord Vale bent over each of their hands in turn, a flirtatious smile on his handsome face.

"Lord Vale. Lord Markham." Lucy and Eloisa nodded at the gentlemen, then Eloisa gestured to her mother. "This is my mother, Mrs. Jarvis."

Both gentlemen and Lady Felicia greeted Aunt Jarvis. She looked rather terrified to be so suddenly thrust into such elevated company, but she managed an awkward nod.

"I owe you each a debt of gratitude for entertaining my sister at her dancing lesson yesterday," Lord Vale said, turning back to Eloisa and Lucy. "I can't say if her dancing has improved, but she certainly enjoyed herself."

Lucy felt heat rising in her cheeks and stifled a groan. Lady Felicia was fair-haired like her brother, with wide blue eyes and a sweet face. She was dainty, graceful, and danced like an angel. If Lord Vale thought his sister's quadrille needed improvement, he'd swoon with horror when he saw Lucy's. Her humiliation at Monsieur Guilland's hands would be nothing in comparison.

Well then, she was determined to remain a wallflower, no matter how much it might irritate Uncle Jarvis. No matter what, she refused to set a single toe onto the dance floor this evening—

"Do you care to dance, Lady Lucinda?" Lord Vale turned to her with an extravagant bow and held out his hand, that same teasing smile toying with his lips.

Lucy glanced at the dance floor, saw groups of four couples arranging themselves into a square formation, and smothered another groan. A cotillion? For pity's sake, that was worse than the quadrille!

She winced, and gave Lord Vale an apologetic look. "I, ah…you're very kind, Lord Vale, but I'm…" she leaned closer and lowered her voice. "The truth, my lord, is I'm a perfectly dreadful dancer. Perhaps we can dance together at the next ball, after I've had a few more lessons?"

Lord Vale gaped at her in amazement, but just when Lucy was certain she'd done something horribly rude, he tossed his head back with a hearty laugh. "Such refreshing honesty! Very well, Lady Lucinda. I won't trouble you now, but I'll hold you to your pledge and have my dance very soon."

"Yes, I promise." Lucy beamed up at him. Lady Felicia had hinted her brother was a flirt and a bit of a rogue, but he had such a playful, open smile Lucy couldn't imagine anyone not liking him.

Lord Vale turned and offered his hand to Eloisa. "Miss Jarvis? Will you do me the honor?"

Eloisa's face colored prettily, and she took the hand he offered. "Thank you, my lord."

"Take care of my sister, eh Markham?" Vale tossed over his shoulder as he led Eloisa off to join the other dancers. "There's no telling what sort of mischief she'll get up to if she's bored."

"Yes, she does so hate to be bored. How may I entertain you, my lady?" Lord Markham turned a lazy smile on Lady Felicia. He was fond of her—anyone could see that. His smile was affectionate, even doting, but it was the sort of careless fondness usually reserved for adorable children and overeager puppies.

Lucy's eyebrows rose. *Well, how odd.*

Lady Felicia was lovely, sophisticated, fashionable. She was the kind of lady who struck men dumb with a single glance from her crystal blue eyes—the kind of lady destined to become the belle of her season.

And here was Lord Markham, teasing her as if she were still a schoolgirl in pinafores.

Lucy's gaze shot toward Lady Felicia and she saw her pretty face had darkened with a scowl. "For pity's sake, Edmund," she snapped. "You needn't hover over me as if I'm a child. Why don't you go and ask Miss Fisher to dance?" Lady Felicia nodded toward a dark-haired young lady in a blue gown who was seated several seats away.

"Yes, all right." Lord Markham gave an indolent shrug, then ambled off toward Miss Fisher without a backward glance.

Lady Felicia seated herself in the chair next to Lucy's. "There, isn't this cozy? I confess I'm happy to be rid of the lot of them. That is, not your cousin, of course, but Lord Markham is being tiresome, and my brother... well, he's charming, but he's rather exhausting. One does have to keep one's eye on him, you know, or else he'll fall into mischief."

Lucy laughed. "I believe he just said the same thing about you."

"Yes, he did, the wicked thing, but it's only true for one of us." Lady Felicia gave a tinkling laugh of her own.

Her laugh was a feminine version of her brother's—genuine, and without a hint of self-consciousness. Lucy decided right then and there she liked them both very much. "Well, you needn't worry about that with my cousin. Eloisa doesn't put up with mischief, especially from handsome, charming gentlemen."

Lady Felicia watched Eloisa and Lord Vale for a moment, her head cocked as she considered them. "They look well together, don't they?"

They did. Lord Vale's fair coloring complemented Eloisa's dark beauty. Lucy watched the dancers move through the set for a short time, then turned back to Lady Felicia. "Lord Markham is handsome, and very fashionable."

"He *is* handsome, isn't he? You'd think that careless smile of his would make him less so, yet it suits him, somehow."

"It does. Have you known him long?"

Lady Felicia sighed. "Yes. My entire life. His family owns the estate next to ours in Lewes. Sebastian coaxed Edmund to come to London to help me through my season, but I daresay Edmund's on the hunt for a bride of his own. His father died two years ago, and his mother has been bothering him to secure a wife since Edmund inherited the title."

Lucy thought she heard a note of longing in Lady Felicia's voice, and turned to study her.

Lady Felicia was watching Miss Fisher and Lord Markham move through the set, a dejected look on her face. Lucy followed her gaze and saw Miss Fisher's face was flushed a becoming pink from the exertions of the dance. Lord Markham was gazing down at her with a surprisingly boyish smile.

"I confess I wasn't looking forward to this season." Lady Felicia's tone was gloomy, but then she seemed to gather herself together, and she turned to Lucy with a bright, determined smile. "Now I've met you and your cousin, perhaps the three of us might squeeze some pleasure out of London, after all."

Lucy wouldn't have thought to put "pleasure" and "London" together in the same sentence, but that might change now they'd become acquainted with Lady Felicia. "Yes, we shall! Not at the balls, though. I never realized how tedious it would be to sit about all night and watch other people dance."

Lady Felicia chuckled. "You're not the first lady to say so, I'm certain."

"No." Lucy glanced around them and noted more than one young lady languishing on the gilt chairs scattered around the outer edges of the ballroom. "It's a pity not every lady should have the chance to dance. At least, those ladies who know how, I mean."

"Oh, but they'll all dance, Lady Lucinda. You needn't worry about that. I happen to know the Wallflower Gallant is attending the ball this evening. He'll dance with each and every lady who'd otherwise be obliged to sit out the set."

"The Wallflower Gallant? Who's that?"

"Of course, this is your first season, so you wouldn't know. A gentleman by the name of Mr. Ramsey became famous last season for attending every ball and dancing with every wallflower. He's good fun, and terribly handsome. More than one young lady lost her heart to him."

"How extraordinary." Lucy liked the sound of this gentleman very much, and her lips curved into a smile.

"The belles and beauties tried to catch his attention, but he never so much as glanced at any of them. He danced every single dance of the entire season with London's wallflowers," Lady Felicia went on. "Mr. Ramsey's sister married the Marquess of Pierce shortly after the season ended last year, so I didn't expect he'd spend another season in London, but who should we meet this afternoon but Mr. Ramsey himself? I was ever so glad to see him, and Sebastian wheedled him into attending the ball tonight. Sebastian's very good at wheedling."

Lucy glanced at the dancers again. Lord Vale and Eloisa were twirling in a tight circle together, their hands joined. Whatever it was he was whispering to her was making her smile and blush. "I have no doubt."

"I expected Mr. Ramsey would arrive before now. I do hope he keeps his promise to come tonight, or else I won't stand up for many dances. Edmund never seems to think to ask me, and Sebastian can't, so—oh, wait, there he is!"

"Where?" Lucy craned her neck in the direction Lady Felicia indicated, anxious to see the fascinating Wallflower Gallant, but the room was crowded with gallant-looking gentlemen. "Which one?"

"The dark-haired gentleman, just under the archway there." Lady Felicia gestured discreetly with her fan. "Indeed, you can't miss him, Lady Lucinda. He's the tallest gentleman in the room. He's from northern Scotland. From what I understand, they're all quite large there."

Northern Scotland...

A little frisson of excitement tickled under her breastbone, but Lucy drew in a deep breath to will it away. It couldn't be *him*. Of course, it couldn't be. It was far too much of a coincidence to think she'd stumble upon him again *here*, of all places.

Still…

She was quite anxious to get a peek at the man, just the same.

Lucy abandoned propriety and rose to her feet, then balanced on her tiptoes, her gaze following Lady Felicia's fan. Blast it, the entire ballroom suddenly seemed to be filled with tall, dark-haired gentlemen, and she couldn't see a thing through the sea of jeweled turbans—

Wait, just there. A man, at least a head taller than the gentlemen surrounding him, had paused to speak to an elderly lady who'd stopped him with a hand on his arm. His head was bent toward her, and Lucy couldn't see his face, but he had dark hair, a shade too long, and something about the fluid way he moved…

She froze, willing her eyes to find some disparity between this man and the man she remembered. Willing them to catch up with her brain, which was insisting over and over again that it couldn't possibly be the same man.

No, it couldn't be him. It was impossible.

Except it looked just like him. The dark hair, the broad shoulders, his remarkable size…it *had* to be him. There couldn't possibly be two such enormous gentlemen in England.

Her heart came to a crashing halt in her chest, leaving her breathless.

He hadn't said a word to her about coming to London before leaving for Scotland, but then they hadn't talked much about such mundane things as that, had they? She didn't even know his last name, or he hers—

"Lady Lucinda? Are you all right? You look as if you've seen a ghost."

Not a ghost, no. Just a man. A man she'd thought about every single day since her uncle had dragged her away from Brighton. A man she believed she'd never lay eyes on again.

Lucy shook her head. Her throat was too tight to speak.

Mr. Ramsey. Ciaran Ramsey.

Lady Felicia followed her gaze and let out a little laugh. "Oh, I see. Mr. Ramsey looks a bit terrifying, doesn't he?"

"No," Lucy whispered, too softly for her companion to hear her. He wasn't terrifying at all. Quite the opposite. He was gentle, tender-hearted—a man who saved wallflowers from humiliation and careless young ladies from being trampled in a brawl. A hero on the beach and in the ballroom, with a slightly bent nose and the kindest eyes she'd ever seen.

"He isn't in the least, I assure you," Lady Felicia said. "But there, he's seen me now, so you'll find out for yourself how perfectly lovely he is."

He *was* lovely. The loveliest gentleman Lucy had ever known.

And he was coming straight toward her.

She released the breath she didn't realize she'd been holding and waited for his gaze to find hers. When it did… when it did…Lucy's heart thudded to life again with a sudden, painful leap.

I'm not the sort of lady who falls in love.

That's what she'd told Ciaran, one of those dark mornings on the beach when the friendship between them was still new enough she'd believed those words to be true.

They weren't. All it took was one glance into the blue eyes she remembered so well, and the truth swept over her, too powerful to be denied.

She *was* the sort of lady who fell in love.

She'd fallen in love with Ciaran Ramsey.

Chapter Nine

Ciaran passed under the archway leading into Lady Ivey's ballroom with a sigh of resignation already on his lips. This was all Vale's fault. If it weren't for Vale he'd be at the Pantheon right now, searching for a telltale flash of coppery red hair.

He gulped in a breath of the stale air and made his way into the ballroom. He was here now. It was too late to avoid the inevitable. The sooner he danced with Lady Felicia, the sooner he could escape to Oxford Street, where the first subscription ball of the season was being held in the Pantheon's Assembly Rooms.

If Lucy was in London, that was the most likely place to find her.

She wouldn't be *here*. Lady Ivey was a kind soul, at least as far as fashionable London hostesses went, but she was *haute ton*, and would doubtless have drawn up her guest list from the ranks of the upper ten thousand.

The Earl of Bellamy's daughter wouldn't have been on it.

Ciaran's gaze roamed over the crowd, searching for a glimpse of either Vale or Lady Felicia. He saw a few familiar feminine faces at the edges of the crush—ladies he'd danced with last season, when he'd devoted himself to London's wallflowers—but he didn't see any sign of either Vale or his sister.

Just one evening, Vale had said. A single ball, and no more than that. Surely Ramsey could spare a single evening for his dear friend? It was Lady Felicia's second season, and her first had ended in disappointment. Surely Ramsey thought Lady Felicia deserved another chance to triumph? Surely Ramsey could see Felicia was as lovely a young lady as anyone could find?

Yes, Ciaran could see. That was the trouble. It would be a damn sight more convenient if he couldn't, but God knew it would have taken a harder heart than his to look into Lady Felicia's pleading blue eyes this afternoon and refuse to help her.

Especially after he'd spent all of last season dancing with every wallflower languishing on the sidelines of London's ballrooms—something Vale hadn't hesitated to remind him of. Squiring the wallflowers about last season had been good fun, but he'd never aspired to become the Wallflower's Gallant. Or anyone's gallant, come to that—

"Well, you look grim enough, Ramsey. It's a ball, you know, not a funeral."

Ciaran turned at the low drawl and found Vale at his elbow, an amused grin on his face. "Not much difference between the two, is there?" Ciaran asked.

Vale laughed. "Not for the gentlemen, no. Balls leads to courtships, and courtship to marriage. Either way, a burial awaits."

Ciaran grimaced. "What a cheerful thought. Allow me to thank you again for insisting I come tonight."

Vale slapped him on the back. "Eh, you're safe enough. Felicia doesn't want to marry *you*, so there's no need for you to go about looking like a fox cornered by hounds. Felicia's a good girl, and my sister, you know. Can't leave her at loose ends, can I?"

Ciaran rolled his eyes. He recognized that pathetic, doting expression on Vale's face. He'd worn it himself, every time his own sister Isla wheedled a favor out of him. It was the look of fond elder brothers everywhere.

Of course, that didn't explain why *he* was here. Felicia Wroth wasn't *his* sister.

Ciaran scowled. This was all Isla's fault. If she hadn't twisted him around her finger, he wouldn't be cursed with this irritating protective streak. He shuddered to think what would happen when his baby niece Georgie had her first season. If he wasn't lucky enough to be dead by then, he was doomed.

Vale laughed at his expression. "Never mind that pathetic look, Ramsey. You'll be thanking me soon enough."

Ciaran raised an eyebrow at Vale's smug tone. He glanced at his friend, and found Vale smirking gleefully at him. It was a look Ciaran knew all too well, and he let out a low groan. "Damn it. What have you done this time, Vale?"

"Who, *me*? Why, not a blessed thing." Vale blinked innocently at him. "It's all Felicia's doing. She's made a new acquaintance—a young lady she met at Thomas Wilson's Dancing Academy. Now they're bosom friends, in the way of warm-hearted ladies everywhere. See for yourself. There's Felicia, just there."

Vale nodded toward a row of chairs lined up along one side of the ballroom. Ciaran looked, and his gaze locked on a lady in a bright green gown with a headful of thick, curly red hair. It was a distinctive red—a shade Ciaran had seen only once before. A dark, coppery red that belonged to a single lady, and that lady alone.

All at once he was back in Brighton again, lying on the sand in the early morning, the dying moonlight and the first pale rays of the sun wrestling over which of them would illuminate the white sand. The sound of the ocean in his ears, damp red hair, glittering drops of water clinging to long, dark eyelashes...

A single glance was all it took. He would have known her anywhere.

Lucy.

His ocean siren had reappeared, and in such spectacular fashion his breath stuttered in his lungs when he caught his first glimpse of her.

"Stunning, isn't she? I noticed she was a pretty thing the day of the bout, but she was covered from head to toe in some dark, shapeless cloak or other that day." Vale let out a low whistle. "She's not covered now though, is she?"

No. She wasn't covered now.

Nor was she in her bathing costume, with wet hair dripping down her back. Ciaran had admired her even then—her sparkling eyes and the bright color in her cheeks—but if Lucy was pretty soaked to the skin and smothered in layers of heavy, dark blue linen, out of it, she was...

Breathtaking. An undisputed beauty. In a bright green gown that brought out the glinting threads of red in her hair, she made his mouth water—

Ciaran frowned. In a *friendly* way, that is. Not a lustful one. Certainly not a possessive one. Only a scoundrel leered at his friend.

His *best* friend. He opened his mouth to tell Vale he'd spent hours with Lucy since that day at the bout, but then he closed it again without speaking. Those moments were his—his, and Lucy's—and he didn't want to share them with anyone. Not even Vale.

Instead, he cleared his throat and asked, "What's her name?"

"That lovely lady, my dear Ramsey, is Lady Lucinda Sutcliffe. She's the Earl of Bellamy's daughter. Poor man was madder than a Bedlamite, or so the gossips would have it. He died last year and left her with piles of blunt."

Ciaran stiffened. Lady Lucinda Sutcliffe, heiress, daughter to a dead, mad earl. For the rest of the season, that's all anyone would remember about her.

Jesus. No wonder Lucy had wanted to keep her full name hidden for as long as possible. Which wasn't long at all, as it turned out. If Vale knew who Lucy's father was, that meant all of London knew.

Vale frowned. "Never seen her before that day at the bout. She seems to have come out of nowhere. Felicia says she's never been to London."

Ciaran didn't answer, but stood quietly, watching her. She and Lady Felicia were chatting together as if they were the oldest of friends. She held her head high, a slightly bemused smile on her lips as she watched the couples twirling about the ballroom.

"You do realize, Ramsey, if you'd only move a few paces toward her, you could ask her to dance?" Vale tried to prod him forward with a nudge to the ribs. "Come do the pretty with Felicia, waltz with a wallflower or two, then later we can reward ourselves for our good deeds with a little harmless debauchery. Speaking of debauchery," Vale went on, "There's a gaming hell in Covent Garden we might…"

Vale kept blathering on, but Ciaran didn't hear a word.

He'd come to London only for her, yet a part of him could hardly believe she was actually here—that a few paces would bring him close enough to talk to her, touch her.

He'd thought of Lucy dozens of time—no, hundreds—since she'd disappeared from Brighton. Even after he knew she was gone he'd wandered every secluded stretch of beach, haunted every assembly and endless musical evening, hoping he'd somehow made a mistake—that he'd catch a glimpse of her.

But she'd disappeared without a trace. Without an explanation, and without a single word. His disappointment had been indescribable.

Now here she was, at the first ball he'd happened to wander into, on his very first night in London. Thousands of people flocked to the city during the season but somehow, with all the odds against it, Lucy had found and befriended Vale and Lady Felicia.

A rueful smile drifted across Ciaran's lips. It was just like Lucy to somehow find the only two people in London who'd lead her directly to him.

"Shall we, Ramsey? Felicia's waving us over."

By now Lady Felicia had caught her brother's eye with a few vigorous flutters of her fan. Beside her, Lucy had risen to her feet. Ciaran saw her glance around the ballroom, her lips pressed into a frown. Lady Felicia whispered something in her ear and gestured toward them with her fan.

Lucy rose to her tiptoes, and Ciaran just had time to suck in a breath before her dark gaze caught his.

A spray of gooseflesh rose on his arms. She was looking straight at him. The weight of the velvety brown eyes he remembered so well felt like a caress, as if her fingertips had drifted across his cheek.

As soon as she realized she'd caught his eye, her lips curved in a half-smile.

This time when Vale took his arm to move him forward, Ciaran didn't resist. He did his best not to stare at Lucy, but as they made their way across the ballroom toward her party, he couldn't tear his gaze away from her.

A *friendly* gaze, that is. Not a lustful one.

"Well, Mr. Ramsey. I'd quite given up on you this evening. The ball began an hour ago," Lady Felicia scolded, even as she greeted him with a smile. "May I introduce my friend to you? This is—"

"Lady Lucinda Sutcliffe." Ciaran bowed to both ladies, but it was Lucy's hand he took and raised to his lips.

Lady Felicia looked from one to the other of them, a blonde eyebrow arched in surprise. "You already know each other?"

"Doesn't every lady in London know the gallant Mr. Ramsey, the darling of London's wallflowers?" Lucy's smile widened, and her dark eyes twinkled as she looked up at him. "Tell me, will you dance with the wallflowers this evening, or are you planning some other sort of daring rescue?"

Lucy brushed her gloved fingers discreetly against the side of her nose, and a laugh rose in Ciaran's throat. She was teasing him about his heroic plunge into the ocean to save a lady who knew perfectly well how to swim.

How had he forgotten she'd nearly broken his nose?

"No daring rescues this evening, Lady Lucinda. Just a dance with Lady Felicia, if she'll have me." It took an effort for Ciaran to smother his wild impulse to snatch Lucy up and carry her off to some private corner, but he'd promised Vale he'd dance twice with Lady Felicia. Once he'd done so, he could devote the rest of the evening to Lucy.

"Daring enough, I think, given I haven't left this chair the entire evening." Lady Felicia took his hand with a smile and let him lead her to the dance floor.

When Ciaran glanced back, he saw Vale bow to Lucy. Her eyes widened with alarm and she shook her head, but then Vale said something that made her laugh. After another hesitation she took his hand and let him lead her to a quiet corner of the dance floor. They were on the other side of the ballroom, so Ciaran had to content himself with catching fleeting glimpses of Lucy's burnished head as she moved through the dance.

The dance, which seemed to go on and on and on…

It was a reel, for God's sake. How long could a reel last? Forever, it seemed.

"Your brother tells me you're taking lessons at Thomas Wilson's Dancing Academy," Ciaran managed at last, wrenching his attention back to Lady Felicia. He'd hardly spoken a word to her the entire dance. "I don't remember you having any trouble with the dances last season."

By every rule of birth, fortune, and beauty, Lady Felicia should have had a triumphant first season, but she'd discouraged the attentions of her numerous suitors. Ciaran knew of more than one gentleman who'd sighed after her, but she'd rebuffed them all. She'd gone home to Lewes before the season ended, after refusing two advantageous marriage offers.

"No, no trouble at all, but Sebastian insisted. He thought it might ease my anxiety about returning to London after last season. I was quite put out with him over it, but I'm ever so glad he did, or else I wouldn't have met Lady Lucinda and Miss Jarvis."

"Miss Jarvis?" Ciaran frowned. The name Jarvis sounded familiar, but he couldn't recall why.

"Yes. She's Lady Lucinda's cousin." Lady Felicia titled her head toward the opposite corner of the ballroom. "The young lady who's dancing with Lord Markham."

Ciaran glanced over and saw the pretty, dark-haired girl he'd seen with Lucy at the musical evening in Brighton. "Yes, I remember her, though we were never introduced." Lucy had also mentioned an uncle, but as far as Ciaran knew, he'd never laid eyes on the man the entire time he'd been in Brighton. "I believe Lady Lucinda's aunt is in London, too?"

"Yes, she's just there." Lady Felicia nodded toward the thin, nervous-looking matron Ciaran remembered from Brighton.

The music ended then, but Ciaran kept Lady Felicia on the floor for their second dance. Vale led Lucy back to her aunt, then bore Miss Jarvis off for another dance as soon as Markham returned her to her mother. Markham lingered beside Lucy's chair, chatting amiably with her while Mrs. Jarvis looked on, flushed with pleasure at the compliments being paid to her niece and daughter.

"There's an uncle, too," Lady Felicia went on, "But I haven't met him… oh, but that must be him, mustn't it? The man who's just seated himself on the other side of Mrs. Jarvis?"

Ciaran's gaze slid from Lucy's face to her left, where a rotund little man with greasy dark hair and a petulant twist to his lips had just joined the party.

Ciaran stiffened. *He* was Jarvis?

He recognized the man at once. Had they been introduced? It seemed they must have been, given the number of hours they'd spent across from each other at the card table, but if they had been, Ciaran didn't remember it. Maybe he'd overheard Jarvis's name mentioned once or twice. He'd thought the name was Jarndyce, but he'd never bothered to find out for certain.

Despite the hours they'd spent together at the table, they'd never spoken. Ciaran had disliked Jarvis on sight, and his dislike had quickly turned to scorn when he discovered the man drank to excess, played deep, and wagered recklessly. Of all the men in the world Mr. Jarndyce, or Jarvis, or whatever the devil his name was, was the last man Ciaran would have chosen to turn out to be Lucy's uncle.

"My goodness," Lady Felicia murmured. "I can't say I much care for the look of Lady Lucinda's uncle. He's got a vulgar air about him."

Jarvis *was* vulgar, and it was the best one could say of him. Ciaran studied the man, his eyes narrowed. Mrs. Jarvis didn't seem at all pleased her husband had joined the party. She kept flinching away from him, almost as if she were afraid of him.

"Who's the other gentleman with Mr. Jarvis? The older man, with the walking stick and the sparse gray hair?" Lady Felicia frowned. "I daresay I've seen him before. I can't place him, but I confess I don't much like the look of him, either."

Damn it. It was Godfrey, the worthless scoundrel.

Lord Godfrey had been in Brighton, as well. He was an earl, but from what Ciaran could tell, Godfrey's title was his only claim to gentlemanliness. Ciaran frowned, thinking back to the dozen or so times he'd seen Godfrey in Brighton. He did his best to avoid the man, but Godfrey was an avid gamester, so they inevitably ran into each other at the card games held in the back room of the Castle Inn.

Ciaran's jaw went tight as he watched Jarvis fawn over the older man. Every time Ciaran had seen Godfrey in Brighton Jarvis had been with him, tossing banks notes about the tables as if he had an endless supply of them. Ciaran had been disgusted with them both—Godfrey because he was a grasping scoundrel, and Jarvis because he was just the sort of brainless, drunken cull Godfrey would pluck of every penny he had.

At the time, he hadn't given a damn if Godfrey swindled Jarvis of his last farthing, but that was before he knew Jarvis was Lucy's uncle.

That changed everything.

Now here was Godfrey with Jarvis in London, hanging about Lucy like a leech lusting after fresh blood.

"Mr. Ramsey? The dance is over."

Ciaran jerked his attention back to Lady Felicia. "So it is. I beg your pardon." He escorted her from the floor back across the ballroom, his gaze on Lucy. As they drew near, they heard Mr. Jarvis speaking sharply to her, his voice raised.

Ciaran and Lady Felicia stopped a few paces away, confused. Something was wrong. Mrs. Jarvis's lips were trembling as if she were about to burst into tears, and Markham was gaping at Jarvis with the strangest look on his face—an odd combination of outrage, shock, and fury.

Some sort of argument was taking place between Lord Godfrey, Lucy, and Mr. Jarvis. Mrs. Jarvis looked on, blanching with terror every time her husband's jarring voice rent the air.

"Thank you for the invitation, my lord," Lucy was saying to Godfrey as Ciaran and Lady Felicia joined the party. Lucy's shoulders were rigid, and her lips white at the edges. "But I don't care to dance again this evening."

Ah, so that was what had caused the uproar. Lucy had already danced once with Vale, and etiquette demanded she now dance with whatever gentlemen requested her hand, including Lord Godfrey.

Ciaran didn't give a damn about etiquette. He didn't like the anxious look on Lucy's face, and he didn't want her to dance with Godfrey any more than she wanted it.

"It's a country dance, Lady Lucinda." Lord Godfrey gave Lucy a condescending smile. He was leaning toward her with his arm draped over the back of her chair, as if he had every right to be there, every right to touch her. "I realize you're not familiar with London manners, but surely you can manage a simple country dance?"

Ciaran's scowl deepened. Godfrey was far too close to Lucy, and his arm on her chair was insultingly familiar. Lucy kept edging away from him, but each time she moved Godfrey did, too, closing whatever distance she put between them. He looked like a snake about to wrap itself around its prey.

"I'm afraid I'll have to decline all the same, my lord."

"Don't be silly, girl," Jarvis snapped. "If his lordship wishes to dance, then you'll dance."

Lucy glanced at the dancers assembling for the set, and Ciaran could tell at once what she was thinking. The dance would take an age with such a large number of couples, and she couldn't bear to suffer Lord Godfrey's company for such a long time.

"This instant, Lucinda." Jarvis looked as if he was about to drag Lucy from her chair.

Mrs. Jarvis laid a timid hand on her husband's wrist. "Augustus, I don't think…that is, the child's natural reserve may be such—"

"For God's sake, Harriet, be quiet!" Jarvis snatched free of his wife's grip and turned a fearsome glower on Lucy. "Not another word of fuss, Lucinda, or else—"

"Never mind it, Jarvis." Lord Godfrey rose to his feet and tugged his coat down with icy dignity. "I'm not so desperate for a reel you need to bully the young lady into a dance."

Jarvis's face went from white to red as Godfrey offered Lucy a stiff bow, then turned on his heel and strode away. When Jarvis turned back to Lucy, his face was nearly purple with rage. "By God, Lucinda—"

Markham evidently didn't care for Jarvis's tone any more than Ciaran did. He leapt forward, but Ciaran was there first. He thrust his body between Lucy and her uncle, then stepped up to Jarvis, so close their faces were mere inches apart.

"The lady said she doesn't wish to dance." Ciaran spoke calmly enough, but his voice was frigid with menace.

Jarvis's face drained of color. "The lady is my ward, sir."

Ciaran raised an eyebrow, but he didn't back away. "Even more reason for you to treat her with respect."

Jarvis drew himself up. "Who are *you*, sir, to tell me how to treat my niece?"

Before Ciaran could answer, Lucy made a soft sound of distress. He turned to her to find her dark eyes had gone huge, and her face was paler than he'd ever seen it before. "Lucy, are you all—?"

That was as far as he got before Lucy raised a hand to her forehead. She swayed in her chair, and Ciaran just had time to reach her before her eyelashes fluttered closed, and she fell into a swoon.

Chapter Ten

Goodness, swoons were useful things, weren't they? If Lucy had realized feigning one would lead to such a quick escape she would have fallen into half a dozen of them by now.

"No, never mind coming down from the box, Bexley," she called to the coachman when she reached the carriage. She lowered the stair herself, adding, "Just wait for now, won't you? Mrs. and Miss Jarvis will be out presently."

Bexley, a rough-looking fellow Uncle Jarvis had hired for the season, merely grunted.

Lucy sprang nimbly into the carriage, a long sigh escaping her as she closed her eyes and let her head rest against the seat. Her one regret was she'd worried her aunt with her sudden lapse in consciousness. Or what appeared to be a sudden lapse in consciousness. She'd half-expected to be caught out in her charade, but apparently she was a better actress than she realized.

Uncle Jarvis hadn't bothered to wait and see if she were dead or alive before rushing off after a furious Lord Godfrey, but poor Aunt Jarvis had followed Lucy to the ladies' retiring room, wringing her hands, chastising herself, and clucking nervously the entire way. It had been quite a struggle to persuade her aunt to return to the ballroom and wait for Eloisa to finish her dance with Lord Vale and let Lucy make her own way to the carriage.

"For a lady who swooned not half an hour ago, that was a vigorous leap into your carriage."

Lucy didn't open her eyes, but her lips curved into an involuntary smile. She would have recognized that low, amused drawl anywhere. "Well, Ciaran Ramsey. The Wallflower's Gallant, and hero of ladies in distress everywhere, whether they want saving or not."

Ciaran hauled himself into the carriage, plopped down on the seat across from her and pulled the door closed behind him. "Seems to me you did want saving tonight, lass."

Ciaran's face was half lost in shadow, but Lucy heard the hint of humor in his voice. "Not at all. That is, I don't deny it was an ugly scene, but I found my way out of it. The swoon was a spur of the moment thing, but quite a stroke of genius, really."

Ciaran stretched his long legs out in front of him. He was so tall his knee brushed against hers. "You mean you only pretended to swoon?" He let out a low chuckle. "What a devious thing to do. Yet here you sit without a trace of guilt on your face. Shame on you, Lady Lucinda."

"I'm only happy Eloisa was dancing with Lord Vale at the time. It upsets her when her father falls into a temper, and I don't like to drag her into my scrapes if I can help it." Lucy frowned. "Somehow, though, it seems to happen more often than not."

"I don't doubt it, lass." He was quiet for a moment, then he murmured, "I looked for you, you know. After you disappeared, I searched all over Brighton for you. Quite a lot of effort for the lady who broke my nose."

"I didn't break it! You told me it wasn't..." Her lips quirked when she caught the flash of his smile in the dark. "I think what you mean is it was quite a lot of effort for the lady who kicked you in the face, and *almost* broke your nose."

"Something like that." Ciaran shifted restlessly against the seat. When he spoke again, his voice had grown serious. "I've thought of you every single day since you left Brighton, Lucy. I couldn't believe you'd go without a single word of explanation. I didn't believe it, until I went to your villa and saw it was empty."

Lucy drew in a shaky breath. All her life, she'd always been the one who was left behind. She knew how much it hurt. Without thinking, she reached for his hand. "I didn't choose to leave, Ciaran. You must know that."

He didn't answer right away, but he didn't snatch his hand back, either. After a long, tense silence, he sighed. "I did know it, but it didn't make it any easier. What happened?"

Lucy hesitated She was half-ashamed to admit the disaster in Brighton had been her own fault, but Ciaran was her friend, and one didn't lie to their friends. "My Uncle Jarvis found out about my, er, sunrise beach adventures."

He'd found out, all right, and he'd been livid. Lucy had never seen anyone so angry in her life.

"I should have known that would happen." Ciaran glanced down at their clasped hands. "I never should have encouraged you to keep meeting me there."

Lucy gave him a crooked smile. "Do you suppose there was anything you could have done to stop me? Come now, Ciaran. You know me better than that."

"Was it terrible?" Ciaran sounded as if he wasn't sure he wanted the answer.

Once again, Lucy hesitated. It had, in fact, been terrible, but she didn't intend to tell Ciaran *how* terrible. It might tempt him to another feat of misguided heroism.

Uncle Jarvis had been so overcome with rage he'd frightened her. He'd cursed until spittle was flying from his mouth, and his face had turned such a dangerous shade of red she'd been certain he'd shriek himself into an apoplexy. The next thing Lucy knew their things were packed and loaded into the carriage. They'd left Brighton behind without a second glance.

"N-no, not terrible, but he insisted we leave Brighton at once. We've been in London since then, preparing for the season."

After Uncle Jarvis's fit, neither Lucy nor Eloisa had dared hope they'd get much pleasure from their visit to London. They'd reconciled themselves to a grim time of it, but strangely enough, Uncle Jarvis had seemed to regain his equilibrium as soon as they arrived in the city. His mood had improved at once, and since then he'd been…well, if not pleasant, at least he hadn't locked them in their bedchambers.

Ciaran frowned. "Preparing? What does that mean?"

"It means new clothes, and dress fittings, and dreadful dancing lessons from overwrought French dancing masters." A scowl crept over Lucy's face. "It's been quite awful, really."

Ciaran's lips twitched, but the faint smile was gone as quickly as it appeared. "Why wouldn't you tell me your surname, Lucy? If I hadn't known you were going to London after Brighton, I might never have found you again."

Here it was, the moment Lucy had dreaded since the first day she'd met Ciaran. She squeezed her eyes closed, but there was no escaping it, no hiding from it. All of London knew who she was, and who her father was. Ciaran would find out about it soon enough, and anyway, concealing the truth was just another form of lying. "I didn't want to tell you because my father is…was…the Earl of Bellamy."

Lucy waited for the exclamation, the laughter, the shocked gasp, but it never came.

"Barmy Bellamy? The Mad Earl?" Her brows drew together. "You've never heard of him?"

"Not until I arrived in Brighton. I did hear a few of the rumors while I was there. I've known all along you're his daughter, Lucy." He hesitated, then asked evenly, "Was he mad?"

There was no judgment in the question, no mockery in his voice. He was simply asking. It struck Lucy then no one, not even her cousin or her aunt had ever asked her that. They'd just assumed the rumors were true.

Now he'd asked the question, Lucy wasn't sure how to answer it. Her father had been broken, certainly, and in a way that couldn't be repaired. But madness? Weren't they all mad, in one way or another? Weren't they all broken in some way that couldn't be fixed?

"He was different. People aren't always kind to those who are different, are they? Even before my mother died he wasn't much like other people. Afterward, he became…" She stopped, her breath catching. It was harder to get the words out than she'd thought it would be. "My mother was killed by a highwayman. Her death was sudden and tragic, and my father never recovered. He shut himself up inside our estate in Devon and he never came back out again."

A thick, tense silence fell over the carriage. Lucy knew she'd shocked him. Who'd ever heard of an earl who refused to set foot outside his house? She waited for Ciaran to gather himself, dreading what he'd say, but when he spoke his words surprised her.

"What about you, Lucy? What did it mean for you that your father never left the house again?"

Lucy swallowed. They were going to have this out, it seemed, and she'd just as soon have it all out at once. "It meant he rarely permitted me to leave it, either. Not at first," she added quickly, when she heard Ciaran's sharp intake of breath. "But over the years he grew more restrictive. I loved my father, and I never thought of him as mad, but I may be the only person in England who didn't."

"You're the only one who matters."

Lucy couldn't see him well enough to read his expression, but she'd never heard him speak quite so gently before. Tears rushed to her eyes, but she held them back and forced a laugh. "Yes, well, tell that to the old ladies in Brighton. I thought Lady Essex was going to come after me with a pistol and a burlap sack when she discovered I'm the Earl of Bellamy's daughter."

Lucy sensed more than saw Ciaran smile, felt the tension ease from his body even with the thick shadows dimming the inside of the carriage. Her chest loosened, and the same warmth she'd felt for him when they'd sat together on the beach rushed over her. Impulsively, she reached for him again, until she was holding both his hands. "I can't believe you're in London for the season. When I caught sight of you coming into the ballroom, I thought…well, I've simply never been so happy to see anyone in my life."

"I came to make sure you're safe and to see to it Vale knows you're here. He'll help you this season if you find you need it, but there's something I need to tell you first."

Something in his voice made apprehension dart down Lucy's spine. "What is it?"

He hesitated, then asked, "Lord Godfrey. How well do you know him?"

Lucy blinked. What in the world did Lord Godfrey have to do with anything? "Well enough to know I don't wish to know him any better. My uncle seems to have struck up a friendship with him, though I must say I can't understand why his lordship would bother. They haven't a thing in common. Indeed, I would have been pleased never to lay eyes on him again, but the man's like an unlucky penny, turning up when one least wants or expects him."

"Unluckier than you think. Your uncle and Lord Godfrey aren't friends, Lucy. Godfrey's here to make certain he collects a debt. Your uncle owes him money."

Lucy laughed. "That's impossible. Uncle Jarvis doesn't have any money."

"It *is* possible, Lucy. Lord Godfrey holds your uncle's vowels."

"But how can he have…" Lucy trailed off.

Of course. All those nights in Brighton when her uncle had gone out and hadn't returned until the early morning hours. He'd never deigned to explain his activities to his household, but Lucy knew more often than not he was deep into his cups by the time he arrived home.

If he'd been gaming while he was in that befuddled a state…

"You mean to say he's been wagering. He's been at cards and dice with Lord Godfrey, hasn't he?"

"Yes, and your uncle isn't a skilled gamer. Godfrey's been hanging about Brighton for weeks now, taking the waters by day and your uncle's money by night."

Lucy's head was spinning. "You saw this yourself?"

His smile was grim. "All those mornings I met you on the beach and you teased me about my bleary eyes, I was coming from a private game over at the Castle Inn. Your uncle and Godfrey were there nearly every night, and your uncle was rarely sober."

Lucy shook her head. She couldn't say much in her uncle's favor. He was a weak, selfish man, but a propensity for drink and gaming? It was even worse than she'd realized. "How much? His debt to Lord Godfrey, Ciaran. How much do you think he owes him?"

Ciaran blew out a breath. "I can't say for sure. I didn't pay much attention to their dealings. I didn't know Jarvis was your uncle at the time, or I would have. I only know it went on for weeks, and your uncle played deep. I wouldn't be surprised if it was hundreds of pounds. Maybe more."

"Hundreds of pounds! But my uncle doesn't have it! He hasn't any money at all!"

Lucy knew how foolish she sounded. One couldn't walk down a street in London without stumbling over some gentleman who wagered above his means. Lord Godfrey didn't care whether her uncle's pockets were empty or not. He'd have his money, no matter if he had to ruin her uncle to get it.

And if Godfrey did choose to ruin Uncle Jarvis, her aunt and Eloisa would be caught up in his penury and disgrace.

Ciaran was watching her closely. "Your uncle doesn't have any money, but *you* do, don't you? Forgive me, but Vale tells me you're an heiress. As your guardian and trustee, your uncle is in control of your person and your funds, isn't he?"

Lucy stared mutely at him. Surely, he didn't mean—

"Has it occurred to you he intends to dispose of both to Lord Godfrey? It would be a tidy way to settle his debt."

Lucy gaped at him, protests and denials rushing to her lips, but no matter how her heart tried to make it not so, her brain was busily putting together the puzzle pieces.

Her Uncle Jarvis owed Godfrey a debt he hadn't a prayer of paying. He knew Lucy had the funds to pay it, but he couldn't simply take whatever he liked from her trust. Nor could he force her to do anything against her will. He was her guardian, not her gaoler.

But she was under his care, and there was no question he could put an enormous amount of pressure on her to do his bidding. There was nothing to stop him from choosing a suitor for her and attempting to manipulate her into a marriage she didn't want.

She'd turn twenty-one in a matter of weeks. Once she did, her uncle would lose any control he had over her and her fortune. Whatever it was he intended to do with her, he had very little time left to do it.

But surely her uncle wouldn't go so far as to force a marriage? Lucy shivered, remembering Lord Godfrey's hot breath on her neck tonight, the press of his arm against the back of her chair. For a gentleman who'd never received the least encouragement from her, he seemed awfully certain of himself.

Her first thought was to appeal to the Chancery Court for a change in trustee, but she discarded it at once. There was little point. On what grounds could she object to her uncle's guardianship? That she suspected he wished to marry her to an earl and see her become a countess? The court wouldn't consider Lord Godfrey's age a factor—plenty of young ladies in England married men much older than themselves.

"Godfrey gets an heiress as his bride, and in return he forgives my uncle's debt."

Lucy marveled at her own calmness. Her heart was threatening to burst from her chest, but no one would have guessed it by her steady tone.

"I can't know for sure that's what your uncle intends, but when I saw him this evening, and Lord Godfrey in your party, it was the first thing I thought of."

Lucy couldn't deny it made sense, or that it sounded very much like something her uncle might do. He wasn't a particularly clever man, but he had an instinctual talent for securing his own interests.

Then there'd been Uncle Jarvis's curious behavior tonight. He always displayed an eager obsequiousness to persons of rank, but she'd never seen him as furious as he'd been tonight when she refused to dance with Lord Godfrey.

So furious she'd been afraid he'd grab her and drag her to the dance floor himself.

Ciaran ran a rough hand through his hair. "I don't care for the way Godfrey treated you, either. As if you're some prize piece of horseflesh he's purchasing."

Horseflesh? Lucy shivered. Dear God, what a chillingly descriptive metaphor.

It was out of the question, of course. Her uncle might rage and threaten as much as he liked, but nothing would ever induce her to marry Lord Godfrey. After so many years confined to Bellamy Court, she hadn't gained her freedom at last only to see it snatched away from her.

"My uncle can't make me marry him."

"No, but he can make things unpleasant for you if you don't do as he tells you."

For her, and for Aunt Jarvis and Eloisa.

She could simply leave London and return to Devon. But what would become of her cousin and aunt if she left them at Uncle Jarvis's mercy? No, she couldn't abandon them. They were the only family she had left. It would break her heart to turn her back on them that way.

It was less than four weeks until she turned twenty-one. Surely there was something she could do to hold Lord Godfrey and Uncle Jarvis at bay until then? It would be better still if she could find a way to chase Lord Godfrey off for good. But what? How could she get him to cry off? Feign madness, as she'd feigned a swoon just now? Given the rumors about her father, half of London already believed her mad.

It might work, but Lucy recoiled at the idea. Pretending to madness felt like a betrayal of her father, and if London believed her mad, it would ruin whatever slim chance Eloisa had to make a decent marriage and escape Uncle Jarvis's clutches.

No, madness wouldn't do. A compromised reputation, then? God knew the *ton* was fastidious about a lady's behavior. She could compromise herself simply by walking down St. James's Street, for pity's sake. It was easily done, but then that wouldn't do Eloisa's cause much good, either. Her cousin would be tainted by association.

Marriage to another gentleman? That would certainly do the trick, and yet Lucy flinched away from that idea, as well. She'd made up her mind a long time ago not to marry. A marriage to Lord Godfrey would be the worst possible outcome, of course, but marriage to anyone else, no matter how lovely would be nearly as bad.

Unless it was someone she loved, but…Lucy glanced at Ciaran, then looked quickly away. There was no sense dwelling on what would never be.

But then it wouldn't take an actual marriage, would it?

Lucy's eyes widened as her mind seized on an idea. A courtship would be enough, surely? A courtship that lasted just until her twenty-first birthday, followed by a quick jilting once her fortune was out of reach of her grasping uncle.

A feigned courtship. Wasn't it just possible it would work as well as the feigned swoon had?

"Lucy? Are you all right? You have the strangest look on your face."

Lucy jerked her gaze to Ciaran. "I, ah…"

The Wallflower's Gallant. A gentleman with a decidedly heroic turn, who, against all odds, just happened to be here in London when she needed him most.

A gentleman who just happened to be her dearest friend.

Lucy met his gaze, her teeth scoring her lower lip. "I'm very well, but I have something to ask you, Ciaran. You see, it's just…that is, I'd consider it a great favor if you'd agree to…I need you to help me with…"

Her voice faded, and she lapsed into an embarrassed silence. As it turned out, it was far more difficult to ask your dearest friend to pretend to court you and then jilt you than she'd thought it would be. Truly, how did one ask such a thing? Especially when one was in love with that friend and he hadn't the least idea of returning the sentiment.

"Lucy?" Ciaran leaned toward her. A beam of light from the townhouse fell across his face and she could see his eyes were dark with concern. "What can I do?"

Well, now you ask...

Lucy drew in a deep breath, but while her mind was still working on a delicate way to phrase it her mouth took the liberty of blurting it out. "I need you to pretend to court me this season. Another suitor will discourage Lord Godfrey from pressing his suit. Once I've turned twenty-one and am no longer under my uncle's protection, you'll jilt me."

His smiled vanished. "Lucy..."

Lucy flinched. His voice was gentle. Far *too* gentle. The sort of gentleness one used when they were about to refuse their best friend a favor.

Granted, it was quite a *big* favor.

In the next moment, that was what he did. "I'm not staying in London, Lucy. I'm leaving for Scotland in the next few days."

"Scotland?" Lucy's stomach lurched. "You...you're leaving?"

Of course. He'd told her all about Scotland, about how he'd been longing to go back and see if he could salvage any part of the life he'd left behind. She'd encouraged him to go. She'd scolded him, called him a wastrel, and told him to find something useful to do.

He'd done just as she bid him.

"Will you stay away long?" Lucy had to force the next words past the lump in her throat. "You'll come back to England again, won't you?"

"England?" He blinked, as if the thought had never occurred to him. "I-I don't know, Lucy. I won't know until I see what awaits me in Scotland."

"I see. I...yes, of course." She tried to say something more, to reassure him it was all right—that she'd be all right—but the words wouldn't come. Instead, she tightened her grip on his hands, her eyes closing when his warm fingers wrapped around hers.

Lucy's throat ached. She'd never been one to hide before, but as the sting of tears pressed behind her eyes she leaned back, away from the beam of light from the townhouse.

Just then, she was grateful for the darkness.

Chapter Eleven

To most Londoners, Thomas Wilson's Dancing Academy was a respectable establishment. A place where ladies and gentlemen without the means to hire private dancing masters could learn to shuffle about the dance floor gracefully enough not to attract scorn at the next ball of the season.

To Lucy, it was the ninth circle of hell.

"No, no, Lady Lucinda! You *jetté* forward onto the *left* foot, return to third position, and add an *assemblé* behind!" The dancing master, Monsieur Guilland, patted at his flushed forehead with a damp handkerchief. "I beg you, mademoiselle. Pay attention!"

Lucy *had* been paying attention. She'd paid such close attention her head was spinning and her eyes burning from the strain of trying to follow Monsieur Guilland's gesticulations. Her efforts hadn't made the least bit of difference. Her feet ached, and Monsieur Guilland looked as limp as his ruined handkerchief.

She lowered her right foot to the floor with a defeated sigh. She was tempted to throw her fan in Monsieur Guilland's outraged face, but to be fair, this was also likely *his* idea of the ninth circle of hell, and Lucy the most tormenting of the demons surrounding him.

"If you don't learn the proper foot positions you'll confuse your partner. You risk the entire set falling into confusion!" Monsieur Guilland waved a tragic hand at Lucy's partners in the set, who were all standing about in various states of bewilderment. "Is that what you want, Lady Lucinda?"

Lucy didn't much care whether she ever danced the quadrille again, but she only nodded meekly. "No, Monsieur." She darted a glance at Eloisa, who gave her a sympathetic smile. "I apologize for my clumsiness. I'll do better next time," she promised the other ladies and gentlemen in the set, her cheeks heating with embarrassment.

It wasn't that she objected to dancing, or even to dancing lessons. She'd spent many pleasant hours whirling about the ballroom at Bellamy Park with her father, or, if he was having one of his bad days, their butler Popple, who was quite spry, despite his advanced years.

Indeed, she would have said she already knew how to dance a quadrille before she even set foot in Thomas Wilson's Dancing Academy. Somehow, though, the quadrille she'd learned at home bore little resemblance to Monsieur Guilland's tedious mincing. Every time she began to enjoy herself, Monsieur Guilland fell into a paroxysm of despair. Lucy couldn't understand it. Wasn't dancing meant to be pleasurable?

Monsieur Guilland indulged in a heavy sigh. "I beg you will, Lady Lucinda, but perhaps we'd all benefit from a brief rest first. Ladies, gentlemen!" He clapped his hands for attention, then fluttered his handkerchief toward the row of chairs lining the wall, much in the manner of a man waving a flag of surrender. "My dear Lady Lucinda, do try and pay attention when we resume, won't you?"

"I don't intend to *ever* go through such misery again," Lucy declared as she and Eloisa made their way to the side of the room.

"You have to. You can't refuse every gentleman who asks you to dance the quadrille," Eloisa said. "Father won't like it."

Lucy shrugged. "No, I don't suppose he will, but neither will he like my making a cake of myself in front of all of London, either."

Eloisa sank down in the chair next to her with a sigh. "You're not at all clumsy, Lucy. I daresay you're just more, ah, unpredictable a dancer than Monsieur Guilland's usual pupils."

Lucy shot her cousin a grateful look. "I suppose. I'm sorry my uncle forced you to take these horrid lessons with me, Eloisa. You don't need them. Your quadrille is lovely."

Eloisa let out a short laugh. "My father doesn't think so. He says I dance as if I have hooves instead of feet."

"Why, that's the most absurd thing I ever heard!" Lucy exclaimed, anger sparking in her chest. They'd all be better off if Uncle Jarvis was a touch less free with his opinions.

She'd been willing enough to give her uncle the benefit of the doubt at first. She'd overlooked his boorish manners, his propensity for drink, his insatiable appetite for cards and dice. She'd pretended not to notice his preoccupation with the contents of her bodice, and had borne his frequent tempers without a word of complaint.

But after three weeks in Brighton and another two in London, her patience with him had snapped. She'd suspected he was a villain from the moment she met him, and her first impression was correct.

Uncle Jarvis was about as pleasant as a poisonous snake.

He couldn't lay eyes on his daughter without berating her. As far as he was concerned, Eloisa wasn't pretty enough, charming enough, or accomplished enough to attract an eligible match. He railed at fate for cursing him with such a disappointing daughter. He predicted with much bitterness Eloisa would end a spinster, and he'd be obliged to clothe and feed her until he was laid in his grave.

He was scarcely more generous with his wife. Lucy could hardly blame her aunt for hiding behind a veneer of ill health. She might have done the same if she had such a husband.

Uncle Jarvis was, in short, the most appalling guardian a lady could possibly be burdened with.

But then she'd be out from under his thumb soon enough. Her twenty-first birthday would be here soon enough and then she might do as she pleased. Until then she had no other choice but to tolerate her uncle's slippery attempts to assert control over her.

Or more accurately, over her sixty thousand pounds. There was nothing Uncle Jarvis loved more than money.

"It's not true, Eloisa. Your dancing is wonderful. You mustn't listen to your father when he says things like that." Lucy gave Eloisa's hand a quick squeeze, and Eloisa squeezed back.

"I confess I don't remember the quadrille being so irksome as this. Has it always been so, or is it just Monsieur Guilland's teaching that has me in such fits?" Lucy swung her foot back and forth, her heel striking the leg of her chair. "I tell you, Eloisa, I won't dance the quadrille at all this season if it's going to be such a blasted—"

"Hush, Lucy!" Eloisa hissed, tilting her head toward Lady Felicia, who was making her way over to their side of the room.

"Blessed nuisance," Lucy finished. "Good afternoon, Lady Felicia."

Lady Felicia took the chair next to Eloisa's. "Good afternoon. How do you do?"

Lucy grimaced. "I own I was far better before I tried to dance the quadrille. I beg your pardon for upsetting the dance. Monsieur Guilland has quite despaired of me."

All three young ladies glanced across the room at Monsieur Guilland, who was mopping his brow, waving his handkerchief about, and muttering furiously to himself.

"Oh, dear." Lucy clapped a hand over her mouth to smother the wild giggle that tickled her throat. "I fear I've broken him."

Lady Felicia stared at her in surprise for a moment before dissolving into an answering giggle. "No, it's not so bad as that."

"Bad enough. But I can't think of any reason why *you* should be cursed with Monsieur Guilland's instruction, Lady Felicia," Lucy observed. "Your dancing is as graceful as my cousin's is."

Lady Felicia sighed. "Sebastian insisted I come. I believe he thought it would heighten my enthusiasm for the season. I didn't want to come to London at all, you see."

"Why *would* you want to come? Why would any young lady?" Lucy made a disgusted noise. "I've wanted to see London for an age, but I never imagined a season would be so dreary. It's a wonder to me how any young lady makes her way through it without becoming a nervous wreck."

"A wreck, or a mockery," Lady Felicia said bitterly. "I feel quite sorry for Sebastian, having to drag me through a second season."

Lucy and Eloisa glanced at each other.

"But your brother seemed perfectly happy to act as your chaperone at Lady Ivey's ball last night. He's an ideal escort." Eloisa propped her chin on her palm with a dejected air. She and Lucy, who had to make do with Eloisa's father, weren't quite so fortunate.

Lady Felicia looked from Lucy to Eloisa, a flush rising in her cheeks. "I'm lucky to have him. He's very good to me, yet I daresay I'll disappoint him again this year, just as I did the last."

Eloisa and Lucy glanced at each other again, then back at Lady Felicia.

"Why should that be the case?" Lucy asked. "You're lovely, and the daughter of an earl. You have every advantage. Why shouldn't you make a triumphant match this season?"

Unless, of course, she had no money. Lucy glanced anxiously at her cousin. Eloisa didn't have a penny to her name, and worse, she had a ridiculous, mean-spirited father. She had nothing but her pretty face to recommend her, and London was overflowing with young ladies with pretty faces and empty purses.

If beauty and manners were all that was required for an eligible match, she'd rest easy about her cousin's prospects this season, but there could be no denying Eloisa had only a meager chance at making a decent match.

Lady Felicia looked a bit taken aback at Lucy's blunt assessment. "I only wish it were that simple, Lady Lucinda." She leaned closer and dropped her voice to a whisper. "Unfortunately, my idea of a triumph is to become betrothed to the man I love, and I'm no closer to it now than I was last season."

Eloisa's eyes widened. "What do you mean? Are you in love with someone?"

Lady Felicia caught her lower lip between her teeth, her gaze darting back and forth between Lucy and Eloisa. "Oh, dear. This is terribly humiliating, but I suppose it'll become obvious soon enough."

Lucy and Eloisa huddled closer.

"I thought perhaps…that is, I had hoped Lord Markham might make me an offer last season. I've known Edmund my whole life, and I've loved him for as long as I can remember."

"You…he…you mean…" Lucy gaped at her, trying to gather her wits. She hadn't expected such a blunt confession of love from Lady Felicia.

Lady Felicia sighed. "Dear me. I'm a shocking creature, aren't I? I do beg your pardons."

"No, no. It's quite all right." Lucy wasn't one to pry into others' secrets, having a great many of her own she'd rather not discuss, but there could be little doubt Lady Felicia had just invited them to pry to their heart's content. "Does Lord Markham know you're in love with him?"

Lady Felicia sighed again, this one bleaker than the last. "If he doesn't, then he must be remarkably dim. I haven't been very good at hiding it. He'd fond of me, of course, but he persists in thinking of me as Sebastian's troublesome younger sister."

Lucy tapped a finger against her chin, considering this. "Well, Lord Markham is here with you again this season. Surely that means there's still hope for the two of you?"

Lady Felicia's face was glum. "I'm afraid not. Edmund isn't here with *me* at all. He only came because Sebastian wheedled him into it. I did mention Sebastian is quite good at wheedling, did I not?"

Lucy glanced at Eloisa. "You did, yes."

"Either Edmund's on the hunt for a wife, which means I'll be obliged to watch him dance and flirt with every eligible lady in London, or else he's come to keep an eye out for Sebastian. Either way, I'm in for a grim time of it. Indeed, before I met you both, I'd half made up my mind to insist Sebastian take me back home to Lewes at once."

Eloisa frowned. "Why should Lord Markham have to look after Lord Vale? Does he need looking after?"

Lady Felicia shifted uncomfortably in her chair. "Well, Sebastian was involved with a rather unfortunate incident last season."

"What sort of unfortunate incident?" Eloisa pressed.

"The whole thing was rather absurd, really. Sebastian fell out with Lord Feckham over something to do with Lady Needham, who was Sebastian's *chère amie* at the time."

Eloisa gasped. "Lord Vale has a mistress?"

"Not anymore, no, but he did then. Sebastian ended up calling Lord Feckham out, and he, ah…he shot him in the foot. It caused quite a scandal."

"Lord Vale participated in a *duel*, over his *mistress*?" Eloisa looked horrified. "I don't understand. I thought he was…he seems so…"

"He's a terrible rake," Lady Felicia said matter-of-factly.

"A *rake*!"

"I'm afraid so. Please don't misunderstand me, Miss Jarvis. He's a very good brother, and I'm tremendously fond of him, but there's simply no denying Sebastian's as wicked a gentleman as you'll find in London."

"My goodness." Eloisa fell back against her chair, her mouth open in shock.

None of them seemed to know what to say after that, and they lapsed into silence.

Lucy was the first to rally. "Well, what a sad trio we are, to be sure."

Eloisa frowned. "Nonsense. What's sad about us?"

"Unrequited, poor, and mad." Lucy pointed to Lady Felicia, Eloisa, and herself in turn. "Not quite the cream of London society, are we? It's not any wonder the three of us spent most of Lady Ivey's ball as wallflowers."

"What an awful thing to say, Lucy!" Eloisa huffed, crossing her arms over her chest.

"But true, all the same."

Lady Felicia was staring at her. "Mad? Who's mad? You're the last lady in London I would call mad, Lady Lucinda."

"Oh, I'm not, I promise you, but it hardly matters. My father was the Earl of Bellamy, you see. Damning proof, isn't it? Most of London has already drawn their conclusions about me."

It wasn't the least bit funny, but a grin was stealing across Lucy's lips. It was just so dreadful. What else was there to do but laugh? Surely their prospects were the most dismal of all the young ladies in London.

Not that her own plans had anything to do with the marriage mart. When her uncle had proposed a season she'd agreed to it for Eloisa's sake, and because she'd always wanted to visit London. But a husband? No. A husband didn't figure into her plans. She wouldn't change her mind about that.

Whether her Uncle Jarvis would try to force her to change it, well… that was anyone's guess. "Ironic, isn't it? Of the three of us I'm the most likely to be saddled with a husband, and I'm the only one of us who doesn't want one."

She'd said it more to herself than her companions, but Eloisa and Lady Felicia jerked their attention back to her at once.

"You don't want a husband, Lucy?" Eloisa asked, at the same time as Lady Felicia said, "What husband? Who are you going to marry?"

Lucy hesitated. She'd lain awake for hours last night, her brain jumping from Uncle Jarvis to Lord Godfrey to Ciaran until she felt as if a terrified mouse had been let loose inside her head. She'd woken bleary-eyed, but by the time breakfast was over and she, Eloisa, and Aunt Jarvis were cozily installed in the drawing room, she'd convinced herself Ciaran was exaggerating the danger.

What did they really know about Uncle Jarvis's intentions? Only that her uncle had met Lord Godfrey in Brighton, and likely spent time at the gaming tables with him wagering money he didn't have. They didn't know if he'd actually *lost* substantial sums. That is, it was likely he had, since one didn't usually win when they wagered while in their cups.

That aside, they didn't have any reason to suspect Uncle Jarvis would go so far as to try and force Lucy to marry Lord Godfrey. Yes, Lord Godfrey had turned up in London out of nowhere, but that wasn't so very suspicious. It was the season, after all.

She'd been quite comforted by these reflections, right up until this morning, when Lord Godfrey had appeared on the doorstep of their lodgings in Portman Square, all politeness and insincere charm. He'd paid particular attention to Lucy during the call, hardly sparing a word or a glance for Eloisa.

He'd behaved, in short, very much like a man embarking on a courtship.

The very idea sent a shiver of dread down Lucy's spine.

For his part, Uncle Jarvis didn't even appear to notice Lord Godfrey's rudeness to his daughter. He'd squeezed his bulk into a chair before the fire, a satisfied smirk on his face as Lord Godfrey flattered Lucy and preened like a peacock.

Something was wrong with this business. Lucy could feel it in the pit of her stomach. Uncle Jarvis was as smug as a cat who'd got the cream, and Lord Godfrey wasn't making a secret of what he wanted.

And what he wanted was Lucy.

He wanted to marry her, and he'd begun courting her with her uncle's enthusiastic approval. "Well, there's a chance—just a possibility, mind you—that my uncle means to…"

Lucy trailed off, biting her lip. She didn't want to upset Eloisa by accusing her father of such a loathsome scheme, but as it happened, she needn't have been concerned. Eloisa didn't know about the wagering, but she'd already come to her own conclusions.

"Marry her to Lord Godfrey," Eloisa finished, her face grim.

"Lord Godfrey!" Lady Felicia's voice was shrill with horror. "But that's abominable! He's far too old for you!"

"Three times her age, and with the coldest eyes I've ever seen." Eloisa's lips were tight.

"We don't know for certain, Eloisa," Lucy said. "We may be mistaken about the whole thing. Perhaps we're doing my Uncle Jarvis a disservice."

"We aren't."

Lucy turned to her cousin, surprised at the icy note in Eloisa's voice. Lucy knew well enough Eloisa didn't love her father. Indeed, she had no reason to. But she was devoted to her mother, and in the past the loyalty she'd felt toward one parent translated into, if not love, at least the appearance of respect for the other.

Not anymore.

"My father likely does wish to marry you to Lord Godfrey. No doubt his lordship has offered him something in return for delivering a young, beautiful, wealthy bride into his clutches. The only question is, how far will my father go to achieve his ends? If you refuse Lord Godfrey, will he try and force the marriage? If so, how?"

"I don't like the sound of this at all." Lady Felicia lowered her voice. "Perhaps we'd better learn a bit more about Lord Godfrey."

Lucy leaned closer, and her friends followed until all three of their heads—dark, fair and red—were huddled together. "But who can we ask?"

Eloisa turned to Lady Felicia. "Don't you know anything about him? You never heard even the faintest whisper about him last season?"

Lady Felicia shook her head. "I'm afraid not. As far as I know, he wasn't even in London last season. If he was, there was no gossip or scandal about him."

The three of them were quiet for a moment, considering this. Even if Lord Godfrey had done something perfectly awful, it was quite possible there hadn't been a scandal over it. The *ton* might not hesitate to hold young ladies to a brutal standard of propriety, but they were far more forgiving when it came to the gentlemen, especially the titled ones. The fact that Lady Felicia hadn't heard a whisper to Lord Godfrey's discredit was no guarantee he wasn't an utter scoundrel.

"What of your brother?" Eloisa asked. "Lord Vale is quite the fashionable gentleman about town, and you said he has many acquaintances in London. Might he know something about Lord Godfrey?"

"He might, yes. I can ask him, but I warn you both. If Sebastian suspects there's some kind of mischief afoot, he'll tease mercilessly until he finds out what it is."

"Very right and proper." Eloisa said, trying once again to give Lord Vale credit. "A brother should do his best to protect his sister."

Lady Felicia snorted. "It's more like if there's any mischief to be had, he wants a part of it."

"Oh." Eloisa's face fell. "Well, never mind Lord Vale, then. What of Lord Markham?"

"I've never known a man less likely to listen to gossip than Edmund. He's a terrible disappointment in that regard. Even if he did know anything about Lord Godfrey, I doubt he'd tell *me*." Lady Felicia's tone was bitter. "After all, I'm a mere child, aren't I? I must be protected from anything unpleasant."

"This is absurd." Lucy threw her hands up, disgusted. "Here's poor Felicia with a broken heart, Eloisa with a tyrannical father and not enough funds to escape into a decent marriage, and me, about to be forced to marry a man three times my age who makes my skin crawl. No, it simply won't do. Something must be done."

"Lucy's right." The dejected look fell from Lady Felicia's face and a new, determined light shone in her eyes. "We don't have to let ourselves be tossed about like pieces on a chess board. I'll see what I can get out of my brother, and for Lucy's sake, I'll even try and squeeze some information out of Edmund. Meanwhile, you two must do what you can to discover what Mr. Jarvis means to do."

"But how?" Eloisa worried her lip. "My father's always been secretive, and never more so than when he's doing something wicked."

"I'd start with Mrs. Jarvis. See if your uncle has let anything slip about his plans to see Lucy wed. A little eavesdropping might be helpful, as well. See if you can overhear any of his conversations with Lord Godfrey. Villains always discuss their plans with each other."

Lucy and Eloisa were quiet for a moment, absorbing this, then Eloisa asked, "What of Lord Markham? What shall we do about him? We can't let Lady Felicia wither away from a broken heart."

Lady Felicia tossed her head. "Perhaps it's time I stopped pining for Edmund. There are dozens of handsome gentlemen in London. I'll simply fall in love with one of them, instead."

"And one of them will simply fall in love with Eloisa. Never mind the lack of fortune. We only need to put you forward a bit. Someone is sure to fall victim to your charms. You've all the makings of a belle, cousin." Lucy took Eloisa's hand and gave it a fond squeeze. She was determined to see her cousin safely married. Surely not every gentleman in London was chasing an heiress.

"Oh, nonsense." But Eloisa flushed, pleased at the compliment.

As for Lucy's own problem with Uncle Jarvis and Lord Godfrey... she'd find out what she could from Aunt Jarvis, but she hadn't the least intention of ending it there.

Her idea to have Ciaran pretend to court her had been a good one. A bit reckless, yes, but brilliant all the same. It was a perfect solution to her temporary dilemma. She simply needed to find another gentleman willing to help her.

And she knew just who to ask.

She sighed. If only Ciaran would remain in London a little longer, he could—

No. Lucy cut the thought off before its roots could spread. She couldn't ask that of him. Not when she knew so well how it felt to be trapped and helpless—to want freedom so badly, and see it dangling just beyond your reach.

She cared too much for Ciaran to subject him to that.

He'd waited long enough to return to Scotland. A true friend would wish for him to have everything he wanted.

Even if what he wanted wasn't her.

Chapter Twelve

"It looks like we got here just in time, Markham." Lord Vale strolled into the study and threw himself into a chair in front of the massive oak desk. "What is the trouble, Ramsey? You look a bit green about the gills."

Ciaran grunted. He *felt* green. After his encounter with Lucy in the carriage last night, he'd come home and drunk half a bottle of his brother Finn's very good port. By the time he'd sat down to write what he now imagined was a very incoherent letter to his sister Isla, demanding to know everything she'd ever heard about Godfrey, he could barely keep his eyes open.

Until he'd stumbled into bed, that is. Then he'd lay there staring into the dark, his thoughts in turmoil.

Isobel. Scotland. London. Lucy.

Lucy.

She'd tweaked him about his heroic instincts again last night. She'd reminded him she'd never needed him to save her. Not from drowning, and not from the brawl. But this business with Jarvis and Godfrey…Ciaran couldn't shake the notion that this time, she truly did need him.

She needed him, and he was abandoning her.

On the day of the bout in Brighton, Lucy had insisted a friendship between them was inevitable. She'd said fate had decreed they become friends, whether they liked it or not. Ciaran didn't believe in fate, but he couldn't deny it was odd, the way they kept finding each other. Thousands of people in London, and she'd dropped right into his lap.

That is, not his *lap*. She hadn't a thing to do with his lap.

They were friends, nothing more.

Still, he was starting to believe there was no such thing as coincidence. That there was something inside him that recognized *her*, no matter the occasion or setting, as his final destination.

Like a bird returning to its nest.

"Well, Ramsey?"

Ciaran had been staring out the window, but he looked around to find Vale watching him with an infuriating smirk on his lips. "My green gills—or the reasons for them—aren't any of your bloody business, Vale. Who the devil let you two in here, anyway?"

"A short, roundish fellow. Pleasant enough. I think he said his name was Travers. I believe he's your brother's butler." Vale grinned. "Good thing we're here, too. Ramsey doesn't look quite himself, does he Markham?"

Lord Markham perched on the edge of a chair, folded his hands over his walking stick, and regarded Ciaran in silence for a moment. "Not a bit. You look a wreck, Ramsey."

Ciaran *was* a wreck, but not for the reasons his friends supposed. He dropped into the chair behind the desk, his brow lowering in a scowl. "What do you know about Lord Godfrey, Vale?"

Vale's eyebrow rose. "Godfrey? Bit dry and creaky, isn't he? Not terribly amusing, either. Aside from that, not a blessed thing. Is he the reason you're scowling? What's he done?"

Nothing yet, and Ciaran wanted to keep it that way. "He was at Lady Ivey's ball last night. He asked Lady Lucinda to dance and I didn't like his manner toward her, that's all."

"Ah, so that's it." Vale balanced an immaculate buff-colored leg over his knee. "You know what I think, Markham? I think Ramsey here is preoccupied with Lady Lucinda. I'd wager the guineas in my pocket on it."

Ciaran blinked. All right, then. He was a wreck precisely for the reason his friends supposed.

"That's absurd. I'm not preoccupied." Still, Ciaran couldn't forget the look on Lucy's face when he'd told her he was leaving for Scotland in a few days. Her disappointment, the slight trembling of her lips, the way she'd slid her hand into his as if she'd keep him with her if she could...

He dragged a hand through his hair. If there were another bottle of port to hand, he'd be emptying it right now.

All right, then. He *was* preoccupied.

"Mind you, I don't blame Ramsey a bit." Vale plucked a heavy marble lion off the desk and pretended to study it, but the sly grin was still hovering at the corners of his mouth. "Lady Lucinda is lovely enough to throw any man into a hopeless passion, even an oblivious fellow like Ramsey here. She's good fun, too. What say you, Markham?"

Lord Markham didn't appear to say much at all unless he was prompted, but this time he answered with surprising enthusiasm. "Lovely, indeed, though I prefer dark-haired young ladies to fair ones."

Ciaran lifted an eyebrow, impressed. It was the longest sentence he'd ever heard Markham utter in one breath.

Vale, however, dismissed Markham's declaration with a derisive snort. "Ah, so it's dark-haired ladies is it, Markham? How curious. I would have said it was just the opposite. I suppose we'll see, won't we? For God's sake, Ramsey, what the devil *is* this thing?" He scowled down at the marble lion.

"It's a paperweight, you simpleton."

"Hmmm." Vale turned the lion over in his hands, looking at it from every angle, then plunked it back down on the edge of the desk with a sniff. "Damned ugly one, if you ask me, but never mind. Go fetch your hat and stick, Ramsey. We've come to take you to Old Bailey with us."

Ciaran didn't move. "Old Bailey? Why should I want to go there?"

Vale rolled his eyes. "The better question, Ramsey, is why you should want to stay *here*. It's as dull as a tomb."

"I can't go to Old Bailey. I'm going to Scotland."

"Scotland?" Vale blinked. "What, right *now*? This very second?"

"Not now, but as soon as I'm ready to travel." What Ciaran didn't say was he'd had the entire afternoon to get ready. Long, empty hours had passed since he saw Lucy at Lady Ivey's ball, but he'd hadn't lifted a finger to prepare for his journey, or given a single servant a single order.

Vale waved away this excuse. "Well, as soon as you're ready isn't *now*, is it? Damn cold and rainy in Scotland this time of year, anyway. Can't think why you'd want to go there, Ramsey."

Ciaran rolled his eyes. "I'm Scottish, for one."

"Well, what of it? My great-grandfather was from Cardiff, and you don't see me running off to Wales, do you?" Vale frowned at the marble lion, poking experimentally at it with the tip of his walking stick. "Go to Scotland if you like, but we can't have you moping about in this stupid manner while you remain in London. Can we, Markham?"

Lord Markham shrugged. "May as well come along, Ramsey. You're not any use to anyone lazing about here."

Ciaran doubted he'd be any use to anyone in Old Bailey, either, but he rose reluctantly from his chair. He hadn't anything better to do. He wouldn't leave London until he'd heard back from Isla. Until then, he was trapped here, with the long afternoons stretching out empty before him. "What do you two need to do in Old Bailey? Drop Vale off at Newgate?"

Vale laughed. "Ah, that's much better, Ramsey. Do try and stay amusing today, won't you? There's a good fellow. Our business hasn't a thing to do with Newgate, but with a certain trio of young ladies. My sister is at her dancing lesson with Lady Lucinda and Miss Jarvis. I promised I'd fetch her at Thomas Wilson's Dancing Academy and escort her home."

Ciaran snatched his coat off the back of his chair and shoved his arms into the tight sleeves. It was the perfect chance to speak to Lucy without her bloody uncle hovering over them, listening to every word.

"Vale, stop fussing with that paperweight. You'll hurt yourself. Come on, then. If we're going to Old Bailey, let's go."

* * * *

"What sort of a place is Wilson running here?"

They'd paused at the large window in front of Thomas Wilson's Dancing Academy to take a peek at the ladies inside. Harmless enough, but all of a sudden Markham was clutching his walking stick as if he'd like to smash the window to pieces.

He'd seen something he didn't like, and it had thrown him into a temper.

Ciaran peered through the window. He didn't see anything amiss, but Markham wasn't the sort to indulge in pointless tantrums.

Vale was staring at Markham. "What the devil's the matter with you, Markham?"

"For God's sakes, Vale, are you blind?" Markham's voice was shaking. "Or do you simply not care if someone insults your sister?"

Vale glanced through the window, then turned a blank look on Markham. "Who's insulting her?"

"Lord Nash, of course! He's holding her in his arms!"

Vale pressed his nose to the glass for a longer look, then drew back again. "They're waltzing, Markham. You've heard of waltzing, haven't you? I daresay you've even done it yourself once or twice. It's hardly a scandal. Wilson's is, after all, a dancing academy."

Markham stared at Vale without speaking, but after a few moments he seemed to recall himself, and his cheeks flushed a deep red. "Well, it's nothing to me who Lady Felicia dances with, anyway."

"Clearly not." Vale's voice was gleeful, but when Markham opened his mouth to argue, Vale gave him a hearty slap on the back. "Never mind, Markham. I daresay Felicia's virtue is safe. Just look at Miss Jarvis, would you, Ramsey? I've a notion she's a bit of a scold, but she's a very pretty dancer." Vale's eyes followed Eloisa Jarvis as she drifted gracefully across the floor. "I may have to waltz with her at the next ball."

Ciaran pressed closer to the window, frowning. "Where's Lu—that is, where is Lady Lucinda?"

Vale and Markham crowded closer, and after a quick glance Markham pointed with his walking stick. "She's there, at the back. Who's that she's dancing with? It looks like—"

"It's the dancing master." Ciaran shook his head, a grin curving his lips. God, poor Lucy. It was no wonder she despised dancing lessons. No lady wanted to be made to waltz with her instructor. "She looks miserable."

"So does he, come to that. Shall we rescue them both?" Vale pushed the door open and went inside. Ciaran and Markham followed, and the three of them took seats in the entryway to wait. The music came to an end soon afterward. There was a shuffling of feet as the students filed out the door, but after ten minutes Lucy, Miss Jarvis, and Lady Felicia still hadn't come out.

"What the devil's happened to them?" Vale got to his feet with a long-suffering sigh. "Come on then, lads. We'll have to drag them out."

The room was nearly empty when they entered, the dancing master having made his escape through a door at the back. Lucy, Miss Jarvis, and Lady Felicia were alone, seated on a row of chairs against a wall, their heads close together.

"Well, would you look at that, Markham?" Vale drawled, as they made their way across the room. "Three ladies huddled together, whispering? Why, the three of you look like a trio of thieves."

Lucy, Miss Jarvis, and Lady Felicia all jumped.

"Ah, just the reaction you'd expect from the guilty." Vale strolled to Eloisa Jarvis's side and leaned over her chair. "What are you ladies so deep in conversation about? Discussing your gowns for the next ball, or tittering over the latest sensational novel?"

Lady Felicia shot her brother an annoyed look. "Is that what you think, Sebastian? That ladies discuss nothing but fashions and scandalous books? How dismissive of you. It's not surprising you're not married."

"I'm not married because I don't wish to be, and you know it well, dear sister. However, you never know when a young lady might appear who will inspire me to mend my wicked ways. Perhaps it will even happen this season. What say you, Miss Jarvis?"

Eloisa Jarvis fixed Vale with a cool look. "I haven't the slightest interest in your matrimonial prospects, my lord."

"Pity." Vale's lips curved into a delighted grin as his gaze roamed over her face. "There must be another reason you look so flushed, then. Too much dancing, perhaps?"

"Far too much, from what I saw." Markham shot Lady Felicia a disgruntled look. "What does Nash need with dancing lessons?"

Lady Felicia blinked innocently at him. "Oh, were you watching, Edmund? I can't say I even noticed you." She didn't wait for an answer, but turned away to take Lucy's arm with a toss of her head.

"We were watching from the window." Vale hadn't taken his eyes off Eloisa Jarvis, and now he swept her a mocking bow. "You dance like an angel, Miss Jarvis."

Miss Jarvis's cheeks went pink at Vale's teasing, but she didn't deign to reply. She took Lucy's other arm. "Come, Lucy. We're expected back home."

"Not quite yet, I don't think." Lucy's dark eyes fell on Ciaran. He gave her a slight nod, and she disentangled herself from the two irate ladies on either side of her and walked across the room to glance out the window. "Our uncle's carriage hasn't yet arrived. Mightn't we take a brief stroll to St. Paul's Cathedral? I haven't had a proper look at it yet, and it's just down the street."

To Ciaran's surprise, Markham stepped forward at once and offered Lady Felicia his arm. "If you'll allow me, my lady."

Lady Felicia's eyebrows rose, but she took his arm. "Yes, all right."

Ciaran drew Lucy's arm through his, which left Miss Jarvis no choice but to let Vale escort her. She darted a glance at him, her eyes wide and her cheeks on fire. "It isn't proper to walk with—"

"It's quite all right, Miss Jarvis." This time there wasn't a hint of his usual mocking drawl in Vale's voice. "I promise I'll behave like a perfect gentleman." He offered her a bow, elegant and proper, and held out his arm. "Won't you walk with me?"

Eloisa glanced anxiously at Lucy, but Vale was at his most charming when he was being sincere, and Miss Jarvis wasn't jaded enough to resist him. She took his arm without a word.

"I'm so pleased to see you, Ciaran. I thought perhaps you'd be halfway to Scotland by now," Lucy began, as they made their way through the door and down the street in the direction of St. Paul's Cathedral.

Her tone was teasing, but her words stung Ciaran to the quick. "You thought I'd leave without saying goodbye to you?"

If she *had* thought it, wouldn't she be justified? He hadn't proved to be a very loyal friend. Lucy had brought him back to life. If it weren't for her, he never would have made the decision to return to Scotland at all.

Now he was thanking her by leaving her at the mercy of Godfrey and her despicable uncle.

"No, of course not! I didn't mean it that way, Ciaran."

The hurt in her voice tore at his chest. He squeezed his eyes closed, and for one aching moment wished with everything inside him they were in Brighton still, sitting together on the beach with the sun rising over the water, the cool sand between his fingers and her soft laughter in his ears.

She's the best friend I've ever had...

How could he leave her like this, turn his back on her when she needed him most?

The answer was simple. He couldn't.

Lucy was staring up at him with wide dark eyes. Without thinking, Ciaran brushed the pad of his thumb over her cheek. As soon as he touched her, he realized he'd been wondering if her skin could possibly be as soft as it looked.

It was. It felt like warm silk under his fingertips.

Why are you touching her?

Ciaran jerked his hand away. "I know you didn't mean anything, Lucy. I'm sorry. I wrote to my sister last night and asked her to write back at once, telling me everything she knows about Lord Godfrey. I won't leave London until I hear back from her."

He thought she'd be pleased, but her brows drew down in a frown. "I don't want you to stay here for me, Ciaran. I don't want to be the reason you're made unhappy."

"It's a brief delay, Lucy, nothing more. You can't think I'd leave you alone in London with no one to protect you."

"I'm not alone. I have Eloisa, and Lady Felicia, and Lord Vale."

Lord Vale? What did she mean, she *had* Lord Vale? "What's Vale got to do with anything?" Ciaran demanded, then flushed at his outraged tone. For God's sake, he sounded like a jealous suitor.

Lucy didn't seem to notice. "Well, nothing yet, but I was thinking over my idea to stage a pretend courtship to hold off Lord Godfrey. It'll be a bit tricky to pull it off, but I quite like it, otherwise. I think it might work."

Ciaran froze. It almost sounded as if...

No. She couldn't be suggesting what it sounded like she was suggesting.

Could she? "Once again, Lucy. What's Vale got to do with it?" Ciaran's voice had dropped to a low growl.

"I don't know Lord Vale well, of course, but Lady Felicia was speaking of him, and I couldn't help but think he sounds like just the sort of gentleman I need."

Need? She *needed* Vale? Something dark and tangled rose in Ciaran's chest and crowded into his throat until he was struggling to breathe past it.

"I know he's a bit of a rake, but he's warm-hearted, I think, and Lady Felicia says he loves mischief. He might think a pretend courtship was good fun."

Ciaran's hands clenched into fists. Oh, he'd find it good fun, all right. A pretend courtship with a beautiful lady was just the sort of fun Vale would appreciate.

He knew he wasn't being fair to his friend. Vale might get up to some questionable behavior now and again, but he was no worse than Ciaran was. Lucy was right about him—Vale *was* a good fellow. He'd never hurt Lucy. Would never dream of taking advantage of her.

Ciaran knew that. At the moment, however, he didn't give a bloody damn.

Courtships meant dances, stolen touches, longing glances. Courtships meant whispers, and secrets, and soft smiles. Anything could happen during a courtship, even a pretend one. Two people who had nothing in common could find themselves falling in love.

Lucy was still talking, unaware of the spark she'd lit, oblivious to the fact it was about to burst into a conflagration. "We'll have to be careful. I won't have every gossip in London whispering Lord Vale's a scoundrel who jilted a young lady. It's sufficient if my uncle and Lord Godfrey believe the courtship is real. The rest of London doesn't need to hear of it."

Heat burned up Ciaran's neck, flooded his chest. Why was he so angry? Why—

"So, I thought I might…"

Don't say it.

"Ask him if he…"

Don't say it, Lucy.

"…would pretend to court me. It would be the easiest thing in the world, really, given my and Eloisa's friendship with Lady Felicia. We're sure to spend all our time with Lord Vale anyway, so you see it's…"

"No." Ciaran pushed the word through tight lips.

She didn't appear to hear him. "It's just the thing. I'll speak to Lady Felicia about it first, of course, to make sure she approves. Eloisa won't like it, but nor would she like to see me married to Lord Godfrey. I think I can bring her around."

Ciaran came to a dead stop in the middle of the street. He turned Lucy toward him and raised her face to his with a firm finger under her chin.

"Ciaran?" She stared up at him, baffled. "What's wrong? You look strange."

"You are *not*," he said, biting off each word through clenched teeth. "Asking Sebastian Wroth to pretend to court you."

Her eyes went wide. "I'm not?"

"*No.*" He took a step closer, raising her chin higher so she had no choice but to meet his gaze. "Let me make myself perfectly clear, Lucy. Vale isn't going to be your pretend suitor. Not Vale, and not any other man."

"Well, why not?" Two bright spots of color burned in Lucy's cheeks. She was falling into a temper. Her dark eyes flashed, and her mouth turned down at the corners, exaggerating that stubborn lower lip. Ciaran's gaze darted from her eyes to her lips, and for one wild moment he felt himself leaning closer, and tilting her mouth up to his....

He didn't get very far.

Lucy jerked her chin out of his grasp and planted her hands on her hips. "Well, Ciaran? Why shouldn't Lord Vale be my pretend suitor?"

"Because *I'm* going to do it."

Chapter Thirteen

"*You!*"

Lucy slapped a hand over her mouth, but it was already too late. Her shock had betrayed her into a much louder exclamation than any proper lady would dare to make while standing in the middle of a public street, a block away from St. Paul's Cathedral.

Worse, as soon as she saw the expression on Ciaran's face, she knew she'd said precisely the wrong thing, and in such incredulous tones, too. His jaw was clenched, his eyes a stormy dark blue with anger, and his entire body had gone rigid.

"Are you saying you'd rather have Vale than me?"

His voice was low and throbbing with anger. Lucy, startled by his vehemence, put an instinctive hand on his chest to calm him. "Of course not. I'd rather have *you*, but you can't pretend to court me, Ciaran. You're leaving for Scotland, remember?"

Surprise flashed across his face, as if he hadn't, in fact, remembered it at all. "I don't need to leave right away. That is, of course I'm anxious to...I can wait until you're safe, Lucy."

Gratitude swept over her, but Lucy shook her head. "It's four weeks yet until I turn twenty-one. You can't mean to linger in London for as long as that. I can't ask it of you."

Her hand slid away from his chest. His own hand twitched, as if he were going to snatch if back, but then he stilled. "You're my friend, lass. You can ask anything of a friend."

"Perhaps I can, but I won't. You're my friend, too, and I can't bear to be the reason you're forced to stay when you're so anxious to go."

"No one's forcing me to do anything, Lucy."

Perhaps it didn't feel like it now, but it would soon enough. Ciaran would end up resenting her for it, just as Lucy had ended up resenting her father. Even all the love she'd had for him hadn't kept her from blaming him. "I still think it's best if I ask Lord Vale—"

"*Vale!*" Ciaran's voice echoed in the street. "The devil you will! Why should you ask him when I've just told you I'll do it?"

Lucy's eyes went wide. Dear God, he'd just *cursed* right in front of St. Paul's Cathedral! They were sure to be struck down by a lightning bolt. Or, at the very least, by Eloisa.

"Hush, will you?" Lucy bit her lip and cast a nervous glance at their companions, but they were far enough ahead they hadn't heard his blasphemy.

He drew in a deep breath, and it seemed to calm him down. When he spoke again, his voice was softer. "I'm staying in London, Lucy. Unless you intend to avoid me for the next four weeks, you may as well reconcile yourself to having me as your suitor."

Reconcile herself? Is that what he thought she was doing? Didn't he know how badly she wanted him to stay with her? Lucy gazed up at him, her heart turning over in her chest. He was offering her weeks of his company. Day after day of his conversation, his smile, his laughter, his devoted attention. Day after day of gazing into those blue, blue eyes. She wanted that. She wanted *him*, for as long as she could have him. She wanted it so badly she was trembling with it, her entire body shaking.

Which was the very reason she had to refuse him.

It wasn't fair to keep him here. Not to him, and not to her.

"Ciaran." She laid a tentative hand on his arm. "When we were in Brighton, you told me you'd been waiting for months to return to Scotland. I can't let you—"

"No." He seemed to know what she was going to say. He jerked his arm away from her, and cut her off before she could get the words out. "Scotland can wait."

"Perhaps Scotland can wait." Her gaze held his. "But I'm not certain *you* can."

He frowned. "I don't know what that means, Lucy."

Lucy drew in a deep breath, then let it out in a soft sigh. "The man I knew in Brighton was...unhappy. He wagered too much, slept too little, and was in his cups too often. He ignored his family and neglected his duty to them. I—I don't want that for you, Ciaran. I don't want to see you unhappy again."

She could see at once it wasn't what he'd expected her to say. He stared at her, stunned into silence. Then he reached for her hand and cradled it with infinite care in his own. "Listen to me, Lucy. How can you think I'd just jaunt off to Scotland without knowing you're safe first? Nothing in the world would make me unhappier than that."

Lucy's heart melted in her chest. She gazed up at him, taking in his strong jaw, his dark, silky hair ruffling in the breeze. Emotion rushed over her, so powerful her throat closed. He was such a dear man, and so handsome she could hardly tear her gaze away from him. She didn't know what she'd done to deserve such a friend, but she was tremendously grateful for him.

How could she refuse such a heartfelt plea? "I—if you're sure, Ciaran."

Relief filled those ocean blue eyes. "I am."

Lucy dropped her gaze, afraid he'd see too much in her face. "Very well, then," she murmured, as casually as she could.

He took her hand and brushed his lips across her knuckles. "That's better, lass. I'll call on you tomorrow then, and take you for a drive."

Lucy risked a glance up at him. "You will?"

He grinned. "Yes. That's what a suitor does, Lucy. He dances with his chosen lady, sends her flowers, and takes her for drives."

His chosen lady...

His words cut through her, because she knew she wasn't his chosen lady. All the dancing, flowers, drives, and pretend courtships in the world wouldn't change that.

She didn't say it. Instead, she forced her lips into a smile. "Then I'll expect your call."

There wasn't time for them to say any more. Lord Vale and Eloisa joined them then, with Lady Felicia and Lord Markham close behind, and the six of them made their way back toward the dance academy. When they arrived, they found Uncle Jarvis's hired carriage at the curb waiting for them, a stone-faced Bexley perched on the box.

Lord Vale murmured something to Eloisa that made her blush. She tried to withdraw her hand from his, but Lord Vale held on long enough to hand her into the carriage. Ciaran handed Lucy in after her cousin, and then paused by the open carriage window.

"Tomorrow," he murmured, when Lucy leaned toward him.

She shivered. He was so close his warm breath drifted over her ear. "Tomorrow," she repeated, half in a daze.

Then Ciaran was gone, and Eloisa and Lucy were on their way back to Portman Square. They didn't speak. Each of them was lost in her own thoughts, but when the carriage came to a stop in front of the house, Lucy dragged herself back to the present moment.

They were a trifle late getting back. It was nearly teatime. They'd all been having such a…well, perhaps *pleasant* wasn't quite the right word, but certainly an interesting time that the minutes had seemed to fly by.

"Lord Vale admires you, cousin," she whispered to Eloisa as they handed their cloaks to the butler.

"Lord Vale is a terrible tease, just as his sister says he is, and a wicked rake besides." Eloisa used her sternest, most disapproving voice, but she couldn't hide the tinge of color that stained her cheeks at mention of Lord Vale.

Lucy cocked her head, studying the blush drifting from Eloisa's neck into her face.

Was Eloisa developing a *tendre* for the handsome lord? Lucy wasn't quite sure she liked that. She'd grown quite fond of Lord Vale already, but he was an earl, and a handsome, charming, rakish one at that. Handsome, charming, rakish earls didn't marry untitled, penniless young ladies with vulgar, grasping fathers.

She didn't believe Lord Vale would trifle with Eloisa's affections, but his sophisticated flirtation might prove too seductive for her innocent cousin. "Not so very wicked, I think, and terribly handsome." Lucy watched Eloisa closely. "Such lovely blue eyes, just like his sister's. Don't say you haven't noticed how handsome he is, Eloisa."

"Hush, Lucy! I haven't noticed a single thing about Lord Vale."

Lucy snorted as she followed Eloisa up the stairway to the drawing room. "Eloisa Jarvis, you're the most shameless liar I've ever—"

"Well, here you are at last. I expected the two of you home an hour ago."

Eloisa came to such a sudden halt Lucy stumbled against her. She peered over her cousin's shoulder, and what she saw waiting for them in the drawing room made the smile flee her lips.

Uncle Jarvis was standing in front of the fire, his arms crossed over his barrel of a chest. It was plain to see he was in a towering rage, as he was doing a poor enough job of disguising it. Aunt Jarvis was seated on a settee, a cup of tea balanced on her knee, her pale face pinched with anxiety.

And across from her, cozily ensconced in the best chair in the room sat Lord Godfrey, like a king presiding over his lowly subjects.

Eloisa had frozen in the doorway, so Lucy gave her a gentle little push. "I beg your pardon, Uncle. We didn't realize you were waiting for us."

Uncle Jarvis's lip curled. "It's teatime, isn't it? A few weeks in London, and you're both already so lost to decent manners you no longer appear for tea?"

Aunt Jarvis reached to place her teacup on the table. Her hands were shaking, and the cup rattled in the saucer. "To be fair, Augustus, we never told them to be back for—"

"Be quiet, Harriet." Uncle Jarvis's watery blue eyes narrowed on Lucy. "Lord Godfrey has been waiting for you this past hour!"

Lord Godfrey waved a languid hand. "Now, Jarvis, don't scold the girl. I'm happy enough to wait."

"Beg Lord Godfrey's pardon for your rudeness, Lucinda," Uncle Jarvis demanded, in the tone that always sent his wife and daughter scurrying to do his bidding. Lucy opened her mouth to refuse, but a glance at her Aunt Jarvis's white face made her snap it closed again.

She turned to Lord Godfrey, her jaw tight. "I beg your pardon, my lord, for making you wait. I didn't realize you were joining us for tea this afternoon." He'd spent hours with them this morning, for pity's sake. Wasn't one call from Lord Godfrey enough misery for a day?

For all of Lord Godfrey's gallant protests about being pleased to wait, Lucy could see how gratified he was to watch her grovel before him. "Nonsense, my dear girl. I'd have waited much longer for the chance to see your pretty face."

Lucy had nothing to say in response to such gross flattery, so she only nodded, and took the place beside her aunt on the settee. Eloisa seated herself on her mother's other side. Lucy saw Aunt Jarvis take her daughter's hand and pat it soothingly under cover of a fold of her skirts.

All the pleasure Lucy had felt this afternoon, all the joy she felt in Ciaran's presence drained out of her like air from a balloon, leaving her flat and exhausted. It was clear her uncle wanted this match, and he didn't much care if Lucy shared his enthusiasm.

Was this how she'd feel every day, if she were married to Lord Godfrey? As if someone had stomped on her until all the air rushed from inside her with a sickening whoosh?

Lord Godfrey, for his part, was *far* too enthusiastic. Teatime dragged from one hour into two as he held forth on one topic after the next, all the while ogling and smirking at Lucy as if she were one of the sweets on the tea tray. His conversation was appalling—condescending advice to Uncle Jarvis interspersed with flowery, extravagant compliments to Lucy.

Neither Aunt Jarvis nor Eloisa uttered a single word for the duration of his visit. Lord Godfrey and Uncle Jarvis didn't seem to notice. By the time Lord Godfrey rose to take his leave, Lucy's palms were aching from clenching her fists, and her head was pounding.

"My dear Lady Lucinda. It is, as always, my pleasure to wait on you."

"Thank you, my lord."

Lucy's voice was as cool as she could make it without being downright rude, but Lord Godfrey seemed to take this tepid reply as eager encouragement, because he stepped closer and grasped her hands in his. "No, Lady Lucinda. It is I who should be thanking you for your lovely company."

Lucy tried to draw her hands away, but his hands went so tight around hers she had to smother a cry of pain as the delicate bones in her fingers ground together. Startled, her gaze rose to Lord Godfrey's face, and her breath caught in her throat at the gleam of cold triumph she saw in his eyes.

He'd enjoyed it—enjoyed hurting her.

She jerked at her hands again, and this time he let her go. "I'm very sorry to leave your charming company so soon, Lady Lucinda. Your uncle and I have some business to discuss now, but I will, of course, call on you again tomorrow."

Lucy said nothing. She returned to her seat beside her Aunt Jarvis on the settee. The three ladies watched as Uncle Jarvis led Lord Godfrey from the room, and not one of them said a single word.

* * * *

"Spoiled, headstrong, willful little chit." Lord Godfrey paced from one side of the study to the other, his face a mask of rage.

Uncle Jarvis watched from behind his desk, his lips twisted in a frown. The flickering fire caught at the beads of sweat on his forehead. "You'll soon have her well in hand, my lord."

"Oh, you can be sure of that. I'll break her like I did my last horse, and I'll savor every moment of it." Lord Godfrey swung around and pointed a finger in Jarvis's face. "But I won't be made a fool of in the meantime, Jarvis. It doesn't look to me as if you've got control of her."

Jarvis swallowed. "I assure you, my lord, I've got all the control I need. The girl's my ward, after all."

"Your ward," Lord Godfrey repeated with a sneer. "She may be your ward, Jarvis, but that doesn't mean she'll obey your every command. I'll tell you again, I won't be made a fool of. If I'm going to court that chit in front of all of London, then she damn well better accept me when I ask for her hand. I won't have the *ton* laughing at me."

"She will! You've got nothing to worry about, my lord. I promise you."

Jarvis's voice had disintegrated into a plaintive whine. Lord Godfrey glanced at him, and didn't try to hide his disgust. He tugged his coat down with a jerk, then went to check his cravat in the looking glass hanging on the wall opposite the fireplace. "I admit I'll put up with a good deal of trouble to have her." He smoothed the linen and rearranged the folds to cover the sagging skin under his chin. "She's perfect. Strong-willed and defiant, just the way I like them. That skin, and her hair...delicious. Perfectly ripe."

"Ripe, and not yet *plucked*." Jarvis let out a lewd laugh, pleased with his own wit.

Lord Godfrey's mouth turned down with distaste. "For God's sakes, man, she's your *niece*."

"So she is, but any man would...what I mean is, I'm not blind, my lord. I only wish my own daughter was such a beauty. Perhaps then I could dispose of her as advantageously."

"Miss Jarvis doesn't compare to her cousin, of course, but she's a pretty little bit, just the same. Pity she hasn't a decent portion. If she did, I'd wager you could turn her to account." Lord Godfrey snatched up his hat from Jarvis's desk. He crossed to the door, but paused and turned to Jarvis before opening it. "You're fortunate I'm such a patient man, Jarvis."

Jarvis scrambled to his feet. "Yes, my lord. Thank you, my lord."

"See you get that chit in hand. Don't break her spirit, mind you—I'm looking forward to doing that myself—but do what you must to bring her to heel, understand? I won't be patient forever, and it would be a pity if you found yourself unable to meet your obligations, wouldn't it?"

Lord Godfrey didn't wait for an answer. He settled his hat on his head, tossed one last warning look at Jarvis over his shoulder, and disappeared through the door.

As soon as he was gone, Jarvis fell back into the chair behind his desk. He sat there for a long time, drumming his fingers on the wood surface, thinking. His niece was an obstinate little chit, just as Godfrey had said. He couldn't frighten or coerce the girl into doing his bidding the way he did with his wife and daughter.

Despite his promises to Godfrey, Jarvis wasn't certain he could manage Lucinda at all.

Not in the usual way, that is.

He opened a drawer, drew out a blank sheet of paper and dragged the inkwell closer. "Poor, dear Lucinda," he muttered with a smirk as he dipped the quill into the ink. "Such a pity the girl should be so grievously afflicted."

He began to write.

> *Dear Dr. Willis,*
>
> *I write to you out of a grave concern for my niece, Lady Lucinda Sutcliffe, daughter to the Earl of Bellamy. A gentleman of your profession will, I dare to assume, have heard of the earl's grievous descent into madness after the tragic death of his wife. Alas, doctor, I'm sure I needn't tell you the afflictions of the father are often visited upon his innocent children.*
>
> *As much as it grieves me to say it, such is the case with my dear niece, Lady Lucinda....*

Jarvis wrote until he'd reached the bottom of the page, then signed his name with a flourish. He sprinkled it with sand, then folded and sealed it. When he'd finished, he leaned back in the chair, his lips curling with satisfaction.

Yes, that would do. That would do nicely.

Chapter Fourteen

There was nothing shocking in Ciaran's appearance at Lucy's door the following morning. It was the season, after all. Hopeful gentlemen were darkening the doorsteps of eligible young ladies all over London, eager to pay their calls and prove their devotion.

To the casual observer, it was a perfectly ordinary occurrence.

But Ciaran's jaw was tight as he grabbed the brass ring hanging from the lion's mouth, and let it fall with a resounding thud against the door to the Jarvis's lodgings in Portman Square.

He knew this visit for what it was.

A battle of wills.

He'd told Lucy he'd take her for a drive today. He was determined to do just that, and Jarvis, no doubt, would be just as determined to stop him. Since Ciaran didn't intend to accept a refusal, odds were high this visit would go the way of Brighton's bare-knuckle bout. Ugly, that is, if not actually bloody.

So be it, then. He wouldn't break a promise to Lucy.

He rapped again, more insistently this time, and after another brief wait a butler appeared. He ushered Ciaran into the entryway and disappeared up the stairs to present his card.

Ciaran was fully expecting a large footman or two to descend the staircase and try to toss him onto his arse into the street, so he was surprised when the butler calmly reappeared at his elbow with a polite bow. "This way, sir."

Ciaran followed the man up the stairs, his brows drawn together in a suspicious frown. Likely as not, Jarvis was waiting for him in the drawing room with a loaded pistol.

As it happened, Jarvis wasn't waiting for him at all. There was no sign of Lucy's uncle in the small, overheated room into which he was led, but just as Ciaran was about to celebrate this unexpected stroke of good luck, his satisfaction gave way to disgust.

Jarvis wasn't here, but Godfrey *was*.

Mrs. Jarvis and Eloisa Jarvis were seated on a settee at the far end of the room, their shoulders stiff, their hands clenched in their laps. "Good afternoon, Mr. Ramsey." Mrs. Jarvis offered Ciaran a polite nod, but her eyes were wide with mute appeal.

Ah, so that's what was happening. Mrs. Jarvis had—no doubt against her husband's orders—instructed the butler to admit Ciaran. He was hardly two steps over the threshold before he realized why she'd done it.

To save Lucy.

And not a moment too soon.

Godfrey and Lucy were seated on the settee opposite. Lucy had squeezed herself into a far corner, but her efforts to escape Godfrey had failed. The scoundrel must have chased after her each time she edged away from him, because he was seated in the middle of the settee, his leg pressed against hers.

Ciaran took one look at the flush of misery on her face and was instantly furious. He took a step toward Godfrey, his hands clenching into fists, but before he could tear the man's head off, he caught Lucy's gaze.

She shook her head slightly, her dark brown eyes pleading.

Ciaran sucked in a deep breath and forced a bland smile to his lips. "Mrs. Jarvis, Miss Jarvis." He offered the two ladies a polite bow, then turned to the other settee. "Lady Lucinda, and…Lord Godfrey." His teeth ground together as his gaze fell on Godfrey's smug face.

Jesus, he couldn't recall ever despising another man as much as he despised this one. He wanted to snatch Lucy up into his arms and run off with her.

"Ramsey." Godfrey swept a contemptuous glance from the top of Ciaran's head to his boots, then offered him an icy smile. "How do you do? I didn't realize you were acquainted with the Jarvises."

Bloody liar. Godfrey had seen him with Lucy at Lady Ivey's ball just the other night.

"Yes, very well acquainted. With the Jarvises, and with Lady Lucinda." Ciaran let his gaze linger on Lucy. "Better acquainted every day, in fact."

Godfrey's arrogant smirk faded. "I see. Well then, take a seat, Ramsey." He waved a hand at the settee where Mrs. Jarvis and her daughter were seated, sneering as he inched closer to Lucy.

"Kind of you, Godfrey, but I'm afraid I can't stay." Ciaran paused just long enough for a gleam of satisfaction to enter Godfrey's eyes, then he added, "I'm here to fetch Miss Jarvis and Lady Lucinda for a visit to Bond Street. Lord Markham, Lord Vale, and Vale's sister, Lady Felicia, are in their carriage, waiting for us. Don't say you've forgotten your promise to accompany us?" Ciaran raised a meaningful eyebrow at Lucy. "You said so at Lady Ivey's ball the other night, remember?"

"No, no, of course they haven't forgotten." Mrs. Jarvis leapt to her feet as if the settee were on fire. "Go and fetch your cloaks, dears. You mustn't keep Mr. Ramsey and your friends waiting."

Godfrey's face went an ugly shade of red, but there was little he could do without causing a scene. He rose imperiously to his feet. "I'll take my leave, then." He smiled at Mrs. Jarvis, but it wasn't a friendly smile. More like a threatening baring of his teeth. "You'll be sure to tell your husband I called, won't you?"

Mrs. Jarvis paled, but aside from an anxious wringing of her hands, she remained steady. "Yes, of course, my lord. You're more than welcome to stay until he returns—"

"No. I've other business to attend to." Godfrey glanced between Ciaran and Lucy, his mouth tight. He offered the party a frigid bow, and took his leave.

Once the door closed behind him there was an audible intake of breath, followed by a sigh of relief.

Mrs. Jarvis crossed the room and took Ciaran's hand. "How pleased I am to see you this afternoon, Mr. Ramsey. Such a timely arrival, too. I'm afraid we've all grown a bit...dull. Too much time indoors, I daresay. Some fresh air will do my niece and daughter no end of good. Indeed, I encourage you to call as often as you like."

"Every day, even," Lucy added, rising from the settee. The cornered look Godfrey had put on her face dissolved into a smile as her gaze met Ciaran's.

Ciaran's chest loosened, and an answering smile rose to his lips. "It would be my pleasure."

* * * *

"Are we really going shopping on Bond Street?" Lucy was so elated at her escape from Godfrey she was bouncing on the carriage seat and trying at the same time to tie the ribbons of her bonnet more securely under her chin. "I thought gentlemen despised shopping."

Ciaran looked down at her, tucked closely beside him on the narrow seat, then glanced at the matronly lady sitting across from them. Mrs. Jarvis had sent a servant along for the sake of propriety, but the woman kept her attention fixed on what was passing outside the window, and did her best to ignore them.

Otherwise, Ciaran and Lucy were alone. Vale had claimed Eloisa Jarvis as soon as she appeared and had taken her up into his own carriage with Lord Markham and Lady Felicia.

Ciaran leaned closer to speak directly into Lucy's ear, his voice low. "Does Godfrey call on you every day?"

Lucy frowned. "I don't want to talk about Lord Godfrey. Please, Ciaran. Can't I enjoy my freedom while I have it?"

Ciaran shook his head, his jaw tight. "Answer me first, lass. Your uncle demands you receive Godfrey?"

"Yes," she admitted reluctantly.

Damn it. Just as he'd suspected, Lucy was utterly at their mercy. "I've known men like Godfrey before. He's a predator, and your uncle's no better. Promise me you won't ever let yourself be left alone with either of them."

It wasn't enough, but unless he could find a way to spend every moment at Portman Square until Lucy's twenty-first birthday, it was the best Ciaran could do for now.

Lucy sighed. "I promise to avoid them both as much as I possibly can."

"Good." Ciaran was somewhat pacified, but Lucy's smile had fled. "Don't look like that, Lucy," he murmured, his lips close enough so his breath stirred the wispy tendrils of hair peeking out from the edge of her straw bonnet. "Not another word about either of them for the rest of the day. I promise it."

"Yes, all right." Lucy was quiet for the rest of the drive, but by the time they reached Bond Street she'd recovered her spirits. When Ciaran leapt from the carriage and offered his hand to help her down, she took it with a genuine smile.

"Ah, that's better, lass." Ciaran drew her arm through his and led her toward the walkway in front of Hookham's Library, where the rest of their party was waiting for them.

"My goodness. Where did all these people come from?" Lucy's fingers tightened on Ciaran's coat sleeve as she gaped at the crowds of people bustling up and down Bond Street. "Why, it's like being in the midst of a swarm of very fashionable bees."

"They come from every corner of the city." Vale had somehow managed to coax Eloisa Jarvis to take his arm, and he was looking mightily pleased by it. "Fashionable London haunts Bond Street during the season. The ladies come in search of their corsets and tippets at Madame Devy's, and the gentlemen come to lounge and gawk at the ladies."

Miss Jarvis let out a faint gasp of outrage and turned a frowning countenance on Vale. "I'll thank you to keep a civil tongue in your head, Lord Vale."

"What did I say?" Vale gave her an innocent look, but his lips were twitching.

"Hush, Sebastian!" Lady Felicia glared at her brother. "Corsets, indeed. You're scandalizing Miss Jarvis. You forget not everyone is accustomed to your wild ways."

"Have I offended you, Miss Jarvis?" Vale captured Eloisa Jarvis's hand in his and raised it to his lips. "I beg your pardon."

Miss Jarvis gazed up at him, seemingly spellbound, but when his grin widened she snatched her hand away before his lips could touch her glove. Lord Vale laughed when her cheeks flushed pink, but his gaze lingered on her face.

"He admires her," Lucy murmured to Ciaran. She bit her lip as she watched the scene unfold, as if she were trying to decide whether to be pleased or worried. "I'm not sure I like it. Lord Vale may be a bit much for Eloisa, but one can't deny there's a lovely symmetry about the two of them together."

"Symmetry?" Ciaran snorted. "Your cousin's a high-stickler, and Vale's a scoundrel. What's lovely about that?"

Lucy looked up at him in surprise. "Why, everything, of course. You don't want a stickler with another stickler, or a scoundrel with another scoundrel. Surely you can see they balance each other out? In any case, Lord Vale's not *really* a scoundrel. He's quite gentlemanly when he chooses to be."

As if determined to prove Lucy wrong, Vale spoke up again. "What's so scandalous about corsets? I don't know why you're so offended, Felicia. I didn't say a word about the other sort of gentlemen who come to Bond Street later in the afternoons to—"

"Sebastian!" That was the outside of enough for Lady Felicia, who tugged Vale to a halt in the middle of the walkway to give him a proper scold. "Never mind what wickedness the other sort of gentlemen get up to in Bond Street. Honestly, you're the most dreadful tease—"

"Lady Felicia? I thought that was you! What luck!"

They all turned at once at the low, smooth voice to find Lord Nash bearing down on them, wearing a grin that stretched from one ear to the other.

"Lord Nash. I—I didn't see you there." Lady Felicia colored a bit as she greeted the tall, handsome earl with a smile. "How do you do?"

Lord Markham was walking a few paces ahead of the rest of the party, but he came to an abrupt halt when Lord Nash appeared. His brows rose in surprise, then lowered again in a scowl when Nash offered Lady Felicia his arm.

"Much better, now." Lord Nash's admiring gaze lingered on Lady Felicia. "I've just been round to Park Lane to call on you. I was disappointed to find you not at home, but here you are."

Markham scowled as his gaze fell to Lady Felicia's hand resting on Lord Nash's arm. There wasn't much he could do aside from stand by and watch as Lord Nash led Lady Felicia down Bond Street, both of them chatting and laughing, and Nash carefully shielding Lady Felicia from the more rambunctious gentlemen crowding the walkway.

Lucy let out a quiet laugh. "Oh, that's perfect."

Her husky chuckle made Ciaran glance down at her. She looked so delighted Ciaran's own lips curved in a grin. "What's so amusing? You're not laughing at poor Markham, are you?"

"No, certainly not." Lucy gave him an impish smile. "I'm simply memorizing his scowl so I can describe it in detail to Lady Felicia later."

Ciaran glanced at Markham. He'd dropped a few paces behind Lord Nash and Lady Felicia. He was a stern-looking fellow at the best of times, but Ciaran had never before seen him look so grim. He marched along behind them, glowering at Lord Nash's back.

"Lady Felicia danced twice with Lord Nash at Lady Ivey's ball, you know," Lucy murmured. "She told me afterward she thought him perfectly charming. Those were the exact words she used. Poor Lord Markham! He's not as indifferent to her as he thinks he is."

Markham certainly didn't look pleased, but jealous? Markham was too oblivious to be jealous. "He's just protective of her. They've known each other since they were children."

"Nonsense," Lucy said stoutly. "That's not protectiveness, Ciaran. It's jealousy. Heavens, Bond Street is certainly entertaining, isn't it? We'll have to come here again. It's better than the theater."

Ciaran laughed. "How do you know? Have you even been to the theater yet?"

"No, but real life is always more amusing than a play. Don't you think so?"

Ciaran opened his mouth to say no, but the truth was, he *was* amused. He'd been wearing the same ridiculous grin on his lips since they'd left

Portman Square. No doubt that made him a damned fool, but he'd rather be foolish than miserable. "I didn't used to, no."

"No? Well, I assure you, it is. Now, where shall we shop first? Don't say Madame Devy's, if you please, or Eloisa will insist we go home." Lucy fiddled with the ribbons of her bonnet again, her gloved fingers clumsy on the slippery silk. "Perhaps I should search for a new bonnet."

"I don't know. I think the bonnet you're wearing is very fetching. Pretty ribbons." Ciaran gave one end of the silk a playful tug. They were a dark pink color that flattered her eyes and brought out the delicate flush in her cheeks. "You should wear that color more often."

She arched an eyebrow at him. "You're very gallant today, Ciaran, as befits a suitor, but I can't quite believe you know one sort of bonnet from the next."

"I don't claim to be an expert on bonnets." Far from it, but he did seem to notice everything about Lucy. Bonnets, pelisses, the colors of her gowns. "But I know what I like."

Good God. His sister Isla would laugh herself sick if she could hear him now.

"Well, then it's decided. We'll go to a bonnet shop, and begin your education. You'll find it fascinating, I'm sure." She turned her dark eyes on him, humor shining in their depths.

Ciaran swallowed. How had he ever thought he preferred blue eyes to dark?

Isobel had blue eyes....

But he didn't want to think about Isobel. He shrugged the memory of her aside, and the ghost of his first love drifted away on the breeze. "As tempting as bonnets are, we'll have to shop for them another time. I have something else to show you today."

He tucked her arm more firmly through his elbow, but Lucy hung back. "Wait. Is it proper for me to go off alone with you?"

Ciaran glanced behind him and saw the rest of their party was a few blocks behind. He turned back to Lucy with a sly grin. "Not really, no. Why? Are you suddenly concerned with propriety, Lady Lucinda? I've never known you to be afraid before, especially if it means foregoing an adventure."

Lucy sniffed. "Afraid? Certainly not."

Ciaran chuckled. "Good. Because we're practically betrothed now, and that means we can do all sorts of improper things."

His tone was playful, even a bit suggestive. Lucy noticed it, and her cheeks went such a deep pink they put her ribbons to shame.

Ciaran knew he shouldn't tease her, but he couldn't resist her blushes. He reached out to tweak her ribbon again. "That's a pretty blush, Lucy. You should wear *that* color more often, too."

She peeked at him out of the corner of her eye, blush deepening when she saw his gaze fixed on her face.

Then she did something Ciaran would never forget.

Her pink tongue slipped out, and she dragged the tip of it across her lower lip. It was a little thing, and unconsciously done, but that didn't stop his body from exploding with a sudden rush of fiery heat.

She cleared her throat. "Is Bond Street an adventure, then?"

Ciaran tore his gaze away from her plump, red lips and struggled to gather his wits. "It's not the same sort of adventure as a bare-knuckle bout or a secret dip in the ocean, but genteel ladies don't parade down Bond Street with dubious gentlemen, so you will be challenging propriety in some small way."

She laughed. "Are you dubious, Ciaran?"

Her teasing smile made his heart pound. She was still fussing with the ribbons under her chin, and without thinking Ciaran brushed her hands aside. "Here, let me." He tugged on one end of the ribbon to untie it, then carefully tied them again, his fingertips grazing the soft skin of her neck.

He tucked a stray curl back, then stepped back to study her face. "There. Much better," he murmured huskily. Her hair was so soft, even softer than the silk ribbons. What would it feel like to gather handfuls of it, until it flowed like dark red silk over his palms?

What was he doing, flirting so shamelessly with Lucy? Teasing her, and touching her? And was she…wasn't she flirting back? He could hardly believe she was, but plenty of ladies had flirted with him last season. He knew it when he saw it.

But he and Lucy didn't *flirt*. Ciaran shook his head, confused, but at the same time he was aware of a low hum of pleasure in his belly as their gazes met. Lucy was watching him with wide eyes, and all at once Ciaran realized he was still toying with her ribbons.

Her jerked his hand away, clearing his throat. "I, ah…the shop is this way."

He took her arm and led her down the block to a shop with a large bay window that looked out onto Bond Street. It was separated into multiple panes, with each pane boasting its own colorful satirical print. He waited, strangely nervous, as Lucy's eyes wandered from one print to the next, her brows drawn together.

"What is this place? It looks like…" She trailed off, pausing on the curb to read the sign on the door. "Humphrey's Print Shop." She took her time, studying each print one by one, her mouth open in wonder. "They're all James Gillray. Every one of them."

Ciaran nodded, a flutter of nerves in his belly. He shuffled his feet like an awkward schoolboy, wanting very much to please her. "Yes. You told me once your father was fond of Gillray's work."

"I did tell you that yes, but it was some time ago. You, ah…you remembered." She peeked at him from under the wide brim of her bonnet, the sweetest smile Ciaran had ever seen curving her lips.

Heat flooded his face, then surged a second time when he realized he was actually blushing. He waved a hand at the painted sign over the door of the shop to distract Lucy. "Gillray dealt exclusively with Hannah Humphrey. Admirers of his work purchase his prints here, at Humphrey's Print Shop. Mrs. Humphrey died last year, and now her nephew George has the shop."

"But this is wonderful, Ciaran!" Lucy gripped his arm with one hand and pointed to the window with the other. "Look, it's *Very Slippery Weather*, with the poor gentleman who's fallen down, without a single person lifting a finger to help him, and…" Lucy slapped her gloved hand over her mouth to smother a choked laugh. "*Ladies dress, as it soon will be*. Oh, dear. That's terribly naughty, isn't it?"

The lady in the print had very tall feathers perched on her head, a very low décolletage—so low her breasts were tumbling out of it—and skirts split open nearly to her waist, revealing a plump thigh and the curve of her bottom. "Terribly. Now you see why this is such a scandalous adventure. Shall we go in?"

Lucy hung back. "Are you certain I can? That is, is it proper?"

A few rogues were standing about in front of the shop, guffawing at the prints, but they didn't take any notice of Ciaran or Lucy as he led her to the door of the shop. "Proper enough."

No one would accuse the crowds that often assembled outside Humphrey's to gawk at the prints of being fashionable, or even respectable, but the inside of the shop was the height of elegance. A genteel-looking gentleman—likely George Humphrey himself—was standing behind a wide mahogany counter polished to a high gloss. "Good afternoon." He offered them a polite smile. "May I help you?"

"Yes." Ciaran took Lucy's hand and drew her forward. "Do you have Gillray's *The Famous Battle Between Richard Humphreys and Daniel Mendoza*? The lady here is fond of a bare-knuckle bout, and a pugilist in her own right."

"A pugilist?" The man glanced at Lucy, who was looking particularly ladylike in her dainty straw bonnet with her pink silk ribbons, and chuckled. "She doesn't look much like a pugilist."

Ciaran grinned at Lucy and rubbed his finger over the side of his nose. "You wouldn't know it to look at her, but she's got a vicious kick. Rumor has it she once broke a man's nose."

Chapter Fifteen

Five days later

Lucy was sitting on her bed with her feet tucked under her skirts and the Gillray print Ciaran had given her balanced on her knees. She traced the edges of it with her fingertips. Perhaps not every lady wished to be given a print of a bloody, bare-knuckle bout, but it meant everything to Lucy.

Ciaran was the only person in the world who could have given it to her. The only one who knew her well enough to know how perfect a gift it was. If only—

"Lucy?" There was a soft knock on her bedchamber door, and a moment later Eloisa peered inside. "Oh, you're awake. I thought you might be resting."

"No." Lucy lay the print on the bedside table with a sigh.

They'd been out all afternoon with Ciaran, Lord Vale, Lady Felicia, and Lord Markham, riding in Richmond Park. The day was fine and they'd lingered for some time, but it wasn't Lucy's body that was trembling with exhaustion.

It was her heart.

It was so much harder than she ever could have imagined, acting as though she wasn't in love with her pretend suitor, and it grew harder with every day that passed. Every time he smiled or laughed, every time he touched or teased her, she fell a little deeper under his spell.

Their courtship wasn't real. In her head, Lucy understood that.

But in her heart…

Well, hearts were foolish organs, weren't they? Even now hers gave an insistent thump just at the thought of him.

Lucy hadn't any doubt she'd outwit her uncle and escape Lord Godfrey, but would she ever truly be free of Ciaran? Would her heart ever recover from him? Wasn't she in more danger from him than she'd ever been from Lord Godfrey?

Perhaps this pretend courtship hadn't been such a brilliant idea, after all.

"Where did you get this?" Eloisa had taken up the Gillray print and was studying it, a faint frown on her lips.

"Mrs. Humphrey's Print Shop, on Bond Street. Ciar—ah, Mr. Ramsey gave it to me."

"A print of a prizefight? What an odd gift." Eloisa returned the print to Lucy's table and sank down onto the edge of the bed. "I suppose that's where you and Mr. Ramsey disappeared to the other day. I did wonder."

"Did you? I wonder you noticed anything at all aside from Lord Vale," Lucy teased gently, anxious to turn the subject away from Ciaran.

She expected Eloisa's nose to turn up and a scold to leave her lips, but to Lucy's surprise, her cousin didn't offer her usual immediate denial.

Instead, Eloisa only let out a soft sigh. A soft, *yearning* sigh.

Lucy's eyes went wide. "Eloisa? Is there something you'd like to tell me?"

An unexpected suitor, a hopeless passion, a broken heart? Eloisa hadn't said a word about any of those things, but that soft little sigh said more than words ever could.

Eloisa didn't answer at once, but sat twisting a fold of her skirts between her fingers, her gaze on her lap. Long moments passed in silence before she drew in an unsteady breath, and blurted out, "I'm in love with Lord Vale."

Lucy sat bolt upright against her pillows. "You're *what*?"

It was the last thing she'd expected her cousin to say. Well, no. Not the last. She'd suspected for some days now Eloisa was partial to Lord Vale. But to admit it so bluntly? That wasn't like Eloisa.

"In love with Lord Vale." Eloisa's face flushed with misery. "Madly, hopelessly in love with him."

"*Madly* in love with him? My goodness, Eloisa."

"I don't *want* to be. I—I don't know how it happened, Lucy! I never would have thought myself in any danger from such a man! He's a dreadful tease, and a wicked rake besides. Don't you think he's a tease and a wicked rake?"

Lucy thought about it for a moment. "A tease, yes, but I don't believe he's wicked, or even terribly rakish. I never have thought so. A trifle high-spirited, perhaps, but good-hearted, just like his sister."

Eloisa's laugh was bitter. "Not so good-hearted he wouldn't amuse himself at my expense. He's only toying with me, of course. A meaningless flirtation, in the way of all fashionable London gentlemen."

Lucy hesitated. She'd been watching Lord Vale these past few days. Whenever he looked at Eloisa—which was often—the sweetest, softest smile bloomed on his lips. He didn't look to Lucy like a man who was toying with a lady. He looked like a man in love. "I'm not convinced he *is* toying with you, Eloisa. It looks like more than a meaningless flirtation to me."

"No, Lucy. You know as well as I do the Earl of Vale doesn't marry plain Miss Jarvis."

"He does if he falls in love with her."

Eloisa's voice caught on a sob. "Even if he were in love with me—and I'm not convinced he is—I would never accept his hand."

Lucy frowned. "But why? If he's in love with you, and you're in love with him—"

"Because marrying me would ruin him, Lucy! He'd become a laughingstock among the *ton*. Did you know he has two younger sisters at home? How could he ever bring them out into society with *me* as his countess? Their prospects would be destroyed, and it would be my fault."

To Lucy's horror, a tear ran down Eloisa's cheek.

"Oh, don't cry, Eloisa!" She threw her arms around her cousin's neck. "Why, I can't think of a single young lady in London who'd make a lovelier countess than you."

Eloisa didn't answer, only buried her face in Lucy's neck, her shoulders shaking as she sobbed. Lucy held her, her own eyes filling with tears. She couldn't bear to see Eloisa so devasted, but there was nothing she could do, nothing she could say, unless…

Lucy had been stroking Eloisa's hair, but now her hand stilled. There was *one* thing she could say, and it was nothing but the truth.

She drew in a breath, and took Eloisa by the shoulders to hold her away. "I'm in love with Ciaran Ramsey. Hopelessly, madly in love with him, and he doesn't love me back. You're not alone, Eloisa. Both our hearts are broken. I'm afraid we've made a sad showing for our first season, cousin."

Eloisa stared at her. "Whatever do you mean, he doesn't love you back? He's courting you, for pity's sake!"

"No, he isn't. Not really. He's only pretending to court me, to keep Lord Godfrey at bay until I turn twenty-one and your father is no longer my guardian. He doesn't love me, Eloisa. He's a dear friend, and nothing more."

Eloisa's mouth fell open with shock. "But he…I can't believe he isn't in love with you. No gentleman is that good at feigning a passion."

"Well, it's not as if he's pretending to care for me. He *does* care, but as a friend only."

"My goodness, Lucy. A pretend courtship?" A tiny, rueful smile rose to Eloisa's lips. "That's…well, that's quite a brilliant idea."

Lucy sighed. "It would have been, if I hadn't ruined it by falling in love with him. I think, Eloisa…"

Lucy trailed off as her heart sank in her chest. She'd have to end her pretend courtship with Ciaran. It was the only thing that made sense. A sinking heart was, after all, preferable to an irreparably broken one. "I need to put an end to my pretend betrothal at once."

"What about Lord Godfrey?" Eloisa gripped Lucy's arm. "If you end your betrothal to Mr. Ramsey, you'll have no protection against Lord Godfrey. He's as determined as ever to marry you."

It was true. Lord Godfrey still called on Lucy every day. He'd taken to raising her hand to his lips when he greeted her. It took all of her forbearance not to bring her palm down hard on his cheek.

Lord Godfrey didn't care for Ciaran poaching on his territory—that much was certain—but he was as smug as he'd ever been. It was curious, really. Her uncle wanted the match, yes, and Lord Godfrey was an earl, but Ciaran was far younger, far more handsome, and the brother of a marquess. Given the circumstances, Lord Godfrey seemed awfully confident he'd prevail in the end.

Perhaps it was time to find out why.

She'd suspected for some time there was a good deal more to this business with Uncle Jarvis and Lord Godfrey than she knew. If she intended to outwit them, the time had come to do a bit of investigating.

Lucy's dark gaze met her cousin's blue one. "I think, dear cousin, it's time we followed Lady Felicia's wise counsel."

Eloisa blinked. "What wise counsel is that?"

"How are your spying skills, Eloisa?"

* * * *

"It's fortunate the fate of England never rested in our hands." Eloisa dragged herself across her bedchamber and flopped down on her back on her bed. "We're dreadful spies. We've been prowling about the house like thieves all day and haven't turned up anything incriminating, unless you count the amount of port my father consumes in an evening."

They'd spent the day eavesdropping, interrogating the servants, and prodding Aunt Jarvis for any stray bits of information. They'd lingered at closed doors, and crept down dim hallways. They'd ducked into alcoves and hidden around corners, hoping to glean whatever tidbits they could.

They were both exhausted from the strain, and they'd discovered nothing of any import.

"Dreadful enough. We're not going to get anywhere creeping about and eavesdropping on the servants. We need to change tactics, Eloisa." Lucy stared out the window for a long moment, thinking, then turned to face her cousin. "Your mother said my uncle dines out this evening."

They hadn't gotten anything else of use from Aunt Jarvis, but she had been able to give them the details of Uncle Jarvis's social schedule. It wasn't much, but it was something, and Lucy intended to turn it to account.

Eloisa sat up, bracing herself on her elbows. "Yes, and thank God for it. At least we won't be obliged to sit through dinner with him. Have you noticed he's always watching us, Lucy? He's never paid me the least bit of attention before, but now he can't seem to take his eyes off either of us."

That was true enough. Every time Lucy ventured a glance at her Uncle Jarvis, she found his hard, brown eyes fixed on her and Eloisa, his thin lips turned down in a frown. "Well, he won't be watching us tonight."

"What are you plotting, Lucy? That look on your face is positively sinister."

Lucy crossed the room and sat down next to Eloisa on the bed. "Not sinister. Determined. I'm going to sneak into my uncle's office tonight and rifle through his desk."

"What?" Eloisa struggled upright, horror written plainly on her face. "You can't, Lucy! If he should discover you've been there, he'll...well, I don't know *what* he'll do, but it's bound to be awful. Why, he might lock you in your bedchamber and leave you there for the rest of the season!"

"No, he won't dare. Lord Godfrey's courting me, remember? I can't receive his lordship's attentions if I'm locked in my bedchamber. In any case, my uncle won't discover I've been there. I can be quite stealthy when I choose."

"I don't doubt that, but to sneak into his office, Lucy! What if his desk is locked?"

Lucy had considered that. She knew a way around that problem, but Eloisa would start lecturing if she knew what it was, so Lucy kept the information to herself. "If it is, I'll, ah...I'll find a way around it once I'm there."

Eloisa didn't look convinced. "I don't like this plan."

"Do you have a better one?" Lucy wasn't any surer about the plan than Eloisa was, but she had to do *something*. Lord Godfrey's attentions grew more pointed every day. Without Ciaran to protect her, she'd find herself the Countess of Godfrey by the end of next week.

Lucy shuddered with revulsion. She loathed locked doors, but she'd rather be confined to her bedchamber for the remainder of the season than marry Lord Godfrey. She leaned forward and clasped Eloisa's hands. "You'll help me, won't you? I can't do it without you."

Eloisa's gaze met Lucy's pleading one. She let out a resigned sigh, then rose and crossed the bedchamber to make sure the door was closed. When she turned back to Lucy, her face was grim with determination. "Very well. Tell me what you want me to do."

* * * *

As was the case with most villains, the hours between Lucy and Eloisa's decision to commit the crime and the actual act seemed to drag on forever. As expected, they were not obliged to endure Uncle Jarvis's company at dinner, but Aunt Jarvis's high spirits at having escaped her husband's presence for an evening made her chattier than usual. By the time she took herself off to bed, Lucy's nerves were stretched tighter than piano wire.

"We won't have to worry about my mother catching us out tonight." Eloisa had gone upstairs to bid her mother goodnight, but now she joined Lucy in front of the fire in the library. "She took a dose of Dr. Digby's Calming Tonic. I left the bottle on the table beside her bed."

Lucy nodded. "Good. Let's wait another hour, though, just to be sure. Your father won't be back for ages still, and in an hour the servants will have settled."

They waited in the library for what felt like an eternity, but at last one of the downstairs maids snuffed the candles, leaving the hallway that led to the study and the library dim. Lucy waited until the house was quiet, then rose from her chair and signaled Eloisa to follow her. They crept down the hallway to Uncle Jarvis's study. Lucy grasped the door handle, then paused, squeezing her eyes closed and praying it wasn't locked.

Ah, a stroke of luck! The handle turned easily in her hand, and within seconds she and Eloisa were inside.

"It looks as if a hurricane blew through here," Eloisa hissed. "How are we meant to find anything in this mess?"

Lucy gaped at the untidy piles of paper stacked on top of her uncle's desk, and her heart began an anxious pounding. She was terrified to touch a single sheet lest the entire mountain toppled over.

"If we disarrange his things, he'll notice it." Eloisa eyed the papers. "Light the lamp, Lucy, but keep it low. We'll see if we can read some of them without touching the piles."

"Yes, that's a good start." Lucy, who was impressed with Eloisa's calm demeanor, did as she was bid. They held the lamp over the center of the desk and cast a quick eye over the stacks. "The papers on the top seem to be mostly tradesman's bills." Lucy leaned closer to read one of them. "My goodness, Eloisa. Your father can't have spent that much on a single coat, can he?" She pointed to a bill from Weston that was balanced on the top of the pile.

Eloisa leaned closer, saw the number and gasped. "You don't think..." Eloisa swallowed as she took in the dozens of papers scattered across the desk. "You don't suppose these are all bills, do you?"

Lucy saw the dawning despair on her cousin's face and wished with all her heart she could say no, but she *did* suppose it. How her uncle planned to pay for all his luxuries was a mystery, unless...

"My uncle appears to be expecting a windfall, doesn't he?" Odd, considering he was in debt to Lord Godfrey.

Lucy caught Eloisa's gaze, and saw she and her cousin were thinking the same thing. They both knew there was only one place Uncle Jarvis could lay his hands on the sort of money it would take to pay all these bills.

Lucy's trust.

She hadn't any idea how he thought he could manage it. He was required to give an accounting of expenditures from the trust to the court every quarter. He couldn't just plunder it at will.

Unless, of course, he found some way to do it without arousing suspicion.

Lucy swept her gaze over the piles of papers. They might not all be bills—it was impossible to tell with the mess—but even at a cursory glance she could see there were dozens of them. Weston. Lock & Company Hatters. J Floris, perfumer. An extortionate bill from Berry Brothers & Rudd. Well, that explained the dozens of bottles of port. Rundell & Bridge—

Rundell & Bridge! Lucy pressed her lips together. Why should her Uncle Jarvis have a bill from Rundell & Bridge? He hadn't given her aunt any new jewels.

Not really a mystery, was it? Impotent anger rose in Lucy's breast, but she forced herself to stay focused. There would be time enough to hold Uncle Jarvis accountable for his sins, but for now, they needed to see what he was hiding in his desk. Surely, a man careless enough to leave a chaos of tradesman's bills lying about was also careless enough to leave his drawers unlocked?

Lucy slid her fingers under the lip of one of the drawers on her side of the desk and pulled, but it didn't budge. Not quite that careless then, blast him. "It's locked."

"This one, too." Eloisa was tugging on the drawer on the other side, but to no avail.

"We've made it this far. I refuse to give up now." Lucy scanned the top of the desk. There, laying on one corner was a letter opener.

She seized it and was about to use it to pick the lock when Eloisa grasped her wrist to stop her. "No! You can't break the lock, Lucy. My father will be able to tell."

Lucy blew out a frustrated breath. They were so close. "We have to, Eloisa. There's no telling when we'll get another chance. Perhaps he won't notice it."

"Wait, Lucy. We didn't try this one." Eloisa took hold of the tiny gold knob of the middle drawer and pulled. It slid smoothly open, and both of them leaned over the desk to get a look inside.

Lucy rummaged through the drawer. "Quills, some blank paper, an enameled snuff box...there's nothing of any interest here."

"I beg your pardon, cousin. There is one thing." Eloisa reached into the desk, plucked something up, and held it up to the lamp so Lucy could see it.

Lucy's breath left her lungs in a quiet gasp. It was a small key. The sort of key that might open a gentleman's desk drawers. "Try it."

Lucy watched, her breath held as Eloisa fitted the key into the lock of the larger drawer. It slid right in like it was made for the lock, which, of course, it was. The drawer on Lucy's side of the desk didn't budge, but Eloisa's slid smoothly open.

"Eloisa, you're brilliant!"

She threw hers arms around her cousin and squeezed until Eloisa let out a wheezy chuckle. "You're breaking my ribs, Lucy."

"Yes, of course. I beg your pardon." Lucy released Eloisa and peered inside the open drawer. "There's not much here." An inkstand, dry of ink, and underneath it a slim wooden box that contained stationery, a stick of red wax and a seal.

"There's something underneath the box." Eloisa stuck her hand into the drawer and fumbled around before drawing out a book with a soft leather cover.

"It's an accounting book." Lucy stared at it, her stomach turning over with a combination of excitement and dread.

There was something in that book. She was certain of it.

She held out her hand. Eloisa gave her the book, and they stood shoulder to shoulder as Lucy opened it with shaking fingers. There, right on the first page in black ink, they found what they were looking for.

Neither of them said a word, but they both watched as Lucy ran a finger down the long column of figures. They were insignificant enough at first—a few pounds here, a half-dozen guineas there—but they multiplied with every entry. One-hundred pounds. Three hundred. Five. A thousand...

Eloisa let out a small cry when Lucy's finger stopped at the bottom of the column, where Uncle Jarvis had tallied the figures and written the total.

Five thousand, three hundred and six pounds.

Uncle Jarvis had underlined the figure, and next to it he'd made a small notation.

Godfrey.

Uncle Jarvis owed Lord Godfrey in excess of five thousand pounds.

Lucy swayed where she stood, and Eloisa grasped her by the shoulders to steady her. "Let me see it."

Lucy handed her cousin the book, then slumped against the edge of the desk, her heart racing as Eloisa read through the column of numbers again. When Eloisa looked up from the book, her face was white. "This doesn't mean...you don't think this means..."

Eloisa's voice trailed off, and she fell silent.

Lucy drew a shaky breath. They both knew what it meant. Refusing to say it aloud didn't make it any less true. "It means my uncle intends to sell me to Lord Godfrey in exchange for paying his debt." They'd known it already, of course, but there was something shocking about seeing one's worth reduced to a handful of numbers in an accounting book.

Eloisa's gaze moved from Lucy's face to the open book in her hands. She stared down at it for a moment, then turned and placed it carefully back in the drawer and arranged the inkstand and stationery box on top of it. When she'd closed and locked the drawer, her gaze met Lucy's again, and Lucy saw her eyes were full of tears.

"Oh, Eloisa. It's not as bad as all—"

"It *is* as bad. It's worse. I always knew my father was...well, he's not a good man, but I never imagined he'd do something like this." Eloisa dragged the back of her hand across her cheek. "All these bills he can't pay, and gaming debts besides, and if that weren't wicked enough, he intends to...to s-sell my cousin to a horrible old lord who's so wicked himself he'd actually agree to forgive a debt in exchange for a bride!"

Well, when Eloisa put it that way, it *did* sound rather bad.

Lucy gripped the edge of the desk behind her until her knuckles went white. She felt as if a weight were pressing down on her chest, and her throat started to close with panic. She gulped in a breath—once, again—until she managed a shuddering gasp, and the panic began to recede.

She had to think, that was all. There had to be a way out of this mess.

"You must leave London at once, Lucy."

Lucy met Eloisa's solemn gaze. She started to shake her head, but before she could say a word, Eloisa interrupted her. "*Yes*, Lucy. Don't you see? You don't have a choice! If you remain in London, my father will find a way to force you to marry Lord Godfrey. You don't know what he's like. You don't understand how far he'll go."

For a brief moment Lucy considered heeding Eloisa's advice. A few weeks was all she needed. If she could find a way to disappear until her birthday, she would be free from Uncle Jarvis's power altogether....

But if she did flee, what would happen to Eloisa and Aunt Jarvis? Her uncle would guess Eloisa had helped her. He'd be furious, and there was no telling what he might do. Two weeks was an eternity. Anything could happen in that time.

"No, Eloisa. I won't leave you and my aunt alone with him. There's got to be another way." Lucy pressed her fingers to her temples, but she couldn't *think*. Finally, she looked up to meet Eloisa's anxious gaze. "Tomorrow night is Lord and Lady Weatherby's ball. Mr. Ramsey will be there. He'll help us decide what's best to do."

Chapter Sixteen

"Father's watching us."

At Eloisa's whisper, Lucy glanced toward the archway that led into the card room. Of course, it was just as her cousin said. Uncle Jarvis *was* watching them.

He was *always* watching them.

He'd gone straight toward the card room as soon as they entered the Weatherbys' ballroom. Lucy had breathed a sigh of relief, imagining he'd stay there for the rest of the evening, but he hadn't gone inside. Instead he lingered by the doorway, as if he were waiting for someone.

Lucy could hardly be at a loss to imagine who.

"He doesn't look pleased, does he?" Lucy muttered, for Eloisa's ears only.

"No, but he never looks pleased, except when he's—" Eloisa broke off on a soft gasp, and gripped Lucy's arm. "Oh no, Lucy. Lord Godfrey is here."

Lucy ventured another quick glance behind her and a chill rushed over her skin. Lord Godfrey was indeed here. He'd just joined her uncle in front of the card room. Even from this distance she could feel those cold gray eyes crawling over her skin, making every hair on her arms rise in alarm.

Lucy sucked in a quick breath to steady herself, then jerked around in her chair and gave Lord Godfrey her back. She fixed her gaze on the couples twirling gingerly around the dance floor, their elbows tucked into their sides to keep from jabbing their neighbors.

It was a dreadful crush. It looked as if Lord and Lady Weatherby had invited every person in London to their ball this evening. It would explain why *they'd* received an invitation. The Weatherbys were quite fashionable, and Lucy and the Jarvises…weren't. Perhaps the *ton* had discovered she was an heiress and had decided to forgive her for having a mad father.

Then again, perhaps they hadn't. Not a single gentleman had spared her a glance so far this evening, and no one had asked her to dance. Under any other circumstances, Lucy might have been relieved at that, her dancing skills still not being quite what they should be, despite Monsieur Guilland's frenzied instruction.

But a dance was her only chance to escape her tormentors. Even a humiliating half-hour at the quadrille was preferable to enduring a public encounter with Lord Godfrey.

"I'm going to the ladies' retiring room."

Lucy half-rose from her seat, preparing to flee, but Eloisa grabbed a fold of her skirt to stop her. "Wait, Lucy. Lord Vale is here, and Lady Felicia and Mr. Ramsey with him. They're coming this way."

Lucy followed Eloisa's gaze and saw Ciaran, his dark head towering over the crowd. She sagged back against her chair, nearly dizzy with relief. He'd promised he'd be here tonight, yet it was remarkable, wasn't it, the way he always appeared just when she needed him most?

"I've never been so happy to see anyone in my life." Lucy turned to Eloisa and saw a flood of color was now staining her cousin's cheeks, just as it always did whenever Lord Vale appeared. "Oh, Eloisa—"

"No, Lucy. You needn't look at me like that. I haven't the slightest interest in Lord Vale's arrival. I certainly won't dance with him, if that's what you're thinking, no matter how much he teases."

Lucy said nothing, but she thought, not for the first time, that Eloisa's blush gave her away.

* * * *

Ciaran had hardly taken a step inside the Weatherby ballroom before he was looking for the tell-tale glint of copper hidden among the sea of fair- and dark-haired ladies.

Ah, just there. Flashing dark eyes, red lips, a stubborn chin, and a headful of shining red hair framing a perfect face. Each time he saw Lucy, he thought her more beautiful than he had the time before.

He stood rooted to the spot, a faint smile on his lips as he waited for her to notice him.

It didn't take long. It never did.

Wherever they happened to be—at a prizefight, on a beach in Brighton, at an overcrowded ball in a London ballroom—somehow, they always seemed to find each other. It was as if some irresistible force was determined to pull them together.

Fate, or coincidence? Destiny, or luck? Ciaran no longer cared. He cared only when he wanted or needed her, she was always there.

Was it the same for her?

As if in answer, Lucy's head turned toward them, as though she'd sensed his presence as soon as he entered the room. A smile lit her face when her gaze landed on him. As always, that smile pulled him toward her as surely as if she had him dangling on a string.

Lady Felicia had seen them, too. She let out a little cry of joy and tugged at her brother's arm. "Lady Lucinda and Miss Jarvis are here already, just over there."

"I see them." Vale was hurrying across the room, his gaze locked on Eloisa Jarvis.

Ciaran followed along behind them, his own gaze lingering on Lucy.

Lady Lucinda. He was always momentarily startled when anyone referred to her by her title. He never thought of her as anything but *Lucy.* Maybe it was because of the unconventional way they'd met. It was hard for a man to think of any female who'd kicked him in the face as *Lady* anything.

Or maybe it was just because her title didn't suit her. It didn't fit. *She* didn't fit—not inside this ballroom, or among this company. She looked like some sort of exotic butterfly caught in a net, or a succulent piece of ripe fruit in an otherwise barren orchard.

The taste of her, tart and sweet on his tongue...

Ciaran's mouth flooded with moisture, but he forced himself to swallow it down and gather his wits. Another man might allow himself to be dazzled by those velvety dark eyes, but Ciaran didn't have that luxury.

She was a friend only. Of course, that was all she was. They'd agreed on it. He'd hadn't known Lucy for longer than a week before they'd decided that. It had been a promise—a pact, of sorts—and she'd never asked for anything more from him than friendship. Never given him any reason to think she wanted anything other than that. Revealing his attraction for her would only end in confusion and recriminations.

He couldn't give in to his desire for Lucy, no matter how tempting she was. No matter if he couldn't stop thinking of her lips—

No, damn it.

No lips. No soft, creamy skin. No wavy tendrils of red hair brushing the secret, sensitive place behind her ear...

But it was no use. Ciaran had had this same argument with himself dozens of times since he'd arrived in London, but somehow, he still couldn't get Lucy into the proper place in his thoughts. He couldn't recall ever being so preoccupied with a woman in his life—not even his betrothed.

Isobel Campbell, the lady he was leaving London for. Leaving Lucy for—

"Lady Lucinda looks fetching tonight, eh, Ramsey?" Vale nudged him in the ribs. "You'd better hurry and ask her to dance before her card is filled for the evening."

She did look fetching tonight. She looked fetching every night. Every day, too.

Ciaran took a deep breath to steady himself. Lucy was lovely—there was no denying that. Her beauty hadn't escaped his notice, and neither had his reaction to it. He was a man, after all, and he wasn't blind.

But he was leaving London in the next week or so, with plans to court another lady. He wasn't the sort of man to indulge in fantasies about one lady when he had unfinished business with another. He was a gentleman, not an animal who couldn't control himself.

Still, perhaps it would be better if he didn't dance with Lucy tonight—

"She *is* fetching, and it irks me no end she's slighted by every gentleman other than those in our party, just because her father was the Earl of Bellamy." Lady Felicia's voice was heavy with disgust, and she was plying her fan with far more energy than necessary. "Both of you must dance with her. You promised her a quadrille at Lady Ivey's ball, Sebastian. You haven't forgotten?"

"No. I'd be delighted to dance a quadrille with Lady Lucinda, but not just yet. Right now, I have different quarry in mind."

"For pity's sake." Lady Felicia tugged her brother to a halt in the middle of the ballroom. "I'll have your word right here and now you won't torment Miss Jarvis this evening."

"But it's so delightful to tease her. She becomes adorably flustered, and then there's that pretty blush—"

"Sebastian!"

"Very well. May I at least dance with her?"

Lady Felicia smiled, took her brother's arm, and resumed her trek across the ballroom. "Of course, but be a gentleman about it, if you please."

Vale laughed. "I'll do my best."

When they reached the other side of the ballroom, Vale bowed before the three ladies, his blue eyes gleaming as his gaze fell on Eloisa. "Lady Lucinda. Mrs. Jarvis, and Miss Jarvis. Allow me to say, Miss Jarvis, you look exquisite this evening. Will you dance?"

Eloisa Jarvis had watched Vale's approach with her chin high and her lips pulled into a prim little frown, but as soon as he offered his hand, her disapproval seemed to desert her. "I, ah—"

"Go on, Eloisa." Lucy tapped her cousin's arm gently with her fan. "Mr. Ramsey and Lady Felicia will keep your mother and me company."

"Yes, do go and dance, my dear." Mrs. Jarvis gave Vale a distracted smile, then turned back to the lady on her opposite side, who was listening, enthralled, as Mrs. Jarvis regaled her with a description of the wonderful effects of something called Dr. Digby's Calming Tonic.

"Miss Jarvis?" Vale was standing patiently before Eloisa, his hand still held out to her, his blue eyes soft on her face. Eloisa flushed again, but she accepted his hand and let him escort her to the dancers.

"There's something happening there," Lady Felicia said, taking the seat beside Lucy. "Sebastian likes to act as if it's all in fun, but I've never seen that expression on his face before."

Ciaran studied Vale as he and Eloisa took their places in the set. Vale's expression was certainly telling. "He looks pleased, befuddled, and nervous all at once."

Lucy was watching them as well, an anxious little frown between her eyes. "They look divine together. Is your brother free to, ah…bestow his affections according to his inclination? He's an earl, after all."

Lucy didn't say anything more. She didn't need to. Lady Felicia knew well enough earls didn't generally marry untitled, penniless ladies like Eloisa Jarvis. Ciaran knew Lucy was fond of Vale, but he also knew she wouldn't stand by while Vale trifled with her cousin, or broke her heart.

"Perfectly free," Lady Felicia murmured. "He needn't marry a fortune, or to please anyone other than himself, so—"

"Good evening. How d'ye do, Ramsey?"

Lord Nash had appeared beside Lady Felicia's chair. He offered an affable nod to the rest of the party, then held out his hand to her. "May I claim this dance?"

Lady Felicia blushed and took his hand. "Certainly."

Lord Nash bowed to Lucy and Mrs. Jarvis, then led Lady Felicia to the floor, looking for all the world as if he were bearing off a prize.

Markham appeared a moment later, following so closely in Nash's wake Ciaran suspected he'd chased Nash across the ballroom to get to Lady Felicia first. Unfortunately, he arrived just in time to watch Nash take Lady Felicia away.

Ciaran slapped him on the back. "Bad luck, Markham. You'll have to move faster than that next time if you want to dance with Lady Felicia."

Markham scowled. "Every time I turn around, Nash is fawning over her like a spoiled child with a new toy."

Lucy shot Ciaran an amused glance. "Fawning? I believe they're simply dancing, my lord."

Lord Markham grunted, but didn't reply.

"Lady Felicia enjoys his company," Lucy went on. "He's very fashionable, but a lovely, gentlemanly sort, in spite of it, and so *attentive*."

Markham's gaze shifted from the dancers to Lucy's face. "Attentive?"

She gave him a sunny smile. "Oh, yes. Why, just look at his face!"

Markham looked, and his own face fell.

"Better yet, look at Lady Felicia's face," Lucy added. "A lady likes to be fawned over every now and then, Lord Markham."

Ciaran chuckled at Markham's perplexed expression. "The lady enjoys dancing, Markham. Something to keep in mind."

Markham watched Lady Felicia in silence. He looked nearly as befuddled and anxious as Vale did when he looked at Eloisa Jarvis. Ciaran almost felt sorry for him—love was a devil of a business—but just as he opened his mouth to offer some encouragement, Markham stalked off without another word.

"Oh, dear." Lucy turned to Ciaran, a low laugh escaping her lips. "He doesn't look at all pleased, does he? I feel rather bad for him, but I daresay it'll do him good to have a rival. A man needs a gentle push every now and then."

"Or a not so gentle one." Ciaran hadn't taken the seat Lady Felicia had vacated. Instead he stood gazing down at Lucy, admiring the way the candlelight played on her hair. She was wearing a green gown again tonight, with a matching green ribbon woven throughout her copper curls. He'd seen her wear the color many times. It was a similar shade to the green lining of the cloak she'd been wearing the first time he saw her on the beach in Brighton.

Not many ladies could wear such a vibrant shade of green, but not many ladies were Lucy. No color could outshine her, no matter how bright.

Ciaran forgot he'd decided not to dance with her. He forgot everything he'd told himself and held out his hand to her. "Come dance with me, Lucy."

Lucy glanced up at him, her eyebrow raised. "Certainly not. I like you too much to dance with you."

She laughed at his expression, and a tingle of pleasure shot down Ciaran's spine. She had the most engaging laugh—rich and full, but husky, as if she were slightly breathless.

"You agreed to dance with me at the assembly in Brighton," he reminded her. "Why should this be any different?"

"You *know* why. Because I'll make a dreadful mess of it. Brighton is one thing, Ciaran, but London is quite another."

"Come now, Lucy. You owe me a dance." All at once, Ciaran wanted to dance with her more than anything, and he was prepared to tease and cajole until she gave in.

"It had to be the quadrille, didn't it?" Lucy muttered, her gaze dropping to something she held in her lap. She stared down at it, her lower lip caught between her teeth, her brows drawn together with fierce concentration.

Ciaran leaned over her shoulder, curious, and saw a few cramped lines scrawled across the leaves of her fan.

The steps to the quadrille.

He dissolved into a grin. "Ah. Your lessons at Thomas Wilson's Dancing Academy still aren't going well, then?"

Lucy grimaced. "Not unless you'd call nearly knocking a gentleman down 'going well.'"

There wasn't any reason in the world Ciaran should find that endearing, but somehow, he did. He'd felt just as out of place as Lucy did now when he'd first come to London last year. A big, awkward Scot among all the sleek, fashionable London gentlemen. He'd been like a fish out of water.

But if there was one thing he'd learned since then it was how to dance the quadrille. He'd led every wallflower in London through every dance at every ball last season. He was as skilled a partner as any dancing master. "It's not as difficult as it looks. Come dance with me, Lucy, and I'll teach you the steps as we go."

Lucy glanced at the dancers, then back at his face, then back at the dancers. Ciaran could see she wanted to dance, but her forehead was creased with doubt. "You didn't see the disaster I made of the set the other day at my lesson. If you had, you wouldn't ask me. I trod on Monsieur Guilland's foot a half-dozen times, at least."

"I don't care. I'd still ask you, even if you'd trod on dozens of gentlemen's feet." Ciaran realized with a start it was true. Even if she'd knocked a man unconscious—or, more likely, broken his nose—he'd still ask her. He couldn't think of a single circumstance in which he wouldn't want to dance with Lucy.

Dance with her, lie on a beach with her, watch a bout with her, stroll along Bond Street with her on his arm. Images of Lucy flashed through his mind—moonlight on damp red hair, glittering drops of water clinging to long, dark eyelashes—and an odd, breathless feeling swelled inside him.

Anna Bradley

He didn't know what to make of it, but all at once a part of him wanted to flee—to leave London this minute and run off to Scotland before he did something he'd regret.

But that wasn't what he did.

Instead he reached down, grasped her gloved hand gently in his own and urged her to her feet. "I promise I'll take care of you, Lucy. Don't you trust me?"

The tiny frown line between her eyes disappeared and her face went soft. "Of course, I do. More than anyone. It's just…I'm not certain it's a good idea."

"I am." He wasn't, but he smiled down at her as if he was.

She smiled back, and the lovely brown eyes that made his chest ache went soft and warm. She raised her hand to take his, but just as her fingertips grazed the palm of his glove she froze, her smile vanishing as she stared at something over his shoulder.

"Lucy." Mrs. Jarvis turned suddenly toward her niece, her voice high with warning.

Ciaran turned to follow their gaze, and his chest went tight.

Jarvis was coming toward them, with Lord Godfrey on his heels. Ciaran had never seen two men who looked more like villains than these two. Jarvis wore such a smug smirk on his face Ciaran's fist twitched with longing, and Godfrey…

Jesus, he looked like a vulture, salivating as he circled his prey.

Ciaran tensed, his body vibrating with suppressed aggression as Jarvis and Godfrey drew closer. He wanted to leap in front of Lucy, to protect her, but just as he moved to shield her, Jarvis and Godfrey were already upon them.

Ciaran narrowed his eyes as Godfrey sketched an extravagant bow before Lucy. "Good evening, my dear."

My dear? Ciaran stiffened. Who the devil did the old scoundrel think he was, addressing her in such a familiar manner? As much as Godfrey might wish it otherwise, Lucy *wasn't* his betrothed.

"You look as lovely as ever this evening." Godfrey's gaze swept over Lucy, his pale gray eyes glittering with possessiveness. "I'd be honored to escort you to the dance floor."

Godfrey held out his hand to her with an assured air, as if he hadn't the least expectation of being denied. Ciaran saw Lucy try and suppress a shudder of revulsion. "That's kind of you, my lord, but I don't intend to dance this evening. I'm a trifle fatigued tonight."

"Nonsense, girl." Jarvis scowled at Lucy, his face flushing with anger. "Lord Godfrey is honoring you with his attentions. You will dance for as long as he wishes it."

"No, Augustus." Mrs. Jarvis's voice was sharper than Ciaran had ever heard it. "The child looks pale, and she said she's fatigued. I won't let you *force* her."

Jarvis said nothing, but he gave his wife a look that made her shrink back in her chair before he turned his icy gaze back to his niece. "Do as you're bid this instant, Lucinda."

It was the same ugly scene that had played out at Lady Ivey's ball all over again, except this time Ciaran was determined to put a stop to it.

He was about to give in to his fantasy of leaping on Jarvis and pummeling him into the ballroom floor when Lucy gave Godfrey her hand. "Yes, I— yes, of course. I'd be pleased to dance with you, Lord Godfrey."

"Splendid," Godfrey said, darting a look of smug triumph at Ciaran as he clamped his hand over hers and dragged her toward the floor.

Ciaran started to go after them, but Lucy shot an anxious glance at him over her shoulder. It was a plea, and it was as clear as if she's spoken it aloud. *Please don't make a scene.*

Ciaran was shaking with anger, but Lucy was right. A scene would only make it worse for her. So, he stood there helplessly while Godfrey manhandled Lucy as if she were his prized possession, like a pretty piece of art, or an enviable bit of horseflesh.

One dance, and then another…

By the end of the second dance Ciaran was ready to explode with impotent rage, but what happened next was far, far worse.

The last notes of the music faded, but Godfrey didn't escort Lucy off the dance floor. Ciaran saw her disentangle herself from his grip and try to move back toward her aunt, but before she'd taken two steps she stopped, her face going pale.

The other couples shifted, and some left the floor. A new set assembled, and then, unbelievably, the music began again.

A red haze descended over Ciaran as Godfrey swept Lucy into the dance. Their *third* dance.

Ciaran stood on the edges of the ballroom, frozen with fury as Godfrey forced Lucy to waltz with him.

It went on forever. It was the longest waltz in Ciaran's life.

By the time Godfrey led Lucy back to Mrs. Jarvis he was smirking with satisfaction, but Ciaran hardly spared him a glance.

His gaze was fixed on something else.

A dark red handprint on the pale, delicate skin of Lucy's arm.

Godfrey had grabbed her. Hurt her.

A rage unlike any Ciaran had ever felt before swept through him, like a fire devouring his insides. He heard Lucy say something to him, her voice high-pitched and anxious, but he couldn't make out the words through the roaring inside his head. He thought, fleetingly, of the one time he'd seen his brother Lachlan in a rage like this, when another man had laid his hands on the woman Lachlan loved.

Lachlan had seized the man by the throat and nearly shaken the life out of him. Ciaran hadn't understood it at the time. Hadn't understood how a man could feel so much rage, and so much love.

Ciaran thought fleetingly of Lucy. Of moonlight on damp red hair. Of long, dark eyelashes tipped with glittering drops of water. Of an ugly red handprint on smooth, pale skin…

Am I in love with Lucy?

The question stole through Ciaran as quickly as a breath, but then it was gone, and he was moving, following Jarvis and Godfrey, his hands clenched into fists. They were strolling toward the card room, laughing and chatting, satisfied with their success.

He didn't get far.

"Ciaran, don't."

Lucy's voice was soft, but this time it penetrated the roar in Ciaran's head. He turned toward her just in time to see her collapse, a sea of bright green silk falling around her, enveloping her like a wave as she sank to the floor.

Chapter Seventeen

Everything happened so quickly after that, the only thing Lucy could recall later was Ciaran's solid strength. His soft murmurs and gentle hands.

By some miracle, he got her out of the ballroom, called her carriage, and hurried her into it without attracting the attention of the Weatherbys' fashionable guests.

Had she once teased him about his heroism? It didn't seem so amusing now.

"Don't try and tell me you feigned that swoon, Lucy." Ciaran was standing at the open door of the carriage, his blue eyes moving anxiously over her face.

Lucy blinked at him. Had she feigned the swoon, or hadn't she? She hardly knew anymore.

He rubbed her cold hands between his. "Are you all right? You're shivering, and you're whiter than my cravat."

You're the most beautiful man I've ever seen....

It wasn't the first time she'd thought it. Every time she looked at him, Lucy found something new she loved about his face. The angular curve of his cheek, the flecks of gold in his blue eyes. But somehow now, with the light from the townhouse shining on his dark hair and playing over the angular line of his jaw, he took her breath away.

"Lucy?" His fingers tightened over hers.

She tugged gently, urging him into the carriage with her. "I—I'm all right, yes."

"No, I don't think you are." He flung himself down next to her and slammed the carriage door behind him. He ran both his hands down his face, his chest straining with shallow, jerking breaths. He was too agitated to notice how close they sat, with their bodies pressed tightly together on the narrow seat.

But Lucy wasn't.

For the space of a single heartbeat she closed her eyes and let herself sink into the feeling of his warmth enveloping her, his reassuring strength pressed against her. For a heartbeat only, and then she opened her eyes. "I promise you I am, Ciaran. I—I feigned the swoon."

Mostly. There'd been a moment, when Lord Godfrey had grabbed her, that the frantic pounding of her heart had made her chest tighten and her head go dizzy with fear. It was the closest she'd ever come to a real swoon, and she had no wish to repeat the experience.

Ciaran leaned over her, his dark blue eyes holding her gaze as if he could see all she hid from him in her eyes. "I can't let this business with your uncle and Godfrey go on any longer, Lucy. It grows worse every day—" He broke off, his eyes narrowing on her face. "There's more, isn't there? Something you haven't told me."

Lucy dragged in a shuddering breath. Ciaran was going to be furious when she told him she and Eloisa had sneaked into Uncle Jarvis's study, but there was no other way to explain how they'd gotten ahold of his accounting book.

Ciaran had said from the start he thought her uncle was in debt to Godfrey, but he could never have guessed how bad it was. The gaming debt, and all those tradesman's bills…

Five thousand, three hundred, and six pounds.

Lucy dropped her gaze to her lap, but in an instant Ciaran was there, capturing her chin in his fingers and raising her face to his. "He didn't… touch you, did he? Your uncle, or Godfrey? Tell me at once, Lucy! I can't bear—"

"No!" Lucy pressed her fingers to Ciaran's lips to quiet him. "No, that's not it. It's the debt, Ciaran. You were right all along. My uncle owes Lord Godfrey a great deal of money."

"How do you know?" Ciaran's eyes were bleak.

Lucy hesitated. He wasn't going to like this, but a lie would only complicate things. In any case, she couldn't lie to Ciaran. "Eloisa and I went to Uncle Jarvis's study last night and rifled through his desk."

Even in the dim light, Lucy saw Ciaran's face go white. His mouth opened but he remained silent. When he did speak, the words sounded as if they'd been torn from his throat. "Do you know—do you have even the slightest inkling what he would have done to you if he'd caught you, Lucy? You can't…I can't…he might have *hurt* you."

"But he didn't. He was out all evening. We were very careful, and he knows nothing about it. We found his accounting book, and…oh, Ciaran. It's so much worse than we thought."

"How much?" Two words only, but so harsh they sliced through the quiet of the carriage like a whip.

Oh, God, she didn't want to tell him. As soon as she said the number aloud there would be no taking it back, no pretending this wasn't real—

"*How much*, Lucy?"

Lucy tried to jerk away from him, but Ciaran wouldn't let her go. He tipped her chin up higher, so she couldn't avoid that wild blue gaze.

"More than five thousand pounds," Lucy whispered, but she might as well have screamed the words for the effect they had on Ciaran.

He sucked in a shocked breath, and his entire body tensed. She saw his throat move in a swallow before he said in a strangled voice, "Enough. This stops now, Lucy. It has to. You can't deny any longer how dangerous this is."

An image of Uncle Jarvis's red, furious face rose in Lucy's mind, and a shudder passed over her. "I don't deny it, no."

"That isn't all, is it?" He released her chin, but his hand stayed on her face, his fingertips on her jaw. "Tonight, on the dance floor. Godfrey forced you to remain for three dances, didn't he?"

Lucy hesitated. Godfrey had indeed forced her, but she didn't want to admit it to Ciaran. He'd nearly torn Godfrey limb from limb in the ballroom, and now he looked as if he were ready to leap from the carriage and hunt Godfrey down. "He was a trifle insistent, yes, but he didn't precisely force—"

"Stop it, Lucy." Ciaran's fingers remained gentle on her face, but his jaw looked ready to shatter. "Stop acting as if you're not in danger. Do you realize all the *ton* now thinks you're betrothed to him?"

"Betrothed to him?" Lucy stared at him, dumbfounded. "Why should they think that?"

"Because a lady doesn't dance with a gentleman more than twice unless they have an understanding, Lucy. That's why your uncle forced you to allow Godfrey to take you to the floor in the first place. Don't you see? They planned this. They want all of London to think you and Godfrey are betrothed, to try and force you into a marriage."

Lucy stared at him, stunned. How could her uncle be so cruel, so manipulative? She'd never imagined anyone could behave so viciously. A raw, dry laugh tore from her throat. "They don't know me very well then, do they? I don't care a fig for what anyone thinks. If refusing to marry Lord

Godfrey after dancing three times with him ruins my reputation, then so be it. I don't intend to ever marry anyway, so what difference does it make?"

Ciaran let his hand drop away and stabbed his fingers through his hair. "You don't understand. If Jarvis and Godfrey will go so far as to publicly expose you, there's no telling what else they'll do. When I think I might have left you here in London, alone and unprotected…"

He muttered this last part, as if he was speaking more to himself than to her, but Lucy heard him and her spine stiffened. "I told you once before, Ciaran. I'm not alone. I have Eloisa and my Aunt Jarvis, and Lady Felicia, Lord Vale, and Lord Markham—"

"None of whom can do a damn thing to protect you if this business turns any uglier. Your cousin and aunt care for you, but they're terrified of Jarvis, and what do you suppose our friends can do?"

"They could…that is, I can't imagine they'd allow…" Lucy's voice faded. She fell back against the squabs, her heart rushing into her throat. She wasn't a piece of property. Surely Uncle Jarvis couldn't simply do whatever he pleased with her?

"Jarvis is your guardian, Lucy. That doesn't give him a legal right to force you into anything, but practically, what do you plan to do if he attempts it? Complain to the Court of Chancery?" Ciaran let out a bitter laugh. "You'll be married to Godfrey with a half-dozen children clinging to your skirts before they ever get around to hearing your case."

Lucy couldn't deny it was true. She was certain her Uncle Jarvis was already stealing money from her trust, but what could she do to stop him? He'd have to give an accounting of her fortune to the court eventually, yes, but there were dozens of ways he could excuse the withdrawals. Uncle Jarvis was coarse and grasping, but clever when it came to saving his own skin.

"I have an idea." Ciaran took her hand, his large palm swallowing her fingers. "It's not ideal, but it would protect you from—"

"No." Lucy already knew what he was going to say. "I won't leave London, Ciaran."

"Listen to me, Lucy—"

"No! What do you suppose my uncle will do to my aunt and cousin if I leave? He'll take his fury out on them. I'm certain of it."

Lucy thought of the way her aunt had tried to help her tonight, of the fear in her eyes when Uncle Jarvis had spoken to her so harshly. Then there was Eloisa, who'd become as dear to Lucy as the sister she'd always dreamed of having. What would become of her? Uncle Jarvis might drag them out of London, and whatever hopes Eloisa had of Lord Vale would be destroyed.

Eloisa had looked so pretty tonight, with her pink cheeks and bright eyes. She might pretend her heart wasn't bleeding, but Lucy had seen the way her cousin looked at Lord Vale. The more Lucy saw them together, the more persuaded she was Lord Vale loved Eloisa in return. Eloisa had had precious little joy in her life. Didn't she deserve her chance at happiness?

When she raised her gaze to Ciaran, tears were burning behind her eyes. "I can't leave them, Ciaran. I w-won't leave them."

Before Lucy knew what was happening, Ciaran closed the tiny sliver of space between them. He wrapped a warm hand around the back of her neck and eased her head down onto his shoulder. "Hush. I know you don't want to leave them, but it wouldn't be for long. Just a few weeks, until your birthday. Vale will keep an eye on them until then. Your aunt and cousin want you to be safe, Lucy."

Lucy curled her fingers into his coat. It wasn't at all proper to let him hold her like this, particularly when they were alone in a dark carriage, but she didn't draw away. She sagged against him and nestled her face into the hollow of his shoulder. "But where would I go?"

Ciaran didn't answer right away, and Lucy felt his chest move beneath her cheek in a long sigh. His hand slid away from the back of her neck and that huge, warm palm stroked over her hair.

Dear God, it felt divine. *He* felt divine. She squirmed closer, melting into the strength surrounding her. Her senses reeled as the seductive scent of clean linen and something else filled her nose. She inhaled deeply, trying to place it.

Warm skin, clean linen, a faint hint of leather...

She wouldn't have thought it possible, but Ciaran smelled even better than he felt.

His soft breath stirred the wisps of hair at her temple, tickling her skin. "I'll take you to my brother's country seat in Buckinghamshire. Once you're there, you'll be under his protection. Even if your uncle or Godfrey find out where you are, there's a good chance they wouldn't dare to challenge the Marquess of Huntington."

"I can't flee to Buckinghamshire, Ciaran. Your brother and the rest of your family don't even know me. I can't simply appear on their doorstep and beg them to take me in."

"You won't have to. I'm coming with you, of course. How can you think I'd let you tear off to Buckinghamshire alone? I told you I'd protect you, Lucy, and I meant it."

"You want me to leave London—to flee my uncle's protection—with *you*?" Lucy's head was spinning. What he was suggesting didn't make sense. "It'll cause a scandal, Ciaran! Everyone will think we've eloped."

Ciaran let out a short laugh. "We *will* have eloped. Whatever scandal there is will be short-lived, because as soon as you're of age, I'll marry you."

Lucy went utterly still, a strangled breath trapped in her throat. She should have pushed away from him then. She should have raised her head from his chest at once and put some distance between them. Instead, her first impulse was to tighten her arms around him.

Her second impulse…God help her, but her second impulse was to leap into his lap and tell him she'd marry him. Somehow, all her promises to herself, her decision never to marry seemed to dissolve like dew in the morning sun. "You want to m-marry me?"

But of course, he *didn't* want to. He was offering his hand, yes, but not because he loved her. Not in the way a husband should love a wife. They were simply friends, nothing more. His strong arms around her, the solid warmth of his chest under her cheek had confused her, made her wish for things she knew could never be.

If he'd been any other man, or if she'd loved him any less, she might have agreed to marry him. But he was Ciaran, and she loved him far too much to let him give up everything he wanted for her.

Dear God, how selfish she was. She never should have allowed him to remain in London with her. He felt responsible for her now, unable to leave her behind. It would hurt her to see him go, but it would hurt her more to see him sacrifice his dream of returning to Scotland, just for her.

Lucy swallowed the lump in her throat. "I can't marry you, Ciaran."

She lifted her head from his chest and began to gently disentangle herself from his embrace. For a breathless moment his fingers tightened in her hair, as if he wanted to keep her against him, but then he sucked in a breath and released her. She pressed herself into the corner of the carriage, putting a few precious inches between their bodies, and tried to gather her wits.

"Don't do this, Lucy." Ciaran's tone was gruff, but he held out his hand to her. "Stop this, and let me help you."

Lucy didn't take his hand or move toward him, but it was as if he'd wrapped her in his arms once again. Warmth flooded her, and it felt as if her heart were melting in her chest. "I told you before I never intend to marry. You teased me for it at the time, but you see, it was the truth. I haven't changed my mind."

"Not even for me?" His voice was low and hoarse, filled with hurt. "You won't change your mind even for me?"

Oh, she couldn't bear it, that break in his voice.

Lucy did move then. She leapt straight into Ciaran's arms. "How dear you are," she whispered, cradling his face in her hands. Then, without a second thought, she leaned forward and pressed her lips to his cheek. "How dear you are, Ciaran."

He seemed to freeze against her, but then his fingers wrapped gently around her wrists. He didn't move her hands away from him, but he leaned back a little so he could look into her eyes. "I'd do anything for you, Lucy." Again, his voice was gruff, but the lines of his face had softened, and one corner of his lips quirked in that half-smile she'd come to treasure.

They stared at each other without speaking, long silent moments ticking between them. Ciaran didn't pull away again, and Lucy kept her hands on his face. His skin was warm, and the light prickle of his emerging beard tickled her palms.

Her gaze roamed over his face, coming back again and again to his mouth. A faint smile curved her lips. One had only to look at that obstinate jaw, that stubborn lower lip to see how determined a man he was. She'd seen those lips pressed together with irritation more times than she could count.

But not as many times as she'd seen them curved in a grin.

How had she ever managed to resist that full mouth? How had she looked at his beautiful face dozens of times without giving in to the need to touch his lips? She stared, suddenly mesmerized by them. Slowly—so slowly she wasn't sure she even moved—she slid her thumb across his cheek and dragged it over his lower lip.

"It's so soft," she whispered. She'd never imagined a man's lips could be so soft.

Ciaran said nothing, but his blue eyes went as dark as a midnight sky, and then, without warning his lips parted, and he pressed a warm, wet kiss against the tip of her thumb.

A hot ache unfurled in her belly, and Lucy's eyes slid closed.

"Open your eyes, Lucy." Ciaran's voice was rough, husky.

Lucy did as she was told. His gaze held hers as slowly—oh, so slowly—he raised his hand to her face and, very gently, touched a fingertip to the middle of her lower lip, opening her mouth for him. Then he leaned toward her, and before she had a chance to draw a breath, his mouth took hers.

Lucy had never kissed a man before. Never stroked a man's skin, or held his face in her palms. Was it always this sweet, this perfect? Or was this kiss different than any other she'd ever have, because it was her first?

Or was it different simply because it was *him*?

I didn't know. I didn't know....

She'd fallen in love with Ciaran weeks ago, but it wasn't until his lips found hers that she understood how badly she wanted to kiss him. That she'd been thinking about how he'd feel, how he'd taste since the first time they'd stood together on the beach in Brighton, with cold water dripping down her back and Ciaran's nose gushing blood.

It was a soft, tender kiss. Hesitant, his lips merely brushing against hers, almost as if he were asking a question.

Did she *want* to kiss him? Did *he* want to kiss *her*? Were they simply friends, or had Ciaran been right all along about desire turning friends into lovers?

Lucy didn't know the answers to any of these questions. She knew only she found herself balancing on a precipice, her feet edging closer to midair with every stroke of Ciaran's lips over hers.

She was moments away from tumbling over the side, and once she did, once she did…

She'd either fall, or she'd fly.

That was the trouble with love. Until you leapt, you didn't know which.

Chapter Eighteen

Even before his mouth took hers, Ciaran knew Lucy would have the softest, sweetest lips he'd ever kissed. Even before he coaxed her to open for him and stroked his tongue against hers for the first time, he already knew how she'd taste.

Wild and sweet, ocean air and green apples.

It made no sense he should know this, just as it didn't make sense his mouth against hers felt inevitable, as if he'd been waiting all his life to kiss her. It didn't feel strange, kissing Lucy, and that didn't make sense, either. Shouldn't it feel strange to kiss your friend?

Because *this*—this wasn't a *friendly* kiss.

It was deep and hot and maddening, and it was everywhere at once. First a tingle in his lips and then lower, a sweet, pulsing ache in his belly, and higher, spreading inside his chest, wrapping tightly around his heart.

"Lucy." It was more a groan than a word, and so needy, so hungry Ciaran hardly recognized his own voice. His lips were still clinging to hers when he reached out to capture a long, red curl between his fingers. "*Lucy.*"

His head was spinning, his body burning with desire. He could only say her name, the words low and ragged, and hope it was enough.

That she'd understand all the words he couldn't say.

Her mouth curved under his, and for one breathless instant he let his tongue trace her lower lip. He tasted her smile until he coaxed a soft whimper from her throat. Her arms twined around his neck, her fingers sinking into his hair.

All it took was that touch, the light, sensual stroke across the back of his neck and Ciaran was lost to her. "Closer," he begged, his lips against her ear. He wrapped his hands around her slender waist to hold her still against him. Tighter, tighter, until he could feel the soft swell of her breasts against his chest and her curved hips filled his palms.

She shivered at his touch, a gasp catching in her throat as he took her mouth again, ravenous now, his tongue flicking and teasing at her red lips until with a sweet sigh of surrender, she opened fully for him.

Ciaran didn't hesitate. He surged inside with a low growl, his tongue stroking against hers. Once, then again and again until he released her mouth with a tortured groan, certain he'd go mad from the hot, wet caress of her tongue.

He let his forehead rest against hers, his chest heaving as he tried to make himself let her go. He had to let her go, to ease her away from him. Desire was clouding his brain, so thick and seductive he couldn't speak, couldn't think…couldn't find a single reason why he shouldn't tumble her onto her back on the carriage seat and let his body cover hers, their legs tangling together.

"Lucy." He braced his hands on her shoulders and began to ease her back, away from him. "This is…we can't…we have to—"

"Not yet." She kissed her way from the corner of his mouth to his cheek, then his jaw, and then—dear God—his earlobe. Her soft lips slid over his throat and the heated skin of his neck, nipping and teasing until she stole every breath from his lungs. He arched against her, his hands sliding over her ribs to drag her closer, urge her harder against him.

She was so close the loose strands of her hair brushed against his neck, the soft tickle driving him mindless with desire. So mindless when her mouth found his again Ciaran closed his eyes with a groan, his head falling back against the seat, his lips opening helplessly under hers.

The kiss seemed to go on forever, and yet it hadn't gone on nearly long enough when at last she drew away and let her face fall against his chest. Ciaran went still, panting, his chest heaving as he dragged one desperate breath after another into his lungs. He kept his hands firmly wrapped around her waist to keep them from wandering again while Lucy lay motionless against him, her fingers still buried in his hair.

She slid her palm over the sensitive skin of his neck and dragged her fingers down to his chest. She stared down at her own hand resting against him, then looked up into his eyes with a shy smile. "Your heart is beating so quickly."

"It is." Ciaran covered her hand with his to keep it pressed to his body. "Is yours?"

Lucy hesitated, then she closed her slender fingers around his wrist and pressed his palm against the pulse beating in the base of her throat. "Yes."

Long, quiet moments slipped by. Neither of them moved, and everything faded to oblivion around Ciaran except her hand on his chest, her heartbeat fluttering against his palm.

"You have to go, Ciaran," she whispered at last. "My aunt and Eloisa will be here any moment. They can't find us alone in the carriage."

"No. I won't go without you." Ciaran brushed a stray wisp of hair back from her face. "You can't return to Portman Square. It isn't safe. Please, Lucy. Let me take care of you."

"I—I want to, Ciaran, but I can't." A slow, shaky breath shuddered out of her, but she met his gaze without flinching.

Ciaran's hands tightened around her waist, helpless anger and fear rolling over him. "Yes, you can. You have to."

"No, I can't. Not without my Aunt Jarvis and Eloisa. Call on me tomorrow, won't you? As early as you can. I'll be fine until then."

"You don't know that, Lucy. By then you could be the Countess of Godfrey." Ciaran blew out a frustrated breath. "Come with me tonight. *Please.*"

Lucy was as worried about her uncle and Godfrey as he was—Ciaran could see it by the furrow in her brow, the uneasy way she bit her lip, but she shook her head. "No. I won't leave them."

"Damn it, Lucy—"

"Go, Ciaran." She squirmed free of him and shifted to the other side of the carriage. "Quickly. You'll only make it worse if my aunt catches you alone with me."

Ciaran hesitated, but short of tossing her over his shoulder there wasn't much he could do. He dragged a hand down his face and threw open the carriage door with a curse. "Tomorrow, then. I'll come early. Be waiting for me, Lucy."

She nodded. "I promise."

Ciaran leapt down from the carriage. He took one long, last look at her before closing the door, his heart twisting at how small and alone she looked, huddled in her dark corner.

It was less than a day. She'd be all right for such a short time. That was what Ciaran told himself as he took the stone steps leading into the Weatherbys' townhouse two at a time. He'd come with Vale and Lady Felicia, but they'd likely left by now—

"Women are a bloody nuisance."

Ciaran stopped halfway up the steps. That voice—and on occasion that sentiment—belonged to Vale.

"Can't think why I came to London for the season in the first place. Dozens of silly chits on display, being towed around by their marriage-minded mamas. Well, what do I want with a wife? Wouldn't know what to do with her if I had one."

Ciaran turned and bounded back down the steps. He found Vale and Markham a short way down the street, standing under a tree that shielded them from the guests streaming in and out of the Weatherbys' townhouse. "What are you two doing out here?"

"Waiting for my bloody carriage." Vale gave the branch hanging over his head a vicious slap with his walking stick. "What do you think, Ramsey?"

Ciaran ignored Vale's ill-humor. "Where's Lady Felicia?"

"Went off with Mrs. Jarvis and Eloisa." Vale scowled. "No doubt they've told each other all their darkest secrets by now, too."

Ciaran raised an eyebrow. *Eloisa?* Vale referred to Miss Jarvis by her Christian name?

Markham let out a short, hard laugh. "I'm surprised you agreed to let your sister out of your sight, Vale. She's gotten herself into more mischief this season than I would have thought Lady Felicia capable of."

"I don't know. I'd say Lady Felicia's done well enough for herself," Ciaran said, feeling compelled to speak up for her. "Nash is a good sort."

Ciaran's tone was mild, but he slid a curious glance at Markham. Markham was a decent man, but a bit arrogant, not to mention oblivious. Everyone could see Lady Felicia was in love with him—everyone but Markham. Ciaran couldn't blame her for torturing him a bit.

Markham cast him a withering glance. "Good for *what*? Not a husband for Lady Felicia, I can promise you that."

"Well, *someone* has to bloody marry her, because I'm not coming back to London for another season," Vale snapped. "If I never set foot in London again, it'll be too soon."

"I should never have let you talk me into coming to London in the first place, Vale," Markham grumbled. "You persuaded me it would be good fun, but it's been a misery from start to finish."

"I thought it *would* be good fun, but that was before I realized we'd have to spend every minute in a ballroom keeping track of the blasted women." Vale shook his head with a grimace. "Damned if I know how it became such a mess. I blame *you*, Ramsey."

"Me? Christ, Vale. Have you forgotten it was *you* who talked *me* into coming here? If it weren't for you I'd be in Scotland right now, doing what I…"

Doing what? Ciaran broke off, because for the life of him he couldn't think of a single thing of any value he'd be doing in Scotland. His childhood home, his old friends, Isobel…they all seemed further away now than they ever had. Except now, he no longer regretted it. Perhaps it was just as well to put the past away, and turn his attention to the future.

"Scotland," Vale scoffed. "For God's sake, Ramsey, if you truly wanted to go, you'd have done it by now. No, I think your interests lie here, in London." He jabbed Ciaran in the ribs with the head of his walking stick. "Not but what you'll have a hard time bringing Lady Lucinda to heel. She's stubborn, that one, just like her cousin."

Ciaran snorted. "Bring her *to heel*? She's not a hunting dog, Vale."

"No. None of them are, and a damn pity, too, because the three of them would be a good deal easier to manage if they were." Vale was gripping the head of his walking stick so tightly the silver lion threatened to snap off. "Do you know she actually had the gall to say she was refusing me for my own good? My own good, indeed."

She? Ah, it was all starting to make sense now. No wonder Vale was in such a temper. He must have made Eloisa Jarvis an offer, and she'd refused him. Ciaran couldn't imagine why she would, but he predicted her refusal would be short-lived. He'd seen the way Miss Jarvis looked at his friend. "Give it a few days, Vale. She'll come 'round."

"You wouldn't think so if you'd heard her, Ramsey." Vale had been waving his walking stick around wildly, but all at once the fight seemed to go out of him and he subsided with a desolate sigh. "I think a man can decide for himself what's good for him. Don't you think so, Markham?"

Markham gave a loud snort. "Certainly, unless that man happens to be Lord Nash. If *he* knew what was good for him he'd keep a respectful distance between himself and another man's lady."

Another man's lady? Ciaran jerked his attention toward Markham. Good Lord, how long had he and Lucy been gone? A great deal seemed to have happened since they'd left the ballroom. "Does Lady Felicia even realize she's your lady? You might want to tell her, Markham."

Markham's face reddened, but he didn't have a chance to reply before Vale interrupted. "Pathetic fools, all three of us. No, no, don't bother coming down, Nibbs," Vale called to his coachman as his carriage drew up to the curb. "Just get us the devil away from here. You can drop Ramsey in Grosvenor Square."

Vale heaved himself into the carriage with an irritable grunt, and Markham and Ciaran climbed up behind him.

"What do you mean, all three of us?" Ciaran asked, once the carriage started moving. "Don't put me in the same category as you two pathetic, lovesick fools. Lucy and I are friends, nothing more. I'm in perfect control of myself."

There was a moment of stunned silence, then both Vale and Markham burst into uproarious laughter.

"What?" Ciaran looked from one to the other of them. "What the devil's so bloody amusing?"

"Friends!" Vale exclaimed. "Very well then, Ramsey. You're a friend who hasn't spared another woman so much as a glance since you arrived in London."

"A friend who keeps insisting he's off to Scotland at any moment, but can't tear himself away from Lady Lucinda long enough to mount his horse," Markham added with a smirk.

"A friend who gazes at Lady Lucinda as if he's scheming to snatch her away and enjoy her somewhere in private." Vale went off into another peal of laughter.

A friend who'd kissed her. A friend who dreams about her...

But a few kisses, a few vivid dreams—those things didn't mean he loved her. He desired her, yes, but that had been true from the start. What man could know Lucy and *not* desire her? But desire wasn't any closer to being love than dreams were to being reality.

Markham was shaking his head, a faint smile on his lips. "You're the worst of the three of us, Ramsey, and God knows Vale and I are hopeless enough."

"That's ridiculous. No one could be more hopeless than you two." Ciaran opened his mouth to argue further, to deny he had any wicked designs on Lucy, but the words refused to leave his mouth. No, what came out instead was, "Do you suppose she's...that is, do you imagine she feels—"

"The same way? Sorry, Ramsey. Can't help you there." Vale settled back against the seat with a forlorn sigh. "Love is a wretched business. Can't make head nor tails of it, myself."

Ciaran glanced at Markham, but Markham only gave him a helpless shrug.

Ciaran turned his gaze to the window. London was rushing by, but he didn't see it. Instead, he saw Lucy right before he'd left her tonight, her dark eyes soft, her lips red and swollen from his kisses. His mouth went dry, and his stomach tight.

He never should have kissed her. It was this damned courtship—it was confusing him, making him feel things he shouldn't feel for her. He cared for Lucy, but what they had was a friendship, not a love affair.

Wasn't it?

He turned back to face his friends, dragging his hands through his hair with rough fingers. "I'm courting her."

Vale and Markham turned to him in surprise. "Who?" Vale asked.

"Lucy, of course." A frustrated groan left Ciaran's lips.

"You're in love with Lady Lucinda, and you're courting her?" Markham gave him an impatient look. "Isn't that how it's supposed to work? Beg pardon, Ramsey, but I can't see what you're moaning about."

"Damn it, Markham. I'm not in love with Lucy, and even if I were, she's not in love with me. I made her an offer tonight. I offered her my hand, and she…refused me. She told me she wasn't going to marry at all, and sent me on my way."

Vale stared at him for a moment before throwing his hands up in the air, thoroughly disgusted. "Well, of course she did. Do you know why? Because they delight in tormenting us. Damn it, a man has every right to expect a courtship will end with a betrothal. I told you, Ramsey. Women are a bloody nuisance!"

Ciaran shook his head. "No, you don't understand. The courtship isn't real. I've only been pretending to court her to discourage Godfrey's suit."

"Wait." Markham sat up, shaking off his moody silence. "You mean to say Lady Lucinda doesn't even know you're in love with her?"

"I'm not—" Ciaran broke off with a heavy sigh. What was the use in arguing about it? "Christ. I think I've made a mess of this."

"I've no doubt of that. You know, Ramsey, you might want to tell Lady Lucinda you're in love with her," Markham said, throwing Ciaran's own words back at him. "She likely thinks you're only offering for her to protect her from Godfrey."

Ciaran was silent. That *was* why he'd offered for her.

Wasn't it?

"For God's sake, what's all this bloody nonsense about Godfrey and a pretend courtship, anyway?" Vale demanded. "It doesn't make any sense. Start from the beginning, Ramsey."

Ciaran blew out a breath. "I promised to court Lucy to protect her from Jarvis and Godfrey. I was meant to jilt her in a few weeks, after she turns twenty-one and is free of Jarvis's guardianship. But the only way to keep her safe is to take her out of London, and I can't do that without marrying her."

It wasn't just that, though. He didn't *want* to jilt Lucy. He wanted to marry her. They cared very much for each other, and the spark of passion between them burned bright—much brighter than he'd realized until he'd kissed her tonight. He adored her, and he wanted her, badly. Wasn't that enough?

People might go on and on about love, but Ciaran had learned his lesson. Love had shattered his hopes, stolen his happiness, crushed his will. Love had taken everything from him, and left only pain and betrayal in its wake. He'd never be foolish enough to trust it again.

But what he had with Lucy was nothing like that. It was simple, natural, achingly sweet. Not anything at all like he knew love to be.

"I knew Godfrey had been sniffing about Lady Lucinda, but I didn't think he was any sort of serious threat to her." Vale was shaking his head, a worried frown on his face.

"Serious enough. Didn't you see Godfrey dancing with her tonight? He kept her on the floor for three dances, Vale. *Three*." Just thinking about it made Ciaran's fists clench. "He made her do it—grabbed her hard enough to leave a handprint on her arm."

Markham gaped at Ciaran, horrified. "Jesus. What a scoundrel."

Ciaran's blood was burning through his veins. "Lucy despises him, but it hasn't stopped either Godfrey or Jarvis from plotting to force her into the marriage. I don't trust either of them."

"Nor should you. That is, I don't know much about Jarvis aside from his being a troublesome, tyrannical sort of fellow, but Godfrey's an outright villain. You can't let him anywhere near Lady Lucinda, Ramsey."

"I don't want to, but I can't get Lucy to listen to me." Damn it, he never should have let her go back to Portman Square tonight.

"I didn't see Godfrey force Lady Lucinda to dance. I was, er...rather caught up with Eloisa. But I heard Lord Henley talking to Lord Weatherby about it, though I didn't realize they were referring to Lady Lucinda at the time."

Something about the tone of Vale's voice made gooseflesh rise on Ciaran's neck. "What did you hear?"

"Henley must have noticed Lady Lucinda dancing with Godfrey. He said something about what a pity it would be to see another lovely young lady fall into Godfrey's clutches."

"His *clutches*?" Bile rose in Ciaran's throat.

Vale's face was grim. "It's not widely known in London, but Henley's country estate in Wiltshire borders Godfrey's, and there was plenty of gossip about it in their neighborhood."

An apprehensive shudder tripped up Ciaran's spine. "Gossip about *what?*" He was ready to shake the story out of Vale.

"Two years ago, Godfrey married a lady by the name of Alice Trentham. She was much younger than him, very pretty, and possessed of a rather impressive fortune. No title—her father made his money in some trade or other, and he wanted to marry his daughter to an aristocrat. It was a shameful thing, Henley said. The father forced the girl to marry Godfrey in order to turn her into a countess."

"Godfrey bought her with his title," Ciaran spat.

"He bought her, yes, and a year later she was dead."

Ciaran and Markham stared at Vale, both of them struck dumb with shock.

"She took too much laudanum one night, and didn't wake up the next morning. There were rumors afterward. A couple of housemaids swore they saw Godfrey dose the girl that night, but nothing was ever proved, and the matter was dropped."

"So, the marriage ended with her fortune in Godfrey's pocket," Markham hissed. "A wealthy man with no wife to burden him."

Vale gave a tight nod. "Just so. Now here he is again, chasing after Lady Lucinda, another young, beautiful heiress."

Chasing her, and if Jarvis had anything to say about it, catching her. Ciaran thought of Lucy huddled in the corner of the carriage tonight, so small and vulnerable, and his stomach twisted. "I've made a terrible mistake."

Markham and Vale stiffened. "What mistake? Where is Lady Lucinda, Ramsey?"

"On her way back to Jarvis's in Portman Square." Ciaran was already slamming his fist against the carriage roof. "With only Mrs. and Miss Jarvis to protect her."

Vale paled at the mention of Eloisa Jarvis. "Nibbs!"

He began struggling with the window, but Markham already had it open and was shouting to the coachman. "Portman Square, Nibbs, and hurry, man!"

Chapter Nineteen

"Men are vile, loathsome creatures."

Lucy would have sworn nothing in the world could jolt her from her thoughts. She'd been manhandled by Lord Godfrey tonight. All of London now thought her betrothed to him—a man three times her age whom she despised—and Lord Godfrey likely thought so, as well. Meanwhile the man she *was* madly in love with had kissed her with a passion that took her breath away, and then proposed marriage to her.

And she'd refused him.

In short, she had quite a few of her own problems to worry about.

But as soon as Lady Felicia made her announcement, both Lucy and Eloisa jerked their heads toward her, their mouths dropping open in shock. The three of them were in the Jarvises' hired carriage, waiting at the curb outside the Weatherbys' townhouse for Aunt Jarvis, who'd gone in search of her husband in the card room to inform him they were leaving the ball.

"My goodness, Felicia. What's gotten into you?" Lucy asked, surprised to hear such bitter words from sweet-tempered Lady Felicia.

"Do you mean to tell me, Lucy, you don't think men are vile, loathsome creatures?" Lady Felicia turned on Lucy, her blue eyes flashing.

"Well, er…some of them certainly can be." Lucy didn't necessarily disagree with her friend. Some men *were* vile, loathsome creatures. One needn't look any further than Lord Godfrey for proof of that. "Are you condemning a specific gentleman in particular?"

Silly question, and one to which Lucy already knew the answer. It was rare enough for Lady Felicia to fall into a temper. When she did, Lord Markham was generally the reason for it.

"I'm in no humor to defend *any* man," Lady Felicia declared. "The entire sex is dreadful, but Lord Markham is the worst of the lot."

Lucy bit her lip to hide a smile. It was her considered opinion when a lady and a gentleman who were dear friends started flinging insults at each other, love wasn't far behind.

"Dear me." Eloisa's eyes were wide. "What's he done?"

Eloisa gave Lady Felicia's arm a soothing pat, but it didn't do a thing to calm Felicia's temper. Her brow lowered, and her frown turned into a dark scowl. "Do you know what he said to me tonight?"

Lucy opened her mouth to reply, but Lady Felicia cut her off before she got a word out. "He demanded to know my feelings regarding Lord Nash. Then he had the gall to suggest—subtly, mind you, because Edmund is nothing if not restrained—I was trifling with his lordship when my affections truly lay elsewhere!"

The corners of Lucy's lips threatened to curve. "Why, how strange. It's not at all like Lord Markham to say something so ungentlemanly. What could have been the reason for it?"

"You may believe me, Lucy, when I say Edmund isn't always the flawless gentleman he pretends to be. He was in a terrible temper, and behaved like a perfect savage." Lady Felicia fell back against the seat with an outraged sniff.

"Why should Lord Markham suppose you don't care for Lord Nash?" Eloisa's brows drew together. "Why shouldn't you care for such a handsome, charming gentleman? All the young ladies admire him."

Lady Felicia tossed her head. "Well, I suppose he thinks he knows my feelings better than I do myself!"

Lucy glimpsed a flash of consciousness cross Lady Felicia's face, and wondered if perhaps in this one instance, Lord Markham was correct. "Hmmm. What threw Lord Markham into such a terrible temper?"

"Why, nothing at all remarkable, but he's been in a temper since yesterday. He called, you see, and while he was there a servant brought in a bouquet of hothouse flowers from Lord Nash—lovely pink peonies and white lilac. I was exclaiming over them, and Edmund's face kept getting darker and darker, and the next thing I knew he'd fallen into a temper and was saying all manner of unpleasant things."

"My goodness," Lucy murmured. "What did he say?"

"He went on and on, and…well, I couldn't make much sense of it, but something about ladies dancing with the same gentleman twice, then allowing him to take her into supper, and a lot of other incoherent nonsense. He was pacing from one end of the drawing room to the other like a caged animal, and it was all quite awful, and then Sebastian had to have his say, and he only made it worse, and—"

"Why? What did Lord Vale say?" Eloisa's head snapped toward Lady Felicia.

"He agreed with Edmund! He said young ladies are calculating, cold-hearted things who tease and flirt until they gain a man's attention, then they dangle him on a string and rejoice in his misery."

Eloisa sucked in a furious breath. "That's utter nonsense! If anyone's a tease and a flirt, it's Lord Vale!"

"I couldn't agree more, Eloisa. Sebastian's a dreadful tease, and so I've told him dozens of times, but do you suppose he listens to me?"

"Of course, he doesn't! He doesn't listen to anyone!" Eloisa huffed. "Certainly not to any lady who tries to reason him out of making a foolish choice he'll regret for the rest of his life. Never mind she's only trying to help him, and doing it for his own good!"

Lucy stared at Eloisa, her eyes wide. *Foolish choice?* One that would affect Lord Vale for the rest of his life? Surely her cousin could only mean one thing by *that*.

"Vile, loathsome creatures," Eloisa muttered under her breath.

My, it was a season for proposals, wasn't it? Weren't betrothals meant to be happy occasions? "I daresay everything will work out as it's meant to in the end." It would, too—for Eloisa and Felicia, that is. Lucy was far less optimistic about her own situation.

She couldn't stop thinking about Ciaran's face when she'd refused him, the way shadows had darkened the blue in his eyes. He'd looked hurt. If Lucy didn't know better, she would have thought his heart was broken—

"No, it won't work out in the end, Lucy. Things never do." Eloisa's voice was thick, as if she were about to burst into tears. "Everything's a dreadful mess, and likely to stay that way."

Lucy's gaze shot to her cousin's face, and in the next instant she was across the carriage, squeezing into the narrow bit of seat between Eloisa and Lady Felicia. "What's happened tonight?" She took Lady Felicia's hand in one of hers, Eloisa's in the other, and braced herself. "Well, Eloisa? Felicia? Tell me at once."

Silence at first, but it tipped over into chaos soon enough. "Lord Vale made me an offer, but I—" Eloisa began, at the same time Lady Felicia said, "Edmund offered me his hand, and I told him—"

That was as far as they got before the carriage door flew open and Aunt Jarvis scrambled in. "Dear me, girls! I beg your pardon for keeping you waiting. It's such a crush it took me ages to find…oh, aren't you uncomfortable, crowded together on one side?"

Lucy, Eloisa and Lady Felicia all shook their heads at once.

"No? All right, then." Aunt Jarvis settled herself into the opposite seat and spread her skirts with a sigh before squinting at Lucy through the gloom of the carriage. "Lucy, my dear child. Are you quite all right? Such a terrible scene with Lord Godfrey!"

"Yes, Aunt," Lucy said quickly, hoping to end the conversation before Eloisa or Felicia started asking questions. It would only upset them further if they knew about Lord Godfrey's abominable behavior this evening.

But she hoped in vain. As soon as his lordship's name was mentioned she felt Eloisa go stiff beside her, and Lady Felicia asked sharply, "What scene? What has Lord Godfrey done now?"

"It was nothing," Lucy began, but her aunt interrupted her with an energy Lucy had never seen in her before. Perhaps she shouldn't have put so much elderflower in that last batch of Dr. Digby's Calming Tonic.

"It *wasn't* nothing. It was excessively unpleasant, and I don't mind saying I'm not at all pleased with Lord Godfrey. I haven't always approved of his behavior before tonight, but I never imagined he could be so *very* ungentlemanly."

"What happened, Mama?" Eloisa asked, her face pale.

"Why, Lord Godfrey practically dragged poor Lucy into the set, and then what do you think? He insisted on keeping her out for three dances! I didn't know what it meant at first, but then Lady Henley came over and asked when Lucy and Lord Godfrey intended to marry! Did you know, girls, if a gentleman and lady dance three dances together, it means they're—"

"Betrothed," Lady Felicia said flatly. "Or as good as betrothed."

"Betrothed! You mean to tell me everyone at the ball tonight now thinks Lucy is betrothed to *Lord Godfrey*?" Eloisa didn't try to hide her horror.

"It seems so. It must be a mistake, of course. That is, I realize Lord Godfrey's been calling on you, Lucy, but your uncle hasn't said a word to me about…"

Aunt Jarvis trailed off as she came to the same conclusion Lucy, Eloisa, and Lady Felicia had already reached. Uncle Jarvis wasn't in the habit of sharing his plans with his wife. That Aunt Jarvis didn't know a thing about a betrothal between Lucy and Lord Godfrey meant precisely nothing.

"Oh, dear." Aunt Jarvis darted an uneasy glance around the carriage, wringing her hands. "You don't think—"

"No, no. I'm sure it's a simple misunderstanding, Mama." Eloisa shot a warning look at Lucy. "You needn't worry. It'll all be sorted out by morning."

It wouldn't be sorted out. Lucy knew that well enough, and if the heavy silence that fell over the carriage was any indication, everyone else did, too. Even her aunt remained quiet until they drew close to Lord Vale's townhouse in Hanover Square. "Shall we leave you here, Lady Felicia?"

Lucy, Eloisa, and Felicia glanced at each other, then Eloisa shook her head. "No, Mama. Her brother will fetch her from Portman Square on his way home from the Weatherby ball. Lady Felicia is…ah, she doesn't like to stay in the house unless he's there."

Given that Lord Vale had dozens of servants Lucy thought this an implausible excuse, but Aunt Jarvis didn't argue. "Very well, then."

They continued on to Portman Square. Once they were there, Eloisa made quick work of seeing her mother from the carriage up to her bedchamber, where Aunt Jarvis promptly swallowed a dose of Dr. Digby's Calming Tonic, and went to bed.

When Eloisa came back downstairs, Lucy and Felicia were waiting for her in the entryway. "Come with me." Eloisa beckoned to them to follow her down the hall.

As soon as Lucy realized where her cousin was headed, she came to an abrupt halt. "Eloisa, no! We can't risk it. Your father could come home at any moment."

"We can, and we will." Eloisa was already pushing open the door of Uncle Jarvis's study. "This business with Lord Godfrey has gone far enough. There's no longer any doubt Father means to marry you off to that despicable man. The question is, how and when? We need to get into that locked drawer and see what we can find out."

Lucy couldn't help thinking Eloisa sounded very much as Ciaran had when he'd begged her to go with him tonight. She paused on the threshold of her uncle's study, misgivings plaguing her. Perhaps she should have listened to him, and done as he bid her.

That is, not the marriage part—no, not that. Never that, no matter if the thought filled her with longing. She wouldn't be the one to lock him away in a gilded cage. She knew too well the unhappiness and resentment that would follow.

But mightn't she have let him take her off to Grosvenor Street with him, just until they could figure out what else could be done? Eloisa was as worried about this mess with Lord Godfrey as Ciaran was. Lucy couldn't help but notice she was the least worried of the three of them.

Perhaps that was a mistake.

"Where's that dashed letter opener gone to?" Eloisa was tossing the papers on her father's desk about, searching underneath them. She'd clearly decided the time for caution had come and gone, because she was making the sort of mess it would be difficult to hide from her father.

Lucy hurried across the room to her cousin's side. She grabbed for the papers, trying to put them back where they belonged, but Eloisa was tossing them aside faster than Lucy could straighten them. "Stop it, Eloisa! You're making a dreadful mess. Your father will know we've been—"

She was interrupted by a gasp from Lady Felicia, who was standing beside the desk. In her hurry to empty the drawers Eloisa had tossed Uncle Jarvis's ledger onto the desk, and Felicia had snatched it up. She raised a shocked gaze to her friends' faces, the ledger open in her hands. "Five thousand pounds!"

"Five thousand, three hundred, and six pounds, to be exact. Ah, here it is!" Eloisa held up the letter opener, wielding it like a sword. "Now, let's see what else my father's been hiding."

She attacked the lock on the drawer that had resisted them the first time they'd rifled through Uncle Jarvis's desk, but Lucy snatched the letter opener away from her after a few fruitless jabs. "Give that to me. Do you even know how to pick a lock, Eloisa?"

Eloisa looked surprised. "Pick a lock? No. I didn't know there was such a thing. I was just going to break it open." She leaned over Lucy, watching with interest as Lucy prodded delicately at the lock with the tip of the letter opener. "How do *you* know how to pick a lock?"

Picking locks was the sort of skill one acquired when one had an unpredictable father, but Lucy was saved from having to offer this answer when the catch on the inside of the lock clicked. "Ah, here we are."

She placed the letter opener back under the piles of paper where Eloisa had found it, then held out her hand for the ledger book. Lady Felicia handed it over and Lucy put it carefully back in its place under the stationery box while Eloisa and Lady Felicia bent over the opened drawer.

"Papers, and more papers." Eloisa was pawing through them, a frown on her face as she dug through the piles, scanning each paper quickly before putting it back where she'd found it. "Dash it, it looks like it's just more tradesman's bills—"

She broke off as she caught up a small, neat bundle of papers and skimmed the top page. Her gaze moved over it, her face draining of color as she read. "Oh, no. *No.*"

A chill swept over Lucy, puckering her skin. "What is it?"

Lady Felicia was reading the pages over Eloisa's shoulder. When she reached the bottom of the page she looked up, her stricken gaze meeting Lucy's. "Dear God. Your uncle is an utter villain."

"Not a penny of pin money. No jointure." Eloisa was flipping through the pages, her fingers curling into the paper as if she was on the verge of ripping it to shreds.

Pin money? Jointure...

"Marriage settlements." Lucy's legs began to shake, and she dropped into the chair in front of the desk. "My uncle has had marriage settlements drawn up."

"He has. It seems you're not to be suffered to retain one penny of your own fortune once you and Lord Godfrey marry." There was a bitter, angry twist to Eloisa's lips. "Godfrey gets it all, with the likely exception of my father, who no doubt gets all his debts paid, and probably a generous portion of your fortune into the bargain."

"Why should your father get any of Lucy's fortune when she marries?" Lady Felicia asked. "You don't mean to suggest—"

"That my father is selling Lucy to Lord Godfrey? Yes, that's what I mean to suggest." Eloisa came around the side of the desk and kneeled beside Lucy's chair. "You need to leave this house at once, Lucy. Leave London."

Lucy shook her head, but her brain was sluggish with shock. "I can't leave you and Aunt Jarvis. Your father will know, Eloisa. He'll know you helped me, and then what will become of you?"

Eloisa took Lucy's hand, the papers still clutched in her other fist. "Please, Lucy. My father must mean the marriage to happen soon, or he wouldn't have drawn up the settlements. I'm begging you."

"Eloisa's right, Lucy." Lady Felicia abandoned the desk and came to kneel on the other side of Lucy's chair. "My brother and Edmund won't let anything happen to Eloisa or her mother. I promise you we'll take—"

A thundering crash cut Lady Felicia off, and all three ladies shot to their feet.

"My father." Eloisa froze, her face going so white Lucy was certain she'd swoon.

One breath, two...

Another crash, like the pounding of fists on a heavy wooden door, coming from the entryway. There was a slam, and then male voices echoing in the hallway.

"Quickly." Lady Felicia snatched the papers from Eloisa's hand. She ran over to the desk and shoved them back into the drawer, then began frantically tidying the papers on the surface. "Quick! Help me."

Eloisa shook her head. "It's too late."

Indeed, it was too late. None of them had time to draw another breath before footsteps were rushing down the hallway. Heavy footsteps—men's dress pumps echoing on marble floors.

"They've seen the lamplight." Lucy, Eloisa, and Lady Felicia all jerked their heads toward the door at once. The study door was open a crack, and a narrow beam of light from the lamp was spilling into the hallway.

Lucy's heart was thundering in her chest. She swayed, and reached out to grip the back of the chair beside her.

So, this is what a real swoon feels like....

The men burst into the room, each of them looking positively murderous, but when they saw the ladies standing there, they came to a skidding halt.

Lucy stared at them, her entire body shaking.

It wasn't Uncle Jarvis or Lord Godfrey.

"Sebastian. Thank God."

It took a moment for Lucy to realize it wasn't Lady Felicia who'd said it, but Eloisa.

"Eloisa." Lord Vale darted across the room, his face as pale as death, and without the slightest hesitation gathered Eloisa into his arms.

Lord Markham wasn't far behind him. He was at Lady Felicia's side in an instant, his dark eyes burning in his white face. He slid his arms around her, letting out a long, deep breath when she turned into him and buried her face in his shoulder.

Lucy felt more than saw all these dramas unfold. She was conscious of movement, of the soft murmur of soothing words, but her attention was fixed on one face, one man only.

"Ciaran, I—"

She wanted to say she was sorry, that she was grateful to him—so grateful he'd come for her, so grateful he was her friend—but she never got the chance because he was there, his warm body wrapped around hers, his big hands stroking her hair.

Lucy didn't realize she was sobbing until Ciaran's gentle fingers touched her lips. "Shhh. It's all right. I've got you." He kept whispering to her, his lips in her hair until the fear subsided, and she relaxed against him.

As soon as she was calm, he eased her a little away from him so he could see her face. "You'll come with me tonight?"

Lucy gazed up into those devastating blue eyes. For a fleeting moment she thought of Brighton, of the feeling of cool water caressing her skin. All those mornings, alone in the water, and she'd never been in danger of drowning...

Until now.

"Yes. I'll come with you."

Relief flooded Ciaran's face. "We'll leave for Buckinghamshire tomorrow. They won't think to look for you there until it's too late."

He didn't mention his proposals from earlier that night, and Lucy didn't ask. She turned to look at Lord Vale. "Eloisa, and my aunt?"

"They'll be safe. I promise it, Lady Lucinda. Markham and I will make sure of it."

Lord Markham was cradling Lady Felicia against his chest, but his gaze met Lucy's over the top of Felicia's golden head. "I promise it, too."

After that, there was nothing to say but goodbye. It was quick and tearful. By the time Lucy was tucked into Lord Vale's carriage beside Ciaran, she felt as if her heart had been torn from her chest.

She didn't realize she was crying until Ciaran's fingertips swept across her cheeks, gathering up her tears. "Don't cry, sweetheart. I can't bear it."

"Am I crying?"

Ciaran didn't answer. Not in words. But he took her hand, his fingers warm around hers, and pressed her palm against the center of his chest, over his heart.

Chapter Twenty

"Your brother's house is very grand." Lucy's voice was hushed, her steps hesitant as she crossed the marble entryway of the Grosvenor Square house.

It *was* grand. Pity they couldn't stay here, but this was the first place in London Jarvis would come looking for Lucy.

"He's a marquess. They all have grand houses." Ciaran was only half a step behind her, but she didn't turn to look at him when he spoke. She'd been avoiding his gaze since he'd handed her down from the carriage.

Why won't she look at me?

"A marquess," she repeated blankly, as if she weren't quite sure what the word meant. "Yes, of course. I—I forgot."

"Lucy. Look at me." Ciaran drew closer to her, so close he could see the fine red tendrils of hair curling against her neck. He lay a hand on her shoulder and turned her toward him, and understood at once why she'd been hiding her face from him.

Her eyes were red, her lips trembling, her long, thick eyelashes damp with tears.

Ciaran's heart twisted. He'd never been able to withstand a lady's tears. As a child he couldn't bear it when his sister Isla wept. If one of his boyish pranks made her cry, he'd grovel and plead with her to forgive him, his stomach in knots until her tears dried.

That pain was nothing more than a shadow compared to this. Seeing Lucy cry made him feel as if his heart were being ripped from his chest. "Come here." His voice was gruff, but his big hands were careful as he pulled her into his arms.

"I just…I don't understand how my uncle could do this. I never imagined people could be so cruel, Ciaran." She was shuddering against him, her fingers curling into his coat as if she were holding onto him for dear life. "I always thought it was wrong of my father to hide away from the world, but now…perhaps he wasn't so mad, after all."

Ciaran gathered Lucy tighter against him. Mad, or sane—what did it matter if the Earl of Bellamy had been one, or the other? The man had loved his daughter, and Lucy had loved him. That was enough for Ciaran.

So, he said nothing, only wrapped a protective arm around her shoulders and guided her down the darkened hallway to the study. He seated her in a deep chair in front of the fire, then ducked out again. He hadn't summoned the butler, but like all his brother's servants, Travers was well trained. Ciaran asked that Lord Vale's carriage be sent back to Portman Square, and everything made ready for a journey into Buckinghamshire.

The sooner he and Lucy left Grosvenor Square behind them, the better.

Travers hurried off to see Ciaran's things packed and order the traveling coach, and Ciaran returned to the study. He'd had a bottle of sherry and glasses sent here earlier in the evening, and now he paused beside the desk to pour a measure for Lucy. He was turning away when he caught sight of something he hadn't noticed before.

It was a letter from his sister, Isla. She'd written him back at last.

He plucked up the letter and the glass, crossed the room, and handed them both to Lucy before sinking down into the chair across from hers.

"What's this?" Lucy sipped from her glass, frowning at the letter.

"It's from my sister. Read it."

Lucy turned the letter over in her hands, then shook her head and held it out to him. "No, Ciaran. It's not addressed to me, and you haven't even opened it."

"I already know what it says."

She hesitated, but when he didn't reach to take the letter back she shook her head and broke the wax seal. She read a few lines, then glanced up at him. "She begs your pardon for not writing back at once. She and her husband were in Kent, and have just returned."

"I thought so. Go on."

She looked down, and Ciaran watched as her gaze moved farther and farther down the page. It was a short letter—one side only in Isla's neat script—but its effect on Lucy was profound.

Her breath grew short, and she pressed one hand hard against her lips. When she reached the last line the letter fluttered from her slack fingers and drifted to the floor.

Her gaze met Ciaran's. "It's—it's about the first Countess of Godfrey."

"Alice Trentham."

Lucy's eyes widened. "You know about her?"

"I found out tonight. Lord Henley's country estate is in the same neighborhood as Godfrey's. Henley repeated the story to Vale, and Vale told me. That's why we came for you tonight, Lucy. I was worried."

Worried. No, he hadn't been worried. He'd been bloody terrified, panicked he'd be too late. That he'd arrive in Portman Square and find Jarvis and Godfrey had gotten there first, and taken Lucy away.

"She, ah...the Countess of Godfrey. She died very young." Lucy's hands were trembling.

"She did. Far too young. I won't let that happen to you, Lucy." Ciaran leaned forward and steadied her hands in his. "We'll go to Buckinghamshire and marry at my brother's estate the day after your birthday."

Lucy drew her hands away and rose unsteadily from the chair. Ciaran's gaze followed her as she wandered the room, and somehow, even before she said a word, he knew.

She's going to refuse me again.

When she turned to face him, her expression was bleak. "I'll go with you to Buckinghamshire, but I can't marry you, Ciaran."

"If you come to Buckinghamshire with me and we don't marry, your reputation will be ruined." Ciaran spoke through gritted teeth. He was holding onto his control by the thinnest thread.

Lucy shook her head. "I'm the Earl of Bellamy's daughter, Ciaran. My reputation was ruined long ago."

"Stop it, Lucy." Ciaran shot to his feet, his hands clenching into fists. "Stop saying that. You're *not* mad. You're smart, and sweet and funny, and beautiful—"

"Don't." She held up a trembling hand. "Don't make this harder for me. Please, Ciaran."

But Ciaran didn't stop. He couldn't. "I care about you, Lucy. You're the best friend I've ever had."

Lucy smiled faintly, but her dark eyes were sad. "People don't marry their best friends, Ciaran."

Her voice was soft, but it cut through him, puncturing his chest, slashing across his heart. He couldn't explain why it hurt so much, but her words silenced him at once. For long, aching moments they simply stood there, staring at each other across a deep, empty chasm—far deeper and emptier than anything Ciaran would have believed could open between them.

Lucy was the first to break the silence. "I—I'm tired."

He nodded, reaching to take her arm, but his hand dropped to his side before he touched her. He led her back toward the entryway, the dull thud of his shoes echoing in his head as they approached the door.

Travers was waiting for them there. "The coach is in the drive, sir."

"Thank you, Travers."

"I wish you a safe journey, sir." Travers bowed, and then Ciaran and Lucy were alone in the shadowed hallway.

Ciaran reached for the door, but before he could open it, Lucy stopped him with a hesitant touch on his arm. "Wait, Ciaran."

He turned to face her, but said nothing.

"Are you…" Her voice was shaking, and tears once again filled her eyes. "Are you angry with me?"

He *was* angry, but it wasn't the anger that was tearing him apart. The anger was only floating on the surface of something much deeper, and much more painful.

It felt like…heartbreak.

He drew a deep breath and shook his head. "No. I'm not angry." He opened the door, flinching as the cold night air sank sharp claws into his skin. "Come, Lucy. We can't stay here any longer."

* * * *

Ciaran took her to Cheapside, to a small, obscure inn called the Swan and Anchor.

It was a good choice for two people who wished to disappear. No one, least of all her uncle, would think to look for them here.

It was very late by the time they arrived, and Lucy was shivering, either from the cold or the shocking events of the evening. All she wanted was a bed to curl up in, and she was grateful when Ciaran made quick work of securing the rooms.

Or *room*, as it turned out. As in, one room. It appeared they were sharing.

"I'm sorry. I know it's awkward," Ciaran muttered, looking everywhere but at her. "I think we're safe enough, but I'd just as soon not leave you alone."

He looked so tortured Lucy found herself rushing across the bedchamber to reassure him. She touched his hand. "It's fine, Ciaran. We'll manage."

Ciaran glanced at her hand on his and cleared his throat. "I'll sleep there." He nodded toward a chair in the corner of the room.

Lucy stared at it for a moment, then turned back to Ciaran, taking him in from head to toe. It was a very small chair, and Ciaran was a very large man. "I don't think you'll fit."

Ciaran tensed under her gaze, and eased his hand away from hers. "It's just for one night, Lucy."

Lucy suspected it would prove to be an excruciatingly long one for him, but she didn't get a chance to say so before he turned to the door. "I'll just let you..." He waved a vague hand in her direction.

It took her a moment before she understood he was gesturing at her ball gown. "Change into my bedclothes?"

"Yes." Ciaran swallowed. "That."

Was he *blushing*? "Ciaran—"

He was gone before she could finish, scurrying out the door like a naughty schoolboy fleeing a caning.

Lucy stood in the middle of the room for a while after he left, staring blankly at the closed door. Why was he so nervous? Given the circumstances, shouldn't she be the skittish one?

Perhaps she was too exhausted to be skittish. So exhausted she wouldn't have bothered to change out of her clothes at all if she hadn't been wearing a ball gown. The puffed lace sleeves were itchy, the bodice too tight, and she didn't fancy being suffocated under layers of heavy satin once she fell asleep. It took her some time to wrestle her way out of the thing, but at last she was tucked into the bed, the coverlet pulled up to her neck in deference to her maidenly sensibilities.

Or to Ciaran's gentlemanly ones. He seemed to be far more agitated about her shift than she was.

Lucy closed her eyes, but they instantly popped open again.

Blast it. After all the drama of the evening she'd at last managed to find a bed, and now, of course, she was wide awake.

So, she lay there, staring at the ceiling, wondering where Ciaran had gone. Wondering, and wondering, and wondering...

The bedchamber was pitch dark before he returned. Lucy lay quietly, listening as he fumbled around the room. She heard a thud, and then another—Ciaran's boots dropping to the floor. The soft creak of the chair, and then...

Nothing.

Once a gentleman had removed his boots, weren't his breeches next? Was Ciaran sleeping in his breeches, then? What of his shirt? She hadn't heard even the faintest rustle of cloth that might hint at items of clothing being discarded.

He must be mostly dressed still, then. It couldn't be pleasant, sleeping in such tight breeches. Not that his breeches were any business of hers, of course. It was simply a matter of being concerned for his comfort.

"Are you quite comfortable, Ciaran?" Lucy winced at how loud her voice sounded in the quiet room.

There was a moment of frozen silence before Ciaran muttered, "Comfortable enough."

Lucy lay in the dark, biting her lip. "How can you be comfortable? You're stuffed into a chair two sizes too small for you."

Ciaran grunted, but didn't reply.

Lucy plucked at the coverlet. "May I bring you a blanket? I have more than I need here."

Ciaran groaned. "Go to sleep, Lucy."

Yes, that would probably be best, wouldn't it? Lucy obediently squeezed her eyes closed, but now the thought had occurred to her, she found she couldn't stop thinking about Ciaran's breeches. Why would he choose to sleep in them? Did he imagine she'd leap from the bed and ravish him if he dared remove them?

Lucy's eyes flew open.

I could leap from the bed and ravish him.

She sucked in a breath, half-scandalized, half-intrigued.

No, no. It was absurd. Where would she start? She hadn't any idea how to ravish a gentleman, and Ciaran wasn't acting at all like a man who *wanted* to be ravished.

Except...

Lucy pressed her fingers against her lips. Except there'd been that kiss, this evening in the carriage. A kiss that had left her breathless, aching. Ciaran had been the one to put an end to it, but he hadn't wanted to stop kissing her any more than she'd wanted to stop kissing him. Lucy didn't have any previous experience kissing gentlemen in dark carriages, but he'd seemed very much like a man struggling to subdue his passion.

He'd been just as desperate as she'd been, his panting breaths drifting over her skin. The memory of it made her shiver even as her body heated and warmth pooled between her legs. She pressed her thighs together and tried not to squirm, but all at once the bedchamber was too hot, the sheets too rough against her tingling skin.

Lucy smothered a whimper, and kicked one of the coverlets aside.

Ciaran stirred in the chair, but he remained silent.

That kiss had changed everything. The thing was, she was in *love* with Ciaran, so of course, she wanted him. Wherever a lady's heart led, her body followed. But if it hadn't been for that kiss, it never would have occurred to her Ciaran might want *her*. He didn't love her in a romantic sense, but a man experienced desire differently than a woman did. His friendship for her, his deep affection—perhaps they were enough to spark his passion.

Lucy turned over onto her side and rested her cheek against a cool spot on her pillow. She was under no illusions about all she'd chosen to give up when she'd made the decision not to marry. Physical love, desire, passion—she yearned for them as much as any other woman did.

Many women who didn't marry took lovers. She could do the same if she chose, but somehow, in the deepest part of her, Lucy knew she never would. For her, physical love would only ever be an expression of emotional love. She couldn't give her body without her heart, and she'd given her heart to Ciaran. Her love for him had been as inevitable as the waves rolling onto the beach in Brighton.

Inevitable, and final.

Now by a strange twist of fate, she was alone in a bedchamber with the man she adored, the man she wanted above all others, and there was nothing but her own fear stopping her from rising from this bed and taking him into her arms.

Lucy had never been one to succumb to fear.

She loved him, and she ached to give herself to him. Who would it hurt if she went to him now, took him by the hand, and brought him back to the bed? It would devastate her to lose him after sharing a night with him, but the only heart she'd be breaking was her own.

Lucy pushed the blankets aside and slid quietly from the bed. The floorboards were cold beneath her feet as she crossed the bedchamber. The room was so dark if it hadn't been for the fire Ciaran might not have noticed her coming toward him, but the glow of the flames caught at the hem of her fluttering white shift.

A sound fell from Ciaran's lips, a sound unlike any Lucy had ever heard him make before. A strangled breath, a gasp, and a groan all at once, ragged and desperate.

"Lucy." He rose, holding out his hands as if to stop her.

But Lucy wouldn't be stopped. One step, another, until she stood before him, her heart racing in her chest. Slowly, she reached for him, and twined her arms around his neck.

And waited while he decided whether to touch her, or push her away.

Chapter Twenty-one

As if in a dream, Ciaran raised his hand and brushed his fingertips over her cheek. It was a ghost of a touch, so soft he might have believed he'd imagined it but for the flush that rose to Lucy's skin in its wake.

Her skin slid like silk under his fingertips. Her dark gaze roamed his face, her rosy flush deepening as it settled on his mouth.

She's thinking of our kiss.

He was thinking of it, too. The incredible softness of her lips, the hitch of her breath when he'd stroked his tongue against hers, her warm fingers sifting gently through the hair at the back of his neck.

He hadn't meant to kiss her. He hadn't planned it. All the while his lips had been devouring hers he'd kept telling himself to stop, that they were friends only, and he had to release her.…

But he hadn't done it. He hadn't been able to let her go. Now they were alone in a quiet bedchamber, the fire crackling and a large, soft bed only a few paces away.

There was nothing to stop them—nothing but his honor, which was giving way to desire with every rasping breath into his lungs.

He had to get out of this room, *now*.

Ciaran dropped his hand and stepped away from her. He'd sit up all night in the hallway, or at the top of the stairwell—anything, anywhere—to keep himself from touching her.

She wasn't his. She would never be his. He had no right to take anything from her.

He cleared his throat. "I, ah…it's late, Lucy. You need to rest." He kissed her forehead, then set her away from him with unsteady hands. "Sleep well."

He'd already opened the bedchamber door when she caught his hand in hers.

"Don't go, Ciaran."

Ciaran closed his eyes as that soft, inviting voice brushed over him, firing his blood and igniting sparks over every inch of his skin. "I have to, sweetheart."

Lucy reached around him, still holding his hand, and eased the door closed. She took a step toward him, then another, until the hard wood met his back, and warm, soft, fragrant woman filled his arms. "No, you don't. You don't have to go anywhere, Ciaran."

He swallowed. "I—I should—"

"No, you shouldn't," she whispered, her lips right next to his ear. Her breath drifted over his heated skin, and then she was kissing him, those soft, red lips teasing gently across his jaw and down his neck.

He'd dreamed of her lips…

Ciaran never made a conscious decision to touch her. The moment her lips touched his skin, he couldn't think. He couldn't do anything but feel. Everything went hazy around him until there was only Lucy and her soft, coaxing kisses, the seductive slide of her fingers into his hair.

Someone groaned, low and breathless and desperate.

Him. It was him.

Lucy caught one end of his cravat. He arched his neck for her as she loosened it, the smooth fabric sliding across his throat as she tore it free. His head hit the back of the door, but he hardly noticed, he was so desperate to feel the maddening slide of her mouth against his bared throat.

Her kisses were sweet, hot, the lightest caress against his skin until he could stand her teasing no longer, and he took her lips hard. She opened for him at once, her tongue darting eagerly into his mouth to stroke against his. Ciaran kissed her and kissed her, until her lips were plump and swollen and the only sound in the room were her soft whimpers and their ragged, panting breaths.

"Is this what you want, Lucy?" He took her earlobe into his mouth, tickling it with his tongue before scoring it lightly with his teeth. She let out a soft cry, so he did it again, nibbling at her delicate flesh until she was shivering against him. "Do you want me?"

"Yes. Please, Ciaran." She slid her hands under his shirt, her fingernails grazing the skin of his back as she frantically tore the linen from his breeches.

Her tender scratch against his skin ripped an urgent moan from his throat. God, he couldn't get his clothes off quickly enough. He dragged his shirt over his head and tossed it aside.

"Oh," Lucy breathed, and Ciaran had to close his eyes against the hot tease of her breath drifting across his bare chest. Her soft sighs and whimpers made him wild, driving him right to the edge of his control. He wanted to drag his mouth over every inch of her, devour her.

Did she even know what it meant, to want a man? To have him? She'd been sheltered her whole life. If ever a woman was innocent, it was Lucy—

"Warm." She dragged her hands from the base of his throat down his chest, pausing to sift those maddening fingers through the smattering of dark hair. "I like this." She leaned forward and pressed her mouth where her fingers had been, her lips stroking the center of his chest.

"Ah." Ciaran sucked in a sharp breath, his head falling back. She was innocent, yes, but naturally passionate, a red-haired seductress in the making.

And now, at last, she was *his*.

"More, sweetheart. Kiss me there again."

Lucy looked up, her gaze finding his. What she saw there made her lips curve in a smile of such pure, feminine triumph he groaned again. He cupped the back of her head and gently urged her face toward his chest.

She didn't hesitate. Her warm mouth opened over his taut flesh, her lips and tongue kissing and teasing and nipping until Ciaran was writhing with mindless pleasure. He caught her hips in his hands, grasping handfuls of her shift, desperate for the feel of her bare curves against his palms. "Want to feel you."

She let out a low laugh. "Then take it off me."

God, where to begin? He was dying to touch her. He wanted all of her at once, yet there was one thing he'd thought about over and over again—one thing he had to have before they went any further.

"Keep still," he whispered as he raised his hands to her hair. His fingers found the first pin and he slid it loose. One by one he pulled the rest of the pins out, his breath catching as her wild red curls began to tumble free. Her hair was longer than he'd thought, nearly to her waist, a waterfall of burnished copper in the firelight. His breath came quicker as the thick tendrils fell like heavy silk into his hands. Once the pins were scattered across the floor and her hair lay loose over her shoulders he gathered handfuls of it and, groaning, brought it to his lips.

"Beautiful," he choked, burying his face in the fragrant waves. "Nothing could be more beautiful, Lucy."

"Nothing?" She gazed up at him shyly, her dark eyes shining.

He leaned down to drop a kiss onto the corner of her mouth. "Well, one thing, maybe."

"What?" She dragged her nails lightly down his chest, making him shiver.

Ciaran's heated gaze lingered on the smooth, creamy expanse of her neck, the curves of her breasts, the hint of the dark shadows of her nipples under the thin, white muslin shift. "Your hair against your bare skin."

A faint flush rose in her cheeks. Ciaran followed it with his fingers, laughing softly. "Is that a blush, Lucy?"

He reached down, his fingers curling into the hem of her shift. Lucy trembled as he dragged it up the long line of her body, inch by torturous inch. He sucked in a harsh breath when at last she stood bare before him.

"Lucy." He went still, staring down at her, all tormenting curves and flushed, creamy skin. "Look at you, sweetheart. So perfect."

Her breasts were full and lush, her hard nipples a tempting, rosy red. His gaze roamed over her, lingering on every curve, swell, and hollow. Her waist was slender, her hips rounded, her legs long, her skin like ivory silk.

Lucy's own gaze wandered over his bare chest and lower, taking in the flat plane of his stomach. "I've seen you bare once before, you know. Or nearly so."

A sly little smile crossed her lips, and Ciaran couldn't resist tilting her head back to take her mouth again, his tongue tracing the plump curves. "I don't recall ever stripping for you before," he teased, dragging his thumb over her lower lip.

"You didn't have to. The first day we met, on the beach in Brighton, you dove into the water in just a shirt and breeches, and…" Her cheeks went even pinker. "Well, white shirts are transparent when they're wet, you know."

"I do know. Did you look at me that day, Lucy?" Heat flared low in his belly at the thought of that dark gaze moving over him, secretly taking in the sight of his bare skin.

"Yes." It was a husky whisper, barely audible. "I'd never seen a man's body in such detail before. I remember thinking…"

"What did you think, sweetheart?"

"That I'd never known a man who looked like you. I never even realized a man *could* look like you. Your shoulders and chest, the ridges in your stomach." She reached for him, trailing her fingers over his lower belly. "I didn't see this, though." She was staring at his breeches, seemingly fascinated.

Ciaran bit back a groan. "See what, lass?"

"This." She traced a finger over the faint line of hair just visible at the top edge of his waistband.

Ciaran's lips parted, a small, hungry sound escaping.

Lucy raised her gaze to his face, and then, very slowly slid her fingertip under the edge of his breeches. "I think...I think the hair grows thicker lower down, doesn't it?"

"Yes." *And it wasn't the only thing growing thicker....*

Ciaran's cock was hardening, straining for the teasing touch of her finger. She'd never seen a man before, never mind an aroused man. He wondered if it would shock her, and for one fleeting moment he thought of drawing away from her.

But that's not what he did. Instead he brought her hand to one of the buttons of his falls, closing her fingers around it. He kept his hand over hers as she slid the button free, then dragged her hand across to the other button. "See for yourself."

His breath caught hard in his chest as she loosened the second button and his falls dropped open. He was painfully aroused, his cock hard and arching against his belly.

Lucy sucked in a quick breath, flushing as she stared down at him. She didn't look shocked. She looked amazed, and...

Eager.

It was too much for Ciaran. His cock twitched, and a drop of hot moisture rose to the tip. His knees went weak, and a tortured moan fell from his lips.

"Oh." Lucy darted a quick look at his face, taking in his flushed cheeks and parted lips.

And then...

Then, dear God, she touched him.

Ciaran's hips jerked forward as her soft fingers stroked over him, her touch too gentle to satisfy, but just enough to torment.

He groaned again, and she snatched her hand away. "Ciaran?"

"Like this, sweetheart." He took her hand in his, pressed it against himself and showed her how he liked to be stroked. When his hand dropped away she kept up his rhythm, her mouth opening in wonder as he grew hotter and harder against her palm.

"You, ah...you seem to enjoy this." Lucy's gaze darted between his face and her hand moving over him.

Ciaran let out a shaky laugh. "I do." He reached down and covered her hand with his again, but instead of drawing her away, his fingers tightened over hers. "Harder. Yes, just like...ah, God. *Lucy.*"

She was staring down at her hand as it moved over him, her breaths quick. He helped her stroke him once, then again, broken sounds tearing from his chest. Another stroke and he was going to release, spill into her hand—

"Stop, Lucy." He jerked away, shuddering. He tore his breeches down his legs, then caught her up into his arms, crossed to the bed, and lay her gently down in the center of it.

"Ciaran?" She levered herself up on her elbows, her anxious gaze finding his. "Did I hurt you?"

Was that what she thought? Ciaran drew in a deep breath. He only had one first time with Lucy, and he was rushing it, letting his desire for her turn him savage.

She deserved better than that. She deserved everything.

"No, sweetheart." He reached down to stroke her cheek. "I'm just…I want you so much I'm being greedy with you, trying to have everything at once."

"Oh." She gave him a hesitant smile. "I don't mind."

He let out a quiet laugh, then climbed onto the bed. He stretched onto his side, facing her. "Are you nervous, Lucy?"

She bit her lip. "Maybe a little."

Ciaran settled his hand on her hip, but he kept it still, though a part of him wanted to explore every one of her tempting curves. He lay quietly with her, stroking his hand over her shoulders and neck, down the center of her body to rest on her stomach. He touched her this way for a long time, easy and unhurried, until he felt her relax, her limbs going heavy against the coverlet.

Then, he kissed her. Her lips, her neck, the pulse fluttering at the base of her throat. He was gentle with her, careful, building her passion slowly with light strokes of his tongue over her satiny skin. Lucy lay quietly at first, but as he continued to tease her, her body grew restless.

She wrapped her arms around his neck, squirming closer, pressing her hips to his.

"Not yet, sweetheart." Ciaran stilled her with gentle hands, keeping her pinned to the bed as he nuzzled his face into the soft skin between her breasts. Lucy let out a quiet whimper when his tongue darted out to taste her. He cupped one of her breasts in his palm and teased his thumb over her hard nipple.

"*Ciaran*." Lucy's body jerked a little at the caress, and she slid her fingers into his hair.

Ciaran dragged his thumb over her sensitive nipple again, and then again, his breath held. He waited until she was writhing against him, pushing herself harder against his hand.

Then…then he did what he'd been aching to do.

He closed his mouth over the tip of her breast and sucked.

"*Oh.*" Lucy's body arched sharply, her fingers pulling hard at his hair as he licked and teased, abrading the tender peak before he moved to her other breast, sucking and nipping until the straining tip was wet under his tongue.

When he finally drew back his heart was pounding in his chest, each of his breaths strangled and desperate. He stared down at her with heavy-lidded eyes.

She dragged her fingernails across the sensitive skin of his belly, her dark eyes burning. "More, Ciaran."

He couldn't deny that sensual command. "What do you want, sweetheart?" He traced lazy circles over her lower belly, drawing ever closer to the sweet tuft of soft red hair between her thighs with every stroke.

She cradled his face in her hands, dragged his mouth to hers, and murmured against his lips, "You. I want you. All of you." She wrapped her fingers around his wrist and moved his hand lower until each of his strokes grazed her inner thigh.

Ciaran groaned as his cock gave a desperate surge. He let his knuckle slide over the sweet spot between her legs, another tormented groan breaking from his lips when he felt how wet she was. He lowered his face to her breasts and took a nipple back into his mouth as he sank one finger inside her. He worked her slowly, sliding over her slippery center, teasing and stroking until she was pleading, her breath hot in his ear.

He pushed gently against the insides of her thighs. "Open for me, sweetheart."

Her legs fell open, her back arching. Soft whimpers fell from her lips. "Ciaran, please."

"Do you ache for me, Lucy? Right here?" He dragged his body over hers, nudging her legs wider with a twist of his hips. He reached down to take himself in hand and teased the head of his cock against the wet heat between her silky thighs.

They both sucked in a breath. Lucy's fingernails scored his back, and a soft hiss left Ciaran's lips. He hovered over her, dipping his head down to take her mouth while he moved carefully between her legs. "I want you so much, Lucy."

Her hand settled on his cheek and she turned his face to hers. "I want you, too."

He kissed her palm, but held back a few moments more, thrusting gently against her until she grew more used to the rhythm of his body between her legs.

Then, with one quick, powerful surge, he was inside her.

Lucy gasped. Ciaran froze, every nerve in his body screaming with tension as he held himself perfectly still. Lucy was panting under him, her body rigid. "Ah, sweetheart. I'm sorry." He leaned over her, murmuring soothing words as he dropped gentle kisses against her hair, her cheeks, her throat, her lips.

Gradually her breathing steadied, and her body relaxed beneath his. "I'm all right." She caressed his cheek, her mouth opening in wonder as she shifted a little beneath him, accustoming herself to the feel of him inside her. After a few moments she arched against him, a hesitant thrust, and wrapped her legs around his hips.

"Ah God, Lucy." He threw his head back, gritting his teeth against the pleasure. He was already on the jagged edge of release, ready to spill inside her, but he held back, his neck stiff with strain as he moved in slow, restrained thrusts until Lucy's breaths grew ragged, and she was lifting herself against him with every nudge of his hips.

"Ciaran." His name disintegrated into a desperate moan on her lips. "I—I need…"

He gave her what she needed, his hips plunging as he thrust harder and faster into her, urged on by her choked cries in his ears. A groan tore loose as his climax slid closer, the base of his spine tingling, tightening, his vision blurring as he held off his release, waiting for her.

"Come for me, Lucy," he growled, his teeth grazing her neck. He reached between her legs and stroked his fingers over her. One stroke, two, and that was all it took before she was gasping, her body tightening around him as she fell over the edge into trembling, moaning bliss.

Ciaran was right behind her, his back bowing, her name an incoherent plea on his lips as he shuddered over her, his cock jerking as he spilled himself inside her.

Afterward he held her tightly against him, dazed, both of their bodies slick with sweat. He gazed down at her, brushing strands of damp hair away from her face. "I've never…it's never been like that before."

Because he'd never cared for anyone before.

Not in the way he cared for her. With all of himself, with everything inside him.

She touched his cheek, bringing his mouth down to hers. Then she kissed him so softly, so sweetly he was certain his heart was going to burst from his chest.

Ciaran didn't remember falling asleep. He remembered rolling onto his side and gathering her against him. He remembered tucking her head under his chin, and the scent of her hair. He remembered the feel of her slender back pressed against his chest, and her soft, contented sigh before he drifted off, his arms wrapped around Lucy.

Chapter Twenty-two

Ciaran had never given much thought to ladies' undergarments before. Not until the following morning when he woke up and discovered Lucy's shift was the single most seductive article of clothing he'd ever seen.

He'd taken great care to wrap her up in it before he'd fallen asleep in the early morning hours, easing it gently over her head and smoothing it down her legs until it hid every hollow and curve that had driven him to madness the night before.

As it turned out, the thin linen didn't hide a bloody thing. Not the arch of her neck, the long, tempting line of her legs, the gentle swell of her hips and breasts, the sweet shape of her nipples, or the tantalizing shadow between her thighs.

Ciaran rolled onto his back on the bed and threw an arm over his eyes. Flimsy, worthless bit of cloth.

Fine, then. He simply wouldn't look. If he didn't look at her he wouldn't be tempted to touch her again. He was a gentleman, after all, not an animal, and a gentleman didn't trifle with a lady who hadn't yet agreed to marry him.

He certainly didn't do it *twice*.

But then a lady didn't invite a man to her bed unless she intended to marry him, and that meant Lucy had come to her senses at last.

He could wait until they were married to touch her again. It wasn't as if he were some green lad who couldn't control himself. Lucy wasn't the first woman he'd ever had in his bed. He'd tasted smooth, creamy skin before. He'd worshipped every arc and dip and warm, scented valley of a woman's body with his hands, his lips, and his tongue before. This was no different.

She was no different—

He let out a low, tortured groan and rolled onto his side. He propped his head on one hand and gazed down at her. Lucy was splayed out on her back, her lips parted, her hair spilling in a wild red ocean across the pillow. The useless shift had slipped down her shoulder, leaving flushed, naked skin exposed to his heated gaze.

God, how he wanted to kiss that bared neck, run his tongue over that perfect skin, teasing and licking and nipping until her eyelids fluttered open with a moan.

Ciaran squeezed his eyes closed. The truth was she could have been wearing dozens of shifts, one layered on top of the next, and it wouldn't make a damn bit of difference. He'd still want her.

Ache for her. Burn for her...

There was a faint rustle of fabric, soft sheets sliding against his skin. Warm legs wrapped around his, and fingertips dragged down his bare chest. "Ciaran?"

Ciaran opened his eyes to find Lucy gazing up at him, a sleepy smile curving her red lips.

That was all it took. Her smile hit him right in the center of his chest, hurtled into his lower belly, then exploded between his legs like a lightning bolt. He reached for her, groaning when she tumbled willingly into his arms.

Her lips, her skin, her palm stroking over his chest and belly, her breathless murmurs in his ears—everything about Lucy was warm and welcoming and alive. She came to him eagerly, teasing him with soft touches and light brushes of her lips and fingers until he arched and writhed for her.

Ciaran lost himself in her then. His world went fuzzy at the edges until all he knew, all he was, was Lucy. The swells of her breasts in his palms, the hard peaks of her nipples against his fingertips and tongue, her legs tangled with his, her hands tight his hair, the sinuous twist of her body against his.

The taste of her.

God, the sweet taste of her, the slide of her silky skin like cream against his tongue.

When he couldn't stand the torment a moment longer he cupped the curves of her hips in his hands and slid her body on top of his. She gasped when he found her hot center with his fingers, her head falling back as he circled and petted her there until her desire flooded his palm.

A hoarse groan escaped his lips when he surged upward, sinking into the warm, tight embrace of her body. She wrapped her legs around his hips and twined her arms around his neck so every part of her held him. He thought, fleetingly, that it had always been this way with Lucy. She'd been holding him tightly against her from the beginning, and she'd never stopped.

Then Lucy cried out, her lips on his as the pleasure took them, and for long, delirious moments, he didn't think at all.

Afterward, she fell against his chest, her body limp and sated, and he buried his face in her neck, dazed. As his breathing calmed his limbs went liquid, his body melting against hers. He could have stayed like that all day, his parted lips pressed against her throat as they both drifted off to sleep, but it was a full day's drive to his family's country estate in Buckinghamshire.

They'd have plenty of time to linger in bed once they were married.

A sleepy smile drifted over his lips at the thought, and he gathered Lucy closer. "You're not falling asleep, are you?" He teased his mouth over the damp curls at her temple. "Did I wear you out?"

"Shhh." Lucy's eyes were closed, a contented smile on her lips. "Go to sleep."

Ciaran chuckled, stroking his hand down the silky length of her spine. "I swore to myself I wouldn't bother you with my attentions again this morning."

Lucy smiled, opening one sleepy eye. "Do I look bothered to you, Ciaran?"

Ciaran grinned back at her and dropped a kiss behind her ear. "Well, no, but a proper gentleman would have had the decency to wait."

She opened the other eye and gazed at him, suddenly wary. "What do you mean? Wait for what?"

Something in her tone made Ciaran stiffen. "It's obvious, isn't it? Wait until we marry."

An awful silence fell, and then she was struggling out of his arms. "We've been through this already, Ciaran. I told you I can't marry you."

Ciaran sat up, every vestige of sleep dissolving at her words. "I know what you told me, Lucy, but that was before."

"Before what?" A faint flush rose in her cheeks, but otherwise her face gave nothing away.

"Before *what?*" He gestured between them, then waved a hand over the tangled coverlet, the rumpled sheets. "Before *this.*"

Lucy took in the evidence of their passion with cool, dark eyes. "This doesn't change anything."

He stared at her, his skin going cold. "It changes bloody *everything.* Jesus, Lucy. Last night, you...I would never...do you think I would have come to your bed if I didn't believe you'd changed your mind about marrying me? Do you think I'm the sort of man who'd steal a lady's innocence and then abandon her? I'm not a villain."

She was quiet for a moment, her dark eyes unreadable. Then she asked, "Is that why you came to my bed? To lure me into marrying you?"

Lure? Hurt and anger swelled in Ciaran's chest, but he sucked in a quick breath to calm himself. He must be misunderstanding her, because he couldn't believe his Lucy could really be accusing him of trying to manipulate her into marriage.

No, something was wrong. That bland expression on her face was too practiced, too careful. There was something else going on here. She was hiding something from him.

"I took you to my bed for one reason, Lucy." He took her hand and gently laced his fingers with hers. "Because I wanted you. I still want you, and I think you want me, too."

"I do. I—I did. I can hardly deny that while we're still lying in bed together."

She let out a little laugh, but there was something hard and raw about it, and the sound tore at Ciaran's chest. Did she *want* to deny it? He shook his head, a strange, dark foreboding curling into a tight ball inside his chest. "I don't understand what's happening here."

Lucy's face softened. She gripped his hand hard, her fingers curling into his palm. "What happened is we made love, and it was…it was special, Ciaran, but I haven't changed my mind about marriage." Her voice cracked a little, and her gaze dropped to their joined hands. "You haven't changed yours, either. Your future is in Scotland. I gave myself to you because I wanted you. You didn't steal anything from me, and I won't steal your future from you."

He shook his head to try and make sense of his chaotic thoughts. He tried to grasp them, to catch them on his fingertips and line them up in the proper order, but his mind and his heart were in turmoil.

How could she think she was stealing anything from him?

She hadn't stolen a thing.

She'd *given* him something. Something that felt like…everything.

"You're not taking anything away from me. How can you think that? Don't you see? I *want* to marry you. My God, Lucy, you're my dearest friend."

He wanted to take her into his arms then, to explain, to make her understand what he was trying to say—to make *both* of them understand— but she recoiled from his touch. Ciaran froze, his heart rushing into his throat. She'd never done that before—never shrunk away from him as if she couldn't bear for him to touch her.

"And you're mine, but I told you last night, Ciaran. Best friends don't marry each other."

The words cut through Ciaran. Hurt and anger poured from the wound, drowning him in pain and ugliness. "They do if one of them has ruined the other."

Lucy heard the coldness in his voice and she went still. "Is that what you think happened last night, Ciaran? That you ruined me?"

"It doesn't make a damn bit of difference what I think. You've fled your uncle's protection, Lucy. Everyone will assume I've ruined you." A harsh laugh fell from Ciaran's lips. "And they'll be right, won't they?"

An angry flush darkened Lucy's face, and she grabbed at the tangle of blankets and dragged them up to her chin. "Still trying to save me, Ciaran? Ever the hero. This is no different than the prizefight, or that morning on the beach, is it?"

"No! That isn't what this is about. I—it's…" Ciaran dragged a hand through his hair. What was it about? God, he didn't know. He wasn't sure of anything anymore. "You're my *friend*, Lucy. I could never hurt you."

Ciaran saw at once, without understanding that this had been the wrong thing to say. Lucy flinched at his words, her grip on the blankets going so tight her knuckles went white. "I never needed you to save me. I didn't need it then, and I don't need it now."

He leapt from the bed, suddenly so furious he couldn't stay still a moment longer. He snatched up his breeches and tugged them over his hips, not bothering to fasten his falls. "I warned you this would happen. That morning on the beach, I told you men and women couldn't be friends, and damned if I wasn't right all along."

She glared at him over the edge of the coverlet. "No, you weren't! You said a man can't be friends with a woman without someone shrieking at him to marry her. Well, the only one shrieking about marriage here is *you*."

Ciaran threw his hands up in the air, at his wit's end. "Christ, you're stubborn! You were a stubborn friend, and you're an even more stubborn lover."

"I'm not being stubborn. I'm trying to…" She broke off on a sharp breath. When she spoke again, she was nearly pleading. "You think you want to marry me now, but marriage isn't a holiday in Brighton, Ciaran, or an afternoon at Brighton Racetrack. It isn't a few hours this time, or a few weeks. It's your entire life. You don't understand what you're promising."

"No, Lucy. It's *you* who doesn't understand. I know exactly what it means to promise a woman my entire life."

Lucy stiffened. "I—I don't understand what you mean."

Ciaran hesitated. He'd never once mentioned his former betrothed to Lucy. Never once breathed her name, but the words were there now, waiting to be spoken. "I made that promise once before, when I became betrothed to Isobel Campbell."

It wasn't until Ciaran heard himself say Isobel's name aloud that he understood he *wanted* to tell Lucy about her—had wanted it for some time.

Isobel Campbell. His childhood friend, and the lady he was meant to marry. The lady who'd abandoned him when he needed her most. Ciaran went still, bracing himself for a painful wave of memories from his past. Memories of another lifetime, of a love and a promise he'd thought would last forever.

They never came.

He'd been drowning in those memories since the day he left Scotland. They'd rolled and tossed him, left him spluttering, gasping, and choking, a broken bit of wreckage on the sand. But now, when he thought of love, of promises, of lifetimes, he didn't think of Isobel. He didn't see Isobel's face. He saw moonlight on damp red hair, and long, dark eyelashes tipped with glittering drops of water.

He saw Lucy.

He hadn't said anything about Isobel to Lucy because...

Because Isobel no longer mattered to him.

Isobel no longer mattered.

The lady he thought he'd loved beyond measure. The lady who'd hurt him in a way he'd believed he'd never recover from. The lady who'd broken his heart.

Isobel was a part of a painful past, but she had nothing to do with his future. He hadn't thought of her in weeks. No, *months*. Since he'd first set eyes on Lucy, she'd dominated his every thought, his every action.

Lucy was staring at him in shocked silence.

"Lucy." Ciaran held his hand out instinctively, as if he could stop her from drawing the conclusion she was clearly already drawing.

"You...you were *betrothed*?" All at once Lucy's face drained of color, until it was as white as the bedsheet still clutched in her hand. "It's the Scottish lady you told me about that morning on the beach, isn't it? The first lady you ever kissed? The lady you've dreamed of marrying since you were a boy?"

Her face went from white to red, then back to such a stark white Ciaran felt a stab of fear in his chest. "Yes, it's her, but it's been over between us for some time."

Lucy just stared at him, her eyes wide with disbelief.

Ciaran sank down on the edge of the bed. "It ended when my family left Scotland. She jilted me, and I haven't seen or spoken to her since."

Lucy swallowed. "H—how long were you betrothed to her?"

Ciaran winced at the question, knowing his answer would only make things worse. "Three years. I was hardly more than a lad when I offered for her, and our families insisted on a long betrothal."

"Three years." Lucy sounded dazed. "You've known this lady your entire life, and you were betrothed to her for three years. All this time you've been insisting on marrying me, you never once thought to mention her?"

"I wasn't trying to hide her, Lucy. I swear it. I just—she doesn't matter anymore."

"She doesn't matter?" Lucy repeated, as if she couldn't make sense of the words. "I think she matters very much. You must have loved her, or you never would have asked for her hand. I think you still love her, Ciaran. If I'd known about her, I never would have..." She trailed off, but the look she cast at the disheveled bed revealed her thoughts more clearly than words.

If I'd known, I never would have brought you to my bed.

Ciaran dragged a hand down his face. How could he make Lucy understand it had never been about Isobel, when he'd only just realized it himself? "I was besotted with her at one time, yes, but it was a boy's infatuation, not a man's love. We've been apart for more than a year, ever since I left Scotland. I don't love her anymore. This isn't about Isobel, Lucy. I thought it was, but I was wrong."

Lucy let out an incredulous laugh. "Ciaran, don't you see? She's the reason you're so determined to return to Scotland. She broke your heart, and now you're going back for her. It's the only thing that makes sense."

"No! I don't want Isobel back. I thought I did at one time, but...don't you see, Lucy? My past, and Scotland, and Isobel are all tangled together in my mind. I didn't understand it at first, but I was never heartbroken over her. I just...I miss Scotland. I wanted to go back because I wanted my home again."

Except Scotland *wasn't* his home. Not anymore.

It hadn't been for a long time. His family was here—Finn, Lachlan, Isla, baby Georgie, even Lady Chase.

His home was with them. With them, and with Lucy.

"Lucy, please listen to me." He reached for her, surprised to see his hands were shaking. "I've made a mess of this from the start, but I want to fix it. You have to let me—"

"I—I think it's best if I don't go to Buckinghamshire with you, Ciaran," she whispered, drawing away from him.

Ciaran's heart stopped. "No. Don't say that."

She wouldn't meet his eyes. "I'll stay here at the Swan and Anchor until Lord Vale has settled things with Eloisa. Once I know she and my aunt are safe, I'll return to Devon."

"Lucy, please listen to me——"

"Once I'm gone, you'll be free to return to Scotland, and—"

"No!" Ciaran's voice was hoarse with panic. "I don't want—"

He was interrupted by a sharp knock on the door, and the muffled sound of a servant's voice on the other side. "Mr. Ramsey? Lord Vale is here to see you."

Ciaran's gaze didn't leave Lucy's face. "Ask him to wait."

The servant paused, then said, "His lordship says it's urgent."

Lucy tugged her hands free of his. "Go, Ciaran. He might have news about Eloisa and my aunt."

Ciaran hesitated, but then rose to his feet and pulled on some clothes. His knees were shaking. When he reached the door he turned back, his pleading gaze falling on Lucy. "I'll go, but I'll return soon. We're not done with this discussion, Lucy."

She nodded, but the look on her face...

Ciaran thought he might indeed be done, whether he wanted to be or not.

Chapter Twenty-three

Anyone looking at Augustus Jarvis's face would believe him to be a man whose carefully laid plans were falling into ruin right before his eyes.

He cradled his throbbing head in his hands. He'd been so deep in his cups the night before he couldn't quite recall what had happened, but one thing was certain. He'd left the card room at the Weatherby ball four-hundred and nine pounds poorer than he'd been when he entered it, and Godfrey had his vowels to prove it.

It hadn't been a fruitful evening at the tables, but whatever twinge he'd felt at losing a few pounds was nothing compared to the hammering pain in his skull this morning.

Lord Godfrey was stalking back and forth in front of the fireplace, every inch of him quivering with fury. "Call that chit down here at once, Jarvis, and force her to explain herself!"

No need for Godfrey to name which chit he meant. His lordship only ever became this agitated over one chit.

Jarvis's niece, Lady Lucinda Sutcliffe.

A termagant of the first degree. She'd seemed biddable enough at the start, but after that business in Brighton Jarvis had decided Lady Lucinda was a vixen sent straight from hell to torment him.

Vixens must be dealt with. Lady Lucinda certainly would be, but Jarvis had to survive this encounter with Godfrey first.

"Wake up, damn you!" Godfrey's fist slammed down onto the desk in front of Jarvis, making him jump. Papers flew in every direction, tradesmen's bills fluttering to the floor at Jarvis's feet.

It seemed a bad omen, that.

Godfrey's livid face was mere inches from Jarvis's own, so close Jarvis could smell his lordship's hot, fetid breath. His stomach heaved as the bottle of port he'd drunk the night before threatened to reappear, but he managed to gag it back down before it spurted from his mouth and splattered onto the desk between them.

"Now, my lord, I'm certain it's nothing more than a rumor." Jarvis wiped his sweaty forehead with his handkerchief and offered Godfrey a weak smile. "I can't believe my niece would disgrace herself in such a manner, and you know how the *ton* loves their gossip."

Lord Godfrey's eyes narrowed to angry slits. "I warned you once before, Jarvis. I won't be made a fool of. Not by you, and not by some uppity little chit like Lady Lucinda. I won't take a whore as my wife." Godfrey reached into the pocket of his coat, pulled out a piece of paper and shoved it into Jarvis's face.

It was the special license Godfrey had procured at Doctors Commons the day before. Jarvis watched, eyes narrowed, as Godfrey marched over to the fireplace and dangled the paper over the flames.

Jarvis heaved himself up from his chair, but he didn't approach Godfrey, and he made no effort to snatch the paper from Godfrey's hand. "Now, now, my lord. You're being much too hasty. I'm sure it's nothing more than a misunderstanding. Lady Lucinda is, er…a trifle spirited, but she's not a wanton."

Not as far as Godfrey knew, anyway.

"I'll be the judge of that," Godfrey spat. "I can assure you I don't intend to take Ciaran Ramsey's leavings. For your sake, I hope I find Lady Lucinda's explanation satisfactory."

"I've no doubt of it, my lord." The lie slid easily enough from Jarvis's lips, and it did seem to appease his lordship.

For now.

Whether he'd remain so was less certain. Ramsey had been chasing Lucinda for weeks, and if the gossips could be believed, he'd finally caught her. In Jarvis's carriage, no less, outside the Weatherby ball last night. Lady Essex had seen the debauchery with her own eyes, and hadn't hesitated to share it with all of London.

Jarvis's hand was shaking as he pulled the bell for a servant, his voice not quite steady as he instructed a housemaid to fetch Lady Lucinda from her bedchamber and bring her to his study without a moment's delay.

But there *was* a delay, and it was a long one. The minutes ticked by, one after the other, and no one appeared. Godfrey was growing twitchier by the second, and the bile was rising once again, a hot, burning trickle at the back of Jarvis's throat.

Until at last, the door cracked open.

Jarvis leapt forward, a shout already on his lips. "How dare you keep his lordship waiting so long, Lucinda? Come in here at once, and explain—"

When he saw who was on the other side of the door, the words died in his throat.

It wasn't Lucinda who entered the study. It was Eloisa, and with her was Jarvis's wife, Harriet, clutching Eloisa's arm.

"My lord." Eloisa offered Godfrey a brief curtsy, then turned to face her father. "Good morning, Father."

"What the devil do you two want?" Jarvis wheeled around the side of the desk. "Go back up at once and fetch your cousin. I sent for Lucinda."

"She's not here." Eloisa's gaze met his, her chin high.

For a moment Jarvis was too stunned to speak. Not *here*? It was eight o'clock in the morning! Either Lucinda had fled her bed before sunrise, or...

Jarvis's brain gave a sluggish twitch as, very slowly, a suspicion wormed its way through the alcohol haze in his head. If Lucinda wasn't here, then she likely hadn't spent the night in her bed. If she hadn't spent the night in her bed, it was fair to assume she'd fled his protection.

Jarvis eyed his daughter. Yes, Lucinda had fled. He could see the truth in Eloisa's face, in the strange glitter of her blue eyes.

Now he thought of it, it wasn't surprising, really. Anyone could see Lucinda was smitten with Ramsey. Yet Jarvis *was* surprised, all the same, and not at all pleasantly. Up until now everything had gone just as he'd predicted, but he hadn't anticipated this turn of events.

Godfrey didn't say a word, but from the corner of his eye Jarvis saw his lordship's hand clench, the special license crumpling in his fist.

Again, not surprising, but Jarvis was prepared to rage and bluster as though it were. He grabbed Eloisa's shoulders. "What do you mean, she's not here? You will tell me at once where she is, or else—"

"No, I won't tell you." Eloisa's chin shot higher. "And you won't find her."

"Search the house," Jarvis barked, and the servant fled.

"You may send as many servants as you like scurrying over every corner of this house, Father, but it won't do you any good. Lucy's not here, and she hasn't been for hours."

Eloisa didn't say anything more, but her meaning was plain. Lucinda had spent the night somewhere else.

Or, more to the point, *with* someone else.

That was more than enough for Godfrey. "It seems you've lost control of your niece, Jarvis. Pity. She would have made a lovely countess." Before Jarvis could utter a word of protest, Lord Godfrey leaned over, and with one quick flick of his wrist, tossed the license into the fire. When he turned to face Jarvis, his face was hard. "You'll do me the honor of calling on me later today, won't you? I believe we have business to discuss."

Then he was gone, and with him all of Jarvis's plans to get himself out from under Godfrey's thumb lay in tatters at his feet.

Or so it appeared to Lord Godfrey.

Jarvis drew a shaking hand over his damp brow. Good Christ, he'd thought the man would never leave. Now he had, Jarvis was ready to get some answers.

He turned his icy gaze on his wife and daughter. He took several menacing steps toward Harriet, who could be relied upon to crumble like dust between his fingers the moment he started squeezing her. She blanched as he drew closer, but Eloisa darted between them, her eyes flashing. "Don't touch her!"

"You presume to issue orders to *me*?" Jarvis snatched his daughter's arm and clamped down on it until the soft flesh collapsed under the pressure of his fingers.

His wife let out a cry and clawed at his hand. "Stop, Augustus!"

But Jarvis didn't stop. He shoved his wife aside and turned his attention back to Eloisa. "Now, my dear child. Let's try this again, shall we? Where the devil has your cousin gone?"

Eloisa was silent, fear, defiance, and triumph in her eyes.

Jarvis's fingers tightened. "Speak, girl!"

Eloisa flinched, but not a single word passed her lips.

Jarvis stared down at her, his eyes bulging with shock. It had never occurred to him Eloisa would defy him. She'd never done so before.

"Very well, then." He wrenched his daughter toward the door with a twist of her arm and dragged her from the study into the hallway. His wife scrambled after them up the stairs, her shrieks growing louder with every step. Several servants paused to watch, open-mouthed, but none dared interfere.

Jarvis didn't stop until he reached a door at the end of a long hallway on the third floor, in the servants' quarters of the house. "Get in," he hissed. He shoved Eloisa into the bedchamber with enough force to make her stumble before grabbing his wife and shoving her in after. "Don't bloody move, either of you. You'll stay here until you tell me where Lucinda is."

He didn't give either of them a chance to reply, but slammed the door closed and, just for good measure, locked it behind him.

He hurried back down the stairs to his study, closed and locked that door as well, and went straight to the sideboard. His hands were shaking so badly the first glass slid from his fingers and fell to the floor, but he managed to get the port into a second glass. He downed it with one swallow, filled it again, then grabbed the bottle and crossed the room to throw himself into the chair behind his desk.

He had to *think*.

He was halfway through his third glass of port before he realized there was nothing to think about. Until Eloisa became hungry or thirsty enough to tell him where Lucinda was hiding, there wasn't anything he *could* do. Worse, he didn't have much time. Godfrey was going to call in the debt this afternoon. Jarvis didn't have the money, and without Lucinda he hadn't a prayer of getting that much blunt in one go.

Nearly six thousand pounds, at last count.

Too much to steal from Lucinda's trust. A pound or two here and there could be explained easily enough, but Chancery tended to frown on guardians snatching thousands of pounds from their wards. No, the only hope he had of paying the debt was to seize permanent control of Lucinda's fortune, and for that he needed to get his hands on Lucinda.

Trouble was, London was a big city, and he hadn't any bloody idea where to look for her. His first thought was Grosvenor Square, but he discarded it at once. Ramsey's brother was some high-in-the-instep marquess with a fancy house on Grosvenor Street, but Jarvis knew well enough Ramsey wouldn't take Lucinda there.

Ramsey wasn't, alas, a fool. He'd guess that would be the first place Jarvis would look for her. The first and the last, because after Grosvenor Square, he hadn't the vaguest idea where they might be. They could have gone anywhere. If Eloisa was to be believed, Lucinda had been missing the entire night. That was more than enough time for Ramsey to have taken her out of the city.

Even if they were still here, Jarvis didn't have time to chase his niece down every filthy alley in London. Godfrey was waiting, and he wasn't a patient man.

Or a merciful one.

That left Jarvis with one choice only. A quick retreat from London.

He muttered a vile curse and dropped his head into his hands, overwhelmed with self-pity. How had it come to this? He'd planned the thing so carefully, fit each piece into the next with such deftness he'd impressed even himself.

Now here he was, on the verge of leaving London with a vengeful earl and dozens of infuriated London tradesmen on his heels.

How could it all have gone so wrong, so quickly? Less than twelve hours ago he'd been at the Weatherby ball, satisfaction curling through him as Godfrey led Lucinda through three dances while all of fashionable London watched. He'd been so certain it was the beginning of the end for his troublesome niece, but he hadn't anticipated she'd run. He'd expected another Eloisa, and instead he'd gotten a red-haired demon with an iron will and a rebellious streak wider than the Thames.

She was the wiliest, slipperiest chit he'd ever come across. No doubt she intended to remain hidden until her twenty-first birthday. Then she'd marry Ramsey, and take her sixty thousand pounds with her.

As for Jarvis, well…it was looking more and more like he'd be fleeing to the Continent with the bitter knowledge he'd been outmaneuvered by a devious slip of a girl with a sharp tongue and a mad father.

He reached for the bell and stood staring moodily out the window until Harley, the hired butler, appeared. He offered Jarvis a bow, then stood silently, waiting for instructions.

"My family and I are leaving London sooner than expected. Ready the carriage, send a maid to attend to our baggage, and make preparations to close the house."

The man stared. "You mean to leave *today*?"

"I mean to leave well before teatime. Don't stand about gaping, man! Do as I say. Oh, and we're not at home to any visitors. Don't even answer the door. I don't care who it is." Godfrey might turn up again, and the last thing Jarvis wanted was another confrontation with his lordship.

Harley looked as if he wished to say more, but he pressed his lips together and bowed stiffly. After he left there was nothing for Jarvis to do but sit and wait, and finish the rest of his bottle of port.

It never occurred to him to release his wife and daughter from their prison, nor did it cross his mind to inform them they'd be leaving London within a matter of hours. Indeed, he'd have completely forgotten about them both if something unexpected hadn't occurred to remind him of their existence.

There was a knock on the door.

Jarvis's first thought was it was Lord Godfrey, come early to collect his debt. He stumbled to his feet and peered out the window, but the awkward angle only permitted a glimpse of their visitor. He could see it wasn't Godfrey—and thank God for it—but he couldn't tell who it was.

Harley appeared in the study doorway and cleared his throat.

"Who is it?" Jarvis whirled around, nearly losing his balance. "What do they want?"

"It's Lord Vale, sir. I imagine he's here to call on Miss Jarvis."

Jarvis stared blankly at the man. Eloisa? Why the devil would a young, wealthy aristocrat like Lord Vale want to call on Eloisa? Damned if he knew, but whatever it was Vale was after, he was impatient enough to get it. A second dull thud sounded from the front door, this one louder and more insistent.

Jarvis flinched. It didn't sound as if he was going to go away without speaking to someone. "Damn the man. Go on then, Harley, and tell Vale Eloisa isn't—"

Jarvis broke off. He wasn't any cleverer a man than he was a kind one, but even the dullest brain enjoys an occasional flash of illumination.

Vale and Ramsey were friends—as thick as two bloody thieves. A man couldn't lay eyes on one of them without being obliged to look at the other. If anyone in London knew where Ramsey had gone, it would be Vale.

Wasn't there a chance, slim though it might be, that Vale would go straight to wherever Ramsey and Lucinda were hiding once he left here? Mightn't it be worth sending him on his way, and then following him?

"Sir?" Harley was still waiting.

He'd need the carriage. That was the first consideration.

"Sir?" A faint note of impatience had crept into Harley's voice. "Shall I fetch Miss Jarvis?"

The carriage, perhaps a blanket or two, and a bottle of his wife's laudanum—

"Do you wish me to admit Lord Vale, sir, or do you intend to permit him to break the door down?"

Jarvis jerked his attention back to Harley. "Is the carriage ready, Harley?"

Harley blinked. "I believe so. I instructed the groom to ready it."

Jarvis rubbed his hands together as a new plan began to take shape in his head. "Wait until I've gone, then you may answer the door. Tell Lord Vale Miss Jarvis has left London, and won't be returning."

"Left London, sir?"

Jarvis could see by the way Harley's brow lowered he didn't at all care for these instructions. Unfortunately for Harley, Jarvis didn't give a damn whether he cared for them or not. "Impertinent fellow! You heard me. Now do as I say at once."

Harley didn't move. "May I assume, sir, whatever journey you intend to undertake will include Mrs. and Miss Jarvis?"

"Yes, yes. That is, not just yet. I, er...I just recalled I need to make a brief trip to Maidstone. I'll return to London to fetch my family as soon as that business is concluded." Though if things went as he hoped they would, there'd be no need to flee London, after all. "Now, mind what I said. Don't open the door to Lord Vale until I'm out of sight."

Harley didn't look pleased, but Jarvis didn't give him a chance to refuse. After one final peek through the window, he flew from the study down the hallway to the staircase. He went up, grabbed a coverlet and the brown bottle on the small table beside his wife's bed, then lumbered back down the stairs to the kitchen and into the mews behind the house.

Lord Vale's equipage was standing at the curb on the opposite end of the mews. Jarvis instructed his own coachman to wait until his lordship regained his carriage, then to follow him without delay.

They didn't have to wait long. Lord Vale came rushing out less than ten minutes later, looking even less pleased than Harley had. He called something to his coachman, then leapt into his carriage as if his breeches were on fire. The coachman wasted no time, but flew off down the road at such a speed the carriage wheels skidded across the stones.

Jarvis held his breath as they followed Lord Vale's carriage through the streets of London. Once or twice they were delayed in the heavy tangle of conveyances on the road and lost sight of Vale, but each time Jarvis's heart began to fail, they managed to catch him again.

The chase continued until at last Lord Vale's carriage came to a halt. Jarvis peered out the carriage window to find they'd stopped in an obscure London street in Cheapside, in front of an indifferent looking inn called the Swan and Anchor.

Once again Jarvis's heart failed him. What the devil would they be doing *here*? Why would Ramsey have brought Lucinda to some shabby little inn in Cheapside?

Lord Vale seemed to know exactly what he was doing here, however. He leapt from the carriage, rushed up the stone steps to the door, and disappeared into the interior of the inn.

Now Vale was out of sight, there was nothing for Jarvis to do but wait here in the carriage and hope Vale would come back out with Ramsey in tow. Jarvis had left just enough confusion behind him to tempt Vale to bring Ramsey to Portman Square to set everything to rights.

It was the sort of thing they'd do. The sort of thing tiresome heroic types always did.

But if they did leave the inn, mightn't they take Lucinda with them? Jarvis hadn't a prayer of snatching her away if Ramsey and Vale were hanging about. If she slipped through his fingers now, he wouldn't get another chance at her. If he made a muck of this, his only other option would be to leave London at once.

Leave England.

Jarvis perched on the edge of his seat with his breath held, peering out the carriage window. He fixed his anxious gaze on the door, a curse falling from his lips. There was no sign of either Vale or Ramsey.

Jarvis was wasting what little time he had.

If the thing were to be done, it had to be done now. He couldn't linger here all day and wait for Vale and Ramsey to leave the inn. He'd have to make his move now, and hope for the best. Fortunately for Jarvis, he knew just what he needed to do to coax Lucinda outside.

"Bexley!" Jarvis rapped on the roof of the carriage until the coachman slid down from the box and appeared at the window. "Go inside and find Lady Lucinda. Do what you must to get her alone, then tell her Miss Jarvis is outside in the carriage. Say her cousin must speak to her on a matter of grave importance, and urge Lady Lucinda to come out at once."

The coachman, who was a man of few words and even fewer scruples, nodded and turned away to do his master's bidding.

Before he'd gone a step, Jarvis called him back. "Lord Vale and Mr. Ramsey are inside. Take care neither of them sees you. There's a reward in it for you if you manage the thing discreetly, Bexley."

Bexley gave him another nod, then disappeared into the inn.

Cautious hope surged through Jarvis. Or perhaps it wasn't hope, but something darker. Jarvis didn't trouble himself much over it one way or another. He had one bothersome chit locked in a bedchamber at Portman Square and the other soon to be on her way to Kent, from whence she wouldn't return. The whole thing was proving to be almost too easy.

Jarvis's one regret was he wouldn't be there to see Ramsey's face when he found Lucinda was gone.

Chapter Twenty-four

Ciaran had been gone longer than Lucy had expected he would be. Either that, or she'd become such a fool over Ciaran Ramsey, every moment without him now felt like an eternity.

I'm not the sort of lady who falls in love....

She'd actually told him that, hadn't she? Even more astounding, she'd truly believed at the time it was the truth. Now, looking back, Lucy was amazed she could have known herself so little, been so deceived about her own nature.

She *was* the sort of lady who fell in love. Worse, she was the sort of lady who fell deeply, helplessly, and irrevocably in love, and as humiliating as it was, it seemed she could do this without it being at all a requirement the object of her affections love her back.

That is, Ciaran *did* love her. She knew he did, but as he'd reminded her on many occasions, his love was the love of one friend for another. It wasn't a romantic love, or a love one built a life upon. It wasn't a love that dwelt in every corner of his heart.

It wasn't the sort of love Ciaran had felt—and likely *still* felt—for his former betrothed, Isobel Campbell. Ciaran was as much a victim of his heart as Lucy was. It might be over between him and Isobel, but he must be still in love with her, whether he realized it or not.

Lucy fell across the bed with a sigh, then leapt up again. She retreated to a chair on the other side of the room, as far away from the bed as she could get. Even then, she couldn't stop staring at it. Staring, and remembering what had happened there.

Twice. Last night, and then again this morning. Goodness, what a wanton she was!

That was another thing she hadn't known about herself. Lucy shifted a little, squirming on her chair. Her body was alive with dozens of unfamiliar twinges and aches, each one more delicious than the last. She flushed as she recalled all the places Ciaran had touched her with his hands, his fingers....

His mouth.

He'd given her so much last night. Pleasure, tenderness, that playfulness that was his alone. Then afterward, he'd held her in his arms, so closely his warmth became her own. To wake up every morning that way, with his arms wrapped around her, the gentle fall of his breath against her neck...

Tears burned behind Lucy's eyes, but she squeezed them shut before any could fall. She didn't want Ciaran to find her red-eyed and sniffling when he returned. It would hurt him to see it, and one broken heart between the two of them was enough.

She owed him that much, at least.

How could she have taken everything Ciaran offered her last night without sparing a single thought for tomorrow? How selfish she was, how thoughtless! She hadn't been thinking of Ciaran at all. She'd simply wanted him for herself, and so she'd taken him, knowing he didn't belong to her. That he'd never belong to her.

She *knew* him—far too well to persuade herself he would have succumbed to her awkward advances last night if he'd known she still didn't intend to marry him. Even now she could hardly believe she'd succeeded in seducing him. She'd touched and kissed him and he...he...

Well, he'd touched and kissed her *back.*

She could marry Ciaran, just as he'd asked her to. She could return to Buckinghamshire and become his wife, and even then, he'd still never really be hers. No matter how much she wanted him, she couldn't steal his chance at a love that took his breath away—a love that lived in every corner of his heart.

Before they'd become lovers, they'd been friends. What kind of friend would she be if she snatched his freedom away from him? Not the kind of friend Lucy had always promised herself she'd be.

No kind of friend at all.

She had to convince him a marriage between them would be a mistake—that she only loved him in the way a friend loved another friend. As much as it would hurt her, she had to try and persuade him she'd rejected his proposals because she didn't care about him enough to marry him.

Not because she cared too much.

The idea of *that* discussion made her want to dive into the bed and pull the coverlet over her head. But she was no coward. As soon as he returned she'd say what she had to say, and pray he'd listen to her this time.

If he ever *did* return. Why hadn't he returned?

He'd said he'd be back soon. In Lucy's opinion "soon" meant in less than half an hour. She wasn't quite sure how long he'd been gone, but it had been long enough for her to bathe, drink a cup of tea, take a few nibbles of toast and dress herself.

Lucy paced around the room for a while, then forced herself to resume her seat in the chair. He'd promised he'd return soon, and she trusted him. For once in her life she was going to do just as she'd been told, and wait patiently.

Five minutes passed, then another five, then Lucy was up from her chair again, pacing from one end of the room to the other. Perhaps she'd just slip out—just for a tiny moment, mind you—just to see if any of the servants happened to know where Ciaran had gone. She wouldn't venture beyond the hallway outside the bedchamber.

Except there wasn't anyone in the hallway. It was deserted. She'd dismissed the maid Ciaran had sent to attend her, and the girl had promptly vanished.

Very well, then. She'd go just to the top of the staircase. No farther than that. Someone must be stirring on the floor below. She'd call to them, ask her question, then return to her room at once.

But when she got to the top of the stairs, she didn't see anyone below. There was no sign of either Ciaran or Lord Vale anywhere.

Well, there was no help for it, then. She hurried back to her bedchamber, snatched up her cloak, and ran back into the hallway. She didn't intend to go far, of course—no, indeed—but if Lord Vale was still here his carriage would be in the drive. It wouldn't do any harm to creep down to the ground floor and have a peek outside the window.

Right, then. She'd just tiptoe down another flight of stairs, and have a bit of a look around the innyard. It wouldn't do to venture any further than that, though. She'd promised Ciaran she'd stay—

"Begging yer pardon, miss." The maid who'd attended her earlier was coming up the stairs.

Lucy paused on the landing. "Yes?"

"I've a message fer ye."

At last, a word from Ciaran! "Yes? What is it?"

"A lady who says as she's your cousin is in the yard in her carriage, waiting to speak to you. She says it's important, like, and ye must come at once."

Lucy's heart dropped right into her stomach.

What was Eloisa doing outside the Swan and Anchor in Uncle Jarvis's carriage? ? It didn't make sense. How had Eloisa managed to escape Portman Square, and with the carriage, no less? It would have taken a near-miraculous stroke of luck. Uncle Jarvis would never have permitted her to leave the house.

Had something happened to her uncle then, or God forbid, her aunt? Had something happened with Lord Vale? Lucy had hoped Eloisa and Lord Vale would have peacefully concluded their tumultuous courtship with a happy betrothal by now, but perhaps they'd quarreled and Eloisa had followed Lord Vale here.

One thing was certain. If Eloisa was here, then something must be wrong. All at once Ciaran's prolonged absence took on a more sinister cast. Ciaran was missing, and Lord Vale with him, and Eloisa had suddenly appeared at the Swan and Anchor....

Lucy gathered her skirts, flew past the maid and down the stairs to the front door, her heart racing. As soon as she stepped outside, she saw it. Her uncle's carriage, and perched on the box, her uncle's coachman. She hurried down the steps and without any hesitation darted across the yard.

She was out of breath by the time she reached the carriage. She snatched the door open without a second thought, and—

"Oh!" Lucy let out a faint cry as someone inside the carriage grabbed her arm in a merciless grip and hauled her roughly into it with one vicious tug.

It wasn't Eloisa.

Lucy scrambled instinctively for the door, ready to leap out and fly back across the yard, but before she could so much as twitch a heavy arm wrapped around her neck, and a low, threatening voice muttered in her ear. "Not happy to see me, niece? I'm certainly happy to see you."

Lucy's blood went cold.

No. It couldn't be her Uncle Jarvis. He hadn't any idea where she was, and no reason at all to look for her *here*, of all places. He couldn't have found her. No, it couldn't be him. This couldn't be happening—

"What a pity you're not pleased to be back in my company. I'm afraid you've no choice but to tolerate me, however, because we're going on a bit of a journey together, you and I."

A panicked gasp left Lucy's lips and she struggled in earnest to get loose. She clawed at the arm pressed to her neck, her fingers digging into flesh until she felt a smear of blood against her fingertips. Uncle Jarvis dropped his arm, cursing, and for one breathless moment, she was free. She kicked out wildly and made another leap for the door. She managed to tear it open, but by then carriage was already moving.

Her uncle had her now, and he had no intention of letting her go. "No, no. Can't have that, can we? You could get hurt." He reached across her and slammed the carriage door closed. He wrapped his arm around her throat again, pressing hard enough to make it difficult for her to breathe. He shoved his hand over her face, pressed his palm against her nose and held it there until her head began to go fuzzy.

Lucy opened her mouth with a gasp, desperate for air, but as she sucked in a breath she felt something cold against her lips. She instinctively jerked her face away, but her uncle grabbed her hair with his other hand and held her still. "Open your mouth, damn you."

He squeezed until her mouth opened. She expected the sharp, bitter flavor of laudanum, but the liquid that rolled over her tongue was sweet, with a hint of elderflower.

Dr. Digby's Calming Tonic.

"There. That'll keep you quiet for a bit."

His voice rang with triumph, and Lucy understood at once her uncle didn't realize it wasn't laudanum in the bottle. Thinking quickly, she forced her limbs to go lax. Uncle Jarvis loosened his grip and she let her body slump against the carriage seat, seemingly lifeless.

Her uncle thought he'd dosed her, and Lucy intended to keep it that way.

She was trapped in a carriage with a man who wished her ill—a man who would stop at nothing to get his hands on her fortune. There was no telling how long it would take before Ciaran discovered she was gone. Once he did, he wouldn't have the first idea how to find her. After their argument this morning he might even believe she'd left him, and gone off to Devon alone. Would he even come after her? Or would he consider himself well rid of such a troublesome friend, and leave for Scotland and Isobel Campbell?

A chill rushed over Lucy as the gravity of her situation sank in. Her one advantage was her uncle mistakenly believed he'd rendered her insensible.

It wasn't much, but it was all she had.

* * * *

"Something's wrong, Ramsey." Vale met Ciaran's gaze across the inn's small back parlor. "Something's terribly wrong."

Ciaran paused at the threshold, his shoulders sagging. Yes, something was bloody wrong, all right. He'd just left Lucy alone in the bedchamber where they'd made passionate love not half an hour earlier, looking so miserable his heart hurt to think about it.

He'd left his dearest friend confused, angry, and unhappy.

And ruined. Mustn't forget ruined. Of all the terrible consequences of last night's loss of control, that was by far the worst. Why wouldn't she listen to him? He had to find a way to persuade her to marry him. He refused to be the man who ruined his best friend and then left her, alone and unprotected—

"Ramsey!" Vale's voice was sharp. "Are you listening to me? Something's *wrong*, I tell you. I've just been to Eloisa's and the servant told me she's left London!"

Ciaran's head jerked up. For the first time since he'd entered the room he focused on Vale, and good Lord, his friend looked an utter mess. His coat was rumpled, his cravat askew, and his hair was standing up in every direction, as if he'd been clutching it in his hands.

"That's impossible." Ciaran strode into the room and steadied Vale with a hand on his shoulder. "She was in Portman Square just last night, Vale. She can't have disappeared from London so quickly."

Vale shrugged off Ciaran's hand and began to pace, too agitated to remain still. "She could if that disaster of a father of hers decided to disappear her. I don't put it past him to have shoved both Eloisa and Mrs. Jarvis into a carriage and sent them to God only knows where."

Ciaran couldn't help but agree. He hadn't the faintest doubt the scoundrel would do whatever was in his own best interests, his family be damned. "Was Jarvis there?"

"I don't know. I didn't see him, or anyone else aside from the servant. It looked as if—" Vale broke off, his frantic gaze meeting Ciaran's. "It looked as if the servants were closing the house, Ramsey. As if the entire family really had left London."

Ciaran dropped into a chair and braced his hands on his knees as he considered the possibilities. "If Jarvis has left London, there can be only one reason for it. Godfrey's found out Lucy's fled her uncle's protection. He's told Jarvis there will be no marriage, and he's after Jarvis to settle his debt."

Vale let out a bitter laugh. "Jarvis is a bloody fool. He won't escape the debt that way. Godfrey's the sort who'll chase him to the edges of England for a single shilling."

Ciaran didn't argue that point. He'd never come across a greedier man than Godfrey. "True enough, but it's a good way for Jarvis to escape the London tradesmen he owes, and it gives him some time to think about what to do about Godfrey."

"Do? What can he do? It's a debt of honor. He's obliged to pay it, unless he takes the coward's way out, and…" Vale had been pacing again, but now he froze, his face going pale.

"Flees to the Continent," Ciaran finished grimly.

Vale stared at Ciaran, horrified. "He'll take Eloisa with him if he does. He'll drag her off, and I'll never see her again. I can't bear to stand about helplessly while she's left at the mercy of Jarvis's sinister schemes. I can't lose her, Ramsey."

The anguish in Vale's voice, the torment…

Ciaran understood it. He recognized it as the same anguish he'd felt when Lucy had been at Jarvis's mercy. It was unbearable. He'd have done anything, gone anywhere he needed to go to keep her safe.

To the edges of England, and beyond.

"Enough of this. I'm going after them."

Vale turned on his heel and was halfway out the door before Ciaran caught him, stopping him with a hand on his arm. "Vale, wait. We can't be sure where they've gone, or even *if* they've gone. Jarvis's servant might be lying for him."

"We have to find her, Ramsey. I'm in—" Vale's voice broke. "I'm in love with her. I won't lose her."

Ciaran's chest went tight. It did Vale credit that he'd fallen in love with a lady like Eloisa Jarvis. She would be the making of him.

If they found her.

"You won't lose her. I promise you that, Vale, but it won't do any good to go rushing off in whatever direction strikes your fancy. Just give me a moment to think."

Vale didn't argue, but he paced and sighed in an agony of impatience while Ciaran tried to sort out what was best to do. The truth was, neither he nor Vale had the faintest idea where Jarvis had gone. He might be on his way back to his home in Berkshire, or, if he truly did intend to flee England he'd be headed in the opposite direction, toward Dover. This was provided he'd actually left London at all.

"We need to return to Portman Square and question the servants before we do anything else," Ciaran said. "You can depend on it, the servants know what Jarvis is about."

Vale shook his head. "I already tried that, Ramsey. The fellow who answered the door was as tight-lipped as they come. I couldn't squeeze a single word out of him."

"They're hired servants, Vale, and you can be sure Jarvis hasn't paid them a farthing for their service. The man will find his tongue once we make it clear they'll get their wages from us, not Jarvis."

Vale blew out a breath, then wheeled around toward the door. "Yes, all right. That makes sense. Come on, then."

Once again Ciaran stopped him. "Wait, Vale."

"Damn it, Ramsey! What now?"

"Where's Lady Felicia? If you're obliged to chase after Miss Jarvis, what becomes of your sister?"

To Ciaran's surprise, a slight smile rose to Vale's lips. "There's no need to worry about Felicia. Markham is taking her back to Lewes this afternoon. I don't want her tangled up in this mess, and her season is over in any case. Markham offered for her again last night, and this time Felicia accepted him."

"Ah. Markham finally came to his senses, did he?"

Vale waved a hand in the air. "Markham's been in love with Felicia for years now. He simply didn't know it, the fool. Why do you suppose I dragged him to London for Felicia's season? I knew he'd come to his senses as soon as some other gentleman tried to take her away from him."

Ciaran shook his head. "Poor Nash."

Vale shrugged. "Eh, Nash will recover. He isn't in love with Felicia. He wants Miss Fisher. He has since the season started."

"Miss Fisher?" Ciaran stared at him. "Good Lord, Vale. You seem to know a great deal about who's in love with whom."

"I'm more observant than you think, Ramsey." Vale gave him a considering look. "Speaking of love, where is Lady Lucinda?"

Unfamiliar heat rose in Ciaran's cheeks. "She's, ah...she's upstairs in her bedchamber."

Ciaran was careful to say *her* bedchamber rather than *our* bedchamber, but he could see by Vale's raised eyebrow his friend guessed the truth. Fortunately for Ciaran, Vale was too distracted at the moment to press him. He simply nodded, then asked, "Will you go up and tell her you're going out?"

Ciaran hesitated. The moment he stepped into the bedchamber Lucy would read his expression, and she'd know at once something was wrong. "She'll want to come with us, but it will only worry her if she has any inkling her cousin's in danger. There's a chance Jarvis is at Portman Square still, as well. Lucy's much safer staying here."

"Alone? I don't think that's a good idea, Ramsey."

Damn it. Ciaran didn't like the idea of Lucy being anywhere near Jarvis, but he liked the idea of leaving her here alone even less. "You're right. I'll go fetch her. Go to the carriage, Vale, and wait for us there, will you?"

"Yes, but hurry, Ramsey."

Ciaran took the stairs two at a time. When he reached their bedchamber he threw open the door with such force it crashed into the wall behind it. "Lucy? Lucy!"

No answer.

He ventured further into the room. The bed was made, the coverlet neatly drawn up. The fire had burned down to embers in the grate. A breakfast tray stood on a low table, with the meal mostly untouched.

Ciaran's footsteps echoed in the empty room. "Lucy?"

Silence, so loud his ears rang with it.

The bedchamber was deserted.

Lucy was gone.

Chapter Twenty-five

Every servant Ciaran questioned had noticed the redheaded lady.

One of the upper housemaids was sure she'd seen her coming down the staircase. A footman thought she'd been in the entryway. Another was certain she'd seen her standing on the second-floor landing.

They'd all seen her, yet not one of them could tell Ciaran where she'd gone. One moment she'd been there, and the next she'd disappeared.

He ran into the innyard and found Vale standing beside his carriage, impatiently tapping his walking stick against his boot. When he saw Ciaran he started forward, but then he caught sight of the expression on Ciaran's face and stopped. "Ramsey? What's happened?"

"I—I can't find Lucy. She's missing."

The color drained from Vale's face. "Missing? Eloisa and Lucy, both missing? Jesus, Ramsey. Did you question the servants?"

"A half-dozen servants, dozens of questions, and not one useful piece of information. No one saw her leave the inn, but she must have, Vale." Ciaran dragged a hand down his face, his gaze darting up and down the street in front of him.

That was when he saw it.

The color caught his eye first. Bright green silk peeking out of a limp bundle of dark gray wool, lying in the middle of the innyard.

Ciaran darted across the yard, only narrowly avoiding a collision with a heavy wagon.

"Ramsey, what the devil?" Vale shouted, following on his heels. "Are you trying to get yourself killed?"

"Look, Vale." Ciaran caught up the cloak and stood in a daze, gazing down at the bundle of dusty fabric in his hands. "It's Lucy's. She must have left the inn and come out into the yard."

Then she'd disappeared.

Ciaran clutched the cloak to his chest. "He took her, Vale. Jarvis. Snatched her right out of the yard and shoved her into his carriage. It's the only explanation for why her cloak would be lying out here in the dirt."

Except, was it really the only explanation? Lucy might have left him and gone off to Devon alone—

No. Lucy would never have done that. She wouldn't leave London without knowing her aunt and cousin were safe.

She wouldn't leave him.

Not like this. He was as sure of that as he was of the sun rising tomorrow morning.

"How could Jarvis have found her, Ramsey? He couldn't have simply stumbled across the Swan and Anchor. Only Eloisa and I know where you—"

Vale broke off and met Ciaran's gaze. Ciaran saw his own panic reflected in his friend's eyes, and knew they were both thinking the same thing. Jarvis had threatened his own daughter. He'd made Eloisa tell him where Lucy was, and then he'd come after her.

Now Eloisa and Lucy had both vanished.

Icy fear filled Ciaran's heart, but only for a moment before it exploded in shuddering, trembling, burning rage. His jaw went tight, and his hands fisted. If Jarvis laid a finger on Lucy, touched even a single hair on her head, he'd spend the rest of his life answering to Ciaran for it.

But first he had to find them.

"Portman Square, Ramsey," Vale said through gritted teeth. "Portman Square, and if I have to I'll shake the truth out of the servants."

Within minutes they were in Vale's carriage and on their way to Portman Square. Ciaran's stomach twisted tighter and tighter with every agonizing mile. The carriage was still rolling into the drive when he leapt from it and flew toward the front door, with Vale right behind him.

The house was dark and silent, but nothing could have stopped either of them from pounding on the front door.

Or, if that failed, knocking it down.

As it happened, force turned out to be unnecessary. Vale's fist hardly had a chance to touch the wood before the door flew open. On the other side stood Eloisa Jarvis, her hair disheveled and her eyes wild.

"Eloisa," Vale whispered, stunned. "I thought…God, I was terrified you'd been—"

"Sebastian! Thank goodness." Eloisa grasped his arm and tugged him into the entryway. Ciaran followed, and she slammed and locked the door behind him. "I heard the carriage, and I was afraid you were my father."

Vale glanced at Ciaran, his expression troubled. "Your father isn't here, then?"

"No." Mrs. Jarvis stepped forward, darting a glance behind her as if she were afraid Jarvis would leap from the shadows. "He left in the carriage a while ago."

Ciaran's heart sank like a stone in his chest. "Lucy?" he asked, his voice hoarse. "Is Lucy here?"

But he already knew the answer. As soon as he'd walked into the bedchamber at the inn and heard the dull thud of his footsteps in the empty room, a part of him knew Jarvis had found her—that he'd taken her. But knowing it was one thing. Hearing Mrs. Jarvis say it aloud was another.

Mrs. Jarvis stared at him, her face going white. "No. I thought…isn't Lucy with you?"

For one helpless moment, Ciaran let his head drop into his hands. How could he have let this happen? He should have known Jarvis would find a way to track her. Now she was gone, and Ciaran felt as if his chest had been hollowed out—as if a hand had plunged inside him and ripped out his heart.

Mrs. Jarvis was trembling with shock, and Ciaran caught her arm to steady her. It took every bit of his control, but his voice was calm when he asked, "Did Mr. Jarvis tell you where he was going?"

"He didn't even say he *was* going, much less where." Eloisa Jarvis let out a bitter laugh. She wasn't at all unsteady. Her blue eyes were flashing with fury. "We weren't in a position to ask him, since he locked us in a bedchamber at the top of the house before he left."

"Eloisa," Mrs. Jarvis began, but then she fell silent again, her lips tight. Even she was in no humor to defend her husband.

Vale's face had turned an ominous shade of red, but when he spoke, his voice was soft, controlled. "Your father *locked you up*?"

Ciaran darted a glance at Vale, alarm bleeding through his panic. Vale didn't often lose his temper, but when he did, he didn't rage or shout. Instead, he went oddly quiet. It was a lucky thing Jarvis wasn't here, because Vale looked ready to tear the man limb from limb.

"Easy, Vale."

Ciaran reached out to lay a restraining hand on Vale's shoulder, but Eloisa Jarvis was already there, speaking in soft, soothing tones to Vale. She cupped his cheeks, cradling his face and whispering to him until gradually Vale's hectic breaths began to slow. The rigid line of his shoulders relaxed, and his forehead met hers.

Mrs. Jarvis gasped softly, shocked to see her daughter on such intimate terms with the Earl of Vale. After a moment, though, her arm relaxed beneath Ciaran's fingers, and a tentative smile rose to her lips.

Ciaran left the lovers to their tender moment for as long as he could before clearing his throat. He was happy for Vale, but right now he could think of nothing but Lucy. Jarvis had her, and he was taking her God-knew-where. What if he abandoned her on a remote country road somewhere? Or took her to a place Ciaran would never find her?

What if he *hurt* her?

"Do you have any idea at all where your father's gone, Miss Jarvis?" Fear made Ciaran's voice harsher than he'd intended, and he forced himself to take a deep breath. "Forgive me, but we have to find him."

Eloisa Jarvis looked stricken. "Oh, I don't know! By the time we got out of the bedchamber he was already gone."

"How much time has passed since you escaped?" The situation was growing worse with every moment, and Ciaran's chest was pulling tighter and tighter.

"I—I'm not sure, but perhaps two hours? Our first thought was to go to Sebastian and Lady Felicia in Hanover Square, but then we discovered my father had left in the carriage." Eloisa raised her face to Vale's. "We were just trying to decide what to do when you and Mr. Ramsey appeared."

Vale brushed Eloisa's hair gently back from her face. "How did you manage to get free from the bedchamber?"

"Did a servant let you out?" Whatever servant had freed them was the one most likely to reveal what they knew about Jarvis's whereabouts. But Eloisa shook her head, and Ciaran's heart sank even lower.

"No." She flushed, and held up her hand. She was clutching a hair pin between her fingers. "I picked the lock."

Vale blinked. "You know how to pick a lock, Eloisa?"

Eloisa blushed. "Lucy showed me how to do it. She's, ah...very good at that sort of thing. She picked the lock on my father's desk."

Of course, she had, because it was just the sort of thing Lucy would know how to do. For the first time since they'd arrived at Portman Square, hope swept over Ciaran. Lucy was, without question, the most capable woman he'd ever known.

I never needed you to save me, Ciaran.

It was the truth. Lucy had always known how to save herself. It wouldn't stop him from going after her, because nothing in the world could stop him from that, but that didn't change who she was.

How special she was.

Intriguing, kind, passionate, beautiful...

Yes, she was all those things, and so many others as well.

She was everything.

He thought of her, with her stubborn chin and those dark eyes that had held him spellbound since he'd first looked into them all those weeks ago, and something in his chest unfurled its wings and soared into sudden, glorious life.

He swallowed.

His heart. It was his heart.

The truth swept over him then—soft, like a breath from parted lips.

He was in love with her. He was in love with Lucy.

Madly so. Not friendly love, but passionate, delirious, weak-kneed love. The sort of love he'd never felt before, never imagined he *could* feel. The sort of love where nothing would ever be right again if her face wasn't the first thing he saw when he woke, and the last before he fell asleep.

Those mornings they'd sat together on the beach, when he'd told her his secrets and listened to hers in return. His first night in London, when he'd walked into Lady Ivey's ballroom and found her again. Their kiss in the carriage, the trembling of her lips against his...

All that time he'd been falling, falling, falling deeper with every day that passed.

How could he not have seen it? He'd fallen in love with Lucy without ever realizing it.

When he'd held her last night, it hadn't been just his arms wrapped around her.

It had been his heart.

That was what he should have told her this morning. He'd talked of marriage, friendship, stubbornness, obligation, but he'd never breathed a single word about love. God, it was unbearable she could be out there somewhere without knowing how much he loved her. Unbearable to spend another moment without her in his arms.

"How long ago did Mr. Jarvis leave the house?"

"A little more than an hour ago," Mrs. Jarvis replied. "The bedchamber he locked us in looks down on the mews. I saw him leave."

"An hour ago?" Vale frowned. He pulled his pocket watch free, consulted it, then met Ciaran's gaze. "I was here an hour ago, Ramsey. I should have crossed paths with him."

"You *did* cross paths, but you didn't realize it."

The voice came from the far end of the hallway. All of them turned toward it and watched as a man made his way to them. "Mr. Jarvis was here when you arrived, my lord."

Vale stared at the man. "You're the servant who answered the door."

"Harley, my lord. The butler." The man bowed. "Mr. Jarvis was here all morning. He ordered me to answer the door and tell you the family had left London and didn't intend to return."

Eloisa gasped.

"He told you to lie, you mean." Vale had gone eerily quiet again, and he took a menacing step toward Harley. "You were ordered to lie, and you did exactly as you were told."

Harley didn't flinch. "I did, my lord, and I beg your pardon for it. I… didn't like to do it, and I've come now to help if I can."

Ciaran was struggling with his own anger, but giving into it wouldn't do Lucy any good, and she was all that mattered. "Good man," he said, stepping between Vale and the butler. "What else can you tell us? How did Jarvis know how to find Lady Lucinda? She was safely tucked up at an obscure inn in Cheapside. He wouldn't have thought to look for her there."

Harley turned a wary look on Vale. "My lord, you didn't happen to go to this inn after you left here this morning?"

"I did, yes. Why would that—"

"Mr. Jarvis followed you. He thought you'd lead him to Lady Lucinda, and I'm afraid he was right."

Ciaran froze. It was a far cleverer plan than he would have thought Jarvis capable of. Lucy had warned him Jarvis was dim enough in general, but had an uncanny ability to secure his own interests.

The best way for Jarvis to save his skin was to marry Lucy to Lord Godfrey. Ciaran had assumed Godfrey would beg off the marriage when he discovered Lucy had placed herself under Ciaran's protection, but he'd never known a more avaricious man than Godfrey. Wasn't there a chance he'd made up his mind to overlook it to gain Lucy's fortune?

Even now, Jarvis could be delivering Lucy into Godfrey's hands.

A fear unlike any he'd ever known before lodged in Ciaran's throat. For one awful moment he couldn't think, couldn't breathe. "Do you know where Jarvis has gone?"

"Yes, sir. He went to Kent. He said he'd forgotten he had business in Maidstone."

"Maidstone?" Ciaran turned to Eloisa and Mrs. Jarvis, but they looked as baffled as he was. What kind of business could Jarvis have in Maidstone? Of course, he could have lied to the butler, or the butler could be lying to them, but Ciaran's instincts told him the man was telling the truth.

If Jarvis was traveling into Kent, he could be headed for Dover as easily as Maidstone, but it seemed unlikely, given he'd left his wife and daughter behind. If he wasn't fleeing to the Continent via Dover, then he must have some other reason for heading south to Maidstone.

"Mr. Ramsey." Ciaran felt a slight tug on his coat sleeve and looked down to find Mrs. Jarvis at his elbow, her face gray. "Please, I—I'm worried about Lucinda. Lord Godfrey was here this morning, and he...my husband sent for Lucinda to wait on him, but she wasn't...Lord Godfrey got angry, and my husband was even angrier, and I'm afraid he'll take it out on Lucinda."

Ciaran couldn't make much sense of this incoherent ramble, but he took Mrs. Jarvis's hand and patted it. "I won't let your husband hurt Lucy. I promise you, Mrs. Jarvis."

"You mustn't let him take her!" Mrs. Jarvis managed, before she burst into tears.

"Please, Sebastian." Eloisa clutched at Vale's coat. "You must go after them! There's no telling what my father will do if he—"

"No." Ciaran met Vale's gaze. "Take Mrs. and Miss Jarvis to Hanover Square, Vale, and stay there with them. I'll go after Lucy."

A horse—it would be faster than a carriage. Jarvis had more than two hours start on him, but if he rode hard, he'd catch them. He had to.

Because if he didn't...if he didn't...

Ciaran refused to acknowledge the possibility, even to himself. He wouldn't even think it. He'd go after her, and he'd find her.

As far as direction, he had precious little to go on, but he'd take the butler at his word, and head for Maidstone. Jarvis would have to stop at some point to change horses. A gold coin or two, and whatever innkeeper happened to see them would be pleased to tell Ciaran which direction they'd taken. Someone would have noticed Lucy. She wasn't the sort of lady you overlooked.

Maidstone, Dover—it didn't matter. He'd go all the way to the edge of England if he had to, but he'd find Lucy, and he'd get her back.

She was *his*, and no one, least of all Jarvis, was going to take her away from him.

Chapter Twenty-six

"Unconsciousness suits you, Lucinda. If you were even a fraction as obedient when you're awake, you wouldn't be in your current predicament. Alas, I'm afraid it's too late now."

Lucy flinched away from her uncle's cruel words, the hot drift of his breath. Her mouth was as dry as dust. She tried to swallow, but a starburst of pain exploded in her throat, and a faint moan escaped from between her bruised lips.

"You're a bit heavy-headed, I expect." Uncle Jarvis drew back, the carriage seat giving a protesting squeak as he settled his bulk against it. "It's a pity, but it won't be much longer now. We're almost there."

Almost there.

Where? She'd tried to stay awake, to keep track of her surroundings, but the panic and exhaustion had caught up to her. How long had they been traveling? Judging by the way her body ached, it must be hours.

Lucy cracked an eye open. The inside of the carriage was dim, the view outside the window shrouded in dusk. Hours, yes. It had been late afternoon when they'd changed horses in Rochester. She tried to pull together a coherent guess as to their final destination, but she kept losing the threads of logic in the cotton wool inside her head.

"It might comfort you to know, Lucinda, that you made all this much easier than I imagined it would be." Uncle Jarvis's grating voice scraped at the inside of her skull.

Lucy peeled the other eye open and struggled upright against the squabs. Her uncle was seated across from her, one foot balanced negligently on his knee, an arm thrown across the back of the seat.

A picture of casual ease.

It was terrifying. More so even than the dark isolation into which he'd brought her. Uncle Jarvis was never at ease unless he was very certain whatever scheme he had in hand was sure to succeed.

"Easier, Uncle?"

"Oh, yes. At first, I thought the easiest thing would be for you to marry Godfrey, but once I had a chance to reflect on it, I realized it's far better this way." Uncle Jarvis picked a bit of lint off the sleeve of his coat. "Why should I settle for the paltry ten thousand Godfrey was going to give me when I can have the whole lot?"

Have the whole lot?

He meant her fortune, of course. Uncle Jarvis would hardly exert himself to a kidnapping for anything less than the entire sixty thousand pounds.

Lucy waited in silence. Her uncle was in a chatty mood, so she'd let him talk.

"It *is* gratifying when things work out, isn't it, Lucinda? I confess I wasn't sure they would until I saw you emerge from the Swan and Anchor this morning. It all fell into place after that."

Lucy remembered his arm pressing into her throat, and then…nothing. Not for a while. By the time she came back to herself, they'd left London behind.

"Laudanum's a fine thing, isn't it? I never thought I'd see the day when your aunt would prove useful, but here we are."

Lucy ran her tongue over her dry lips. He'd forced her to drink from a brown bottle several times over the past few hours. She'd obligingly feigned a collapse each time, but thanks to Dr. Digby's Calming Tonic, she'd remained awake and alert for most of the drive. She shuddered, thinking how much worse off she'd be now if he'd really given her laudanum.

Unfortunately, consciousness hadn't done her much good. She hadn't gleaned any information aside from a general impression they were moving south. "Where are we?" Lucy's voice was so hoarse she hardly recognized it as her own.

She didn't expect him to tell her, but to her surprise, he answered readily. "In Kent, near Maidstone. Nice county, Kent. Lovely countryside. I think you'll like it here, Lucinda."

A rough laugh scraped over Lucy's abused throat. "I don't intend to stay, Uncle."

"But you won't have a choice, my dear. I'm afraid Dr. Willis will insist on it. I've been writing to him for weeks now, since I learned of your troubling behavior in Brighton. He's heard your entire sad history."

His smile made the hair on Lucy's neck rise.

"Madness so often runs in families, doesn't it?" Uncle Jarvis went on in a low, satisfied purr. "Such a pity the daughter should suffer from her father's illness, but hardly a surprise, really."

Madness...

Lucy went still, her blood turning to ice in her veins. She could only stare at him, frozen with horror. He was taking her to a madhouse, leaving her there so he could retain control over her fortune. Lucy's throat worked, but she was so shocked at his perfidy she couldn't produce a sound.

From the first moment she'd met her Uncle Jarvis she'd known he wasn't a good man, but this...this was far, far beyond any line she'd ever imagined he'd cross. To lock her away, knowing full well she was perfectly sane—dear God, she could hardly credit such treachery.

"There's a flaw in your plan, uncle." It was an effort to keep her voice steady and meet her uncle's eyes, but Lucy managed it. "Rather a fatal flaw, I'm afraid."

He shifted his weight, settling himself more comfortably against the squabs. He looked as if he were enjoying himself. "Is there, indeed? What's that?"

"I'm not mad."

He waved a desultory hand. "That's neither here nor there."

"I'm afraid it is. You need two doctors to testify I suffer from madness before you can have me committed." Lucy had made it her business to discover all there was to know about madhouses and commitment, given her father's situation.

If Uncle Jarvis had relied on her ignorance, he'd made a mistake.

But any hope Lucy might have had vanished when she saw the smirk on his face. "No need to fear, my dear. Dr. Willis is prepared to declare your wits well addled, and I've no doubt his colleagues will follow suit. In his last letter he expressed himself very concerned about your sanity, and urged me to bring you to him as soon as the thing could be managed."

Lucy didn't move or answer. She kept still, waiting, but desperation was clawing at her, its talons growing sharper with every word out of her uncle's mouth.

He leaned across the carriage and fixed his cold blue eyes on her face. "He could hardly think otherwise, could he? You see, Lucinda, I felt it my duty to explain your recent erratic behavior to him, in some detail."

"I don't..." Lucy swallowed. "What e-erratic behavior?"

He shrugged, but those hard eyes were gleaming with satisfaction. "That business in Brighton, sneaking onto the beach every morning at dawn. The fainting fits at balls—half of London witnessed those. Your unreasonable aversion to Lord Godfrey."

Lucy pressed a hand to her mouth. Every pitch and lurch of the wheels over the rough roads made her stomach twist with nausea.

Uncle Jarvis sighed as if he were disappointed in her. "Really, my dear, this is all your own fault. You must see that. Naturally I predicted you'd balk at a match with Godfrey—indeed, that was why I chose him—but I confess it never occurred to me you'd react so violently, or *publicly*. But as I said, you've made it all quite easy for me."

The thick press of bile burned Lucy's throat as Uncle Jarvis revealed the depths to which he'd sunk to steal her fortune.

He'd never intended to marry her to Lord Godfrey at all. It had been a ploy to push her to extreme behavior—expose her to the notice and censure of the *ton*, so he'd be justified in declaring her insane. He'd planned to lock her up in a madhouse from the very start, and she...

She'd foolishly played right into his hands.

Uncle Jarvis gave a mournful shake of his head. "I explained to Dr. Willis the care I took to find you an advantageous match, only to be faced with your flagrant disobedience. Really, Lucinda. What sane young lady balks at becoming a countess?"

Panic rushed through Lucy, making her dizzy. "Plenty of sane young ladies would balk at becoming Lord Godfrey's countess!"

Uncle Jarvis went on as if she hadn't spoken. "But what really alarmed me, as I explained to Dr. Willis, is your unnatural fixation on Mr. Ramsey. I told him I was afraid it would lead you to do something rash, and you see, I was right. To leave your uncle's kind protection and throw yourself on the mercy of a rake like Ramsey!" Another shake of the head. "Wantonness in a female is a sure sign of madness."

Lucy collapsed against the seat, her chest tightening at mention of Ciaran's name. What must he have thought when he returned to the inn and found her gone? Would he suspect her uncle had snatched her away, or would he think she'd left on her own? What if she were locked away forever, and never saw him again? He'd think she'd left him, abandoned him.

Despair washed over Lucy, but she faced her uncle with her chin raised. "He'll come after me. He'll find out what you've done, and he'll follow us."

"Oh, I hope not. He has a bit of a temper, that one. I wouldn't want to be on the receiving end of it. That's why I took care no one should know anything about my plans. Not your aunt, and not Eloisa. Certainly not Mr. Ramsey. They'll be distressed when they find you gone, of course, but they won't have the first idea where to look for you."

She couldn't breathe. Her lungs were folding, collapsing. The darkness of the carriage pressed in on her, and her fists opened and closed helplessly. She darted a glance at the carriage door. If she could get it open before Uncle Jarvis knew what she was about, she could—

"That's not a wise choice, Lucinda." Uncle Jarvis clamped a hand down on her arm with a mirthless laugh. "Even if you land in one piece, where do you suppose you'd go? Now, be a good girl and stay where you are. We're here."

Lucy hadn't noticed the carriage had slowed. She pressed her face to the glass as the coachman made a turn, and her heart rushed into her throat. They were driving up a long, tree-lined road, at the end of which loomed a massive, gray stone building. A trio of arches graced the ground floor entryway, atop which stood a columned portico. Two giant wings were attached to the main building, with endless rows of windows looking onto the drive below.

Lucy shrank into a corner of the carriage, as far away from that forbidding place as she could get, but it did her no good. As soon as they stopped her uncle seized her arm and pulled her out of the carriage and onto the drive.

"Now, my dear niece. You can come along quietly, or I can have Bexley here take your other arm, and we'll drag you inside." Uncle Jarvis nodded at the coachman, who stared down at Lucy, his face utterly expressionless.

Lucy was painfully aware it would only make her look more of a lunatic if she forced them to drag her. She opened her mouth to say she'd go quietly when her gaze fell on the brown bottle lying on its side on Uncle Jarvis's seat. Desperation cleared the haze in her mind, and in its wake rose an idea, sharp and blindingly clear.

If she kicked up a fuss, they might decide to dose her again to keep her quiet. Once they did…well, even madwomen succumbed to laudanum, didn't they? All she need do then was stage a strategic collapse, and they wouldn't expect much more trouble from her. After all, how much havoc could one unconscious madwoman raise?

Except it wasn't laudanum, and she wouldn't be unconscious. On the contrary, she was beginning to feel quite alert, indeed.

Her mind made up, Lucy launched into a fit that would have put the maddest Bedlamite to shame. There was a great deal of screaming, kicking, and squirming on her part, and scrambling and cursing on Bexley's and Uncle Jarvis's. Bexley leapt from the box into the carriage, fetched the brown bottle, and held her down while her uncle forced her to swallow such a deep draught Lucy suspected it might have killed her had it truly been laudanum.

She didn't waste any time afterward, but fell into a such a determined swoon her uncle was forced to carry her up the stairs to the entrance of Oakwood Asylum.

Through a narrow slit in her eyelids Lucy saw a gentleman waiting for them there. Dr. Willis—or so she assumed him to be—cast her a pitying look, and instructed several large, raw-knuckled nurses to take her to an upstairs chamber while he consulted with her uncle.

Quicker than a breath, Lucy was half-dragged, half-carried up three flights of stairs and deposited on a bed in the corner of a chilly, sparsely furnished room. The nurses didn't linger, but left her there alone. She flinched at the metallic click of the lock, but as soon as their footsteps faded she scrambled up from the bed and darted toward the window.

The locked door didn't trouble her. She could free herself easily enough with one of the dozens of hairpins in her hair.

The vast emptiness outside the window was another matter.

She could see a good distance from her vantage point, but not a light glimmered in the pressing darkness. The good people of Kent must prefer to keep those afflicted with madness at a distance, because the Oakwood Asylum was as remote a place as Lucy had ever encountered. She'd been groggy still when they passed through Maidstone, but she calculated it must be five or more miles away.

She could pick the lock on the bedchamber door, sneak down the corridors, and gain the entryway, but once she escaped into the night, where could she go? She wasn't such a fool as to think her uncle would take her sudden absence lightly. She wouldn't get far before he came after her and dragged her back here, and it would prove far more difficult to escape a second time.

No, if she were going to flee, she had to make certain she'd get away.

And get away she would, no matter what it took. Lucy bit her lip, the last of her panic dissipating as she considered and then discarded various escape scenarios.

There was a thick line of trees on either side of the drive. They'd hide her well enough until she was out of sight of the asylum, but which direction should she take when she reached the end of the drive? If she did manage to make it to Maidstone, what then? She hadn't a single shilling in her pockets, or even a cloak to—

What in the world?

A gasp broke from Lucy's lips. She pressed her face to the glass, her heart pounding. She could have sworn she saw something—a flash of movement on one side of the drive, close to the tree edge. She stared, her breath catching hard in her chest as she waited, hoping against hope....

Please let it be him. Please.

She strained to see into the darkness, her eyes watering with the effort. She sucked in one ragged breath after the next as her gaze darted over the drive below, waiting, waiting—

There! Further up the drive now, but still clinging to the shadows, another flash of movement, the flick of a man's hands on a horse's reins.

Lucy gasped again, her fingers clawing at the cold glass as he moved closer, weaving cautiously through the trees.

It was *him.*

She couldn't see his face—couldn't even make out the color of his horse—but Lucy knew it was him. She knew, because who else would have come for her but the same man who always did? The man who'd been there time and time again, arms wide open and ready for her, even when she thought she didn't need him?

She *did* need him. She'd teased him about his gallantry and poked fun at his heroics, but there'd never been a single moment when Lucy hadn't needed him. He was her best friend. Her lover. The man she'd gifted with her heart, the man she treasured above all others. He was the hero she'd never thought she'd find, the hero she never thought she'd need.

Now he was here, about to embark on another rescue. His most dramatic one yet.

But he couldn't do it alone.

Lucy assessed her options, her brain churning out one idea after another as Ciaran drew closer and closer to the building. He paused before clearing the tree line to dismount and tie his horse, then she saw him creep closer on foot, his face turned up toward the massive stone building looming over him.

She was too far above to make out his expression, but she could see the tautness in his body, sense the fury pouring through him, the grim resolve, and she knew what he was going to do even before he took another step.

He was coming in after her.

She knew Ciaran as well as she knew herself. Once he was inside, he wouldn't leave until he had her. He'd made up his mind she'd be with him when he went back out that door, no matter what he had to do.

Lucy couldn't prevent the foolish little leap of her heart just then. To have such a man as this risk everything to save her was heady. But even as her heart throbbed, she knew she couldn't allow him to do it.

There was another way, a much better one.

She'd go to *him.*

Unfortunately, this required getting his attention and stopping him before he stormed the gates, as it were. How she'd manage it without making any noise that would attract attention, well…that was the difficult part.

She peered down into the drive, her heart sinking. It felt as if she were miles above him, with an eternity of empty space between them. Too far to shout or pound on the window without every madhouse nurse in the place flooding into her bedchamber.

How could she catch Ciaran's attention without alerting anyone else? No one expected any trouble from her. They believed her to be in a laudanum-induced stupor, and she had a far better chance at escape if she kept it that way.

Lucy never made a conscious decision about what to do. She saw Ciaran creeping across the drive, inching closer and closer to the front entrance, and the next thing she knew she was tugging at the window, amazement sweeping over her when it slid open under her clawing fingers. Not locked? It seemed incredible it wouldn't be, but then even a lunatic would think twice before throwing herself from such a height.

Herself, yes, but any number of other things might be thrown from a window, mightn't they? A book? Lucy glanced around the room. No, no books. Not the lamp, either. It would make an awful noise when it shattered. Oh, if only she had her cloak still—

Lucy froze as the answer slammed into her. No cloak, but she did have her shoes. She dropped onto the floor, tore a shoe off her foot, then braced herself on the sill and poked her head out. She closed one eye, took aim, and…

Hurled her shoe out the window.

It seemed to hover in mid-air, as if making up its mind whether to challenge gravity or succumb to it, but then it was falling, falling, and… yes! It hit the ground with a thud, right at Ciaran's feet.

He halted mid-step, his head jerking upward.

Lucy knew the exact moment when he saw her. The shock, anger, and panic melted from his face at once, and his lips curved in a slow smile…

Oh, such a smile!

Her heart threatened to melt inside her chest, but this wasn't the moment to fall into a besotted swoon. Instead she pressed a finger to her lips and held up her hand to signal he should remain silent and motionless.

He didn't move, and he didn't make a sound. He stood below her, his face turned up to hers, waiting.

She pointed toward the side of the drive from where he'd come, then made a shooing gesture to indicate he should return to his horse and wait for her. His shoulders stiffened, and he gave a sharp shake of his head.

"Yes," Lucy whispered. She laced her fingers together under her chin. *Please.*

He hesitated, frowning, but after a moment he did as she bid him and vanished back into the shadows.

Lucy snatched a hairpin from her hair, rushed to the door and knelt before it. There was no time to lose. If she didn't appear on the drive in the next few minutes, she hadn't the slightest doubt Ciaran would come after her.

Fortunately, she'd picked so many locks she didn't need much time.

Escaping the asylum undetected proved a great deal more difficult than escaping the bedchamber. Three flights of stairs had never seemed so many before, but between diving into alcoves and around doors—and, at one point—into an unlocked room with a sleeping occupant—Lucy made it to the first-floor landing.

She eyed the entryway just below her. Every doctor, nurse, and servant in Oakwood Asylum seemed to be gathered there. She was obliged to wait for some time, one eye on the staff milling about and the other locked fearfully on the front door, dreading the moment when Ciaran would burst through it.

After a long, torturous, breathless wait, a bell rang. It seemed to be some sort of signal to the staff, because within minutes they'd all dispersed, some down corridors and others up the stairs. Fortunately, none of them spotted Lucy quivering behind a half-closed door.

Once the sound of footsteps faded, Lucy took a deep breath, threw her shoulders back...

And fled.

If anyone called after her, she didn't hear them. If anyone chased her, she didn't notice them. She simply ran, as fast as her legs could carry her, a muttered prayer on her lips.

Down the final set of stairs and across the entryway, her one stockinged foot slipping over the slick marble floor, and through the door. Once she was outside she skidded around the corner, heading blindly for the side of the drive where she'd last seen Ciaran, and...

Flew straight into his arms.

"Ciaran." She hurled herself against him and clung to him tighter than she'd ever clung to anything in her life. She couldn't speak, couldn't look at him, could hardly breathe, but she pressed her face into his chest, dragging in great gulps of him, the dark, rich scents of wood and leather.

"Lucy. Thank God." He didn't say anything more, but he was trembling as he gathered her against him and buried his face in her hair.

She could have held him like that for hours, days, a lifetime, but the front drive of the Oakwood Asylum wasn't the place to bare her heart to him.

They had to get away at once. Uncle Jarvis's carriage still lingered in the drive. There was no sign of Bexley, thank goodness, but either of them could appear any moment. Lucy didn't intend to be there when they did.

Ciaran seemed to come to this realization at the same time she did. Without a word he led her toward the trees and lifted her onto his horse. He mounted behind her and wrapped a muscular arm around her waist. "Lean back on me," he murmured, his warm breath drifting over her cheek.

Lucy didn't argue. Why should she? There was no other place in the world she'd rather be. So, she snuggled closer, her back pressed against his chest. Then she closed her eyes, and let her hero take her away.

Chapter Twenty-seven

Under the best of circumstances, it was a full day's ride from Maidstone to Windsor. Two people on one horse, both of them dazed and exhausted, weren't the best of circumstances.

Even so, Ciaran pushed on, riding for hours through the night until his thighs burned and Lucy was a limp bundle of shivering limbs in his arms. It was midnight by the time they reached Sevenoaks, but they only paused long enough to exchange their horse for a carriage. They followed a southern route from there, skirting around London to evade any pursuit by Jarvis.

Ciaran looked over his shoulder the entire time.

It wasn't until they rode into Windsor that he was able to draw an easy breath. The sun had been peeking over the horizon for an hour or more before he found a tiny inn off the main road and led Lucy upstairs to a small but clean bedchamber tucked under the eaves.

Once again, he asked for one bedchamber only. It wasn't any more proper now than it had been before, but there was no way Ciaran was letting Lucy out of his sight after what had happened with Jarvis. Even now the villain might be chasing them across Kent, determined to drag her back to that godforsaken asylum. Lucy wouldn't be safe until they reached Buckinghamshire. He wouldn't leave her alone until then.

Not *even* then, if he had his way.

She wouldn't ever truly be safe from Jarvis until she married. Jarvis was her only male relative. If he got his hands on her again he could have her locked away, regardless of her age.

Ciaran didn't say so to Lucy. There was no need. She knew the danger as well as he did.

So, he said nothing. In fact, they both remained strangely silent on the subject of a marriage between them. Ciaran wasn't certain why. His love for her, his wish to marry her never wavered. A plea hung constantly on the edge of his lips, but he didn't speak it aloud, and Lucy didn't question him.

In his worst moments, Ciaran took this as a bad sign—proof that Lucy intended to refuse him again, and was building her strength for the inevitable battle between them. In his better moments, he was able to convince himself they were both simply too exhausted to talk.

In his best moments, his heart soared with hope.

The first of these breathtaking moments happened in Windsor, after they'd retired to their bedchamber. There was no chair this time, so Ciaran had made a pallet for himself in front of the hearth with a pillow and a few blankets from the bed. He was removing his boots when Lucy turned from the wash basin, frowning.

"What are you doing, Ciaran?"

"Going to sleep." Ciaran made an awkward gesture toward the pallet. He certainly wasn't going to crawl into bed next to her again. It would drive him mad to know her warm, sweet curves were a mere arm's length away, and not be able to touch her.

And he damn well wouldn't touch her. Not now, and not ever again unless she was his wife. There would be no gathering her into his arms, no covering her mouth with his, no tasting her soft whimpers and sighs with every breath between them—

"No." Lucy met his gaze, her chin raised. "You're exhausted, Ciaran. You're not sleeping on the floor."

"Yes, I am. Lucy! Stop it!"

Lucy had darted across the room and was snatching up the pillow and blankets. She tossed them onto the bed, then marched back across the room and took his hand in hers. "Come with me."

Ciaran didn't move. "This isn't a good idea, Lucy. I—"

She quieted him with her fingers against his lips. "Please. I won't be able to rest otherwise."

Ciaran closed his eyes against the burning need to kiss her fingertips—take her delicate fingers into his mouth, one by one. He opened them again when she drew her hand away, his anxious gaze darting between Lucy and the bed.

It looked so soft, so tempting. *She* looked so soft, so tempting. "I don't think—"

"Well, then there's no reason to start now." She tugged him across the bedchamber until his knees hit the edge of the bed, then braced her hands on his chest and gently pushed him down. "Stop being so stubborn, Ciaran."

"*You're* calling *me* stubborn? I wonder you can say that with a straight face," he grumbled, but he stretched out on the bed, too exhausted to argue with her.

Too exhausted to do anything else with her, either. Or so he told himself.

"Hush. Close your eyes and go to sleep." Lucy made her way to the other side of the bed and slid in beside him.

Ciaran's eyes fell to half-mast, his entire body going hot and tight as she wriggled and squirmed and fussed with her pillow. At last she lay down and nestled into the covers, for all the world as if she'd never been more comfortable in her life.

He wasn't comfortable. He felt like one of the burning logs trapped in the fireplace.

Hot. Rigid. Moments from bursting into flames.

But he didn't touch her. He wanted to. God, he wanted to.

Every inch of him ached to gather her against the length of his body until her arms wrapped around his neck and her legs cradled his hips. Instead he lay on his back, arms at his sides, staring at the ceiling with wide-open eyes. His entire body was taut, attuned to her every tiny movement, her every breath and sigh.

Ciaran froze as Lucy turned onto her side, facing him. He could feel her gaze on him, burning every inch of skin it touched. Then she was sliding toward him, closing the slender gap still open between them. Ciaran's breath caught as her hand landed on his chest and she nestled her head into the hollow of his shoulder.

It wasn't a seduction. Within minutes Lucy's breath evened out and her body relaxed into sleep.

Ciaran's didn't. No matter how he tried to convince it otherwise, his body insisted it was indeed a seduction, and it behaved as any young, healthy male body tended to when a warm, inviting female pressed against it.

A warm, inviting female with whom he happened to be madly in love.

It tormented him.

Oh, God. It was the sweetest agony he'd ever experienced. Her soft body molded to his, her hair tickling his chin, her breath on his neck, her scent enveloping him, drowning him. He'd never fall asleep like this, might never sleep again just from the memory of this.

Don't touch her.

But he was already moving. He wrapped one arm around Lucy and pressed her tightly against him. It wasn't until he had her in his arms that he slept. Slept, and dreamed. The most tender, heartbreaking dream where Lucy promised to be his, and he spent every night forever after just like this one, with her cradled safely in his embrace.

Ciaran woke much later, and for one groggy moment he thought his dreams had come true. Lucy was beside him, still wrapped in his arms.

Hours had passed. The one window in the tiny room was dark. Ciaran blinked at it, confused, until understanding dawned.

They'd slept the entire day.

He glanced down at her. She was clinging to him, her head on his chest, a handful of his shirt clutched in her fingers. Her face was turned up to his, her eyes wide open. "I wondered when you'd wake. Your stomach has been rumbling for half an hour now."

She gave him a sweet smile, and Ciaran's heart melted. Unable to resist, he leaned down and pressed a lingering kiss to her forehead. "Are you hungry?"

She nodded, but she made no move to pull away from him. She seemed perfectly content to remain in his arms. She did loosen her grip on his shirt, then dragged her fingers over the cloth, smoothing it. She did this for a long time, and Ciaran remained as still as he could, hypnotized by the soft stroke of her fingers. He would have stayed with her like this forever, but then one of her fingernails scraped lightly against his chest. He caught his breath, and her hand stilled, as if she'd only just realized she was stroking him.

A flush spread over her cheekbones, and then she did pull away from him.

"Lucy." He tried to hold onto her, his fingers tightening over hers, but she swung her legs over the side of the bed and rose before he could stop her.

"I'll ring for a servant." She escaped to the other side of the room, beyond his reach, and pulled the bell. A serving girl appeared after a short time, and Lucy asked for the fire to be tended and a supper tray brought up.

After the door closed behind the girl, an awkward silence fell.

Lucy wandered aimlessly around the room, darting anxious glances at him, glances he returned with anxious ones of his own. They seemed not to know what to say to each other. There was too much to say, and neither of them knew how to begin.

Or maybe they both knew once they did begin, there would be no going back to who they'd been on that beach in Brighton, when they'd sworn to be friends.

Friends. The idea seemed ludicrous to Ciaran now. He should have known from the start he'd never be able to settle for mere friendship with Lucy. That he'd grow to want her with a soul-deep ache he'd never be free of. He'd already been half in love with her by the time she left Brighton; he just hadn't known it.

And he'd thought Markham was the oblivious one.

He and Lucy dined in front of the fire, the scrape of their forks across the plates the only sound in the room. It wasn't awkward, precisely—he and Lucy had spent many moments on the beach in comfortable silence—but the space between them was heavy with unsaid words.

He half-expected her to banish him to the pallet for the night, but when he spread the pillow and blankets across the hard floor in front of the hearth Lucy fetched them back again and returned them to the bed. She didn't insist he join her—she simply curled up under the coverlet and waited, her dark eyes on his face.

Since there was nowhere else in the world Ciaran wanted to be than tucked into a warm bed beside her, he also didn't say a word. He simply crossed the room, climbed into the bed, and held out his arms until she nestled against him with a soft sigh, her cheek pressed to his chest.

* * * *

The next morning, they left Windsor before sunrise and pushed relentlessly toward Aylesbury, stopping only briefly to dine and change horses.

It was an eleven-hour journey. By the time they reached Huntington House, the sky had gone dark. Lucy should have been exhausted. Perhaps she *was* exhausted, but at the same time she was wide awake.

Wide awake, and panicking.

"There's no reason for you to look as if you're facing the gibbet, Lucy." Ciaran frowned as his gaze roamed over her face, lingering on the marks she'd bitten into her lower lip. "My family will welcome you here. They won't credit any of the rumors about your father, if they've even heard them at all."

"My father?" Lucy had been staring out the window at the grand estate spread out before her, but now she jerked her gaze to Ciaran and a despairing groan left her lips. "I'd forgotten all about that! As if it weren't bad enough a strange lady appears out of nowhere on their doorstep in the middle of the night, but now there's a mad father thrown into it, too!"

Why, the Marquess of Huntington would likely send her back to Oakwood Asylum without so much as a by-your-leave.

"I wouldn't say you're strange. A little unconventional, yes, but not strange." Ciaran tried a tentative grin, but when he saw the expression on her face he sobered again.

"Are they even expecting us? That is, I know they're not expecting *me*, but did you send word you were leaving London?" Lucy asked, twisting a fold of her cloak between her fingers.

Ciaran shifted uncomfortably in his seat. "Well, no. That is, there wasn't time to—"

Lucy closed her eyes and fell back against the seat with another groan. "This couldn't be worse, Ciaran!"

"Lucy." Ciaran plucked her wrinkled cloak from her fingers and took her hand in his. "It's going to be all right, I promise you. Do you truly think I'd bring you here if I didn't think it would be?"

"I—no. No, of course not." Lucy clutched at his hand, trying to absorb his warmth into her chilled skin.

Ciaran let her pet and squeeze him as the carriage made its way to the end of the long drive and stopped in front of a set of wide, stone steps. Lucy had regained some of her courage by then, but it fled again when the front door opened and a small group emerged, astonishment plain on their faces.

Lucy gaped at them. Her heart stuttered in her chest, then shuddered into a frantic pounding. There were four of them, and they were...glorious.

Well, not *quite* that, perhaps, but they were certainly an impressive-looking quartet. The gentlemen were both exceptionally tall and more than exceptionally handsome. The taller, darker gentleman resembled Ciaran. The two ladies were fair-haired, blue-eyed, and both of them far more beautiful than any one lady had a right to be.

Two exquisite china dolls and their majestic giants.

"It's nearly midnight!" the first giant spluttered. "Who the dev—"

"Hush, Finn." The lady at his side quieted him with a hand on his arm, then came down the steps and peered into the carriage. "Ah, I thought so! It's Ciaran!" Her blue eyes lit up, and her lips curved in a delighted smile, but it faded into a puzzled frown when she noticed Lucy. "Ciaran and a... er, a young lady."

The other three exchanged baffled looks, then hurried down the steps to crowd around the carriage. "What young lady?" The darker-haired giant demanded, poking his head through the carriage window. His eyes widened when he saw Lucy. "Well, I'll be damned. It is a young lady."

"What sort of young lady?" The younger of the two blondes rose to her tiptoes and tried to see over the giant's shoulder.

"For God's sake." Ciaran rolled his eyes, an expression of affection and exasperation on his face. "If you'd give us room we could come out of the carriage and you can all see for yourselves. Get off, Lach," he added as he swung the carriage door open and leapt down onto the drive.

Lucy peeked out the window at the circle of strange faces and for one shameful, cowardly moment she shrank back against her seat. But then Ciaran's face appeared at the open door, and he held out his hand to her with a breathtaking smile that made her heart squeeze inside her chest.

She took his hand. His warm fingers wrapped around hers, and Lucy realized, with that peculiar sort of clarity born from anxiety and exhaustion, that whenever Ciaran offered her his hand, there'd only ever be one choice for her. Since the first moment she'd laid eyes on him, there'd only ever been one thing she wanted to do.

Take it.

He drew her gently forward until she was out of the carriage and standing on the drive. "This," he said, his blue eyes soft as they caught hers, "is Lady Lucinda Sutcliffe."

There was no mistaking the pride and affection in his voice, or the way it dropped to a husky murmur when he said her name. Lucy stared at him in wonder, her heart fluttering madly.

One of the gentlemen cleared his throat, and offered Lucy a polite bow. "Lady Lucinda."

"My brother Finn, the Marquess of Huntington," Ciaran said, then introduced the rest of his family one by one.

They welcomed her warmly, but Lucy could see they were all astonished at her sudden appearance among them. Still, she gathered her wits and managed proper curtsies for each of them. "How do you do?"

After the introductions they all stood staring at each other. The silence stretched until they were all fidgeting, then finally the marquess asked, "You and Lady Lucinda are betrothed, Ciaran?"

Lucy froze. She'd expected the question—of course, she had. The marquess was only speaking aloud what they were all thinking.

Beside her, Ciaran stiffened. "No."

The marquess and Ciaran's other brother, Lachlan, exchanged glances. "Married, then?" Lachlan asked in hopeful tones.

"*No.*" Ciaran growled, but neither of his brothers seemed to notice the warning in his tone.

Both handsome faces grew darker and the marquess flushed, as if he were a moment away from falling into a temper. "You mean to say you've traveled all the way from London with Lady Lucinda—that you've taken her into your protection—and you're neither betrothed, nor married?"

"Finn!" Lady Iris, the Marchioness of Huntington, gasped. "For pity's sake!"

Her exclamation came too late to save Lucy, however. Heat washed over her, so intense she was certain she'd burst into flames in the middle of the Marquess of Huntington's carriage drive.

Ciaran's sisters-in-law noticed her embarrassment. They both stepped toward her, but Ciaran was already there, drawing her close, his arm wrapped protectively around her waist. He faced his elder brothers, his expression warning them not to say another word. "This isn't the place to discuss it."

The marquess's glance lingered on Ciaran's face, then dropped to the arm Ciaran had wrapped around Lucy's waist. He exchanged another glance with Lachlan, this one puzzled, then nodded. "Very well. My study, then. Iris, will you and Hyacinth please take Lady Lucinda upstairs and see her settled?"

"Yes, of course. You must be exhausted, Lady Lucinda."

Lucy managed one last wide-eyed glance at Ciaran before Lady Iris eased her gently out of his embrace, and she and Lady Hyacinth led her away.

* * * *

She was whisked upstairs to an elegant bedchamber. They bustled about until the bed was aired and the fire lit, then fussed and soothed a dazed Lucy into a soft, warm night rail, and tucked her under the covers.

They were kind to her. Too kind to ask any questions, though Lady Iris did pause on her way out the door and turn back to Lucy, her expression thoughtful.

Lucy waited, resisting the urge to dive under the coverlet.

"We trust Ciaran," Lady Iris murmured, her deep blue gaze holding Lucy's dark one. "If he's brought you here, Lady Lucinda, he's done so for a reason."

Then she was gone, the door closing with a soft click behind her.

Lucy stared at it for a moment, then flopped back onto the bed and tugged the coverlet up under her chin. Ciaran had his reasons, yes, each one more noble than the last.

She was his best friend. She needed his protection. He'd compromised her.

So many reasons, but not one of them the right one.

He'd never said a word about love.

He'd held her in his arms last night. She shivered as she remembered how his warmth had surrounded her, the strong, steady thump of his heart echoing against her cheek. It had felt so real—so close to being what she'd always imagined love should be.

She'd felt as if she belonged there, wrapped in his arms.

The entire ride from Windsor to Huntington House, her head had been trying to convince her heart it was enough.

It almost worked.

Almost.

Lucy let her eyes fall closed on a deep sigh. She expected sleep to prove elusive, but for once, her body overruled her mind and heart. The faint crackle of the fire faded as sleep stole over her, gathering her into its soothing embrace.

Tomorrow. She'd think about what to do tomorrow...

She woke with a start some time later. She wasn't sure how long she'd been asleep, but the bedchamber was lost in shadows. Still nighttime, then. She blinked into the dark. Why had she woken?

There'd been a noise—

"Lucy." Ciaran's voice was the quietest whisper, but he was so close she could feel him, the softest tickle of his breath against her face.

Lucy struggled to sit up, but Ciaran stopped her with a gentle hand on her shoulder. "Lie back down, sweetheart."

Sweetheart.

His voice was so soft when he said it, almost reverent, and a delicious shiver drifted down Lucy's spine. He'd never spoken to her in quite that tone before, his voice like fingertips dancing over her skin.

It didn't occur to her to wonder why Ciaran was in her bedchamber in the middle of the night. She simply reached for him, her fingers slipping into his hand. "Ciaran? Is everything all right?"

He stared down at her without answering, then he sank onto the edge of the bed with a sigh. "Well, I'm still breathing. My brothers haven't killed me yet, so I suppose that's a good sign."

Lucy winced. "I imagine they aren't pleased."

"They're concerned, and they have reason to be. I'm concerned too, Lucy."

"Me, too." Not about the same things Ciaran was, though. She was concerned about heartbreak, loneliness, a lifetime of being haunted by the man sitting beside her, the faint glow of moonlight on his beautiful face.

Ciaran was concerned with honor, duty, friendship, obligation. All worthy things, but none of them enough, no matter how much she loved him. She'd spent years of her life locked inside a gilt cage, all in the name of love. She knew the truth.

You couldn't trap love inside a closed fist.

She sighed. "What did you tell them? Your brothers, I mean."

To Lucy's surprise he reached out to trail a finger down her cheek. "The truth, Lucy. I told them the truth."

Lucy's lips ached to kiss his fingertip. "What is the truth, Ciaran? I hardly know anymore." She knew her own truth, but she wasn't sure she knew his. "Tell me what you told your brothers."

The moonlight caught a glint of humor in his blue eyes. "I told them we met on a beach in Brighton, that I saved you from drowning, and the only thanks I got for it was a broken nose."

Lucy let out an outraged squeak. "I wasn't drowning! And I didn't break your nose. Only bent it."

"Then I told them about how you wandered into a bare-knuckle bout to do some sketching, and were nearly trampled in a brawl," Ciaran went on, as if she hadn't spoken. "I explained how I saved you from certain death a second time, and all I got for that was another kick, this time to the chest."

Lucy's mouth dropped open. Dear God, she'd never be able to look his brothers in the eyes again. "That's not how it—"

"I told them despite your numerous assaults on me, we somehow became best friends. I told them we met on the beach every morning afterward, and watched the sun rise together. That we talked for hours." He was quiet for a moment, looking down at their entwined hands, but then he looked up. His gaze caught hers, and there was something there—something she'd never seen before. "I told them you brought me back to life, Lucy."

A sound broke from Lucy's lips—a sigh, a gasp, a sob. Oh, how could she refuse him, when he looked at her like that? He was stealing her will, melting her heart.

"I told them if it hadn't been for you, I'd be in Scotland right now. They didn't care for that, especially Lachlan. So, I begged their pardons for nearly betraying their trust. Then I told them I was grateful, Lucy—so grateful I hadn't gone. Grateful I was still here with the people I love."

Lucy caught her breath. That look on his face, the break in his voice when he'd uttered that last word. She could almost imagine he'd meant it…

For *her*.

"Ciaran—"

"No. Let me finish." He raised her hand to his mouth and brushed his warm lips over her knuckles. "I told them you disappeared from Brighton without a trace soon afterward, and I followed you to London because I was worried for you. I must have known, even then, that if anything happened to you, I'd never forgive myself for it."

Words crowded onto Lucy's tongue, words of love and fear and hope, but she didn't speak them yet. Instead she lifted his hand to her mouth and returned his kiss with a press of her lips to his palm.

Ciaran's eyes darkened to a stormy blue. "I didn't explain much about what happened with Jarvis and Godfrey, but I did tell them I stayed in London to court you, because the idea of Vale doing it made me wild with jealousy."

Lucy's eyes went wide. She recalled Ciaran had been inexplicably angry when she'd told him her plans for Lord Vale, but she'd never guessed it was jealousy.

"My brothers found that part hysterically funny." Ciaran gave her a wry smile. "It seems I may have boasted in the past about never being such a fool as to be jealous over a woman, but I never have been before, Lucy. Not even with Isobel. Only with you."

Lucy didn't realize she was crying until Ciaran brushed a tear from her cheek. "I told my brothers you'd refused to marry me. That you didn't want to marry at all, and that I—I couldn't make you change your mind. Not even for me. I told them…I told them you'd broken my heart."

"I—I've broken your heart?" If she'd broken his heart, that meant… didn't that mean…

His heart was *hers*?

"Shattered it. I'm in love with you, Lucy." Ciaran tried to smile. "But I'm still your friend. I'll always be your friend, no matter what else happens."

"But Scotland, and…and Isobel Campbell. I thought…you told me—"

"I told you I wanted to return to Scotland. I told myself that, too." Ciaran raised her hand to his lips again. "I was wrong. I haven't thought about Isobel in weeks. Not since I met you."

"You don't love her anymore? You were wrong?"

"I was wrong. Can't a man be wrong?" Ciaran let out a shaky breath, and then he started speaking very quickly, the words pouring out of him in an incoherent stream. "Isobel is my past, Lucy, but you…you're my future. There's only one reason I want to marry you, and it has nothing to do with our friendship, or your uncle, or because I've compromised you, or because I think I have to save you. How could it be, when it's you who's saved me?"

Tears were flowing freely down Lucy's face now. "W-we saved each other, I think."

Ciaran took her face in his hands. "I want to marry you because I'm in love with you, Lucy. I've been in love with you for weeks, ever since you kicked me in the face."

"If I'd known that's all it would take to make you fall in love with me, I would have kicked you in the face a dozen more times by now." A broken sound left her lips, and then she was in his arms. "I love you too, Ciaran. I've been in love with *you* for weeks, ever since that morning on the beach when I broke your nose."

"You didn't break it. My nose, or, thank God, my heart. Say it again."

She twined her arms around his neck, laughing even as tears flowed down her cheeks. "I love you, Ciaran."

A smile quirked his lips, but his blue eyes were serious when they met hers. "You told me once you never wanted to marry. Is that still true? I'd never try to take your freedom away from you, Lucy. I only want to give you things—to make you happy. I want to give you everything."

Lucy laid a tender hand on his cheek. "Give me yourself, then. You're all I need to make me happy. I love you, Ciaran. I never wanted anything but you."

His eyes drifted closed, as if he needed a moment to gather her words into himself, to lock them inside his heart. "You love me enough to marry me, then?"

Lucy rested her forehead against his. "Will you come swimming with me, and take me to bare-knuckle bouts, and teach me the quadrille?"

His warm mouth covered hers, and he kissed her until they both were breathless. "I'll do anything you ask me to," he murmured, when they finally drew apart. "Though you won't mind if I keep my nose out of the way of your foot, will you?"

She laughed softly, and leaned forward to kiss his perfectly imperfect nose. "Not as long as I have your heart."

Epilogue

Three months later.

Le Pantalon, L'été, La Poule...

They were the same steps Lucy had despaired of mastering during her brief, eventful season, but this wasn't like any quadrille she'd ever danced before.

There was no music, no Monsieur Guilland, and no fan with incoherent instructions written in cramped letters on the sticks.

There was only Lucy and Ciaran. They'd long since abandoned the proper steps, and were simply swaying together in the middle of the empty ballroom at Bellamy House, their arms wrapped around each other.

"Ciaran?" Lucy's fingers curled into the broad shoulder under her hand. "Are you certain you're teaching me to dance the quadrille? Because I don't remember Monsieur Guilland holding me quite so tightly when he partnered me."

"No?" Ciaran dropped a kiss onto the top of her head. "How strange."

"Yes, isn't it? I also don't recall him nuzzling my neck, or nipping at my ear. If I didn't know you to be the Wallflower's Gallant and an honorable gentleman, I might suspect this wasn't a proper quadrille at all."

Ciaran pulled back slightly to look down at her, his lips quirking in a slow, seductive smile. "Not proper for a dancing master, no, but perfectly proper for a husband."

"Hmmm." Lucy let her head fall to his shoulder with a contented sigh. There was nothing in the world she loved more than being held in her husband's arms, and she might have drifted along in this dreamy state for hours if Ciaran's hands hadn't started to wander.

When he paused in a very improper place to give her a gentle squeeze, Lucy squealed. "Ciaran! I'm certain Monsieur Guilland never did *that*!"

"Damn good thing for him he didn't." Ciaran's other hand slid from between her shoulder blades down to the arch of her back to urge her more closely against him. "He seems like a decent enough fellow. It would have been a pity if I'd had to challenge him to a duel for laying his hands on the lady I love."

"You didn't love me at the time." Lucy attempted an indignant look, but the effect was somewhat spoiled by the teasing glint in her eyes.

"Yes, I did," he murmured, drawing back again to look into her eyes. "From the first day I met you, there has never been a moment when I didn't love you, Lucy."

He'd said as much to her many times since that memorable night at Huntington House, but Lucy never got tired of hearing those words. She was tempted to sink back into his arms, but she held back and offered him a sly grin instead. "Yes, but you didn't know it. Perhaps I should have encouraged Monsieur Guilland to flirt with me. It might have brought you to your senses sooner."

He smiled and swept her into a graceful turn. "It worked for Markham."

It had, indeed. So well Lady Felicia had become the Countess of Markham a few months after Lucy and Ciaran had married at Huntington House. Lady Felicia had never been happier, and Lord Markham's sternness had given way to an enraptured expression Ciaran and Lord Vale found endlessly amusing.

"Odd, how Vale was the only one of us who had any sense. He even guessed the truth about Lord Nash and Miss Fisher." Ciaran chuckled. "I never would have thought he'd turn out to be so wise in the ways of love."

"Wise enough to choose Eloisa as his bride." Lucy nestled her head into the hollow of Ciaran's shoulder. Whenever she thought about Eloisa and Lord Vale, the same contented smile rose to her lips. Just as Lucy had predicted, Eloisa made a lovely countess.

Ciaran and Lucy had traveled from Huntington House to Lord Vale's estate in Lewes for the wedding. Afterward, they'd gone off to Brighton, where they'd spent every morning on the beach together, watching the sun rise over the ocean. The gouty old gentlemen and phlegmatic old ladies had been scandalized, but neither Lucy nor Ciaran cared a bit what anyone thought.

Indeed, they might have stayed in Brighton longer, but Lucy had been anxious to return to Devon. She had grand plans to update Bellamy House, but since their arrival three weeks earlier she and Ciaran had spent most of their time in their bedchamber.

Ah, well. They had all the time in the world to make Bellamy House their home.

A lifetime, in fact.

"Has Eloisa written recently?" Ciaran trailed his lips down Lucy's neck, dropping tiny kisses over every inch of bare skin he could reach.

"Yes, she…ah, I had a letter from her just yesterday." Lucy's breath caught as he paused to nip at the curve between her neck and shoulder. "She said…she, ah…I can't think when you do that."

Ciaran laughed softly. "She and Vale are still coming here next month, aren't they?"

"Coming here?" Lucy sank her fingers into Ciaran's hair and tilted her head to encourage him to kiss her throat. "I mean, yes. Yes, of course. I remember now. Eloisa, Lord Vale, and my aunt will arrive at the end of next month, and my aunt will remain through Christmas."

Aunt Jarvis was rarely at her home in Berkshire these days. She traveled a good deal, dividing her time between Lewes and Devon. Her nerves were doing wonderfully well. She credited her improved health to judicious doses of Dr. Digby's Calming Tonic, but Lucy suspected Uncle's Jarvis's absence was the real reason for her aunt's miraculous recovery.

"Jarvis remains in Berkshire?" Ciaran asked, as if he'd read her mind. He hadn't forgotten or forgiven Lucy's uncle for his treachery, and he'd made it clear the man wasn't welcome in their home.

Which seemed to suit Aunt Jarvis just fine.

"He does, indeed." Lucy lay a palm on Ciaran's cheek. "In Berkshire, where he can't cause any mischief."

After that ugly business in Kent, Ciaran and his brother Finn had put a swift end to Jarvis's machinations. Uncle Jarvis had slinked back to Berkshire with thousands of pounds of debt still hanging over his head. Lord Vale had paid the debt, and since then he'd kept tight control over Uncle Jarvis's purse strings.

Once he was put on a strict allowance, Uncle Jarvis's behavior had improved dramatically. Lucy had never known him to be so obedient, but it wasn't so surprising, really. Uncle Jarvis had never cared for anything as much as he did his own comfort.

But Lucy hardly thought of her uncle at all these days. She was far too taken up by her life with Ciaran to spare him a thought.

"Good." Ciaran turned his head to press an open-mouthed kiss to Lucy's palm. She sighed at the warm press of his mouth, and he looked down at her, eyes gleaming. "It's getting late."

Lucy glanced toward the window. "It's not yet dusk."

Ciaran raised her hand to his lips and, one by one, pressed warm kisses to each of her fingertips. "Quadrille lessons are over, Lucy. Come to bed."

"Ah. So that *was* meant to be the quadrille, then?" Lucy gave him a playful smile. "How curious. I don't remember it being anything like that at Thomas Wilson's Dancing Academy."

Ciaran was already drawing her toward the door. "This is how we dance the quadrille at the Wallflower Gallant's Dancing Academy."

Lucy rose to her tiptoes and brushed her lips over the hollow of his throat. "I see. I can't imagine you have many pupils, with such a scandalous quadrille as that."

"Just one." Ciaran captured her chin in his hand and raised her face to his. He gazed down at her, his blue eyes soft with love. "And she's the only one who matters."

Printed in the United States
by Baker & Taylor Publisher Services